JAMES PATTERSON

OMNIBUS

VIOLETS ARE BLUE

FOUR BLIND MICE

Typeset in Palatino Light by
Letterpart Limited, Reigate, Surrey

Printed and bound in Great Britain by
Mackays of Chatham plc, Chatham, Kent

CONTENTS

VIOLETS ARE BLUE

This is for my friend, Kyle Craig, who doesn't work for the FBI, but who has, I think, a really cool name. I should mention a few other patrons of the arts: Jim Heekin, Mary Jordan, Fern Galperin, Maria Pugatch, Irene Markocki, Barbara Groszewski, Tony Peyser, and my sweet Suzie.

Prologue

Without Any Warning

Chapter One

Nothing ever starts where we think it does. So of course this doesn't begin with the vicious and cowardly murder of an FBI agent and good friend named Betsey Cavalierre. I only thought that it did. My mistake, and a really big and painful one.

I arrived at Betsey's house in Woodbridge, Virginia, in the middle of the night. I'd never been there before, but I didn't have any trouble finding it. The FBI and EMS were already there. There were flashing red and yellow lights everywhere, seeming to paint the lawn and front porch with bright, dangerous streaks.

I took a deep breath and walked inside. My sense of balance was off. I was reeling. I acknowledged a tall, blonde FBI agent I knew named Sandy Hammonds. I could see that Sandy had been crying. She was a friend of Betsey's.

On a hallway table I saw Betsey's service revolver. Beside it was a printed reminder for her next shooting qualifier at the FBI range. The irony stung.

I forced myself to walk down a long hallway that led from the living room to the back of the house, which looked to be close to a hundred years old. It was filled with the kind of country clutter that she'd loved when she was alive. The master bedroom was situated at the end of the hall.

I knew instantly that the murder had happened in there. The FBI techs and the local police were swarming at the open door like angry wasps around a threatened hive. The house was strangely, eerily quiet. This was as bad as it gets, worse than anything else. Ever.

Another one of my partners was dead.

The second one brutally murdered in two years.

And Betsey had been much more than just a partner.

How could this have happened? What did it mean?

I saw Betsey's small body sprawled on the hardwood floor and I went cold. My hand flew to my face, a reflex over which I had no control.

The killer had stripped off her nightclothes. I didn't see them anywhere in the bedroom. The lower body was coated with blood. He'd used a knife. He'd punished Betsey with it. I desperately wanted to cover her, but I knew I couldn't.

Betsey's brown eyes were staring up at me, but they saw nothing. I remembered kissing those eyes, and that sweet face. I remembered her laugh, high-pitched and musical. I stood there for a long time, mourning Betsey, missing her terribly. I wanted to turn away, but I didn't. I just couldn't leave her like this.

As I stood in the bedroom, trying to figure out something coherent about Betsey's murder, the cell phone in my jacket pocket went off. I jumped. I grabbed it, but then hesitated. I didn't want to answer.

'Alex Cross,' I finally spoke into the receiver.

I heard a machine-filtered voice and it cut right through me. I shuddered against my will.

'I *know* who this is and I even know where you are. At poor, dear, *butchered* Betsey's. Do you feel a little bit like a puppet on a string, Detective? You should,' said the Mastermind, 'because that's what you are. You're my favorite puppet, in fact.'

'Why did you kill her?' I asked the monster on the other end of the phone line. 'You didn't have to do this.'

He laughed a mechanical laugh and the hairs on the back of my neck stood up. 'You ought to be able to figure that out, no? You're the famous Detective Alex Cross. You have all those big, important cases notched on your belt. You caught Gary Soneji, Casanova. You solved Jack and Jill. Christ, you're impressive.'

I spoke in a low voice. 'Why don't you come after me right now? How about tonight? As you say, you know where I am.'

The Mastermind laughed again, quietly, almost under his breath. 'How about I kill your grandmother and your three kids tonight? I know where *they* are, too. You left your partner with them, didn't you? You think he can stop me? John Sampson doesn't have a chance against me.'

I hung up and sprinted out of the house in Woodbridge. I called Sampson in Washington and he picked up on the second ring.

'Everything okay there?' I gasped.

'Everything's fine, Alex. No problems here. You don't sound too good, though. What's up? What happened?'

'He said he's coming for you and Nana and the kids,' I told John. 'The Mastermind.'

'Not going to happen, sugar. Nobody will get past me. I hope to hell he tries.'

'Be careful, John. I'm on my way back to Washington *right now*. Please be careful. He's crazy. He didn't just kill Betsey, he defiled her.'

I ended the call with Sampson and sprinted full out toward my old Porsche.

The cell phone rang again before I got to the car.

'Cross,' I answered, still running as I spoke, trying to steady the receiver against my chin and ear.

It was him again. He was laughing maniacally. 'You can relax, Dr Cross. I can hear your labored breathing. I'm not going to hurt them tonight. I was just fucking with you. Having some fun at your expense.

'You're running, aren't you? Keep running, Dr Cross. But you won't be fast enough. You can't get away from me. It's you I want. You're next, Dr Cross.'

Part One

The California Murders

Chapter Two

United States Army Lieutenant Martha Wiatt and her boyfriend, Sergeant Davis O'Hara, moved at a fast pace as the evening fog began to roll in like a sulfurous cloud across Golden Gate Park in San Francisco. The couple looked sleek, even beautiful, in the waning light of day.

Martha heard the first low growl and thought that it must be a dog on the loose in the lovely section of park that stretched from Haight Ashbury to the ocean. It came from far enough behind them that she wasn't worried.

'The Big Dawg!' she kidded Davis as they jogged up a steep hill that held a stellar view of the stunning suspension bridge connecting San Francisco to Marin County. 'Big Dawg' was a pet expression they used for everything over-sized – from jet-liners, to sexual apparatus, to very large canines.

Soon the thick fog would blanket the bridge and bay completely, but for now it was a gorgeous sight, incomparable, one of their favorite things in San Francisco.

'I love this run, that beautiful bridge, the sunset – the whole ball of wax,' Martha said in a steady, relaxed cadence. 'But enough bad poetry. It's time for me to kick your well-formed, athletic-looking butt, O'Hara.'

'That sounds like cheap-shot female chauvinism to me,' he grunted, but he was grinning, showing off some of the whitest teeth she had ever seen, or run her tongue across.

Martha kicked up her pace a notch. She'd been a cross-country star at Pepperdine University, and she was still in great shape. 'And that sounds like the beginnings of a gracious loser's speech,' she said.

'We'll see about that, won't we. Loser buys at The Abbey.'

'I can already taste a Dos Equis. Mmm, mmm, good.'

Suddenly the two runners' playful exchange was interrupted by a much louder growl. It was closer, too.

It didn't seem possible that a dog had covered so much ground so fast. Maybe there were a couple of 'Big Dawgs' loose in the area.

'There aren't any cats in this park?' Davis asked. 'I mean, like a *mountain* lion variety of cat?'

'No. Of course not. Get real, pal. We're in San Francisco, not the middle of Montana.' Martha shook her head.

Moisture jumped off her close-cropped reddish-brown hair. Then she thought she heard footsteps. *A runner and a large dog?*

'Let's get out of these woods, okay?' Davis said.

'I hear you. I don't necessarily disagree. Last one to the parking lot is dog chow.'

'Not funny, Lieutenant Martha. Bad joke. This is getting a little spooky.'

'I don't know about big cats around these parts, but I think I just spotted a little pussy.'

Another loud growl – and this time it was really close. Right on the heels of the two of them. Gaining ground fast.

'C'mon! Let's go. Let's move it,' said Martha Wiatt. She was a little afraid now, running as fast as she could, and that was very fast.

Another eerie growl pierced the gathering fog.

Chapter Three

Lieutenant Martha Wiatt had definitely picked up her pace. She put some distance between herself and Davis. It wasn't that hard. She did triathlons *for fun*. He worked behind a desk, though, God knows, he certainly looked good for an accountant.

'C'mon, c'mon. Keep up with me, Davis. Don't fall back,' she called over her shoulder.

Her boyfriend for the past year didn't answer. Well, that settled any future debate about who was in better shape, who was the real athlete. Of course, Martha had known that all along.

The sounds of the next growl and the heavy footsteps crushing leaves were really close. They were catching up to her.

But *what* was catching up to her?

'Martha! There's something behind me. Oh God! Run!

Run, Martha!' Davis shouted. 'Get the hell out of here!'

Adrenaline charged through her. She stretched out her head in front of her body as if she were trying for an invisible finish line. Her arms and legs moved in synch like efficient pistons. She leaned her weight forward, the way all good runners do.

She heard screams behind her and looked back – but she couldn't see Davis anymore. The screams were so terrifying that she almost stopped running. But Davis had been attacked by something vicious. Martha rationalized that she had to get help. The police. Somebody.

Her boyfriend's screams were ringing in her ears and she was running in total panic, unaware of where she was going. She stumbled over a pointy rock and cartwheeled down a steep hill, crashing into the base of a small tree, but at least it stopped her fall.

In a daze, she managed to pull herself up. Jesus, she was pretty sure she'd broken her right arm. Cradling it with the left, she ran forward in a clumsy stumble.

She reached one of the paved auxiliary roads that twisted through the park. Davis's screams had stopped. What had happened to him? She had to get help.

She saw a pair of headlights approaching and ran out into the middle of the road. She straddled the double center lines and felt like a total madwoman. *For God's sake, this is San Francisco!*

'Please stop, please stop. Hey! Hey! Hey!' She waved her good arm and shouted at the top of her voice. 'Stop! I need help!'

The white van sped straight for her, but then, thank God, it skidded to a stop. Two men jumped out and ran to her. They would help. The van said 'Red Cross' on its hood.

'Help me. Please,' Martha said. 'My boyfriend is hurt.'

Things went from bad to worse. One of them hit her with a closed fist. Before Martha realized what was happening, she went down hard. Her chin struck the pavement, bouncing like a wet ball. She was knocked almost unconscious by the powerful blow.

She looked up, tried to focus her eyes, and wished she hadn't. Blazing red eyes stared down at her. A mouth was open wide. *Two* mouths. She had never seen such teeth in her life. They were like sharpened knives. The incisors were huge.

She felt the teeth bite into her cheek, then her neck. *How could that be?* They tore into her and Martha screamed until her throat was raw. She rolled and twisted and kicked out at her attackers, but it did no good. They were incredibly strong. Both of them were growling.

'Ecstasy,' one of them whispered against Martha's ear. 'Isn't it exquisite? You're so lucky. You were chosen out of all the beautiful people in San Francisco. You and Davis.'

Chapter Four

It was a perfect, blue-skied morning in Washington – well, almost perfect. The Mastermind was on my cell phone. 'Hello, Alex. Did you miss me? I missed you, partner.'

The bastard had been making obscene, threatening phone calls to me every morning for over a week. Sometimes he just cursed at me for several minutes; this morning, he sounded positively civil.

'What's your day look like? Any big plans?' he asked.

Actually, yes. I was planning to catch him. I was inside an FBI van that was already on the move. We were tracing his call and would have the exact location very soon. A court order had been put through the FBI and the phone company was involved in 'trapping' the call. I was in the rear of the speeding van with three Bureau agents and my partner, John Sampson. We had left my house on Fifth

Street as soon as the call came in; we were heading onto I-395 North. My job was to keep him on the line until the trace was completed.

'Tell me about Betsey Cavalierre. Why did you pick her instead of me?' I asked him.

'Oh, she's much, much prettier,' the Mastermind said. 'More fuckable.'

One of the techie agents was talking in the background. I tried to listen to both conversations. The agent said, 'He's living up to his name. We've got a wire tap and *should* be able to trace the call immediately. It *isn't* happening for some reason.'

'Why the hell not?' Sampson asked and moved closer to the agents.

'Don't know exactly. We're picking up different locations, but they keep changing. Maybe he's on a cell phone in a car. Cell phones are harder to trace.'

I could see that we were getting off the D Street Exit. Then we headed into the Third Street tunnel. Where was he?

'Everything all right, Alex? You seem a little distracted,' the Mastermind said.

'No, I'm right here with you. Partner. Enjoying our little breakfast club.'

'I don't know why this is so goddamn hard,' the FBI techie complained.

Because he's the Mastermind, I wanted to yell at him.

I saw the Washington Convention Center on the right. The van was really clipping along, doing sixty or seventy on the city streets.

We passed the Renaissance Hotel. Where the hell was the Mastermind calling from?

'I think we have a fix on him. We're real close,' one of the young agents said in an excited voice.

Suddenly the FBI van stopped; it was chaos inside. Sampson and I pulled out our guns. We had him. I couldn't believe we had him.

Then everyone inside the van groaned and cursed. I looked outside and saw why. I shook my head in disgust.

'Jesus Christ, do you believe this shit!' Sampson yelled and pounded the wall of the van. We were at 935 Pennsylvania Avenue, the J. Edgar Hoover Building. FBI headquarters.

'What's happening now?' I asked the agent in charge. 'Where the hell is he?'

'Shit, the signal is roaming again. It's moving outside Washington. Okay, now it's back in the city. Christ, it just skipped out of the country.'

'Goodbye, Alex. For now anyway. As I told you before, you're next,' the Mastermind said. Then he hung up on me.

Chapter Five

The rest of my day was long, hard, and depressing. More than anything, I needed a break from the Mastermind.

I'm not exactly sure when, where or how I got up the nerve, but I had a date that night. It was with a lawyer for the DA's office here in Washington. Elizabeth Moore was wickedly funny and nicely irreverent. She was a large woman with a really sweet smile that made *me* smile. We were having dinner at Marcel's in Foggy Bottom, a good spot for this kind of thing. The food is French, with a Flemish flair. The night couldn't have been going any better. I thought so, and I was pretty sure that Elizabeth would agree.

After the waiter left with our orders for dessert and coffee, Elizabeth put her hand lightly on top of mine. Our table was lit by a simple crystal votive candle.

'All right, Alex. We've gone through all the preliminaries.

I *enjoyed* the preliminaries,' she said. 'Now what's the catch? There has to be a catch. Has to be. All the good ones are taken. I know that from experience. So why are you still playing the dating game?'

I understood exactly what Elizabeth meant, but I pretended to look slightly puzzled.

'Catch?' I shrugged, then I finally started to smile.

She laughed out loud. 'You're what – thirty-nine, forty?'

'Forty-two, but thanks,' I said.

'You passed every test I could possibly throw at you . . .'

'Such as?'

'Such as picking a great spot for dinner. Romantic, but not too romantic. Such as being right on time when you arrived to pick me up. Such as *listening* to some of the things that actually interest me. Such as being very handsome – not that it matters to me. Yeah, right.'

'I also like children, wouldn't mind having more,' I added. 'I've read all of Toni Morrison's novels. I'm a decent plumber. I can cook if I have to.'

'The *catch*?' she said again. 'Let's leave it.'

Our waiter returned, and right as he was pouring a steaming cup of coffee for Elizabeth, the beeper on my belt went off.

Oh Jesus.

Busted!

I looked across the table at her – and I blinked. I was

definitely the first one to blink.

'You mind if I take this? It's important. I recognize the number – the FBI in Quantico. I won't be long. I'll be right back.'

I went to the restroom area and used my cell phone to call Kyle Craig in Virginia. Kyle has been a solid friend for many years, but ever since I became liaison between the Bureau and the DC police, I've seen way too much of him. He keeps dragging me into the nastiest murder cases on the FBI's docket. I hated taking his calls. *Now* what had happened?

Kyle knew who was calling back. He didn't even bother to say hello. 'Alex, do you remember a case you and I worked about fourteen months ago? A runaway girl was found hung from a lighting fixture in her hotel room. Patricia Cameron? There have been two murders in San Francisco that match up. Happened last night in Golden Gate Park. This is a very bad scene – the worst I've heard about in a while.'

'Kyle, I'm having dinner with an attractive, very nice, interesting woman. I'll talk to you tomorrow. *I'll call you*. I'm off duty tonight.'

Kyle laughed. I amused him sometimes. 'Nana already told me. Your date's a lawyer, right? Listen to this one. The devil meets with this lawyer. Says he can make the lawyer a senior partner, but the lawyer has to give him his soul *and* the soul of everybody in his family. The lawyer stares at the devil and asks, "So what's the catch?" ' After he told his joke, Kyle went on to tell me more than I wanted to hear about the similarities connecting the awful murders in San Francisco to the one I had investigated in DC. I remembered the victim, Patricia Cameron. I could still see her face. I shook off the image.

When he was finished, and Kyle tends to be thorough if a bit long-winded, I went back to join Elizabeth at our table.

She smiled ruefully and shook her head. 'I think I just figured out the catch,' she said.

I did my best to laugh, but my insides were already tied up in knots. 'Honestly, it's not as bad as it looks.'

It's much worse, Elizabeth.

Chapter Six

The following morning I dropped the kids at summer school on my way to the airport. Jannie is eight; Damon just turned ten. They're really good kids, but they're kids. You give them a tiny advantage, they take a lot, and then they take a little more. Someone, I don't remember who, said that 'American children suffer too much mother and too little father.' With my kids, it's been the exact opposite.

'I could get used to this,' Jannie said as we pulled up in front of the Sojourner Truth School. Helen Folasade Adu – *Sade* – was singing softly on the CD. Very nice.

'Don't get used to it. It's a five-block walk from our house to school. When I was a little boy in North Carolina, I used to walk five miles through tobacco fields to school.'

'Yeah, right,' Damon scoffed. 'You forgot that you used to walk *barefoot*. Left that part out.'

'I did. Thanks for reminding me. I used to walk barefoot through those nasty tobacco fields to school.'

The kids laughed and so did I. They're usually good to be around, and I'm always videotaping them. I do it in the hopes that I'll have nice movies to watch when the two of them go bad in their teenage years. Also, I'm afraid I might get CRS someday – the *can't remember shit* disease. It's going around.

'I have a big concert on Saturday,' Damon reminded me. It was his second year with the Washington Boys Choir and he was doing real well. He was going to be the next Luther Vandross, or Al Green, or maybe he was just going to be Damon Cross.

'I'll be home by Saturday, Damon. Trust me, I wouldn't miss your concert.'

'You missed quite a few already,' he said. It was a sharp little dig.

'That was the old me. This is the new and improved Alex. I've also *attended* several of your concerts.'

'You're so funny, Daddy,' Jannie said, and laughed. Both kids are smart, and smart-assed as well.

'I will be home for Damon's concert on Saturday,' I promised. 'Help your grandma around the house. She's almost a hundred years old, you know.'

Jannie rolled her eyes. 'Nana's eighty years young, or so she says. She *loves* to cook, do the dishes, and clean up after us,' she said, imitating Nana's wicked cackle. 'She truly does.'

'Saturday. I can't wait,' I said to Damon. It was the whole truth and nothing but. The Boys Choir was one of Washington's secret treasures. I was ecstatic that Damon was good enough to sing with the group, but most of all that he loved what he was doing.

'Kisses,' I said. 'Hugs too.'

Damon and Jannie groaned, but they leaned in close and I wondered how much longer they would be willing to give me hugs and pecks on the cheek. So I took an extra few while I could get them. When the good times come with your kids, you've got to make them last.

'I love you two,' I said before I let them go off to school. 'What do you say?'

'We love you too,' Damon and Jannie chorused.

'That's why we let you embarrass us to death in front of our school and all our friends,' Jannie said, and she stuck out her tongue.

'This *is* your last ride to school,' I told her. Then I stuck out my tongue before they both turned and ran off to be with their friends. They were growing up way too fast for me.

Chapter Seven

I called Kyle Craig from the airport and he told me his élite crew at Quantico was busy checking for related murders and biting attacks from sea to shining sea. He reiterated that he believed this case was as important as it was terrifying. I wondered what else he knew. Usually more than he tells.

'You're up early, Kyle, and you're busy. This case has caught your full attention. Why is that?'

'Of course it has. It's totally unique. I haven't seen anything remotely like it. Inspector Jamilla Hughes will meet your flight if she can. It's her case and she's supposed to be competent. She's one of two women in Homicide in San Francisco, so she probably is fairly good.'

On the plane trip from DC I read and reread the faxes I'd gotten that morning about the horrific murders in Golden Gate Park. Inspector Hughes' preliminary crime-scene notes were precise and detailed, but most of all gut-wrenching.

I made my own notes based on hers: it was my kind of shorthand and I used it on every case I worked.

Male and female victims found dead at 3:20 A.M. in Golden Gate Park, San Francisco. Why there? Visit park if possible.

Victims hung by feet from oak tree. Why hung? To drain the bodies? Why drain the bodies? Rite of purification? Spiritual cleansing?

Bodies naked and covered in blood. Why naked? Erotic? Sex crimes? Or just brutal? Exposing the victims to the world for some reason?

Male's legs, arms, chest severely gouged – victim appears to have been bitten repeatedly. Male actually died from bites!!!

Female bitten – but not as severely. Also cut with sharp object. Died from massive blood loss, Class IV. Female lost over 40% of her blood.

Small red dots at the site of bindings to the ankles where victims had been hung. Called petechiae by the ME.

Teeth marks on male appear to be those of large animal. Is that even remotely possible? What animal would attack a jogger in a big city park? Seems far-fetched to say the least.

White substance on male victim's legs and stomach. Could be semen. What game were the killers playing? Auto-erotic?

I remembered the related case in Washington. How could I forget it?

A sixteen-year-old runaway girl from Orlando, Florida, had been found dead and severely mutilated in a hotel room downtown. Her name was Patricia Dawn Cameron. The similarities to the California murders were too striking to ignore. The girl in DC had suffered savage bites all over her body. She had been hung by her feet from a hotel room lighting fixture.

Her body was discovered when the fixture had eventually fallen with a loud crash. Patricia Cameron had died of blood loss, another Class IV. She had lost nearly seventy percent of her blood supply.

The first question was an obvious one.

So why did somebody need all that blood?

Chapter Eight

I was still thinking about the strange, terrible bites, and all that blood, as I walked off the plane and into crowded San Francisco International Airport. I looked around for Inspector Jamilla Hughes. Rumor had it that she was an attractive black woman.

I noted that a businessman near the gate was reading *The Examiner*. I could see the bold headline on the front page – HORROR IN GOLDEN GATE PARK, TWO MURDERED.

I didn't see anyone waiting, so I began to look for signs directing me to public transportation. I only had a carry-on bag; I had promised to be home by Saturday for Damon's concert. I had my marching orders and I planned to keep my promises from now on. *Cross my heart.*

A woman walked up to me as I started away from the gate. 'Excuse me, are you Detective Cross?'

I had noticed her just before she spoke to me. She was wearing jeans, a black leather car coat over a powder blue T-shirt. Then I spotted the tell-tale holster under her jacket. She was probably in her mid-thirties, nice looking, down-to-earth, pleasant for a homicide detective, who often come on a little gruff.

'Inspector Hughes?' I asked.

'Jamilla.' She extended her hand and smiled as I took it. Nice smile, too. 'It's good to meet you, Detective. Ordinarily, I'd resist the sell out of any idea that originated with the FBI, but your reputation precedes you. Also, the murder in DC was awfully similar, wasn't it? So – welcome to San Francisco.'

'Good to be here.' I returned the smile as I shook hands with her. Her grip was strong, but not overly so. 'I was just thinking about the murder in DC,' I told her. 'Your crime-scene notes brought it all back to me. We never got anywhere with the murder of Patricia Cameron. You can add that to the file on my so-called reputation, the one that preceded me.'

Jamilla Hughes smiled again. Sincere. Nothing overdone about it; nothing overdone about her either. She didn't particularly look like a homicide detective, and that was probably good. She seemed a little too normal to be a cop.

'Well, we'd better hurry. I've contacted a veterinary dental specialist and he's meeting us at the city morgue.

He's a good friend of the medical examiner. How's that for showing you the sights of San Francisco?'

I shook my head and grinned. 'Actually, it's exactly what I came out here to see. I think I read about it in one of the tour books. When you're in San Francisco don't pass up a chance to see the morgue.'

'It's not in the tour books,' Jamilla said, 'but it should be. It's a whole lot more interesting than any trolley-car ride.'

Chapter Nine

L ess than fifty minutes later, Jamilla Hughes and I were inside the morgue at San Francisco's famed Hall of Justice. We had joined the chief medical examiner, Walter Lee, and the dental expert, Dr Pang.

Dr Allen Pang took his time examining both bodies. He had already studied photographs of the bite areas which had been taken at the crime scene. He was a small man, completely bald, with very thick black-rimmed glasses. At one point during his examination, I noticed Inspector Hughes give a wink to the ME. I think they found Dr Pang just a little strange. So did I, but he was very thorough, and obviously serious about the job he had taken on.

'Okay, okay. I'm ready to talk about the nature of the bites now.' He finally turned to us and made his pronouncement. 'I understand you're making casts of the bite marks, Walter?'

'Yes, we lifted the marks with fingerprint powder. The casts should be ready in a day or two. We swabbed to gather saliva, of course.'

'Well, good. That's the right approach, I think. I'm ready to state my piece, my educated guess.'

'That's excellent, Allen,' Lee said in a soft, very dignified voice. He wore a white coat with the nickname Dragon stitched on one pocket. He was a tall man, probably six-two, and weighed at least two-fifty. He carried himself with confidence. 'Dr Pang is a friend I have used before,' Lee continued. 'He's a veterinary dental expert from the Animal Medical Center in Berkeley. Allen is one of the best in the world, and we're lucky to have him on this case.'

'Thank you for your time, Dr Pang,' Inspector Hughes said. 'This is terrific of you to help.'

'Thank you.' I joined in with the hallelujah chorus of praise.

'It's perfectly all right,' he said. 'I'm not exactly sure where to start, other than to say that these two homicides are most interesting to me. The male was severely bitten, and I'm relatively sure the attacker was, well, it was a tiger. The bites on the female were inflicted by two humans. It's as if the humans and the large cat were running together. Like they were a pack. Extraordinary. And bizarre, to say the least.'

'A *tiger*?' Jamilla was the one to express the disbelief we were all feeling. 'Are you sure? That doesn't seem possible, Dr Pang.'

'Allen,' Walter Lee said. 'Explain, please.'

'Well, as you know, humans are heterodonts; that is, they have teeth of different sizes and shapes, which serve different functions. Most important would be our canines, which are situated between the lateral and the first premolar on each side of each jaw. The canines are used to tear food.'

Walter Lee nodded, and Dr Pang continued. He was speaking solely to the ME at this point. I caught Jamilla's eye, and she gave me a wink. I liked that she had a sense of humor.

Dr Pang now seemed in his own world. 'In contrast to humans, some animals are homodents. Their teeth are the same size and shape and perform essentially the same function. This is not true of large cats, however, especially tigers. The teeth of tigers have been adapted for their feeding habits. Each jaw contains six pointed cutting teeth; two very sharp, recurved canines; and molars that have evolved into cutting blades.'

'Is that important in terms of these murders?' Jamilla Hughes asked Dr Pang. I had a version of the same question.

The small man nodded enthusiastically. 'Oh, of course. Certainly. The jaw of a tiger is extremely strong, able to clamp down hard enough to crush bone. The jaw can only move up and down, not side to side. This means the tiger can only tear and crush food, not chew or gnaw.' He demonstrated with his own teeth and jaw.

I swallowed hard, and found my head shaking back and forth. *A tiger was involved in these murders? How could that possibly be?*

Dr Pang stopped talking. He reached up and scratched his bald pate rather vigorously. Then he said, 'What completely baffles me is that someone commanded the tiger away from its prey after it struck – *and the tiger obeyed*. If that didn't happen, the prey would have been eaten.'

'Absolutely amazing,' the medical examiner said, and gave Dr Pang a pat on the back. Then he looked at Jamilla and me. 'What's the saying – "catch a tiger, if you can"? A tiger shouldn't be all that hard to find in San Francisco.'

Chapter Ten

The large, white, male tiger was making a chuffing sound, a muted, backward whistle. The sucking noise came from deep inside its wide throat. The sound was almost unearthly. Birds took flight from a nearby cypress oak. Small animals scampered away as fast as they could.

The tiger was eight feet long, muscular, and weighed just over five hundred and eighty pounds. Under ordinary circumstances its prey would have been pigs and piglets, deer, antelope, water buffalo. There were no ordinary circumstances in California. There were lots of humans, though.

The cat pounced quickly, its lithe, powerful body moving effortlessly. The young blond male didn't even try to resist.

The tiger's massive jaw opened wide, then clamped down onto the man's head. The cat's jaws were strong enough to pulverize bone.

The man screamed, 'Stop! Stop! *Stop!*'

Amazingly the tiger stopped.

Just like that. On verbal command.

'You win,' the blond man laughed and patted the animal, which released his head.

The man twisted sharply to the left. His movements were almost as quick and effortless as the cat's. Then he pounced. He attacked the tiger's vulnerable creamy-white underside, grabbing onto flesh with his teeth. 'Got you, you big baby! You lose. You're still my love slave.'

William Alexander stood off in the distance, watching his younger brother with a mixture of curiosity and awe. Michael was a beautiful man-child, incredibly graceful and athletic, strong beyond belief. He wore a black pocket T-shirt and powder blue shorts. He was already six feet three and a hundred-eighty-five pounds. He was flawless. Both of them were, actually.

William walked away, staring into the distance at the rich, green hills. He loved it out here. The beauty and the solitude, the freedom to do anything he wanted to do.

He was very quiet inside – an art that he was still mastering.

When he and Michael were small boys, this whole area had been a commune. Their mother and father had been hippies, experimenters, freedom lovers, massive drug-takers. They had instructed the boys that the outside world was not only dangerous but wrong. Their mother had taught William and Michael that having sex with anyone, even with her, was a good thing, as long as it was consensual. The brothers had slept with their mother, and their father, and many others in the commune. Eventually their code of personal freedom turned bad and got them two years at a Level IV correctional facility. They had been arrested for possession, but it was aggravated assault that put the brothers behind bars. They were suspected of much more serious crimes, but none could be proved.

As William stared off at the foothills, he marveled at the concept of the *unbridled mind*. Day by day he left behind the shabby baggage of his past life. Soon he would have no false morals, or ethics, or any of the other bullshit inhibitions taught in the civilized world.

He was getting closer to the truth. So was Michael.

William was twenty.

Michael was only seventeen.

They had been killing together for five years, and they kept getting better and better at it.

They were invincible.

Immortal.

Chapter Eleven

That night, the two brothers hunted in the town of Mill Valley in Marin County. The area was beautiful, small mountains teeming with strapping, healthy evergreen and eucalyptus trees. The redwood house was maybe a hundred yards ahead, up a steep, rocky slope that they climbed with ease. A brick walkway led to an entryway with double wooden doors.

'We have to go away for a while.' William spoke without turning around to Michael. 'We have a mission from the Sire. San Francisco was just the start.'

'That's excellent,' Michael said, and he began to smile. 'I enjoyed what went down there very much. Who are these people, the ones in the big, fancy house?'

William shrugged. 'Just prey. They're nobody.'

Michael began to pout. 'Why won't you tell me who they are?'

'The Sire said not to talk, and not to bring the cat.'

Michael asked no further questions. His obedience to the Sire was complete.

The Sire told you how to think, feel, and act.

The Sire was accountable to no one, to no other authority.

The Sire despised the straight world, as did they.

This definitely looked like the 'straight world'. The large house had all the trappings: gardens tended and watered daily; a small pond filled with koi; several layers of terraces leading up to a large house with over a dozen rooms – for just two people. How obnoxious could anyone be?

William walked right in the front door and Michael followed. The foyer had a twenty-foot ceiling, a ridiculous crystal chandelier, a spiral staircase to heaven.

They found the couple in the kitchen, preparing a late meal, both of them sharing the preparations like the goodie-goodies that they were.

'Yuppies at play,' William said, and smiled.

'Whoa!' the male said, and threw up both of his hands. He was close to six-four and well-built. He was working like kitchen help at the vegetable sink. 'What the hell do you guys think you're doing? Let's take it outside.'

'*You're* the trouble-making lawyer,' William said, and pointed at the female. She was early thirties, short blond hair, high cheekbones, slender, with small breasts. 'We came for supper.'

'I'm a lawyer, too,' the domineering male said. 'I don't think you two were invited. I'm sure of it. Get out! You hear me? Hey, you assholes, hit the road.'

'You threatened the Sire.' William continued to talk to the female. 'So he sent us here.'

'I'm going to call the police.' The woman finally spoke. She was upset now, the nubs of her breasts rising and falling against her shirt. She had a small cell phone in her hand and William wondered if she had pulled it out of her ass. The thought made him smile.

He was on her in an instant and Michael took down the husband almost as easily. The brothers were incredibly fast and strong – and they knew it.

They growled loudly, but that was only an element of surprise, a scare tactic.

'We have money in the house. My God, don't hurt us,' the male shrieked loudly, almost like a woman.

'We're not after your obscene money – we have no use for it. And we're not serial killers, or anything common like that,' William told them.

He bit down into the struggling woman's luscious pink neck – and she stopped fighting. Just like that, she was his. She gazed into his eyes, and she swooned. A tear ran down her cheek.

William didn't look up again until he had fed. 'We're vampires,' he finally whispered to the murdered couple.

Chapter Twelve

O n my second day in San Francisco, I worked out of a small cubicle near Jamilla Hughes' desk at the Hall of Justice. I attended a couple of her briefings on the Golden Gate Park murders, which were thorough and highly professional. She was impressive.

Everything about the murder case was weird and wrongheaded, though. No one had a fix on it yet; no one had a good idea, at least none that I'd heard so far. The only thing we knew for sure was that people were being murdered in particularly horrible ways. It happens more and more frequently these days.

Around noon, I got a call on my cell phone. 'Just checking in,' the Mastermind said. 'How is San Francisco, Alex? Lovely city. Will you leave your heart there? Do you think it's a good place to die?

'Or how about Inspector Hughes? Do you like her?

She's very pretty, isn't she? Just your type. Are you going to fuck Jamilla? Better hurry then. Tempus fugit.' He hung up.

I went back to work. Lost myself for a couple of hours. Began to make some minor progress.

Around four o'clock, I was staring out at the start of rush hour San Francisco-style – pretty mild, actually – while I talked to Kyle Craig. He was still at Quantico, but he was definitely heavily involved in the case.

Kyle was in a position to choose the cases he became personally connected with, and he told me this was going to be one of them. We'd be working together again. I looked forward to it.

I caught a movement out of the corner of my eye and saw Jamilla approaching. She had her leather jacket half on and was struggling into the second sleeve. Going somewhere? 'Hold on, Kyle,' I said into the receiver.

'We have to go,' she said, 'to San Luis Obispo. They're going to exhume a body. I think it's related.'

I told Kyle that I had to leave right away. He wished me happy hunting. Jamilla and I took the elevator down to the parking garage beneath the Hall of Justice. The more I saw of her work, the more I was impressed; not just by her savvy, but by her enthusiasm for the job. A lot of detectives lose that after a couple of years. She obviously hadn't. *Are you going to fuck Jamilla? Better hurry then.*

'Are you always this pumped up?' I asked her once we

were inside her blue Saab and heading out toward Highway 101.

'Yeah. Pretty much,' she said. 'I like the work. It's tough, but interesting, honest most of the time. I could do without the violence.'

'This case in particular. The hangings give me the creeps.'

She looked over at me. 'Speaking of life-threatening situations, you'd better buckle up. We've got a hike ahead of us, and I used to drive funny cars as a hobby. Don't be fooled by the Saab.'

She wasn't kidding. According to the road signs, it was about 235 miles to San Luis Obispo. Heavy rain peppered the car most of the way. She still got us there by eight-thirty.

'In one piece, too.' She nodded and winked as we whisked off the highway at the San Luis Obispo exit.

It looked like an idyllic spot, but we were there to exhume the corpse of a young girl. She had been hung and her blood had been drained.

Chapter Thirteen

San Luis Obispo is a very pretty college town, at least from the outside looking in. We found Higuera Street and drove down it to Osos, past small local shops, but also Starbucks, Barnes & Noble, the Firestone Grill. Jamilla told me that you could always tell the time of day in San Luis Obispo by the scents and aromas: like barbecue smoke in the afternoon on Marsh Street, or the aroma of wheat and barley at night outside the Slo Brewing Co.

We met Detective Nancy Goodes at the police station in town. She was a petite, attractive woman, with a nice California tan, very much in charge of her homicide investigation. In addition to contacting us about this exhumation, she was also the lead on the murders of two students from Cal Poly that didn't seem related to our case, but who could tell for sure. Like most homicide detectives these days, she was busy.

★ ★ ★

'We've got the permissions we need to exhume the body,' Goodes told us on the way out to the cemetery. At least the rain had stopped for now. The air was warm, thanks to Santa Ana winds.

'What can you tell us about the murder, Nancy? You worked the case yourself, right?' Jamilla asked.

The detective nodded. 'I did. So did just about every other detective in town. It was very sad, and an important case here. Mary Alice Richardson went to the Catholic high school in town. Her father's a well-liked doctor. She was a nice kid, but a bit of a wild child. What can I tell you, she was a *kid*. Fifteen years old.'

'What do you mean she was a wild child?' I asked Detective Goodes.

She sighed and worked her jaw a little. I could tell this case had left a wound. 'She missed a lot of school, two or three days a week sometimes. She was bright enough, but her grades were just terrible. She hung with other kids who liked to experiment – drugs like Ecstasy, raves, black magic, heavy drinking, all-night parties. Maybe even a little free-basing. Mary Alice was only arrested once, but she was giving her parents a lot of premature gray hairs.'

Jamilla asked, 'Were you at the crime scene, Nancy?' I noticed that she was respectful of the other detective at all times. Very non-threatening toward Nancy.

'Unfortunately, I was. That's one of the reasons I worked so hard getting the permissions we needed to dig up her body. Mary Alice died a year and three months ago, but I will never, ever forget how we found her.'

Jamilla and I looked at each other. We hadn't heard the particulars of the murder yet. We were still playing catch-up.

Goodes continued. 'It was pretty clear to me that she was meant to be found. Two kids from Cal Poly were the ones who actually discovered the body. They were parking out near the hills. It's a popular spot for submarine races. They went for a little moonlit stroll. I'm sure they had nightmares after what they saw. Mary Alice was hanging from a cypress tree by her bare feet. Naked. Except the killers left her earrings, and a small sapphire in her belly button. This wasn't a robbery.'

'How about her clothes?' I asked.

'We found the clothes: UFO parachute pants, Nikes, Chili Peppers T-shirt. No trophies were taken to our knowledge.'

I glanced at Jamilla. 'The killer trusts his or her memory. Doesn't need trophies for some reason. Or so it seems. None of this follows any of the usual paths for serials.'

'No, it doesn't. I agree with that one hundred percent. Do you know what scarification is?' Detective Goodes asked.

'I've come across it,' I said. 'Scars, wounds. Most often on the legs and arms. Occasionally the chest or back. They avoid the face, because then people might make them stop. Usually the scars are self-inflicted.'

Detective Goodes nodded. 'Mary Alice had either cut herself over the past couple of months, or someone else did it for her. She had over seventy separate cuts on her body. Everywhere but the face.'

The detective's white Suburban pulled onto a gravel road, then we passed between rusted wrought-iron gates.

'We're here,' Nancy Goodes announced. 'Let's get this over with. Cemeteries make me twitchy. I hate what we're going to do. This makes me so sad.'

It made me sad, too.

Chapter Fourteen

I have yet to meet a relatively sane person who is anything but twitchy in a cemetery late at night. I consider myself to be mildly sane, therefore I was twitchy. Detective Goodes was right, this was a very sad affair, a tragic conclusion to a young girl's life.

The backdrop for the cemetery was the rolling foothills of the Santa Lucia Mountains. Three patrol cars from the police department in San Luis Obispo were already parked around the gravesite of Mary Alice Richardson. The medical examiner's van was parked nearby. Plus two beat-up trucks without any clear identification on them.

Four cemetery workers were digging in the bright light cast from the patrol-car headlamps. The soil looked rich and loamy and was thick with worms. When the hole was of sufficient depth, a backhoe was brought in to finish the job.

The police observers, including myself, had nothing to do but stand impatiently around the grave. We drank coffee, exchanged small talk, cracked a few dark jokes, but nobody really laughed.

I turned my cell phone off. I didn't need to hear from the Mastermind, or anybody else, here in the cemetery.

Around one in the morning, the container of the casket was finally uncovered by the cemetery workers. A lump rose in my throat, but I looked on. Beside me stood Jamilla Hughes. She was shivering some, but sticking it out. Nancy Goodes had retreated to her Suburban. Smart lady.

A crowbar was used to pry off the top of the liner. It made an unpleasant groaning noise, like someone in deep pain.

The hole in the ground was approximately six feet deep, eight feet long, less than four feet wide.

Neither of us spoke. Every detail of the exhumation held our attention now. My eyes blinked too rapidly in the eerie light. My breathing was uneven and my throat felt a little raw.

I was recalling crime-scene pictures of Mary Alice that I'd seen. Fifteen years old. Hung two feet off the ground by her ankles, left that way for several hours. Drained of nearly all her blood. Another Class IV death. Viciously bitten and stabbed.

The victim in Washington hadn't been stabbed. So what

did that mean? Why the variations on the murder theme? What did they do with all the blood? I almost didn't want to know the answers to the questions throbbing inside my head.

Tattered gray canvas straps were carefully secured to the casket and it was finally, slowly raised out of the ground.

My breathing was ragged. Suddenly I felt guilty about being here. I had the thought that we shouldn't be disturbing this poor girl in her grave. It was an unholy thing to do. She had been violated enough.

'I know, I know. This sucks. I feel the same thing,' Jamilla said out of the side of her mouth. She lightly touched a hand to my elbow. 'We have to do it. No other choice. We have to find out if it's the same killers.'

'I know. Why doesn't that make me feel any better about this?' I muttered. 'I feel all hollowed out.'

'That poor girl. Poor Mary Alice. Forgive us,' Jamilla said.

A local funeral director, who had consented to be on hand, carefully opened the casket. Then he stepped back, as if he had seen a ghost.

I moved forward to get my first look at the girl. I nearly gasped, and Jamilla's hand went to her mouth. A couple of the cemetery workers crossed themselves and bowed their heads low.

Mary Alice Richardson was right there staring up at us. She was wearing a flowing white dress and her blond hair was carefully braided. The girl looked as if she had been buried alive. There had been virtually no decay of the body.

'There's an explanation for this,' the funeral director said to us. 'The Richardsons are friends of mine. They asked me if anything could be done to preserve their daughter for as long as possible. Somehow they knew their little girl would be seen again.

'The condition of the body, once interred, can be in any state of decay. It depends on the ingredients. I used an arsenic solution in the embalming process, the way we used to in the old days. You're looking at the result.'

He paused as we continued to stare.

'This is the way Mary Alice looked the day she was buried. This is the poor girl they murdered and hung.'

Chapter Fifteen

We got back to San Francisco at seven in the morning. I didn't know how Jamilla could drive, but she did just fine. We forced ourselves to talk most of the way back, just to keep awake. We even had a few laughs. I was bone-tired and could barely keep my eyes open. When I finally closed them inside my hotel room, I saw Mary Alice Richardson in her coffin.

Inspector Hughes was drinking coffee at her desk when I arrived at the Hall of Justice at two o'clock that afternoon. She looked fresh and alert. None the worse for wear. She seemed to work as hard as I did on a case, maybe harder. I hoped it was a good thing for her.

'Don't you ever sleep?' I asked as I stopped to talk for a moment. My eyes went to the clutter at her work-space. I noticed a photograph of a smiling, very good-looking man propped on her desk. I was glad that she had time for a love life at least. It made me think of Christine Johnson, who was now living out here on the West Coast. I felt a stab of rejection. The love of my life? Not anymore. Unfortunately, not anymore. Christine had left Washington and moved to Seattle. She liked it there a lot, and was teaching school again.

Jamilla shrugged. 'I woke up around noon, couldn't get back to sleep. Maybe I'm too tired. The ME in Luis Obispo says he'll send us a report late today. But listen to this. I just got an e-mail from Quantico. There have been eight murders in California and Nevada that bear some resemblance to the Golden Gate Park ones. Not all of the victims were hung. But they were bitten. The cases go back six years. So far. They're looking back even further than that.'

'What cities?' I asked her.

She glanced down at her notes. 'Sacramento – our esteemed capital. San Diego. Santa Cruz. Las Vegas. Lake Tahoe. San Jose. San Francisco. San Luis Obispo. This is so goddamn creepy, Alex. One murder like this would be enough to keep me sleepless for a month.'

'Plus the murder in Washington,' I said. 'I'm going to ask the Bureau to look at the East Coast.'

She grinned sheepishly. 'I already did. They're on it.'

I teased, 'So what do we do now?'

'What do cops always do when they wait? We eat doughnuts and drink coffee,' she said and rolled her dark brown eyes. She had a natural, very attractive beauty, even on just a few hours' sleep.

The two of us had a late breakfast at Roma's around the corner. We talked about the case, then I asked her about other cases she'd solved. Jamilla had a lot of confidence, but she was also modest about her contributions. I liked that about her. She definitely wasn't full of herself. When she had finished her omelet and toast, she sat there nervously tapping her finger against the table. She had several tics, seemed wired most of the time. I knew she was on the job again.

'What's the matter?' I finally asked. 'You're holding something back, aren't you?'

She nodded. 'I got a call from KRON-TV. They're close to doing a story revealing that there have been several murders in California.'

I frowned. 'How the hell did they find out?'

She shook her head. 'Who knows? I'm going to give a reporter I know at *The Examiner* the okay to break the story first.'

'Hold on a second,' I said. 'You sure about that?'

'I'm sure. I trust my friend as much as I trust anybody. He'll ground the story in reality at least. Now help me figure out if there's anything we want the killers to read in the newspapers. It's the least my friend can do for us.'

When we got back to the Hall of Justice there was bad news. The killers had struck again.

Chapter Sixteen

I t was another bad one, another hanging. Two hangings, actually.

Jamilla and I split up as soon as we arrived at the murder scene in Mill Valley. We had different ways of doing things, different crime-scene techniques. Somehow, though, I thought we would arrive at the same conclusions about this one. I could see the signs already – all of them bad.

The two bodies were hung upside down from a rack used to hold copper pots. The scene of the murders was a contemporary kitchen inside a large, very expensive house. Dawn and Gavin Brody looked to be in their mid-thirties. Like the other victims, they'd been drained of most of their blood.

The first curiosity: although the Brodys were naked, the killers had left behind their jewelry. A pair of Rolex watches, wedding bands, a large diamond engagement ring, hoop earrings studded with countless small diamonds. The killers weren't interested in jewels or money, and possibly they wanted us to know it.

So where were the victims' clothes? Had they been used to clean up the mess, to mop up blood? Was that why the killers had taken the clothing with them?

They seemed to have interrupted the Brodys, who were both successful lawyers, while they were preparing a meal. Was there some symbolism involved here? Or dark humor? Was it a coincidence, or had they purposely attacked the couple at dinner time? Eat the rich?

Several small town police officers and FBI techies were crowded into the kitchen with us. I figured that the damage had already been done by the Mill Valley police. They were well-intentioned, but had probably never worked a major homicide before. I saw a few dusty footprints on the natural stone kitchen floor. I doubted they belonged to the killers, or the Brodys.

Jamilla had made her way around the large kitchen and now she came up to me. She'd seen enough already. She shook her head, and really didn't have to say what she was thinking. The local police had messed up this crime scene pretty badly.

'This is beyond strange,' she finally said in a low whisper.

'These killers have so much hatred in them. I've never seen anything like it. The rage. Have you, Alex?'

I looked into Jamilla's eyes, but said nothing. Unfortunately, I had.

Chapter Seventeen

The story detailing a 'rampage' of West Coast murders dominated the front page of the San Francisco *Examiner*. All hell had broken loose. Literally.

William and Michael watched it unfold on TV that night. They were impressed with themselves, though they had expected the news story to break soon. They were counting on it in fact. That was the plan.

They were *the special ones*. The chosen team to get the job done. Now they were on their mission. On the road again.

They were chowing down at a diner in Woodland Hills, north of LA, off Highway 5. People in the restaurant noticed the two of them. How could they not? Both were over six feet two, blond ponytails, strapping, well-muscled bodies, dressed completely in black. William and Michael were the archetypes of modern boyhood: *wild animal* meets *entitled prince*.

The news was playing out on TV. The murders were the lead story of course, and the sensationalized coverage lasted for several minutes. Frightened people in Los Angeles, Las Vegas, San Francisco and San Diego were interviewed on camera and had the most incredibly insipid things to say.

Michael frowned and looked over at his brother. 'They got it all wrong. Mostly wrong anyway. What idiots, what fucking drones.'

William took a bite of his dreary sandwich, then he stared up at the TV again. 'Newspapers and TV always get it wrong, little brother. They're part of the larger problem, of what has to be fixed. Like those two lawyers in Mill Valley. You finished here?'

Michael wolfed down the remainder of his extra-rare cheeseburger in a voracious bite. 'I am, and I'm also hungry. I need to feed.' His beautiful blue eyes were glazed.

William smiled and kissed his brother on the cheek. 'C'mon then. I have a good plan for tonight.'

Michael held back. 'Shouldn't we be a little careful? The police are out looking for us, right? We're a big deal now.'

William continued to smile. He loved his brother's naïveté. It amused him. 'We are an incredibly big deal. We're the next big thing. C'mon, little brother. We both need to feed. We deserve it. And besides, the police don't know who we are, always remember this, the police are incompetent fools.'

William drove their white van back down the road they had traveled on through Woodland Hills, before they stopped at the diner. He was sorry they hadn't brought the cat, but this trip was too long. He pulled into an obnoxiously lit shopping mall and studied the signs: Wal-Mart, Denny's, Staples, Circuit City, Wells Fargo Bank. He despised every one of them as well as the people who shopped there.

'We're *not* looking for prey here?' Michael asked. His bright blue eyes darted around the mall and he looked concerned.

William shook his head. The blond ponytail wagged. 'No, of course not. These people aren't worthy of us, Michael. Well, maybe that blonde girl in the tight blue jeans over there is marginally worthy.'

Michael cocked his head sideways, then licked his lips. 'She'll do. For an appetizer.'

William hopped out of the van and walked to the far end of the parking lot. He was strutting a little, smiling, his head held high. Michael followed. The brothers crossed through the back yard of the Wells Fargo Bank. Then the full parking lot of the Denny's restaurant that William thought smelled of bacon grease and fat people.

Michael began to smile when he saw what his brother was up to. They had done this kind of thing before.

A somber black-and-white sign loomed straight ahead of them. It was backlit. *Sorel Funeral Home.*

Chapter Eighteen

It took William less than a minute to crack open the back door into the funeral home. It wasn't a problem since security was minimal.

'Now, we feed,' he said to Michael. He was starting to get excited and his sense of smell led him to the embalming room. He discovered three bodies stored in the refrigerators. 'Two males and a female,' he whispered.

He quickly examined the bodies. Two had been embalmed, one hadn't. They were fresh. William knew about necrology, including what went on in funeral homes. The embalming process involved draining blood from the veins, then injecting a formaldehyde-based fluid. Tubes connected to pumps were inserted into the carotid artery and the jugular vein. The next step involved empty-ing the internal organs of their fluids. After that, much of the work was cosmetic. The jaws of the dead were wired shut. The lips were arranged and sealed with some kind of glue. Eye caps were placed under each eyelid to prevent the eyeballs from sinking into the head.

William pointed to a centrifuge, which was used to drain bodies of blood and other fluids. He began to laugh. 'We won't be needing *that* tonight.'

All his senses were heightened. He felt larger than life. His night vision was excellent. Nothing more than the illumination from a table lamp would be needed.

He walked to the last of three stainless steel tables and took the unembalmed body in his arms. He carried the dead, a woman in her early forties, to a nearby porcelain table.

William looked at his brother and gently rubbed his hands together. He took a deep breath. They had raided funeral homes before, and though it didn't compare to a fresh kill, prey was prey.

Besides, the dead woman was a fairly good physical specimen for her age. She was attractive and compared favorably to the female they had attacked and fed upon in San Francisco. There was a nametag on the body: *Diana Ginn*.

'I hope some funeral director didn't have Diana first,' William said to his brother. Pathetic geeks sometimes took jobs at funeral homes so that they could ravage the dead at their leisure. They'd do unnecessary searches into vaginal and anal cavities. Another kinky pastime was to have sex with the dead in a coffin. It happened more than people could imagine.

William found that he was excited. There was nothing to compare to this. He climbed up on the embalming table and positioned himself above the woman.

Diana Ginn's naked body was ashen, but pretty enough in the dim light. Her lips were full and blue. He wondered how she had died, since she didn't look sick. There were no obvious wounds. She hadn't been in an accident.

William carefully pried open the eyelids, looked into her eyes. 'Hello, my sweet girl. You're beautiful, Diana,' he whispered dreamily. 'That isn't just a cheap pickup line. I mean it. You're extraordinary. You're worthy of tonight, of Michael and me. And we will be worthy of you.'

He let his fingers lightly graze her cheeks, then the long neck, her breasts, which weren't pert now but more like sacs of pudding. He studied the intricate lines of her veins. So beautiful. He was almost dizzy with lust for Diana Ginn.

While William crouched low over the body, his brother lightly stroked the woman's bony feet, her thin ankles, then slowly, lovingly moved his hands up the long legs. He was moaning softly, as if he were trying to waken her from the deepest sleep.

'We love you,' Michael whispered. 'We know you can hear us. You're still here in your body, aren't you? We know, Diana. We know exactly how you feel. We're the undead.'

Chapter Nineteen

I continued to be impressed with the tremendous discipline and hard work of Jamilla Hughes. What drove her? Something buried in her past? Something more obvious in the present? The fact that she was one of two women homicide inspectors in the San Francisco Police Department? Maybe all of the above? Jamilla had already told me that she hadn't taken a day of comp time in almost two years. That sounded kind of familiar.

A couple of times during the next day at the Hall of Justice I mentioned her incredible work ethic, but she shrugged it off. She was well respected by the other homicide inspectors. She was a regular person. No false airs. No bullshit about her. I found out that she had a nickname. It suited her – *Jam*.

I spent a couple of hours in the afternoon finding out what I could about tigers. Area zoos and shelters were being canvassed in an attempt to locate every single tiger in California. The murderous cat was our best lead so far.

I was keeping my own list of facts, different things that struck me.

Someone had been able to command and control the tiger before and after it had attacked and bitten Davis O'Hara in Golden Gate Park. An animal trainer? A vet?

The jaw of a tiger was so strong that it could crush bone, and then pulverize it. And yet, someone had been able to call the tiger off its prey.

All tiger species were considered endangered. Their existence was being challenged by both loss of habitat and poaching. Could the killers also be environmentalists?

Tigers were being poached for their suspected healing powers. Almost every part of the cat was considered valuable, and in some cases, sacred.

Tigers had magical significance in some cultures, especially in parts of Asia. Could that be important to the case?

I had lost track of the time, and when I looked up from my note-taking it was already getting dark outside. Jamilla was striding down the corridor in my direction.

She had on a long black leather jacket, and looked ready to leave. She'd put on lipstick. Maybe she had a date. She looked terrific. 'Tyger, Tyger, burning bright,' she recited a line from Blake's poem.

I answered with the only other line I could remember.

'Did He who made the Lamb make thee?'

She looked pensive, then she smiled. 'What a team. The poet detectives. Let's get a beer.'

'I'm pretty beat and I have a few more files to check. I think I'm still jet-lagged.' Even as I was saying the words, I wasn't sure why the hell I was saying them.

She put up her hand. 'All right already. You could have just said *no, you're not my type*. Jeez, man. I'll see you in the morning. But thanks for all your help. I mean that.' I saw her smile as she turned, then walked away, down the long hall to the elevators. But then I saw her shake her head.

After she was gone, I sat at the desk overlooking the streets of San Francisco. I sighed, and then I shook *my* head. I could feel a familiar weariness settling in. I was alone again and I had no one to blame. Why had I turned Jamilla down for a couple of beers? I liked her company. I didn't have any other plans; and I wasn't *that* jet-lagged.

But I thought I knew the reason. It wasn't too complicated. I had gotten close to my last two partners on homicide cases. Both Patsy and Betsey were women I liked. Both had died.

The Mastermind was still out there.

Could he be in San Francisco right now?

Was Jamilla Hughes safe in her own city?

Chapter Twenty

The ringing of the telephone in my hotel room woke me early the next morning. I was groggy, still half-asleep when I picked up.

It was Jamilla, and she sounded a little breathless. 'I got a call late last night from my friend Tim at *The Examiner*,' she told me. 'He's got a lead for us. This could be good stuff.' She quickly filled me in on the sketchy details of an attempted murder, an old case. We had a witness this time. She and I were going on the road again. She didn't ask if I wanted to go – it was apparently a done deal.

'I'll pick you up in half an hour, forty minutes at the latest. We're going to LA. Wear black. Maybe you'll get discovered.'

United flies an hourly shuttle between San Francisco and Los Angeles. We just made the nine o'clock and were in

LA an hour or so later. We didn't stop talking for the entire trip. We rented a car at Budget and headed to Brentwood. I was as pumped up about the new lead as she was. The FBI was also in on the game in LA.

On the way to Brentwood, she checked in with her pal Tim at *The Examiner*. I wondered if Tim was a boyfriend. 'You find out any more for us?' she asked. She listened, then repeated what she heard for me. Part of it we already knew.

'Two men attacked the woman we're going to see. She managed to get away from them. Lucky girl, incredibly lucky. They bit her severely. Chest, neck, stomach, face. She thought the perps were in their mid-forties to mid-fifties. The attack occurred over a year ago, Alex. It was a big story in the supermarket tabloids.'

I didn't say anything, just listened to her, took it all in. This case was so strange. I hadn't seen anything quite like it.

'They were going to hang her from a tree. There was no mention of a tiger in any of the articles my friend was able to dig up. A detective from the LAPD is meeting us at the station house. I'm sure we'll hear more details from him. He was the lead detective on the case.'

She looked over at me. She had something here, something good. 'Here's the kicker, Alex. According to my source, the woman believes her attackers were vampires.'

Chapter Twenty-One

We met with Gloria Dos Santos at the police station in the Brentwood section of LA. It was a one-story concrete building, about as non-descript as a post office. Detective Peter Kim joined us in a small interview room, which was about six by five feet, soundproof, with padded walls. Kim was slender, around six feet, in his late twenties. He dressed well, and seemed more like an up-and-coming Los Angeles business executive than a policeman to me.

Gloria Dos Santos obviously knew Kim, and they didn't seem too fond of each other. She called him 'Detective Fuhrman', and she used the name over and over, until Kim told her to 'can it' or he would lock her the hell up.

Dos Santos wore a short black dress, high black boots, leather wristbands. There were about a dozen earrings in strategic locations on her body. Her frizzy black hair was piled high, but some also cascaded down to her shoulders. She was only an inch or two over five feet and had a hard face. Her lashes were thick with mascara and she used purple eye shadow. She looked to be in good physical shape – like all the other victims so far.

She stared at Kim, then at me, and finally at Jamilla Hughes. She shook her head and smirked. She didn't like us, which was fine – I didn't much like her either.

She sneered. 'Can I smoke in this rat-trap? I'm going to smoke, like it or not. If you don't like it, then I'm going the hell home.'

'So smoke,' Kim said. 'But you're not going home under any fucking circumstances.' He took out some David's ranch-style seeds and started to eat them. Kim was a strange boy himself.

Dos Santos lit up a Camel and blew out a thick stream of smoke in Kim's face.

'Detective *Fuhrman* knows everything that I know. Why don't you just get it all from him? He's brilliant, y'know. Just ask him about it. Graduated with some cumma honors from UCLA.'

'There are a few things we aren't clear about,' I said to her. 'That's why we came all the way from San Francisco to see you. Actually, I came from Washington, DC.'

'Long trip for nothing, Shaft,' she said. Gloria Dos Santos had a zinger for every occasion. She wiped her hand over her face a few times as if she were trying to wake herself up.

'You're obviously high as a kite,' Jamilla cut in. 'That doesn't matter to us. Relax, girl. These men who attacked you hurt you pretty bad.'

Dos Santos snorted. 'Pretty bad? They broke two ribs, broke my arm. They knocked me down 'bout six times. Fortunately, they knocked me right down a goddamn hill, side of a mountain, actually. I started rolling. Got up. Ran my ass off.'

'The initial report said that you didn't see either of them very well. Then you claimed that they were in their forties or fifties.'

She shrugged. 'I don't know. It was foggy. That's an impression I had. Earlier that night, I went to the Fang Club on West Pico. It's the only place where you can meet real vampires and live to tell about it. So they say. I was going to a lot of Goth clubs back then – Stigmata, Coven 13, Vampiricus over in Long Beach. I worked at Necromane. *What's Necromane?*' she asked, as if it were a question we would want answered. She was right. 'Necromane is a boutique for people who are really into the dead. You can buy real human skulls there. Fingers, toes. A full human skeleton if that's your thing.'

'It's not,' Jamilla said. 'But I've been to a shop like that in San Francisco. It's called the Coroner.'

The girl looked at her contemptuously. 'So I'm fucking impressed? You must be very cool. You must live right on the edge.'

I spoke again. 'We're trying to help you. We—'

She cut me off. 'Bullshit, you're trying to help yourselves. You've got another big case. Those kinky murders in San Francisco, right? I can *read*, man. You couldn't care less about Gloria Dos Santos and her problems. I got lots of them. More than you know. Who gives a shit, right?'

'Two people were killed in Golden Gate Park. It was a massacre. Did you read that? We think it might be the same men who attacked you,' I told her.

'Yeah, well let me tell you something you better get straight. The two men who attacked me were *vampires*! Got that? I know this is impossible for you to wrap your little minds around, but there are vampires. They set themselves apart from the human world. That means – they aren't like you!

'Two of them almost killed me. They were hunting in Beverly Hills. They kill people *every fucking day in LA*! They drink their blood. They call it feeding. They chew on their bones like it's KFP, that's Kentucky Fried People, chumps. I can see you don't believe me. Well, *believe me*.'

The door to the interview room opened quietly. A uniformed patrolman popped in and whispered something to Detective Kim.

Kim frowned and looked at us, then at Dos Santos. 'There was a killing on Sunset Boulevard a short time ago. Someone was bitten and then hanged at one of the better hotels.'

Gloria Dos Santos's face twisted horribly. Her eyes grew small and very angry. She flew into a rage, started to scream at the top of her voice. 'They followed you here, you assholes! Don't you get it? They followed you! Oh my God, they know I talked to you. Oh Jesus Christ, they'll get me. You just got me killed!'

Part Two

Blood Lust

Chapter Twenty-Two

I always liked working tough murder cases with Kyle Craig, so I was glad that he would be joining Jamilla Hughes and me in Los Angeles later that day. I was surprised, however, when I saw him already at the murder scene in Beverly Hills when we arrived. The body had been found at the Chateau Marmont, the hotel where John Belushi had overdosed and died.

The hotel looked like a French castle and rose seven stories over the Sunset Strip. As I entered the lobby, I noticed that everything looked to be authentic 1920s, but dated rather than antique. Supposedly, a studio boss had once told the actor William Holden, 'If you have to get into trouble, do it at the Chateau Marmont.'

Kyle met us at the door of the hotel room. His dark hair was slicked back and it looked like he'd gotten a little sun. Unusual for Kyle. I almost didn't recognize him.

'This is Kyle Craig, FBI,' I told Jamilla. 'Before I met you, he was the best homicide investigator I ever worked with.'

Kyle and Jamilla shook hands. Then we followed him into the hotel room. Actually, it was a hillside bungalow: two bedrooms, a living room with a working fireplace. It had its own private street entrance.

The crime scene was as depressingly bad as the others. I recalled something typically pessimistic that a philosopher had written. I'd once had this same thought at a grisly crime scene in North Carolina: 'Human existence must be a kind of error. It is bad today and every day it will get worse, until the worst of all happens.' My own philosophy was a little cheerier than Schopenhauer's, but there were times when he seemed on the mark.

The worst of all had happened to a twenty-nine-year-old record company executive named Jonathan Mueller, and in the worst possible way. There were bites on his neck. I didn't see any knife cuts. Mueller had been hung from a lighting fixture in the hotel room. His skin was waxy and translucent and I didn't think he had been dead very long.

The three of us moved closer to the hanging body. It was swaying slightly, and still dripping blood.

'The major bites are all in his neck,' I said. 'It looks like role-playing vampires again. The hanging has to be their ritual, maybe their signature.'

'This is so goddamn creepy,' Jamilla whispered. 'This poor guy had the blood sucked out of him. It almost looks like a sex crime.'

'I think it is,' Kyle said. 'I think they seduced him first.'

Just then the cell phone in my jacket pocket went off. The timing couldn't have been worse.

I looked at Kyle before I answered the call. 'It could be him,' I said. 'The Mastermind.'

I put the receiver to my ear.

'How do you like LA, Alex?' the Mastermind asked in his usual mechanical drone. 'The dead pretty much look the same everywhere, don't they?'

I nodded at Kyle. He understood who was on the line. The Mastermind.

He motioned for me to give him the phone and I handed it over. I watched his face as he listened, then frowned deeply. Kyle finally took the phone away from his ear.

'He broke off the connection,' he said. 'It was like he knew you weren't on the line anymore. How did he know, Alex? How does the bastard know so much? What the hell does he want from you?'

I stared at the slowly revolving corpse, and I didn't have any answers. None at all. I felt drained myself.

Chapter Twenty-Three

It was Friday already and we were in the middle of a nasty, sordid mess that wasn't going to be over soon. In the afternoon I had to make a tough phone call home to Washington. Nana Mama answered after a couple of rings, and I immediately wished that one of the kids had picked up instead.

'It's Alex. How are you?'

She said, 'You're not coming home for Damon's concert tomorrow, are you, Alex? Or did you forget all about the concert already. Oh, Alex, Alex. Why have you forsaken us? This isn't right.'

I love Nana tremendously, but sometimes she goes too far to make her point. 'Why don't you put Damon on the phone?' I said. 'I'll talk to him about it.'

'He's not going to be a boy for very much longer. Pretty soon he'll be just like you, won't listen to a word anybody says. Then you'll see what it's like. I guarantee you won't like it,' she said.

'I feel bad enough already, guilty enough. You don't have to make it worse, old woman.'

'Of course I do. That's my job, and I take it as seriously as you obviously take yours,' she said.

'Nana, people are dying out here. Someone died a horrible death in Washington to get me involved in this mess. It keeps happening. There's a connection I have to find, or at least try to.'

'Yes, people are dying, Alex. I understand that. And other people are growing up without their father around as much as they need him to be – especially since they don't have a mother. Are you aware of that? I can't be mother and father to these children.'

I shut my eyes. 'I hear what you're saying. I don't even disagree with you, believe it or not. Now, would you please put Damon on?' I asked again. 'As soon as I get off the phone, I'll go out and see if I can find a mother for my children. Actually, I'm working with a very nice female detective. You'd like her.'

'Damon's not here. He said if you called, and weren't coming home, to tell you *thanks a lot.*'

I shook my head, and finally smiled in spite of myself. 'You got his inflection down perfectly. Where is he?'

'He's playing basketball with his friends. He's very good

at that, too. I think he'll be an outstanding two guard. Have you even noticed?'

'He has soft hands and a quick first step. Of course I've noticed. You know which friends he's out with?'

'Of course I do. Do *you*?' Nana shot back. She was relentless when she was on the attack. 'He's with Louis and Jamal. He picks good friends.'

'I have to go now, Nana. Please give Damon and Jannie my love. Give little Alex a big hug.'

'Alex, you give them love and hugs yourself,' she said. Then she hung up the phone on me. She had never done that before. Well, she hadn't done it very often.

I sat there, pinned to my chair, thinking over what had just been said, wondering whether or not I was guilty as charged. I knew that I spent more time with the kids than a lot of fathers, but as Nana had so skillfully argued, they were growing up fast, and without a mother. I had to do an even better job and there were no goddamn excuses.

I called home a few more times. There was no answer, and I figured I was being punished. I finally caught up with Damon around six that night. He had just gotten home from a rehearsal for his concert with the Boys Choir. I heard his voice come on the line, and I sang a little Tupac rap ditty he likes.

He thought that was funny so I knew everything was okay. He had forgiven me. He's a good boy, the best I could have hoped for. I suddenly remembered my wife, Maria, and was sad that she wasn't here to see how well Damon was turning out. *You would really like Damon, Maria. I'm sorry you're missing it.*

'I got your message. I'm sorry, Damon. I wish I were going to hear you tomorrow. You know I do. Can't be helped, buddy.'

Damon sighed dramatically. 'If wishes had wings,' he said. It was one of his grandmother's pet sayings. I had been hearing it for years, ever since I was around his age.

'Beat me, whip me, beat me,' I told him.

'Naw. It's all right, Daddy,' Damon said, and sighed again. 'I know you have to work, and that it's probably important stuff. It's just hard for us sometimes. You know how it is.'

'I love you, and I should be there, and I won't miss the next concert,' I said to him.

'I'll hold you to that,' Damon said.

'I'll hold myself to it,' I told him.

Chapter Twenty-Four

I was still at the precinct house in Brentwood at around seven-thirty that night. I was tired and finally looked up from a thick sheaf of police reports on the sadistic murders that had taken place in nine West Coast cities, plus the one in DC, that we knew about. The case was scaring the hell out of me, and certainly not because I believed in vampires.

I *did* believe in the weird and horrible things people could sometimes do to one another: savage bites, sadistic hangings, draining blood out of bodies, tiger attacks. For once, I couldn't begin to imagine what the killers might be like. I couldn't profile them. Neither could the FBI's Behavioral Science Unit. Kyle Craig had admitted as much to me. That was one reason why he was out here himself. Kyle was stumped, too. There was no precedent for this string of murders.

Jamilla appeared at my desk around quarter to eight. She had been working down the hall. She has a very pretty face, but tonight she just looked tired. There is a simple fact of life about police work. Adrenaline starts flowing during bad cases. It makes everybody's feelings more intense. Attractions grow and can cause unanticipated problems. I had been there before, and maybe so had Jamilla. She acted like it. Perhaps that was why we were a little tentative around one another.

She leaned over my desk and I could smell a light cologne. 'I have to go back to San Francisco, Alex. I'm heading out to the airport now. I left *beaucoup* notes for you and Kyle on some of the files I was able to get through. I'll tell you what, though, it doesn't seem, *to me*, that all the murders were committed by the same killers. That's my contribution for today.'

'Why do you say that?' I asked. Actually, I'd had the same feeling. Nothing to substantiate it, though. Just a gut reaction to the evidence we had gathered so far.

Jamilla rubbed the bridge of her nose, then she wrinkled it some. Her mannerisms were funny, and made me smile. 'The patterns keep changing. Especially if you look at the most recent murders versus the ones from a year or two ago. In the earlier murders the killers were methodical, very careful. The last couple of murders are slapdash, Alex. More violent, too.'

'I don't disagree. I'll look at all the files carefully. So will Kyle and his folks at Quantico. Anything else bothering you?' I asked.

She thought about it. 'A strange crime was reported this morning. Might be something. Funeral home in Woodland Hills. Somebody broke in, ravaged one of the bodies. Could be a copycat. I left the file for you. Anyway, I have to run if I want to catch the next shuttle . . . You'll keep in touch?'

'Of course I will. Absolutely. You're not getting off the hook this easily.'

She waved once, and then she was gone down the hallway.

I hated to see her leave.

Jam.

Chapter Twenty-Five

Ten minutes after Jamilla left to catch her plane back to San Francisco, Kyle appeared at my desk. He looked like a rumpled, tweedy, forty-something professor who had just emerged from his library carrel after days of researching a scholarly piece for the criminal justice journals.

'You crack the code?' I asked him. 'If you did, can I get a flight out of here tonight? I'm catching hell at home for being here.'

'I didn't crack a goddamn thing,' he complained. Then he yawned. 'My head feels a little cracked. Like there's a slow leak or something.' He rubbed his knuckles back and forth against his skull.

'You believe in New Age vampires yet?' I asked. 'Role-players?'

He gave me one of his crooked little half-smiles. 'Oh, I

always believed in vampires. Ever since I was a boy in Virginia and then North Carolina. Vampires, ghosts, zombies, other diabolical creatures of the night. Southerners believe in such things. It's our Gothic heritage, I suppose. Actually, ghosts are more our specialty. I definitely believe in ghosts. I wish this was only a ghost story.'

'Maybe it is. I saw a ghost the other night. Her name was Mary Alice Richardson. These bastards hung and murdered her during one of their pleasure fests.'

Around nine, Kyle and I finally left the station house in Brentwood to get some grub and maybe a few beers. I was pleased to have some time with him. Bad thoughts were buzzing in my head: disconnected feelings, suspicions, and general paranoia about the case. And, of course, there was always the Mastermind to worry about. He might call, or send a fax, or e-mail.

We stopped at a small bar called The Knoll on the way back to the hotel. It looked like a quiet place to have a drink and talk. Kyle and I often did this when we were on the road together.

'So how are you doing, Alex?' Kyle asked after he'd taken a sip of Anchor Steam. 'You all right? Holding up so far? I know you don't like being away from Nana and the kids. I'm sorry about that. Can't be helped. This is a big case.'

I was too tired to argue with him. 'In the words of Tiger Woods, "I didn't have my A game today." I'm a little stumped, Kyle. This is all new and all bad.'

He nodded and said, 'I don't mean today. Overall. In general. On balance. How the hell are you doing? You seem tense to me. We've all been noticing it, Alex. You don't volunteer much at St Anthony's anymore. Little things like that.'

I looked at him, studied his intense, brown eyes. He was a friend, but Kyle was also a calculating man. He wanted something. What was he after? What thoughts were going through his mind?

'On balance, I'm totally fucked. No, I'm okay. I'm happy with the way the kids are doing. Little Alex is the best antidote for anything. Damon and Jannie are doing fine. I still miss Christine, I miss her a lot. I'm troubled about how much time I spend investigating the sickest, most fucked-up crimes that anyone can conjure up. Other than that, I'm just fine.'

Kyle said, 'You're in demand because you're good at this. That's just the way it is. Your instincts, your emotional IQ, *something* sets you apart from the other cops.'

'Maybe I'd rather not be so good anymore. Maybe I'm not. The murder cases have affected every aspect of my life. I'm afraid they're changing who I am. Tell me about Betsey Cavalierre. Anything on the case? There must be something.'

Kyle shook his head. His eyes showed concern. 'There's

absolutely nothing on her murder, Alex. Nothing on the Mastermind either. That prick still calling you any time of day or night?'

'Yeah. He never mentions Betsey or her murder anymore.'

'We could set up another trace on your phones. I'll do that for you.'

'It won't do any good.'

Kyle continued to look deep into my eyes. I sensed he was concerned, but it was hard to tell with him. 'You think he might be watching you? Following you?'

I shook my head. 'Sometimes I get that feeling, yeah. Let me ask you something, since I have you here. Why do you keep pulling me into these messed-up cases, Kyle? We worked Casanova down in Durham, the Dunne and Goldberg kidnapping, the bank robberies. Now this piece of shit.'

Kyle didn't hesitate to spell it out. 'You're the best I know, Alex. Your instincts are almost always on target. You give these investigations the best shot they could get. Sometimes you solve them, sometimes not, but you're always close. Why don't you come join us at the Bureau? I'm serious, and yes, this *is* an offer.'

There it was, Kyle's agenda for the meeting. He wanted me at Quantico with him.

I roared with laughter, and then he did too. 'To tell you the truth, I don't feel close on this one, Kyle. I feel lost,' I finally admitted.

'It's still early in the game,' he said. 'The offer stands, win or lose out here. I want you to come to Quantico. I want you working close to me. There's nothing that would make me happier.'

Chapter Twenty-Six

This was a good break. Better than they could have expected or hoped for. William and Michael followed the two hotshot police dicks from the station house in Brentwood. They stayed a reasonable distance back in their van. The brothers didn't particularly care if they lost them. They knew which hotel they were staying at. They knew how to find them.

They even knew their names.

Kyle Craig, FBI. A DIC from Quantico. A 'big case' man. One of the Bureau's best.

Alex Cross, Washington PD. Forensic psychologist to the stars.

There was a saying that William wanted to whisper in their ears: *If you hunt for the vampire, the vampire will hunt for you.*

That was the truth, but it also sounded too much like a

rule. William fucking hated rules. Rules made you predictable, less of an individual. Rules made you less free, less authentic, less yourself. And in the end, *rules could get you caught.*

William touched down lightly, tentatively, on the van's brake pedal. Maybe they shouldn't hunt the two cops down, then kill them like dogs, he was thinking. Maybe they had better things to do while they were in LA.

There was a special place here where he and Michael often went. It was called the Church of the Vampire, and it was for those who were 'searching for the Dragon within'. It actually was a church: vast, high-ceilinged rooms filled with funky old Victorian furniture, elaborate golden candelabras, human skulls and other bones, tapestries that portrayed stories of famous old blood seekers. The usual dreaded role-players came to the Church, but so did real vampires. Like William and Michael.

Exciting, very exotic, sado-erotic things happened inside the Church of the Vampire. Excruciating pain was transformed into ecstasy. William remembered his last visit, and it sent electricity shooting through his body. He had found a blond boy of seventeen. An angel, a prince. The boy was dressed all in black that night; he even had black eye contacts, absolutely gorgeous from every angle. To show William that he was a real vampire, the darling boy had punctured his own carotid artery and then drunk his own blood. Then he had asked William to drink, to be one with him. When he and Michael had hung the boy to drain him completely, it was out of love and adoration of the angel's perfect body. They were merely fulfilling their nature – to be sado-erotic.

William came out of his delicious reverie as the two cops entered a bar called The Knoll. It was just off Sunset Boulevard. Very mundane, a nothing spot. Perfect for the two of them.

'They're going drinking together,' William said to Michael. 'Cop camaraderie.'

Michael snickered and rolled his eyes. 'They're just two old men. They're harmless. Toothless,' he said, and laughed at his joke.

William watched Alex Cross and Kyle Craig disappear inside. 'No,' he finally spoke again. 'Let's be careful with them. One of them is extremely dangerous. I can feel his energy.'

Chapter Twenty-Seven

I finally had a lead, courtesy of Jamilla's contact at the San Francisco *Examiner*. The chase was on, or so I hoped. The next morning I drove up Route 1 to Santa Barbara, which is located approximately sixty miles north of LA.

It was sobering and a little depressing to watch the sky actually grow bluer as I traveled away from Los Angeles and the copper-gray cover of smog thickly spread over the city.

I was to meet a man named Peter Westin at the Davidson Library in the University of California, Santa Barbara. The library was supposed to contain the most extensive collection of books on vampires and vampire mythology in the United States. Westin was the expert who had been recommended by Jamilla's contact. She warned me that Westin was thoroughly eccentric, but a definitive source on vampires, past and present.

He met me in a small private sitting room just off the library's main reading room. Peter Westin looked to be in his early forties and was dressed completely in deep purple and black. Even his fingernails were painted a shade of mauve. According to Jamilla, he owned a clothing and jewelry shop in a small mall on State Street in Santa Barbara, El Paseo. He had long black hair streaked with silver, and he was dark and dangerous looking.

'I'm Detective Alex Cross,' I said as I shook hands with Westin. His grip was strong, lacquered fingernails or no.

'I am Westin, descended from Vlad Tepes. I bid you welcome. The night air is chill and you must need to eat and rest,' he said in overly dramatic tones.

I found myself smiling at the prepared speech. 'Sounds like something the count might have said in one of the old Dracula movies.'

Westin nodded, and when he smiled I saw that his teeth were perfectly formed. No fangs.

'In several of them, actually. It's the official invitation of the Transylvania Society of Dracula in Bucharest.'

I immediately asked, 'Are there American chapters?'

'American and Canadian. There's even a chapter in South Africa, and in Tokyo. There are several hundred thousand men and women with an avid interest in vampires. Surprise you, Detective? You thought we were a more modest cult?'

'It might have a week ago, but not now,' I said. 'Nothing surprises me much anymore. Thanks for talking to me.'

Westin and I took seats at a large oak library table. He had selected a dozen or more volumes on vampires for me to read, or at least leaf through.

'I especially recommend Carol Page's *Bloodlust: Conversations with Real Vampires*. Ms Page is the real deal. She gets it,' he told me, and handed over *Bloodlust*. 'She has met vampires, and records their activities accurately and fairly. She started her investigation as a skeptic, much like yourself I expect.'

'You're right, I'm very skeptical,' I admitted. I told Peter Westin about the most recent murder in Los Angeles, and then he let me ask whatever questions I wished about the vampire world. He answered patiently, and I soon learned that a vampire subculture exists in virtually every major city as well as some smaller ones, such as Santa Cruz, California; Austin, Texas; Savannah, Georgia; Batavia, New York; Des Moines, Iowa.

'A real vampire,' he told me, 'is a person born with an extraordinary gift. He, or she, has the capacity to absorb, channel, transform, and manipulate pranic energy – the life force. Serious vampires are usually very spiritual.'

'How does drinking human blood fit in?' I asked Peter Westin. Then I quickly added, 'If it does.'

Westin answered quietly. 'It is said that blood is the

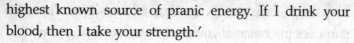

highest known source of pranic energy. If I drink your blood, then I take your strength.'

'My blood?' I asked.

'Yes, I would think you'd do nicely.'

I recalled the nocturnal raid on the funeral parlor north of LA. 'What about the blood of corpses? Those dead for a day or two?'

'If a vampire, or a poseur, was desperate, I suppose blood from a corpse would suffice. Let me tell you about real vampires, Detective. Most of them are needy, attention seeking and manipulative. They are frequently attractive – primarily *because* of their immorality, their forbidden desires, rebelliousness, power, eroticism, their sense of their own immortality.'

'You keep emphasizing the word *real*. What distinction are you trying to make?'

'Most young people involved with the underground vampire lifestyle are merely role-players. They are experimenting, looking for a group that meets their needs of the moment. There's even a popular mass-market game – Vampire: The Masquerade. Teenagers especially are attracted to the vampire lifestyle. Vampires have an incredible alternative way of looking at the world. Besides, vampires party late into the night. Until the first light.' His lips curled into a smile.

Westin was definitely willing to talk to me, and I

wondered why. I also wondered how seriously he took the vampire lifestyle. His clothing shop in town sold to young people looking for alternative trappings. Was he a poseur himself? Or was Peter Westin a real vampire?

'The mythology of the vampire goes back thousands of years. Actually, it's present in China, Africa, South and Central America. And central Europe, of course. For a lot of people here in America it's an aesthetic fetish. It's sexual, theatrical, and very romantic. It also transcends gender, which is an attractive idea these days.'

I felt it was time to stop his spiel and focus on the murders. 'What about the murders – the actual violence taking place in California and Nevada?'

A mask of pain came over his face. 'I've heard Jeffrey Dahmer called a vampire/cannibal. Also, Nicolas Claux, whom you may not be familiar with. Claux was a Parisian mortician who confessed to murders in the mid-nineties. Once he was captured he took great pleasure in describing eating the flesh of corpses on his mortician's slab. He became known all over Europe as the Vampire of Paris.'

'You've heard of Rod Ferrell in Florida?' I asked.

'Of course. He's a dark hero for some. Very big on the Internet. He and his small cult bludgeoned to death the parents of another member. They then carved numerous occult symbols into the dead bodies. I know all about Rod Ferrell. He was supposedly obsessed with opening the

Gates of Hell. Thought he had to kill large numbers of people, and consume their souls, to be powerful enough to open up Hell. Who knows, maybe he succeeded,' Westin said.

He stared at me for a long moment. 'Let me tell you something, Detective Cross. This is the absolute truth. I believe it's important for you to understand. It is no more common for a vampire to be a psychopath or a killer than it is for any random person on the street.'

I shrugged. 'I guess I'd have to check your research statistics on that one. In the meantime, one or more vampires, real ones, or maybe just role-players, have murdered at least a dozen people,' I said.

Westin looked a little sad. 'Yes, Detective, I know. That's why I consented to talk with you.'

'Are you a vampire?' I asked him one final question.

Peter Westin paused before he finally answered. 'Yes. I am.'

The words cut through me. The man was completely serious.

Chapter Twenty-Eight

That night in Santa Barbara, I was just a little more afraid of the dark than I had ever been. I sat in my hotel room and read a touching novel called *Waiting* by Ha Jin. I was waiting as well. I called home twice that night. I wasn't sure if I was lonely, or still feeling guilty about missing Damon's concert.

Or maybe Peter Westin had frightened me with his vampire stories and books, and the haunted look in his dark eyes. At any rate, I was taking vampires more seriously now that I had met him. Westin was a strange, eerie, unforgettable man. I had the feeling that I would meet, or at least talk to him again.

My inner fears didn't go away that night, and not even with the first light of morning shining brightly over the Santa Ynez Mountains. Something strange and quite awful was happening. It involved twisted individuals, or maybe an underground cult. It probably had something to do with the vampire subculture. But maybe it didn't, and that was even more disturbing to think about. It would mean we were in a totally gray area with the investigation.

By seven-thirty in the morning, my rented sedan was easing into soupy gray fog, and then the morning traffic clog. I was singing a little Muddy Waters blues, which nicely matched my mood.

I left Santa Barbara and headed toward Fresno. I had another 'expert' to meet.

I drove for a couple of hours. I got on 166 at Santa Maria and continued east through the Sierra Madres until I reached Route 99. I took it north. I was seeing California for the first time and liking most of what I saw. The topography was different to back East, and so were the colors.

I fell into a comfortable driving rhythm. I listened to a Jill Scott CD. For long stretches of the road trip I thought about the way my life had been going over the past couple of years. I knew that some of my friends were starting to worry about me, even my best friend, John Sampson, and I wouldn't exactly classify him as a worrier. Sampson had told me more than once that I was putting myself in harm's way. He even suggested that maybe it was time for a career change. I knew I could go with the FBI, but that didn't seem like much of a sea change. I could also go back into psychiatry full time – either see patients, or possibly teach, maybe at Johns Hopkins, where I'd gotten my degree and still had pretty good connections.

Then there was Nana Mama's favorite tune: I needed to find someone and settle down again; I needed somebody to love.

It wasn't as if I hadn't tried. My wife, Maria, had been killed in a drive-by shooting in DC that had never been solved. That had happened when Damon and Jannie were little, and I guess I'd never really gotten over it. Maybe I never would. Even now, if I let myself, I could get torn up thinking about Maria and what had happened to her, to us, and how goddamn senseless it had been. What a terrible waste of a human life. It had left Damon and Jannie without their mother.

I had tried hard to find someone, but maybe I just wasn't meant to be lucky twice in my lifetime. There had been Jezzie Flanagan, but that couldn't have turned out worse. And then Christine Johnson, little Alex's mother. She was a teacher and now lived out here on the West Coast. She was doing well, loved Seattle, and had 'found someone'. I still had terribly mixed feelings about Christine. She'd been hurt because of me. My fault, not hers. She had made it clear she couldn't live with a homicide detective. And then, not too long ago, I had started to become involved with an FBI agent named Betsey Cavalierre. Now Betsey was dead.

Her murder case remained unsolved. I was afraid to even have drinks with Jamilla Hughes. The past was starting to haunt me.

'Some detective,' I muttered as I spotted the overhead sign: *Fresno*. I had come here to see a man about some teeth.

Fangs, actually.

Chapter Twenty-Nine

The *tattoo/fang and claws* parlor was located on the fringe of a lower middle-class commercial district in downtown Fresno. It was a ramshackle storefront, with an old dentist's chair prominently displayed in the window. In the chair was a girl who couldn't have been more than fourteen or fifteen. She sat with her skinny, pimpled neck bowed toward her lap, wincing with each needle puncture.

On a tall stool beside her sat a young guy with a bright blue and yellow bandanna wrapped tightly around his head. He was applying the tattoo. He reached for a bottle of ink. The array of tattoo inks beside him reminded me of the spin art booth at a school fair.

I watched from the street for the next few minutes. I couldn't help thinking about the role of physical pain in making tattoos, but also in the murders so far.

I knew the basic tattoo process and watched as the

resident artist adjusted a gooseneck lamp toward the nape of the girl's neck. He used two foot-operated tattoo machines: one for outlining, the other for shading and coloring. The round shader between the machines held fourteen different needles. The more needles, the more colorful the flash.

A middle-aged man with a crew cut was passing by on the street, and paused just long enough to mutter, 'That's nuts, and so are you for watching.'

Everybody's a critic these days. I finally went inside and saw the result of the tattoo master's art: a small Celtic symbol, green and gold. I asked him where I could get fangs and claws. He moved his head, his chin actually, to indicate a hallway to his left. Never said a word.

I walked past display cases: tongue and navel studs, including glow-in-the-dark studs; massive knuckle rings; sunglasses, pipes, beaded thingees; a poster for two popular claws – Ogre and Faust.

You're getting warmer, I thought as I entered the hallway, and then met the fang master face to face.

He was expecting me, and he started talking as soon as I entered his small shop.

'You've finally arrived, pilgrim. You know, when you go to the most interesting, and most dangerous, vampire clubs, the ones in LA, New York, New Orleans, Houston, you see fangs everywhere. It's the scene, and what a scene, my man. Goth, Edwardian, Victorian, bondage apparel, anything goes. I was one of the first to custom-make fangs out here. Started in Laguna Beach, worked my way north. And now, here I am, the Fresno Kid.'

As he spoke, I became aware of his teeth, elongated molars. Those teeth looked as if they could inflict severe damage.

His name was John Barreiro, and he was short, painfully thin, and dressed mostly in black, much like Peter Westin. He was probably the most sinister-looking person I had ever met.

'You know why I'm here – the Golden Gate Park murders,' I said to the fangmaker.

He nodded and grinned wickedly. 'I know why you're here, pilgrim. Peter Westin sent you. Peter's very persuasive, isn't he? Follow me.' He took me into a small over-crowded room in the rear of the store. The walls were dark blue, the lighting crimson.

Barreiro had a lot of nervous energy, he moved around constantly as he spoke. 'There is a fabulous Fang Club in Los Angeles. They like to say it's the only place where you can meet vampires and live to tell about it. On weekend nights you might see four, five hundred people there. Maybe fifty of the fuckers are real vampires. Almost everyone wears fangs, even the vampire wannabes.'

'Are your teeth real?' I asked him.

'Let me give you a little nip and we'll see,' the fang-maker said and laughed. 'The answer to your question is yes. I had my incisors capped, then filed to a sharp edge. I bite. I drink blood. I am the real deal bad dude, Detective.'

I nodded, didn't doubt it for a second. He looked and acted the part.

'If I might take a simple cast of your canines, I could make a pair of fangs just for you. That will really separate you from your detective peers. Make you peerless.'

I smiled at his wit, but I let him talk.

'I make several hundred sets of fangs every year. Uppers and lowers. Sometimes double fangs. Occasionally, I make a pair in gold and silver. I think you'd look great with silver canines.'

'You've read about the other killings around California?' I asked.

'I've heard about them, yes. Of course. From friends and acquaintances like Peter Westin. Some vampires are excited by what's happened. They think it signals a new time; perhaps a new Sire is coming.'

I stopped him. A sudden chill ran through me. Something he'd just said. 'Is there a leader of the vampires?'

Barreiro's dark eyes narrowed to slits. 'No. Of course there isn't. But if there was, I wouldn't talk to you about it.'

'Then there *is* a Sire,' I said.

He glared at me and began to move about again.

I asked, 'Could you make tigers' teeth – for a man to wear?'

'I could,' he said. '*I have.*'

Suddenly he lunged up at me with surprising speed. He grabbed my hair with one hand, my ear with the other. I'm six three and a lot heavier than him. I wasn't ready for this. The small man was swift, and he was very strong. His open mouth moved toward my throat, but then he stopped.

'Don't ever underestimate us, Detective Cross,' John Barreiro hissed, then let me go. 'Now, are you sure that you don't want those fangs? No charge. Maybe for your own protection.'

Chapter Thirty

William drove the dusty white van through the Mojave Desert at close to a hundred miles an hour. The Marshall Mathers LP was playing at maximum volume. William was really pushing it along Route 15, heading toward Vegas, the next stop on their tour.

The van was an ingenious idea. It was a damn blood-mobile with all the requisite Red Cross stickers. He and Michael were actually certified to take blood from anyone who volunteered to give it.

'It's up ahead a couple of miles,' William told his brother, who was sitting with one bare leg out the open window.

'What's up ahead? Prey, I hope. I'm bored out of my skull. I need to feed. I'm thirsty. I don't see anything up there.' Michael whined like the spoiled rotten teenager that he was. 'Don't pull any Slim Shady shit on me. I don't see a thing up ahead.'

'You will soon,' William said mysteriously. 'This should snap you out of your funk. I promise it will.'

Minutes later, the van pulled into a commercial parachute center known as a drop zone. Michael sat up, whooped loudly and beat on the dashboard with the palms of his hands. He was such a *boy*.

'I feel the need for speed,' Michael yelled, doing his best imitation of the young Tom Cruise.

The two brothers had been parachuting since they got out of prison. It was one of the best legal highs around, and it took their mind off killing. They hopped out of the van and headed inside a flat-roofed concrete building that had definitely seen better decades.

William paid twenty dollars directly to the pilot for a ride in a Twin Otter plane. There were two of them sitting near the tiny runway at the airstrip, but there was only one pilot and no one else at the parachute center.

The pilot was a dark-haired girl not much older than William. Early twenties at most. She had a tight sexy body but a mean little weasel's face with badly pocked cheeks. He could tell that she liked his and Michael's looks, but hey, who wouldn't?

'No boards, so you're not sky surfing. What are you boys into?' the pilot asked in a strong southwestern accent. 'Name's Callie, by the way.'

'We're into just about everything!' Michael volunteered

and laughed. 'I mean that too, Callie. I'm serious. We're into just about everything that's worth getting into.'

'I don't doubt it,' Callie said, and held Michael's eye for a few seconds. 'Well, let's do it then,' she said, and they climbed up into the Otter.

Less than ninety seconds later, the small plane was pounding down the hardscrabble runway. The brothers were laughing and hollering at the top of their voices.

'You guys really seem pumped up, I'll give you that. You're free-fallers, right? You're both certifiable,' Callie shouted over the airplane noise. She had a throaty rasp that William found, frankly, a little irritating. He wanted to rip a gaping hole in her neck, but he resisted the urge.

'Among other things, yes. Take her up to sixteen thousand,' William shouted back to her.

'Whoa! Thirteen thousand's plenty. You know, temperature at thirteen thousand feet's under forty degrees. You lose 'bout three degrees every thousand feet. Hypoxia sets in at sixteen. Too much for you thin-skinned boys.'

'We'll tell you when it's too much for us. We've done this kind of thing before,' said Michael, a little angry now, his teeth bared, but maybe she took it for a seductive little smile. It wouldn't be the first time that had happened.

William slid the pilot another twenty dollars. '*Sixteen* thousand,' he said. 'Trust me. We've been there before.'

'Okay, you'll be the ones with frostbitten fingers and

ears,' Callie told them. 'I warned you.'

'We're hot-bodied boys. Don't worry about us. You an experienced pilot?'

Callie grinned. 'Well, we'll just have to see, won't we. Let's just say that I'm probably not losing my cherry up here.'

William watched the gauges to make sure she took them high enough. At sixteen thousand feet, the Otter leveled off smoothly. Not too much wind up there today and a view to die for. The plane was practically flying itself.

'This is not a real good idea, guys,' the pilot warned again. 'It's cold as a motherfucker out there.'

'It's a great idea! And so is *this*!' William shouted.

He took her on the spot, biting deeply into Callie's exposed throat. He held her neck firmly with his teeth and strong jaw and began to drink, to feed at sixteen thousand feet.

It was the height of sado-eroticism. Callie screamed and kicked, struggled fiercely, but she couldn't get him off. Bright red blood splattered around the cockpit. He was so powerful. She tried desperately to get out of her cramped pilot's seat and dislocated her hip.

Her knees cracked against the instrument panel several times, and then they stopped suddenly. Her brown eyes glazed over and became still as stones. She gave in. Both of them drank her blood greedily. They fed quickly and efficiently, but couldn't come close to draining the prey inside the cockpit.

William then opened the plane's door. He was struck with a blast of freezing cold air. 'C'mon!' he yelled. The two brothers jumped out of the plane – free falling.

It wasn't an appropriate name for what they were experiencing. The sensation wasn't like falling, it was more like flying your body.

When the two of them went horizontal, they were soaring at about sixty miles an hour. But when they went vertical, they zoomed up to over a hundred, closer to a hundred and twenty, William figured.

The thrill was incredible, absolutely amazing to experience. Their bodies trilled like tuning forks. Callie's fresh blood was still pumping through their systems. The rush was otherworldly.

At those speeds, the slightest leg movement to the left jolted the body to the right.

They got vertical quickly, and stayed that way. Almost all the way down.

They hadn't pulled the cords on their chutes yet. That was the best thrill of all: the possibility of sudden, unexpected death.

The wind pushed and pulled incredibly against their bodies.

The only sound they heard was the wind.

This was ecstasy.

They still hadn't opened their chutes. How long could they wait? How long?

The only thing missing, the only thing that kept this from being close to perfect, William was thinking, was the absence of pain. Pain made any experience better. Pain was the secret to pleasure which so few understood. He and Michael did though.

Finally, they pulled the cords, and they couldn't have waited a second more. The chutes opened, yanked hard at their bodies. The ground was flying up at them.

They landed and rolled, just in time to see the Twin Otter crash and burn, maybe a mile away in the desert.

'No evidence,' William said smugly, his eyes glazed with pleasure and excitement. 'That was such fun.'

Chapter Thirty-One

T*he Crimson Tide*. That's what William called their murderous tour. He and Michael were on a roll now and nothing could stop them until the mission was over. Nothing – not rain, nor sleet, nor the FBI.

The Red Cross van drifted slowly along Fremont Street, the original Strip in Las Vegas. It blended into the garish neoned scene. Made them feel invisible. And like so many young males, William and Michael felt invulnerable. They would never be caught, never be stopped.

The killers took everything in – the ridiculous spouting fountains in front of nearly every casino and hotel, a wedding chapel with 'Love Me Tender' crooning tinnily from a loudspeaker, brightly painted tour buses, like the one ahead of the van, from the United Union of Roofers and Waterproofers.

'This is a true vampire's city,' William proclaimed. 'I can

feel the energy. Even these pathetic worms on the street must feel alive when they're here. It's fabulous – so theatrical, glittery, overly dramatic. Don't you just love it?'

Michael clapped his large hands. 'I'm in heaven. We can be choosy here.'

'That's our plan,' said William, 'to be very choosy.'

At midnight they drove out to the new Strip, Las Vegas Boulevard. They stopped at the Mirage, where the *Daniel and Charles Magic Show* was advertised on a large, neon billboard that rose high over the busy street.

'Is this such a good idea?' Michael asked as they approached the box office inside the hotel. William ignored him and picked up two reserved tickets for the magic show. They were both dressed in black leather with black engineering boots. Nobody really cared what you wore in Vegas anyway. The show was about to begin as they took two seats near the front.

Everything about the theater was spectacular and over the top. An enormous stage had been covered in spray-on black velvet. The backdrop was a thirty-foot-high metallic structure covered in rear-projection pictures that kept changing. Half a dozen techies worked the spotlights. The lighting conveyed spatial grandness if nothing else.

William used the candle on their table to light a cigar. 'It's showtime, my dear brother. Remember what you said – we can be choosy. Don't forget that.'

The magicians' grand entrance onto the stage was a glittery nugget of eye candy. Daniel and Charles literally flew down from the rafters, at least a fifty- or sixty-foot drop.

Then the magicians *disappeared*, and the spellbound audience erupted in applause.

William and Michael cheered as well. The sheer speed with which the hydraulic mechanisms worked was impressive.

Daniel and Charles appeared again. The magicians led two small elephants, a white stallion, and a glorious Bengal tiger onto the stage.

'That's me,' William whispered against Michael's ear. 'I *am* that beautiful cat. I am right at Daniel's side. He should be careful.'

The sound system played Led Zeppelin's 'Stairway to Heaven' in computerized surround-sound. The noise was as gaudy as the visual. A powerful exhaust system vented out the odor of urine and horse and elephant dung. A semi-pleasant vanilla-almond fragrance was pumped in.

On the stage, meanwhile, the two magicians were arguing about something.

William leaned toward a handsome young couple who had just been seated at the cocktail table to his left. The male and female were in their mid-twenties. He immediately recognized them from a hit TV show. He couldn't decide which of the two actors was better looking. They were both so fly, so full of themselves. He knew that their names were Andrew Cotton and Dara Grey. Hell, he read *EW* and the tabloids in his spare moments.

'Isn't this amazing?' he said. 'I love magic. It's so kinky, and *funny*. This is hilarious!'

The female glanced his way. Dara Grey was about to put him in his place when she looked into William's eyes. Just like that – he had her. Only then did he bother to check out the rest of her: an electric blue slip dress, vintage belt and jeweled shoes, embroidered Fendi bag. Nice, very nice. He wanted to feed on her.

This was going to be so good, so delicious.

Now he would seduce the boyfriend. Andrew, dear sweet Andrew.

Then – then they would party until dawn.

Chapter Thirty-Two

The two magicians continued to taunt each other mercilessly on stage. William's eyes drifted back toward the bright lights and the loud bickering. He smiled, couldn't help it. The magicians were part of tonight too, a big part, actually. Important as hell.

Daniel and Charles were in their early forties. They were handsome in a crude sort of way, confident, especially in the eyes of the tawdry Vegas crowd.

Daniel spoke to the audience as if he were a trial lawyer cleverly engaging a jury. He waved a long, highly polished sword, using it for emphasis.

'We are performance artists, possibly the best now working in the world. We've played at Madison Square, and the Winter Garden in New York, the Magic Castle, the Palladium in London, the Crazy Horse Saloon in Paris. We've headlined in Frankfurt, Sydney, Melbourne, Moscow, Tokyo of course.'

Charles seemed bored by his partner's self-serving speech. He sat down on the edge of the stage and yawned until his tonsils showed.

'They don't care about your pedigree, Daniel,' Charles finally spoke. 'Most of these bumpkins wouldn't know Houdini from Siegfried and Roy. Do a cheap trick, that's what they're here for. Tricks are for kids, and they're all kids! Do a trick! Do a cheap, slick trick!'

Daniel suddenly pointed the tip of his sword at his partner. He waggled it threateningly. 'I'm warning you, chump.'

William looked over at the couple sitting beside him. 'This part is pretty good,' he whispered, 'believe it or not.'

He caught the man's eye, but the actor quickly pulled his gaze away. *Too late. He had him too. The male wanted to get into his pants. Who could blame him? God, he wanted to feed. Right here, right now.*

Onstage, Daniel had begun to yell at Charles. 'I've had enough of your high-handed, condescending bullshit, partner. I've had enough of you! More than enough!'

'*That's too bad,*' William mimicked the next few words spoken onstage, '*because I've only just begun to torment you, and them! The bumpkins!*'

The two actors sitting next to them laughed at William's accurate play by play. He had them utterly charmed. Now the male almost couldn't take his eyes off William. Poor, poor Andrew.

Suddenly, up on the stage, Daniel rushed at Charles. He thrust the sword right into Charles's chest. Charles's scream was piercing and real. Blood erupted from his chest, spilled and splashed everywhere. The frightened audience gasped, and the room went quiet. They were in shock.

William and Michael giggled, couldn't stop. So did the couple beside them. Others *shushed* them.

Daniel began to drag Charles's body across the stage, careful to emphasize how heavy the man was. Very dramatic stuff. He stopped at a small prop that was actually a butcher-block table. He draped the body across the table.

He took an ax, hoisted it high, and chopped Charles's head off!

The room exploded with screams. Some people covered their eyes. 'This is not funny,' someone shouted.

William roared with laughter and clapped and stamped his feet. The loud *shushing* continued all around him. People were horrified, but they wanted more. The two actors beside him were laughing as hard as he was. The woman playfully swatted William's arm.

Daniel now placed Charles's head inside a wicker basket. He did it very theatrically. Then he bowed. The audience finally got it. They had caught up.

William frowned and lowered his head. 'The good part is over. The rest is anti-climax.'

Daniel carried the wicker basket back across the entire length of the stage. He walked very slowly. With great care, he spilled out Charles's head onto a silver platter.

'Just happened to have a platter handy!' William whispered to the couple.

Daniel turned to the audience. 'Any of you figure this out yet? No? . . . Really? . . . He's *dead*.'

'Liar! No he's not!' William shouted from his seat. 'Your act is dead, but Charles is alive! Unfortunately.'

Suddenly, the head on the silver platter moved. Charles's eyes opened. The audience went wild. The illusion was quite stunning, and certainly novel enough.

Charles said, 'My God, look what you've done, Daniel. All these witnesses saw you. You'll never get away with this, you murderer.'

Daniel shrugged. 'Oh, but I will. Nobody out there really cares about you, or anyone else for that matter. They don't like you. They don't even like themselves. You deserved this, Charles.'

The head on the platter spoke again. 'A public beheading? Help me, Daniel.'

'What's the magic word, Charles?' asked Daniel.

'Please help me,' Charles answered. 'Please, Daniel. Help me?'

Daniel carefully placed the basket over Charles's head, and then he carried it back across the stage where, with broad flourishes and theatrical gestures, he reattached Charles's head to his body. Charles then rose up and grasped his partner's hand.

The two magicians stood together and bowed. 'Ladies and gentlemen, we are Daniel and Charles, the best magicians in the world!' they shouted to the rafters.

The applause inside the room was loud and sustained. People stood and clapped and cheered. The magicians took several more bows.

'Boo! Boo! They're fakes!' William and Michael hooted from their seats. They saw a couple of hotel security geeks approaching their table.

William leaned toward Andrew Cotton and Dara Grey. 'You like magic, theater, adventure?' he asked. 'I'm William Alexander and this is my brother, Michael. Let's go somewhere. Let's get the hell out of here. We'll have some real fun.'

The actors rose, and as they were leaving with William and Michael, the security people arrived.

'We want our money back,' William said to them. 'Daniel and Charles are *fakes*.'

Chapter Thirty-Three

'Your place or ours?' William asked the actors, keeping the question as non-threatening as he possibly could. He didn't want to lose Dara and Andrew now. He had plans for them.

'Where are you staying?' Dara asked. She was incredibly sure of herself, a goddess in her own mind, a diva. Yet another one.

William answered, 'Michael and I are at Circus Circus.'

'We're at the Bellagio. We're camped out in a suite. Let's go there. It's fabulous, the best in Vegas. We have drugs,' Andrew said. 'MDMA. You like?'

'We have lots of fun toys,' Dara said and gently brushed William's blond hair with her fingers. He could have killed her for the affront. Instead, he took her hand and kissed it. She was so full of life, and rich, warm blood.

The suite at the Bellagio was on a high floor and it

looked out across a man-made lake with fountains that shot water hundreds of feet into the air. The fountains were choreographed to a song from *A Chorus Line*. William thought it was an incredible amount of water to be wasting in the desert. He glanced around the room and was surprised that he didn't totally hate it – there were no nylon rugs or ultra acrylic-coated walls anyway. Bowls of fruit and fresh flowers had been left out in several places. God, he was hungry, famished, but not for grapes and apples.

Dara slid out of her Bob Mackie party dress as soon as she pranced in the door. The young actress's body was tanned and toned. She shrugged off an expensive bra.

Her small breasts were pert, the nipples erect. She kept on her creamy white thong underwear. And her high heels – Jimmy Choo's.

William smiled at the actors – their primping, their practiced, shallow attempts at seduction and eroticism. He wouldn't be surprised if a make-up person popped out of a closet, and suddenly wondered what Brad Pitt and Jennifer Aniston were like together in bed? Probably a beautiful, blond bore.

'Your turn,' Dara said teasingly to the brothers. 'Let's see what you have. Strut your stuff. Let's all get in the mood.'

'You won't be disappointed,' William said. He smiled and began to peel off his clothes. He took his time with the boots, then slowly unzipped his tight black leather jump-suit. 'You sure you don't want to take this monkeysuit off for me?' he asked Dara.

Her eyes were wide. So were Andrew's.

William unbound Michael's ponytail, letting his brother's wavy blond hair flow down onto his shoulders. He kissed Michael's cheek, then his shoulder blade. He began to undress him.

'Oh my, my, my,' Dara whispered, 'you two *are* beautiful.'

They were both hard. Michael and William were large and their penises pulsed and throbbed as they stood there naked. They weren't shy. The brothers were used to nudity since their boyhoods. They were also accustomed to having sex with strangers.

Dara looked around and said, 'I feel outnumbered, but not over-matched.' She took some coke from her purse.

William gently stayed her hand. 'You won't need that. Lie down on the bed. Trust me a little. Trust yourself, Dara.'

Like a magician, William produced four silk scarves – red, blue, and silver. He tied Dara to the bedposts. She struggled some, pretended to be afraid. They all enjoyed watching her act, and Michael put his arm around Andrew, who was getting lost in the shuffle. He was high, too. His blue eyes were glazed.

'Why don't you get comfortable,' Michael whispered. 'You're among friends.'

Andrew slid a pair of handcuffs from a black leather bag on the floor. 'These are for you. Just for fun. Okay?'

Michael obediently thrust his hands out, ready to be cuffed. 'Just for fun,' he said, and laughed.

'This is going to be so great,' Andrew said, his tongue more than a little thick. 'I can feel a rush already. I think I'm starting to peak.'

'No, you aren't even close,' Michael told him.

It happened so fast that it almost didn't seem possible. Suddenly, Michael had locked the handcuffs onto Andrew's wrists. Then he took the actor down on the carpet. He was all over Andrew. He and William gagged him with silk scarves. They moved so fast. They took off his clothes. They tied his ankles with more scarves.

'Trust us, Andrew. This will be great. You can't imagine,' William whispered. Then he watched Michael bite into Andrew's throat. Just a sip. A few delicious drops. An aperitif.

Andrew Cotton's beautiful eyes became wild with fear and confusion. The look was priceless. He knew that he was going to die. Soon, very soon. Maybe in just a couple of minutes.

Dara couldn't see what was happening on the floor. 'Hey. What are you men doing down there? Is it dirty? Are you buggering one another? I'm feeling neglected up here. Somebody come to bed with me. Bugger me.'

William rose up to her and his penis was large and beautiful, his stomach impossibly flat, his smile enchanting, irresistible, and he knew it.

'Up popped the devil,' he said.

'Kiss me, devil,' she whispered, and fluttered her eyelashes. 'Make love to me. Forget about old Andrew. And Michael. You're not in love with your own brother, are you?'

'Who wouldn't be?' William asked.

He knelt over her and then he lowered his body very slowly. He closed his arms around her. Suddenly, Dara was shaking. She knew, without really knowing. Like so many men and women William had feasted on, she wanted to die, without knowing what it was that she wanted. He knew she could see herself reflected in his deep brown eyes. He knew Dara felt she had never looked more desirable.

And he did desire her. Right now, he wanted Dara more than anything else on the earth. He inhaled her scents – flesh, soap, a citrus fragrance, the rich blood coursing through her veins. Then his tongue gently lapped at her earlobe. He knew that Dara felt as if she had been touched *inside*. It wasn't physically possible – but she had felt William's tongue deep inside her.

Suddenly, Michael was lifting Andrew up onto the immense bed. There was room for everyone. Andrew was bound in colorful scarves and shiny silver handcuffs. There was a harsh, red mark on his neck. And blood running down his chest. The actor was already dead.

Dara was beginning to understand everything. William was right – this was so much better without the cocaine. He was touching her everywhere and he was so warm, so hot, this was exquisite. She was writhing, ready to come already, bursting with yearning and desire.

'This is just the beginning,' William whispered against her throat. 'Your pleasure is only just starting. I promise, Dara.'

He licked away her bittersweet perfume. He kissed her again and again. Then he bit down into her throat.

It got better and better.

The ecstasy of pain.

Dying like this.

No one understood that until the end.

Chapter Thirty-Four

I t had happened again. Jesus. Two more ungodly murders. An FBI helicopter was waiting for me at the airport in Fresno. I was flown to Las Vegas where an FBI sedan was waiting. The driver, an agent named Carl Lenards, informed me that Director In Charge Craig was already at the crime scene. Then Lenards filled me in on the rest.

The latest murders had taken place at a five-diamond luxury hotel, the Bellagio. When it had opened in 1998, the Bellagio was the most expensive hotel ever built. It was upscale, and family friendly, until now anyway. There was hardly a trace of the old Las Vegas – no naked ladies, no mobsters in shiny, sharkskin suits.

Las Vegas police cars and EMS vehicles were parked all over the approach driveway from Boulevard South, Route 604. There were also at least a half dozen TV vans on the property. I estimated that five to six hundred onlookers were gathered outside the hotel. Why was the crowd so large? Exactly what had happened inside? All I had so far were sketchy details of the murders. I knew that the bodies had been drained. *But not hung.*

As I made my way through the onlookers, I saw something that bothered me, shook me up even more than the news of the murders.

There were at least a dozen men and women dressed in Goth attire: black frock coats, top hats, leather pants, long boots. One of them smiled right at me. He showed off a set of sharpened, very nasty-looking fangs. He had on blood-red contacts that glowed. He seemed to know who I was. 'Dude,' he smirked. 'Welcome to hell.'

There was nothing I could do about the ghouls. I kept on walking toward the Bellagio. These strange role-players seemed to have no qualms about being at the crime scene. Were the killers here? Were they watching? What did they expect to see next? What did the murders mean?

I hoped that the Vegas police or the FBI was filming the crowd gathering outside the hotel. I figured that Kyle would have taken care of that. I was here for one reason: I can put together details at a murder scene that other cops usually can't. It was why Kyle Craig had asked for me. He understood my strengths, and probably also my weaknesses.

The suite where the couple had been murdered was

large and relatively tasteful by resort standards. The first thing anyone entering the room would notice was a marble bathtub in a tinted glass window overlooking a man-made lake and several fountains.

Two bodies were in the tub. I could see the tops of their heads and a couple of bare feet. As I got closer, I saw that the man and woman had been bitten, and also cut several times. The nude corpses were eerily white.

There hadn't been anywhere to hang them inside the suite.

There wasn't much blood in the tub itself, but it had been stoppered. The room was buzzing with police activity. Too much to suit me. There were LVPD detectives, paramedics, crime-scene scientists, a pathologist, the Coroner's investigative team, and the FBI, of course.

I needed quiet.

I studied the pale, pathetic bodies for several minutes. As was the case with all of the victims so far, the man and woman had been attractive.

Perfect specimens. Chosen for that reason? If not, then why?

The girl looked to be in her early twenties. She was petite, blonde, slender, probably under a hundred pounds. The span of her shoulders was only about a ruler's length. Her breasts were small, and had been bitten, almost shredded. There were bite gouges up and down her legs. The male also appeared to be in his early twenties. He was blond, blue-eyed, with a corn-fed look; his body was toned and sculpted. He too had been bitten. His throat had been slashed and so had his wrists.

I could see no defensive bruises on either of their hands. *They hadn't fought back.* They knew the attackers.

'You saw the ghouls lurking outside?' Kyle asked. 'The semi-human freak show?'

I nodded. 'It's daylight, though. The ones out there must be harmless. The ghouls in their crypts are the ones we need to find.'

Kyle nodded, then he walked away.

After most of the police technicians left I wandered around the hotel suite for hours. It's a ritual for me, part of my own obsession. Maybe I feel I owe it to the dead. I stopped and stared out at the view of the lake that the victims had enjoyed. I noticed everything – the creamy whites, blushing pinks, and Sixties Parrish yellows that engulfed the room. Framed mirrors spotlighted with recessed lights. Fresh fruit and flowers.

The victims had unpacked and put away their clothes. I went through the labels: Bob Mackie dresses, high-heel shoes by Jimmy Choo and Manolo Blahnik, a couple of skirts. Expensive, chic, the best of everything.

The last thing either of them had expected was to die.

A stack of fifty- and hundred-dollar markers from the Venetian and New York-New York were in plain view on the dresser. The killers had left the chips. Also, two full vials of cocaine in the woman's purse. A carton of Marlboro Lights.

Was it to tell us they weren't interested in money and drugs? In gambling? In cigarettes? What are they interested in – murder? Blood?

There were ticket stubs inside the woman's purse. Souvenirs? Passes to MGM Grand Adventures. Tickets for shows at Circus Circus, the Folies Bergère in the Tropicana, the magicians Siegfried & Roy. A half-full bottle of Lolita Lempicka perfume.

The male kept a few restaurant receipts: Le Cirque in the Bellagio, Napa, the Palm, Spago at Caesars.

'There are no tickets or receipts for last night,' I said to Kyle. 'We need to find out where they went. Could be where they met the killers. They must have gotten friendly with them. They let the killers in here.'

Chapter Thirty-Five

The cell phone in my pocket went off. *Shit! Damn it! Why do I carry these infernal gadgets?* Why does anybody in their right mind need to constantly be on call?

I glanced at my watch as I took the phone in hand. It was already seven in the morning. What a life. So far, we knew that Andrew Cotton and Dara Grey had gone to the Rum Jungle for drinks and then a magic show at the Mirage. They were seen talking to two people, but it had been dark in the theater. That was what we had so far, but it was still early.

I had been at the Bellagio murder scene since a little past four in the morning. The case was really getting under my skin. The murders were brutal, primal.

'Alex Cross,' I spoke into the phone. I turned toward the picture window revealing the lake and the desert in the distance. The view was soothing, an incredible contrast with what had happened in the hotel room.

'It's Jamilla, Alex. Did I wake you?'

'No, not hardly. I wish you had. I'm at a murder scene. I'm in Las Vegas, staring out at the desert. You're up pretty early yourself,' I said.

It was good to hear her voice. She sounded sane and normal. She *was* sane and normal. I was the one in trouble.

'Oh, I sometimes get in to the office before six. That way I can get a day's work done before everybody else arrives here. Alex, I have some information to share on the biting attacks.'

From the sound of her voice, I suspected this wasn't going to make things any easier for me.

'Go ahead, Jamilla. I'm listening.'

'Okay,' she said. 'I've been working with a couple of medical examiners from the other places where the bloodsuckers struck. I think we may have hit on something important in San Luis Obispo and then again in San Diego.'

I was listening; Jam had my full attention.

'In both of the cities, the medical examiners really got into the case, really tried to help. As you know, we exhumed in San Luis Obispo. Then Guy Millner, the ME in San Diego, did the same. I won't bore you with all the details right now, though I can overnight it to your hotel.'

'That would be great. Obviously, no faxes on any of this material.'

'Here's what we've found out. In both these murders, the teeth marks are different to those in San Francisco or LA. The marks were made by human teeth. But the killers were not the same ones. The evidence is pretty conclusive.

'Alex, there are at least *four* killers out there working. *At least* four. We've identified four different sets of human teeth so far.'

I was trying to make some sense of what I'd just heard. 'These are bodies that were exhumed? Human teeth could leave bite marks on bone?'

'Yes. The MEs all agreed on that. The enamel on teeth is the hardest substance in the human body. Also, as you know, the killers might have been wearing enhancers.'

'Fangs?'

'Right. There was *gnawing* on the bones found in San Luis Obispo and San Diego. That's another reason why there were clear marks.'

'Gnawing?' I winced.

'You're the psychologist, not me. Gnawing entails strong, repetitive, intentional action. It could definitely account for teeth marks. One of the victims was an adolescent, the other was in his fifties. That helped us some, too. According to my sources, the adolescent's bones had less density; so did the older person's due to osteoporosis. Thus the clear marks. But why gnaw on the bones? You tell me.'

I was thinking about it. 'How about this. Inside the bone is the marrow. And the marrow is rich in blood vessels.'

'Oh, Alex, *yuk*,' Jamilla said. 'That could be it. How perfectly awful.'

Chapter Thirty-Six

The murders of the two actors exploded media awareness of the case.

Suddenly, we had hundreds of tips to check and way too many bogus leads to follow. According to the tips; Dara Grey and Andrew Cotton had been spotted in nearly every club and hotel in Vegas. It was just what we didn't need to deal with. We had decided not to release the information that there might be more than one set of killers. California and Nevada weren't ready for it.

Kyle Craig had decided to stay out west for the next couple of days. So did I, of course. I didn't have much of a choice. The case was too hot, and seemed to be revving up even more. Over a thousand local police and FBI agents were involved on some level.

Then the killings simply stopped.

The pattern that had seemed to be escalating and

building ended; the killers, who had seemed to be getting bolder, just vanished. Or maybe we weren't finding the bodies anymore.

I was talking daily to profilers in Quantico, but none of them could discern a pattern that made sense to any of us. Jamilla Hughes couldn't come up with interesting leads and theories either.

Everyone was completely stumped.

The killers just stopped killing.

Why? What was going on? Had the publicity scared them off? Or was it something else? What? Where had the killers disappeared to? How many were there?

It was time for me to go home. That was the good news, and I took it for what it was. Kyle agreed, and I headed back to Washington with the uncomfortable feeling that I had failed, and that maybe the murderers would get away with what they had done.

I got to the house on Fifth Street at four on a Friday afternoon. The home front looked a little worn, but also comfortable. I made a mental note to paint the outside this coming spring. The gutters needed work. Actually, I looked forward to it.

Nobody was home. Nobody was there. I'd been away for twelve days.

I had wanted to surprise the kids, but I guess that was

another bad idea. They seemed to be coming in clusters lately.

I wandered around the house, taking it all in, noting little things that were different. The kids' all-the-rage Razor scooter had a broken back wheel. Damon's white choral robe, sheathed in a plastic dry-cleaning bag, hung over the banister.

I was feeling guilty as it was, and the quiet, empty house didn't help. I looked at a few framed photos on the walls. My wedding photo with Maria. School portraits of Damon and Jannie. Snapshots of little Alex. A formal picture of the Boys Choir taken by me at the National Cathedral.

'Daddy's home, Daddy's home.' I sang an old fifties tune as I peeked into the upstairs bedrooms. 'Shep and the Limelights,' I muttered.

Nobody was around to care that I was singing old rock-and-roll tunes and trying to lighten the mood. The Capitol and the Library of Congress were within walking distance, and I knew Nana liked to take the kids there sometimes. Maybe that's where they were.

I sighed and wondered once again whether it was time for me to get the hell out of police work. There was always one catch: I was still passionate about it. Even though I'd failed on the West Coast, I usually got some kind of result. I had saved some lives in the past few years. The FBI brought me in on some of their toughest cases. I figured this was my bruised ego talking, so I stopped the internal bullshit, cut it right off.

I took a hot shower then changed into a Men's March T-shirt, jeans and flip-flops. I felt a lot more comfortable, like I was back in my own skin. I could almost make myself believe that the lurid vampire killers were gone from my life for good. I think that's what I wanted to happen. Just let them crawl back into their hole.

I went down to the kitchen and grabbed a Coke from the fridge. Nana had taped a couple of the kids' master-pieces to the door. 'Inner Galactic Encounter' by Damon, and 'Marina Scurry Saves the Day – Again' by Janelle.

A book was laid out on the kitchen table: *10 Bad Choices That Ruin Black Women's Lives*. Nana was doing a little light reading again. I peeked inside to see if I was one of the ten bad choices.

I wandered out to the sun porch. Rosie the cat was asleep on Nana's rocker. She yawned when she saw me, but didn't get up to rub against my leg. I had been away too long.

'Traitor,' I said to Rosie. I went over and scratched her neck and she was okay with it.

I heard footsteps. I walked to the foyer and opened the front door. Lights of my life.

Jannie and Damon looked at me and screeched, '*Who are you?* What are you doing in our house?'

'Very funny,' I said. 'Come give your daddy a big hug. Hurry, hurry.'

They ran into my arms and it felt so good. I was home, and there was no place like it. And then I had a thought I didn't want to have: did the Mastermind know that I was here? Was our house safe anymore?

Chapter Thirty-Seven

At its best, life can be so simple and good. As it should be. On Saturday morning, Nana and I packed up the kids and we headed over to their favorite place in all of Washington, the huge and wonderful and occasionally elevating Smithsonian complex. We were all in agreement that the Smithsonian, or 'Smitty', as Jannie has called it since she was a very little girl, was where we wanted to be today.

The only issues were where to go first, and, ultimately, where to go during the day.

Since Nana would be there for only a few hours with little Alex, we let her pick out the day's first stop.

'Let me guess,' Jannie said, and rolled her eyes. 'The Museum of African Art?'

Nana Mama shook a finger at Jannie. 'No, Ms Weisen-heimer. Actually, I'd like to go to the Arts and Industries

Building. That's my choice for today, young lady. Surprised? Shocked that Nana isn't the creature of habit you thought she was?'

Damon piped up. 'Nana wants to see the History of Black Photographers. I heard about it at our school. They got cool black cowboy pictures. Isn't that right, Nana?'

'And much, much more,' said Nana. 'You'll see, Damon. You'll be proud and amazed, and maybe stimulated to take a few more photographs than you do. You too, Jannie. And Alex as well. Nobody takes pictures in this family except me.'

So we went to the Arts and Industries Building first and it was very good, as it always is. Inside, the dull roar of air-conditioning and the cries of a gospel album mixed nicely. We saw the black cowboys, and also a lot of exceptional photos from the Harlem Renaissance.

We stood in front of a twelve-foot photo of ambitious-looking black men in suits, ties and top hats taken from a bird's eye view. A stunning shot that would be hard to forget.

'If I saw that scene on the street,' Jannie said, 'I would definitely take the picture.'

After Arts and Industries we appeased Jannie and returned to the Einstein Planetarium, where we watched 'And a Star to Steer Her' for the fourth or fifth time, or maybe the sixth or seventh time, but who's counting. Nana took little Alex home for his nap then, and we trekked on over to the Air and Space Museum. Now began the portion of our journey that Jannie called 'Damon's macho planes-and-trains trip'.

But even Jannie enjoyed Air and Space. The Wright Brothers' plane floated high above us, suspended by long wires, and it was magnificent – light spruce beams and stretched white sheets of canvas. To its right, the Breitling Orbiter 3, another important page from aeronautic history – the first nonstop balloon flight around the world. And then – 'one small step for man' – the thirteen-thousand-pound Apollo 11. You can be cynical about all this or go with it. I choose to go with it. Makes life a lot easier and more rewarding.

After we had studied several of the aeronautic miracles, Damon insisted we catch *Mission to Mir* on the IMAX screen at the Langley Theater.

'I'm going to outer space one day,' he announced.

'I have news,' Jannie said, 'you're already there.'

In honor of Nana, we stopped at the Museum of African Art and the kids got a kick out of the masks and ceremonial clothes, but especially the old currency exhibit – cowrie shells, bracelets, and rings. It was incredibly quiet inside, spacious, colorful, cool as could be. The last stop of the day was to see the Dinosaur House at the Museum of Natural History. But then both Jannie and Damon said we *had* to see the tarantula feeding at the Orkin Insect Zoo. There was a sign on walls painted to resemble a rain forest: *'Insects won't inherit the earth – they own it now.'*

'You're in luck,' Jannie teased her brother. 'Your kind rules.'

Finally, around six, we crossed Maryland Avenue to the Mall. The kids were quiet, tired and hungry by then – and so was I. We ate a picnic supper under spreading shade trees at the foot of the Capitol.

It was the best day I'd had in weeks.

No calls from anybody.

Chapter Thirty-Eight

As he had done so many times before, probably a dozen times by now, the Mastermind watched Alex Cross and his family.

Love equals hate, he thought. What an incredible equation, but so true, absolutely true. It made the world go round and it was a lesson Alex Cross needed to learn. Christ, he was such a fucking optimist. It was infuriating.

If anyone had cared enough to carefully study *his* past they would have discovered the keys to everything that had happened so far. His personal crime and murder spree was one of the most daring in history. It had lasted for over twenty-eight years. He could count the mistakes he'd made on one hand. The keys were right there for anybody to see:

Narcissistic personality disorder.

That's where it all began. That's where it would end.

A grandiose sense of self-importance.

That was him, all right.

Expects to be recognized as superior without commensurate achievements.

Preoccupied with fantasies of unlimited success, power, brilliance, or ideal love.

Interpersonally exploitive.

Yes, indeed. He lived for it.

Lacks empathy.

To put it mildly.

But please note, Dr Cross and others who might wish to study the long and winding trail – this is a personality disorder. There is no psychosis involved. I am an organized, even obsessive, thinker. I can work out elaborate plots that serve my need to compete, criticize, and control. The three Cs. I am rarely impulsive.

Questions you should be asking about me:

Are my parents alive? Answer: *Yes and no.*

Was I ever married? Answer: *Yes.*

Any siblings? Answer: *Oh, absolutely.* Note bene.

If I'm married, do I have any children? Answer: *Two genuine American beauties. I saw that movie by the way. Loved Kevin Spacey. Adored him.*

And am I attractive, or physically flawed in some minor way? Answer: *Yes and yes!*

Now do the homework! Draw the love and the hate

triangles in my life, Doctor. You're *in* the triangles, of course. But so is your family – Nana, Damon, Jannie, and Alex Jr. Everything you care about and think that you stand for is right there in those beautiful triangles, wrapped up in my obsessions.

So unravel it, before it's too late for both of us. Not to mention everybody you care about in the world.

I'm right outside your house on Fifth Street, and it would be so easy to barge inside right now. It would have been easy to kill you and the family at the Smithsonian, the 'Smitty', as your daughter calls it.

But that would be too easy, too small, and *as I've been trying to tell you*—

The phone in the Mastermind's hand was ringing, calling, reaching out to touch somebody. Patiently, he let it continue.

Finally, Cross picked up.

'*I have a grandiose sense of self-importance,*' the Mastermind said.

Chapter Thirty-Nine

I settled back into my duties in Washington, where I took some abuse from my detective pals about how much I seemed to enjoy working with the Federal Bureau lately. They didn't know that I had been approached about becoming an FBI agent, and was actually thinking it over. But I was still drawn to the mean streets of DC.

I had a decent week on the job, and when another Friday rolled around, I also had a date. It had struck me a long time ago that the best thing that had ever happened to me was being married to Maria and having two great kids with her. It's not an easy thing to play the dating game at any age, especially when you have kids, but I was committed to it. I definitely wanted to be in love again if I could, to settle down, to change my life. I suppose that most people do.

Occasionally I would hear my aunts say, 'Poor Alex, he

doesn't have anyone to love, does he? He's all alone, poor baby.'

That wasn't exactly true. Poor Alex, my butt. I have Damon, Jannie, and little Alex. I also have Nana. And I have lots of good friends in Washington. I make friends easily – like Jamilla Hughes. So far, I haven't had trouble getting a date either. So far.

Macy Francis and I had known each other since we were little kids growing up in the neighborhood. Macy went on to get a couple of degrees in English and Education at Howard and Georgetown. I went to Georgetown, then Johns Hopkins for my doctorate in psychology.

About a year ago, Macy returned to the Washington area to teach English Lit. at Georgetown. We met again at one of Sampson's parties. We talked for an hour or so that night and I found that I still liked her. We agreed to get together again soon.

I'd called Macy when I got home from my bust of a trip to California. We met at the 1789 restaurant for drinks and maybe dinner. Macy's choice. It was near her place in Georgetown.

The restaurant is set in a Federal-style town house at Thirty-sixth and Prospect. I got there first, but Macy arrived a few minutes later. She came up, gave me a sweet kiss on the cheek before we sat down in the cozy pub. I liked the fleeting touch of her lips, the smell of a citrus fragrance on her neck. She had on a lilac turtleneck sweater – sleeveless, a black skirt that lightly hugged her, suede slingback heels. She had small diamond studs in her ears.

As far back as I can remember, Macy had always dressed well. She'd always looked nice, and I guess I had always noticed.

'You know, I'll tell you a secret, Alex,' Macy said once we had ordered glasses of wine. 'I saw you at John Sampson's party, and I thought to myself, Alex Cross looks better than he ever did. I'm sorry, but that's what went buzzing through my head.'

We both laughed. Her teeth were even and shiny white. Her brown eyes were bright and intelligent. She had always been the smartest in her classes.

'I thought the same thing about you,' I told her. 'You like teaching okay, the new job at Georgetown working out? The Jesuits leaving you alone?'

She nodded. 'My father once told me you're lucky if you *ever* find something you like to do. Then it's a miracle if you can find somebody who'll *pay* you to do it. I found it, I guess. How about you?'

'Well,' I said seriously, 'I'm not sure if I love my job, or if I'm just addicted to it. No, actually I do like it most of the time.'

'You a workaholic?' Macy asked. 'Tell the truth now.'

'Oh no . . . well, *maybe* . . . some weeks I am.'

'But not this week? At least not tonight.'

'No, last week was the bad one. This week has been mostly relaxed. Tonight is very relaxed. I need a whole lot more of this,' I said, and laughed.

'You look relaxed, Alex. It's so nice seeing you again.'

Macy and I continued to talk easily. A few people were eating at banquettes in the pub room, but it was mostly quiet. Parents of Georgetown students often take their kids to 1789 for a special meal. It *is* special. I was glad I was meeting Macy here. She'd made a good choice.

'I asked some girlfriends about you,' she confessed, then giggled. 'Alex Cross is "not available" a few of them said. "He's kind of a coconut," one sister said. The other girls said she was crazy as a loon. But – *are you*?'

I shook my head. 'People are funny, how they need to make judgments on everybody else. I still live in the old neighborhood, don't I? No coconuts live in Southeast. I don't think so.'

Macy agreed with that. 'You're right, you're right. Not too many people understood how we grew up here, Alex. I was named after a damn department store. You believe that?'

'I do. I grew up here, Macy.' We clinked our glasses and laughed.

'I guess I'm lucky my name isn't Bloomingdale.'

A couple of times, I brought up dinner, but she was

more comfortable sitting and talking. I know Chef Ris Lacoste, and I love her cooking. I had my heart set on crab cakes garnished with her special slaw. But we drank another couple of glasses of wine, and then Macy started to get a little ahead of me with the wine orders.

'You sure you don't want to eat something?' I asked a little later.

'I think I already told you that I didn't,' she said. Then she forced a smile. 'I like what we're doing here, just talking, chilling. Don't you?'

I did like talking to Macy but I hadn't eaten since breakfast, and I needed to get some solid food in me pretty soon. I was hungering for some of the thick, luscious black bean soup. I glanced at my watch and saw it was already ten-thirty. I wondered what time 1789 stopped serving.

Macy began telling me about her marriages. Her first husband had been a bum and a loser; the second, a younger man from Grenada, was even worse, she said. She was getting a little loud and people at the bar were starting to notice us.

'So here I am, thirty-seven years old. I had to go back to work even though I didn't want to. I'm teaching freshmen, Alex. English composition, World Lit. God knows, seniors are bad enough.'

I was sure she said that she liked teaching, but maybe I heard her wrong, or she was being sarcastic. I wasn't doing much talking anymore, just listening to her stories, and eventually Macy noticed. She put her hand over mine. She had the smoothest brown skin. 'I'm sorry, I got carried away, Alex. I talk too much, don't I? So I've been told. I'm really sorry.'

'We haven't seen each other in a long time. Lots to talk about.'

She looked at me and she had such beautiful brown eyes. I was sorry that she'd been hurt in her marriages, hurt by love. It happens to the best of people sometimes. Macy was obviously still hurting.

'You do look great,' she said. 'And you listen pretty good for a man. That's important.'

'You too, Macy. I like your stories.'

Her hand was back on top of mine, her nails lightly grazing my skin. It felt nice, actually. There was nothing too subtle going on here. She let her tongue wet her upper lip, then she lightly bit down. I was finally starting to forget that I was hungry for the crab cakes and black bean soup at 1789. Macy was quietly staring into my eyes. We were both adults, unattached, and I was definitely attracted to a lot of things about her.

'My place isn't far, Alex,' she said. 'I don't usually do this. Come home with me. Jus' walk me home.'

Her place was only ten blocks away, so I walked Macy there. Actually, she had a little trouble walking and her speech was slurred. I put my arm around her, held her steady.

Macy's apartment was on the ground floor of a town house near the university. It was minimally furnished. The walls were painted a pale green. Against one wall was a black lacquered upright piano. A framed magazine article about Rudy Crew caught my eye. The educator's words were set in large type: 'Education is about the distribution of knowledge . . . and to whom we actually distribute this particular commodity is a major question in this country.'

Macy and I held each other and cuddled for a moment on the living-room couch. I liked her touch, the way she kissed. This wasn't right, though. I knew that I didn't want to be there. Not tonight anyway. Macy wasn't at her best right now.

'Good man's hard to find,' Macy said, drawing me close. She was still slurring her words a bit. 'You have no idea, no idea. So hard out there. It's hell.'

I did have some idea about how hard it was to find someone to be with, but I didn't pursue the point. Maybe some other time.

'Macy, I'm going to head home,' I finally said. 'I liked seeing you again. I liked it a lot.'

'I knew it!' she exploded on me. 'I expected as much! Just *go*, Alex. Go. I don't want to fucking see you again!'

Before the anger had welled in her eyes, I had seen

something beautiful and nearly irresistible. Now it was gone again. Maybe she could get back in touch with it, maybe not. Then Macy started to cry and I knew enough not to try and comfort her. I didn't want to be condescending.

I left the apartment, with its beautiful piano and the wonderful quote from Rudy Crew. This woman wasn't right for me to be with. Not now anyway.

Sad night.

A good woman is hard to find too, I wanted to tell Macy.

God, I hated dating.

Chapter Forty

The night with Macy Francis kept bothering me for the next couple of days. It was like a sad song that played in my head. I hadn't expected it to turn out that way. I hadn't liked what I'd seen, or felt. The look in Macy's eyes stayed with me: a terrible mixture of hurt, vulnerability, and anger that would be hard to soothe.

I grabbed Sampson on Thursday night after work. We agreed to meet at the Mark for drinks. The bar was a couple of streets down from Fifth. Local hangout. Tin ceiling, wideboard pine floors, long, worn mahogany bar, ceiling fan turning lazily.

'Sugar, damn,' Sampson said when he arrived and found me sitting by myself, nursing a Foggy Bottom lager while studying the old Pabst clock on the wall. 'You don't mind me saying, you look like shit, man. You sleeping all right? You still sleeping *alone*, aren't you.'

'Good to see you too,' I said to him. 'Sit down and have a beer.'

Then Sampson wrapped one of his mammoth arms around me. He hugged me as if I were his little kid. 'What the hell is going on with you?' he asked.

I shook my head. 'Don't know exactly. The manhunt on the West Coast went real bad. I mean, it dried the hell up. There's no word on Betsey Cavalierre's murder either. Had a date the other night. Just about has me swearing off dating for the rest of my life.'

Sampson nodded. 'I know the words to that sad song.' He ordered a Bud from the bartender, an ex-cop we both knew – Tommy DeFeo.

'The case I was working on in California ended real badly, John. The killers just disappeared. Thin air. So. How are you doing? You look good. For you.'

He raised an index finger. Then he pointed it right between my eyes. 'I always look good. It's a given. Don't try to change the subject on me. We're into something here.'

'Oh hell, you know I don't like to talk about my troubles, John. So tell me about yours.' I started to laugh. He didn't.

Sampson just looked at me, said nothing, waited me out.

'You'd probably make a decent shrink,' I told him.

'Speaking of which, have you been to see the good Doctor Finaly lately?' Adele Finaly is my psychiatrist.

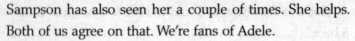

Sampson has also seen her a couple of times. She helps. Both of us agree on that. We're fans of Adele.

'No, she's really pissed off at me. Says I'm not trying hard enough, says I won't embrace my own pain. Words to that effect.'

Sampson nodded and smiled thinly. 'So why is that?'

I made a face. 'I didn't say that I agree with Adele.'

I sipped my Foggy Bottom. It wasn't too bad, and I liked being loyal to a local brewer.

'When I *try* to embrace the goddamn pain, I keep coming back to the conflict between the job and the life I think I want to lead. I missed another one of Damon's concerts while I was out in California. Stuff like that keeps happening.'

Sampson punched my shoulder. 'That's not the end of the world, you know. Damon knows you love his little ass. The young dude and I talk about it sometimes. He's over it. Now you get over it.'

'Maybe it's just that I've worked on too many bad murder cases in the past few years. It's changing me.'

Sampson nodded approval. He liked that answer. 'Sounds like you're feeling a little burnt-out.'

'No. I'm feeling like I'm caught in a scary nightmare that won't go away. Too many coincidences whirling around me. The Mastermind howling my name, threatening me. I don't know how to make it all stop.'

Sampson stared into my eyes. He locked into them. 'Back there a little bit you said coincidences, sugar. *You don't believe in coincidences.*'

'That's what makes it so scary. If you want to know the truth, I think that someone really is after me, and they've been after me for *a long time.* Whoever it is, he's scarier than the vampires. I keep getting calls from the Mastermind, John. He calls me every day. Hardly misses a day. We still can't trace the calls.'

Sampson ran a hand across his forehead. 'I just can't work out who would be stalking you. Who would dare to take on the Dragonslayer? Must be some kind of fool.'

'Believe me,' I said, 'this is no fool.'

Chapter Forty-One

Sampson and I stayed at the Mark later than we should have. We drank a lot of beer, and finally closed the place down at around two. We were smart and sane and sober enough to leave our cars in the parking lot instead of driving home. John and I walked home under a bright moonlit sky. It reminded me of the two of us growing up in Southeast. We had to walk just about everywhere we went. Maybe we'd take a city bus if we were feeling flush. He dropped me off at my house and continued toward the Navy Yard and his place.

Early the next morning, I had to retrieve my car before I went to work. Nana was up with little Alex and I drank a half pot of her coffee, then put the boy in his stroller. He and I walked to my car.

The morning was clear and bright and the neighborhood seemed peaceful and quiet at around seven o'clock.

Nice. I've lived on Fifth Street for thirty years, ever since Nana moved there from her old place on New Jersey Avenue. I still love the neighborhood, and it is home for the Cross family. I don't know if I could ever leave.

'Daddy was with Uncle John last night.' I bent down and talked to the boy as I pushed his blue- and white-striped stroller along. A nice-looking woman passed us on her way to work. She smiled like I was the best man in the history of the world, because I was walking my child this early in the morning. I didn't believe it for a second, but I enjoyed the romanticized fantasy.

Little Alex likes to watch passing people, cars, the clouds streaming above his little head. He loves rides in the stroller and I like pushing him, talking or singing kiddie ditties as we go about our business.

'See the wind blowing the tree leaves?' I said, and he looked up as if he understood every word.

It's impossible to tell how much he understands, but he seems responsive to what I say. Damon and Jannie were the same way, though Jannie was constantly babbling as an infant. She still loves to talk, and to get in the last word, and the next to the last, just like her grandmother, and also, now that I remember, her mother, Maria.

'I need your help, buddy.' I stooped down and talked to little Alex again.

He looked up at me, smiled beautifully. *Sure, Daddy, you can count on me.*

'It's your job to hold me together for a little while. You give me something precious to focus on. Can you do that?'

Alex continued to smile. *Of course I can, Daddy. It's no problem. Consider it done. I am your precious. Lean on me.*

'Good boy, I knew I could count on you. Just keep doing what you're doing. You're the best thing that's happened to me in a while. I love you, little buddy.'

As I was talking to my son, though, a little of the feelings of the night before rolled over me like some cold, wet fog coming up from the Anacostia River. *Coincidences*, I remembered. *The bad things that had happened around me for the past two years. A real bad run. The murder of Betsey Cavalierre. The Mastermind. The vampire killers.*

I needed for it to let up some, needed to come up for air.

When I got to headquarters that morning, a message was waiting for me. There had been another vampire murder. But the game had just changed, taken another turn.

This one had taken place in Charleston, South Carolina.

The killers were on the East Coast again.

Part Three

Murder In The South

Chapter Forty-Two

I flew to Charleston and arrived a little before nine in the morning. The local murder story was splashed boldly across the front pages of the *Post* and *Courier* and also *USA Today*.

I could feel uncertainty and fear in the bright, sterile, overly commercialized confines of the airport. Travelers I passed seemed nervous and wary. Several looked as if they hadn't slept well the night before.

I'm sure that some of them felt that if the mysterious killers could strike in the heart of Charleston, they could do it in an airport waiting room or food court just as easily. No one was feeling safe anywhere.

I rented a car at Charleston airport, and then I set off for a spot called Colonial Lake in town. A male and female jogger had been murdered there at around six the previous morning. The couple had been married for just four months. The similarities to the murders in Golden Gate Park were unmistakable.

I had never been to Charleston, though I'd read books set in the city. I soon discovered for myself that Charleston is physically gorgeous. Once upon a time, it had been a city of incredible wealth, most of which came from cotton, rice, and slaves, of course. Rice had been the biggest export, but slaves, who were brought into Charleston Port and sold throughout the South, were the import that proved the most profitable. Wealthy planters had traveled frequently between the plantations in the lowlands and their homes in Charleston, where the important balls, concerts, and masquerades were held. Relatives of Nana Mama's had been brought into Charleston Port and sold there.

I found a parking spot on Beaufain Street, which was lined with Victorian-style houses. I even spied a few English gardens. This wasn't the kind of place where ghoulish murders ought to happen. It was too pretty, too idyllic. Was that what drew the killers here? Did they appreciate beauty – or hate it? What were they revealing to us with each new murder? What was their dark fantasy? Their horror story?

If Charleston as a whole was suspicious and fearful about the murders, then the streets around Colonial Lake seemed close to terror. People eyed each other warily and coldly. There was nothing even close to a welcoming smile, no southern hospitality on display anywhere.

I had left a message for Kyle to meet me at the lake. It was surrounded by wide sidewalks and wrought-iron benches. Yesterday, it had probably appeared picture perfect and completely safe. Today, bright yellow crime-scene tape was set up near the intersection of Beaufain and Rutledge. The Charleston police had surrounded the area and were watching everybody as if the killers might return today.

I finally saw Kyle waiting under a spreading shade tree and I walked toward him. The morning was warm, but there was a breeze off the ocean that smelled of salt and fish. Kyle had on his usual attire: gray suit, white shirt and nondescript blue tie. He looked like the playwright and actor Sam Shepard, even more so than usual. He also looked gaunt, tired, almost as haunted as I felt. The murders were getting to him, too. Something was.

'It must have been like this yesterday morning, though it was earlier when they struck the couple,' I said as I came up to Kyle. 'No one saw anything? No witnesses in an area like this? That's what I read in the police briefs.'

Kyle sighed. 'We actually have a witness who saw two men hurrying out of the park. Older man in his mid-eighties. He said he thought he saw blood on the shirts of the men, and he felt he was mistaken. Then he found the bodies.'

I quickly surveyed the scene at Colonial Lake again. The sun was shining brightly and I was forced to shade my eyes. Birds were twittering in several of the trees. The park was wide open to scrutiny. 'They were out in broad daylight. Some vampires,' I muttered.

Kyle eyed me. 'You're not starting to believe in vampires.'

'I believe that there are people who practice a vampire lifestyle,' I told him. 'I know some of them believe they're vampires. Some of the role-players even sport very sharp teeth. Fangs. They can be very violent. I haven't seen any shape changers yet. Otherwise our witness might have seen a couple of furry bats winging it out of here instead of two men. That's supposed to be funny, Kyle. What else did our witness say about the men he saw?'

'Not a lot. He thought they were young, Alex. Twenties or thirties, which covers a hell of a lot of territory. They were walking quickly, but didn't seem alarmed that he saw them. He's eighty-six, Alex. He seems, shall we say, distracted by all the attention he's getting.'

'Whoever the killers are, they're certainly bold. Or stupid. I wonder if these are the same bastards we chased through California and Nevada.'

Kyle lit up a little. He had something to tell me. 'My people in Quantico were up half the night. Again. Alex, they've come up with a dozen East Coast cities with unsolved murders that could be connected to the others.'

'What's the time frame of the murders?' I asked.

'That's the really interesting part. This may have been going on for a long time. Nobody seems to have put these cases together before we came along. The time frame is at least eleven years.'

Chapter Forty-Three

That night, Kyle and I had dinner with a good friend in Charleston. Actually, Kyle made the arrangements, including reservations at the Capital Grille on North Tyron.

Kate McTiernan hadn't changed much since we had been thrown together during the Casanova murder spree in Durham and Chapel Hill, North Carolina. When the murderer Casanova had kidnapped Kate in her house outside Chapel Hill he'd believed she was the most beautiful woman in the South.

Not only that, Kate was extremely smart. She was a doctor now, a pediatrician, but she was thinking about becoming a surgeon.

When she arrived at our table, Kyle and I were deep in conversation. Actually, we were arguing about possible next steps in the investigation.

'Hi, guys.' Lustrous brown hair framed Kate's face. She

was wearing it longer these days. Her eyes were dark blue with a nice sparkle. She was still in terrific shape, but I knew she was a softie deep inside.

'Give it up,' Kate said. 'You boys are working way too hard. We're going to have some fun tonight.'

Seeing her there got us both up out of our chairs and grinning like idiots. We'd gone through a lot together, and survived to be together again for this unlikely dinner in Charleston.

'This is a great coincidence. I was at a medical conference just outside town,' Kate said as she sat down with us.

'Alex doesn't believe there are coincidences,' Kyle said.

'Well, fine. So here we are again, brought together by divine intervention or whatever, praise the Lord,' Kate said, and grinned.

'You seem in excellent spirits, Kate,' Kyle said. He was actually pretty buoyant himself.

'Well, Kyle, this is just such a nice, unexpected treat. I get to see the two of you. Plus, I *am* in excellent spirits. I'm getting married next year in the spring. My Thomas proposed two nights ago.'

Kyle fumbled out a congratulation, and I called over our waiter and ordered a bottle of champagne to celebrate. For the next few minutes, Kate told us all about her Thomas, who owned and ran a small, nicely snooty bookstore in North Carolina. He was also a landscape painter, and Kate said he was exceptional at both his jobs.

'Of course I'm hugely biased, but I'm also a picky little bitch, and he really is good. He's a fine person too. How are Nana and the kids? How's Louise, Kyle?' she asked. 'C'mon, tell me everything. I've missed you two.'

By the end of dinner, we were all in good spirits. The champagne and the company did the trick. I had noticed before how Kate could raise up everyone around her – even Kyle, who usually isn't the most social person. All through dinner he rarely took his eyes off her.

The three of us hugged outside of the restaurant at around eleven.

'You two are coming to my wedding,' Kate said, and stamped her foot. 'Kyle will bring Louise, and Alex, you'll bring the new love of your life. Promise?'

We promised Kate. She left us no choice. We then watched her walk away toward her car, an old blue Volvo that she made house calls in.

'I like her a lot.' I couldn't help stating the obvious.

'Yes, I like her too,' said Kyle, who didn't stop watching until Kate's car was gone from sight. 'She's a very special girl.'

Chapter Forty-Four

We were connecting some of the dots now. *Finally.* I hoped we would be able to put together the whole vampire puzzle soon. By the following afternoon, the FBI had identified twelve cities on the East Coast where murders involving vampire-like bites had occurred as early as 1989. I put the names on one of my index cards. Then I stared at the list long and hard. What could possibly link these cities?

Atlanta
Birmingham
Charleston
Charlotte
Charlottesville
Gainesville
Jacksonville
New Orleans

Orlando
Richmond
Savannah
Washington, DC

The breadth of the list was a problem. Scarier and more mystifying was the fact that the murders might have been going on for over a decade.

Next I made an even longer list of cities where non-lethal attacks by supposed 'vampires' had been reported and investigated. I stared at the list and got a little depressed. This was starting to look like an impossible conspiracy.

New York City
Boston
Philadelphia
Pittsburgh
Virginia Beach
White Plains
Newburgh
Trenton
Atlanta
Newark
Atlantic City
Tom's River
Baltimore
Santa Cruz

Princeton
Miami
Gainesville
Memphis
College Park
Charlottesville
Rochester
Buffalo
Albany

The Violent Crime unit in Quantico was working round the clock on the murders. Kyle and I were pretty sure that other cities would turn up, and that the pattern might even go back further than eleven years.

In Atlanta, Gainesville, New Orleans, and Savannah there appeared to have been murders in at least two different years. So far, Charlotte, North Carolina, was the worst hit: there were three suspicious murders going back to 1989. It was even possible that the killing spree had started in Charlotte.

The FBI had moved agents into the twelve cities where the murders had taken place, and special task forces had been set up in Charlotte, Atlanta and New Orleans.

I finished up with my investigation in Charleston. It didn't accomplish too much. At this point, the media didn't have the story about the wide net of murder locations, and we wanted to keep it that way for as long as we could.

That night, I visited Spooky Tooth, the only club in the Charleston area that was a hangout for Goths and vampire wannabes. What I found there was a nest of young people, mostly under twenty. They were still in high school or college. I interviewed the owner of the nightclub, and questioned some of the clientele. They were definitely angry and restless, but no one seemed a likely murder suspect.

I made sure I was back in Washington the next afternoon. At seven-thirty, Nana, Jannie, little Alex and I went to one of the Boys Choir concerts.

The choir sounded better than ever. Damon was one of the featured singers. He had a beautiful solo, 'The Ash Grove'.

'See what you've been missing,' Nana leaned in close and said.

Chapter Forty-Five

William and Michael liked being in the South. It was wild and free-spirited just like they were. Most important, they were right on schedule.

They had arrived in Savannah, Georgia. William drove the van along Oglethorpe Street, and stopped at the famous Colonial Park Cemetery. Then he went on to Abercorn. Then along Percy Street, passing Chippewa and Orleans Squares. He told Michael, lectured to him, 'Savannah is built on its dead. A whole lot of this port city is built on the graveyards.' Also that Savannah had been spared in the Civil War and was now one of the best-preserved southern cities.

William liked this beautiful city very much, and was pleased that they had to take a victim in Savannah. It would be a pleasure to feed here, and to fulfill their mission. He lost track of the street names as he took in the sights of the historic district. Magnificent Federal-period town houses, nineteenth-century churches, fancy scrolled ironwork and Greek motifs, flowers everywhere. He admired the famous old houses: Green-Meldrim, Hamilton-Turner, Joe Odom's first house.

'It's beautiful and elegant,' he told his brother. 'I could live here. You think we should settle down one day? Would you like that?'

'I'm famished. Let's settle down soon,' Michael replied with a laugh. 'Let's settle down and feast on the finest that Savannah has to offer.'

William finally parked the van on a street called West Bay, and he and his brother got out and stretched their arms and legs.

Two young girls in Savannah College of Art and Design T-shirts and blue jean cutoffs came strolling up to the van. They had long, shapely legs, butterscotch tans, and seemed not to have a care in the world.

'Can we give blood here?' the smaller of the girls asked with a conquering smile. She looked to be around sixteen or seventeen. She had lip studs and wild cherry Jello-dyed hair.

'Aren't you the dainty morsel,' said Michael as he locked eyes with the girl.

'I'm a lot of things,' she said, and looked over at her friend, 'but dainty sure isn't one of 'em. Don't you agree,

Carla?' The other girl nodded and rolled her green eyes.

William looked the girls over and thought they could do better in Savannah. These two tramps weren't worthy of him and Michael.

'We're closed for business right now. Sorry.' He was polite and smiled graciously, even seductively. 'Maybe a little later, ladies. Why don't you two come back tonight? How about that?'

The short girl snapped, 'You don't have to get an attitude. We were just making conversation.'

William ran his hand lazily back through his long blond hair. He continued to smile. 'Oh, I know that. So was I. Who could blame me for chatting up two beautiful girls like yourselves. Like I said, maybe we'll see you later tonight. Of course we'll take your blood for the cause.'

William and Michael decided to take a stroll toward the Savannah River and an area called Riverfront Plaza. They barely noticed the freighters and tugs on the water, or the gaily festooned paddleboat, the Savannah River Queen, or even the 'Waving Girl' statue, towering and bronze, a young woman waving a sad farewell to departing sailors. They preferred to check out the men and women walking through the Plaza. They were looking for prey, even though they knew it would be dangerous to strike here in broad daylight. A flea market was in progress and the various local artists had drawn a respectable crowd – a few soldiers, but mostly women, some of them very attractive.

'I do want to take someone. Maybe right here in this oh-so-fucking-pretty river park,' William finally said.

'He'd do nicely,' Michael said, pointing out a slender male in a black T-shirt and blue jean cutoffs. 'Or maybe just a snack. How about that delectable two-year-old in the sandbox there? Yum. Much better than that sickly sugar sweetness I smell everywhere.'

William enjoyed his brother's humor. 'That's pralines you smell. The barbecue is supposed to be especially good here, too. Very spicy,' he said.

'I don't want any stringy pork or beef.' Michael wrinkled his nose.

'Well,' William finally began to relent, 'maybe we could have a quick bite. What do you see that you like? You can have anything that you want.'

Michael pointed out his choice.

'Perfect,' whispered William.

Chapter Forty-Six

This was bad. There had been another grisly vampire-style murder – in Savannah. Kyle and I rushed down to Georgia in a shiny black Bell Jet helicopter that would have done Darth Vader proud. Kyle wouldn't let the case go. He wouldn't let me go either.

Even from the air, the seaport city was stunningly beautiful, with its clusters of mansions, quaint shopping districts, and the Savannah River winding through golden yellow marshes out to the Atlantic. Why were the attacks taking place in crowded, attractive locales? Why these particular cities?

There had to be a reason why this was eluding all of us so far. The killers had to be playing out a complex story/ fantasy. What the hell was it?

An FBI sedan was waiting and it rushed us to the Cathedral of St John the Baptist. The church was on East

Harris in the historic district of town. Police cruisers were parked everywhere among the antebellum homes. So were EMS vans.

'The highways around Savannah are completely block-aded,' Kyle told me as we made our way through the heavy traffic near the church. 'This is the most bizarre and lurid thing to happen around here since John Berendt's book. Or, I suppose, the murder that inspired it. Should bring in lots more tourists, though, don't you think? Maybe the vampire tour will come to rival the one for *Midnight in the Garden of Good and Evil*.'

'Not the kind of visitors the chamber of commerce, or especially residents, probably want to see here,' I said. 'Kyle, what the hell is going on? The killers are working right in our face. They're telling us something. They strike in beautiful cities. They murder in public parks, in crowded luxury hotels, even in a cathedral. Do they want to get caught? Or do they believe they *can't* be caught?'

Kyle looked at the church spires up ahead. 'Maybe it's a little of both. I agree, though, they are reckless for some reason I don't quite fathom. That's why you're here. You're the profiler. You're the one who understands how their sick minds work.'

I couldn't get the thought out of my head that these killers wanted to get caught. *Why?*

Chapter Forty-Seven

K yle and I got out of the sedan and hurried toward the Cathedral of St John the Baptist. A gold-and-white banner over the main door proclaimed, 'One Faith, One Family.'

The twin spires of the church rose high over the city of Savannah. The style was French Gothic: grand arches and traceries, impressive stained-glass windows, an Italian marble altar. It occurred to me that the neo-vampire culture admired Gothic clothing, trappings, so why not architecture? I was taking everything in – *everything*. But nothing had clicked yet.

The murder had been discovered less than two hours ago. Kyle and I were in the air minutes after we heard the news from the Savannah police. The story was already all over the TV.

The sweet smell of incense was in my nose. I could see

the victim as soon as we entered the cathedral. I groaned and felt a little sick to my stomach. It was a twenty-one-year-old male, which I had known from the early reports; an art history major at the University of Georgia named Stephen Fenton. The killers had left Fenton's wallet and money. Nothing had been stolen – except his shirt.

The cathedral was large and could probably hold as many as a thousand worshipers. A flow of light from stained-glass windows created a pattern of colored light and dark patches on the floor. Even from a distance, I could see that the victim's neck had been torn open. The shirtless body was toned and sculpted, just like the others. It lay at the foot of a Station of the Cross, the thirteenth. The floor was stained with blood, but not much liquid remained.

Did they drink the blood here in the cathedral? Was this about sacrilege? Religion? The Stations of the Cross?

Kyle and I approached Stephen Fenton. A body bag was already laid out in the nave. Technicians from the Savannah Police Department stood by. They were restless and angry, anxious to do their work and get out of there. We were holding them up. The local medical examiner was doing his examination of the body and told us he was certain two people had attacked Fenton – he had found two different sets of teeth marks.

Kyle and I knelt over the body together. I pulled on a

pair of plastic gloves. Kyle almost never used them. He rarely seemed to touch evidence at a crime scene. I had always wondered why. His instincts were good, though.

But if we were both so good, why didn't we have any clue as to where the killers had gone, or where they might strike next? That was the question that nagged me more and more at each murder site. What was this gruesome rampage about?

'They're so goddamn impulsive,' I muttered to Kyle. 'I suspect they're both under thirty. Maybe early twenties, or even younger. I wouldn't be surprised if they were in their late teens.'

'Makes sense to me. They don't seem to have any fear at all.' Kyle spoke softly as he looked at the student's wounds. 'It's as if a wild animal has been turned loose. Like the tiger. First in California. Now here on the East Coast. The problem is that we don't really know how far back the killings go, or how many killers are involved, or even if they're working out of this country.'

'That's three problems. Three sub-sets that require answers we don't have. Your agents still talking to people at the Goth and vampire clubs? The Internet? Somebody has to know something.'

'If anybody knows, they're keeping it to themselves. I have over three hundred agents *full time* on this case, Alex. We can't keep this heat up.'

I looked up at the wooden Station of the Cross. It depicted Jesus being taken down from the cross and laid in his mother's arms. Crown of Thorns. The crucifixion. Piercings. Blood. Was blood the connection here? Eternal life? I wondered. In Santa Barbara, Peter Westin had mentioned that some vampires were spiritual. Was this a ritual killing or a random one? Should I talk to Peter Westin again? He seemed to know more about vampires than anyone else I'd met.

The victim was still wearing khaki trousers and new Reebok sneakers. I examined the wounds to his neck. There were also gouges on his left shoulder, and parts of the upper chest. One or more of the killers was very angry, close to a rage state.

'Why take the shirt?' Kyle asked. 'Same thing in Vegas.'

'Maybe because it was blood-soaked,' I answered as I continued to look at the student's wounds. 'These are definitely human bites. But they're attacking like animals. Perhaps the tiger that attacked the victims in Golden Gate Park is a model, a symbol, something important? What, though?'

Kyle's cell phone sounded and he flipped it open. I couldn't help thinking of the Mastermind – his constant calls to me. Kyle listened to whoever it was for about twenty seconds.

Then he turned to me. 'We're going to Charlotte right

now. There's been another murder, Alex. They struck again. They're already in North Carolina.'

'God damn them! What the hell are they doing?'

Kyle and I raced toward the doors of the cathedral. We ran as if we were being chased.

Chapter Forty-Eight

Every once in a while, a single murder, or a series of murders, horrifies us, catches the public's imagination in an almost obscene way. Jeffrey Dahmer's bizarre spree in Milwaukee, the murder of Gianni Versace and subsequent killings by Andrew Phillip Cunanan, the Russian, Andrei Chikatilo, reputed to be the worst. Now this bloody rampage on opposite coasts of the United States.

It was fortunate that we had the FBI helicopter to get us out of Savannah and over to Charlotte. While we were still in the air, Kyle was in contact with his operators on the ground, who had surrounded a ramshackle farmhouse about fourteen miles outside Charlotte. I had never seen Kyle so animated and excited about a case before, not even Casanova or the Gentleman Caller.

'Looks like we caught a break,' Kyle said to me. 'No one

will get out of that house until we get there. I like our chances.'

'We'll see,' I said. 'I'm still not convinced these are the people we're after.' I had stopped making assumptions about the killers. Why Charlotte, North Carolina? This would be the fourth attack in the same city. Had everything been leading us to Charlotte? Why?

Kyle listened to another situation report from agents on the scene, then he gave me the relevant details. 'A married couple – the parents of a seventeen-year-old Charlotte boy – were attacked in bed late last night. Both bludgeoned to death. A claw hammer was found at the scene. There were bites on the bodies. There's evidence that either a large animal attacked the two adults, or the assailant was wearing sharpened metal fangs.' Kyle rolled his eyes. He still didn't have much truck with vampires.

'Their son was seen leaving the house, with blood dripping from his mouth. The assailant then fled to an abandoned farmhouse near the Loblolly River outside Charlotte. As far as we know, the people loitering in the house are mostly teenagers. Apparently, some are as young as twelve or thirteen. It's a mess, Alex. Everything is on hold until we get there. The age of some of these kids is a real problem.'

A little more than ten minutes later we landed in a wide meadow brimming with wild flowers. We were less than three miles from the farmhouse. This was Bonnie & Clyde stuff. By the time we got to the thick woods surrounding the house it was past five o'clock. It would be dark soon enough.

The house was a two-story, wood-framed structure obscured by an overgrowth of wisteria and myrtle. Pine cones, hickory nuts, and what are known locally as sweet gum monkey balls covered the ground where we hid and watched. Everything about the place brought back memories of where I had grown up in the South. Not too many happy moments unfortunately. My mother and father had both died in their thirties, well before their time. My therapist has a theory that I see myself dying young because both my parents did. The Mastermind seems to hold a similar theory, and perhaps wants to put it into action soon.

The roof of the old house was sharply pitched; a narrow attic window was broken in two places. The peeling, white-painted clapboards were mostly intact, but the asbestos-shingled roof was bare in spots, revealing tar paper. Creepy, creepy, creepy. What in hell was going on here?

The FBI was super-sensitive to the fact that most of those inside the house were probably under twenty years old. They didn't know exactly who they were or if any had police records. There was no actual proof they were involved with the murders. It was decided that as long as we remained undetected, we'd wait until night to see if anyone left or entered. Then we would move on the house. The situation was getting sticky, maybe political, and there would be consequences if a minor got hurt or killed.

In sharp contrast, everything seemed peaceful in the woods around the house. The ramshackle building was strangely quiet, considering all the young people who were supposed to be in there. No loud laughter or rock music, no smells of cooking. Dim lights were flickering.

My growing fear was that we were already too late.

Chapter Forty-Nine

Someone was whispering close to my ear – it was Kyle. 'Let's go, Alex. It's time to move on them.'

At four in the morning, he gave the signal to breach the house. Kyle was calling all the shots. He had authority over the locals, too.

I accompanied a dozen agents outfitted in blue wind-breakers. Nobody was feeling too secure about the raid. We moved cautiously to within seventy-five yards of the house, at the edge of the pine forest. Two snipers, who had dug in about thirty yards from the house, radioed that it was still quiet inside. Too quiet?

'These are mostly young kids,' Kyle reminded us before we went in. 'But protect yourselves first.'

We crawled on our hands and knees until we were as close as the snipers. Then we rushed the house, using three entrances to get inside.

Kyle and I went through the front, the others through the side and back. A couple of flash-bang grenades went off. There was screaming on the ground floor. High pitched. Kids. No gunshots – yet.

It was a weird, chaotic scene. Stoned kids – lots of them, most in their underwear or nude. At least twenty teenagers had been sleeping on the ground floor. No electricity, just candles. The place smelled of urine, weed, mildew, cheap wine, and wax. Clown Posse and Killah Priest posters were hung on the walls.

The tiny front hall and the living room merged into an open area. The kids had been asleep on blankets, or just the wooden floor. Now they were awake, and angry, shouting, 'Pigs! Cops! Get the fuck out!'

Agents were rousting more of them on the second floor. There were fistfights, but still no gunshots. No one seriously hurt. A sense of anti-climax.

A skinny boy screamed at the top of his voice and rushed at me. He seemed to have no fear of my drawn gun. His eyes were blood-red. Color contacts. He was growling and drooling frothy saliva. I took him down in a head lock, cuffed him, told him to chill before he got himself hurt. I doubt that he weighed much more than a hundred and forty pounds, but he was wiry and stronger than he looked.

An agent near me wasn't so lucky – a heavy-set

redheaded girl bit him in the cheek as he was attempting to restrain her. Then the girl bit into his chest. The agent howled, and struggled to get her off. She held on like a dog with a bone.

I yanked the girl away and cuffed her arms behind her back. She wore a black T-shirt with 'Merry Fuckin' Xmas Bitch' printed on it. She had tattoos of snakes and skulls everywhere. She was screaming in my face, 'You are unworthy! You suck!'

'The one we want is in the cellar! The killer,' Kyle called to me. 'Irwin Snyder!' I followed him through a dysfunctional kitchen, then out back to a slanted wooden door that led to a cellar.

We had our guns drawn. From what we knew about the viciousness and suddenness of the Irwin Snyder attacks, nobody wanted to go into the cellar. I yanked open the door and we edged inside.

Kyle, two other agents and I went down three rickety wooden steps.

It was quiet and dark. An agent worked a flashlight around.

Then we saw the killer. He saw us too.

Chapter Fifty

A well-built teenaged boy in a soiled black leather studded vest and black jeans was crouched, waiting for us in the far corner of the cellar. He had a crowbar. He leaped up and began swinging it over his head. He was growling. It had to be Irwin Snyder, the boy who had killed his parents. He was so damn young, just seventeen. What had gotten into his head?

Gold fangs protruded from his mouth. Contacts made his eyes appear blood-red. His nose and eyebrows were pierced with at least a dozen gold and silver tiny hoops. He was tightly muscled and over six feet tall. He'd been a star football player before he suddenly dropped out of school.

Snyder continued to growl at us. He stood in an oozing ground-water puddle and didn't seem aware of it. His eyes were glazed and seemed to be set way back in his skull.

'Back off!' he shouted. 'Y'all have no idea how much shit you're in. Y'all have no goddamn idea! Get the fuck out of here! Get out of our house!' He was serious; he believed every word he said.

He was still swinging the heavy, rusted crowbar. We stopped moving. I wanted to hear whatever he had to say.

'What kind of shit are we in?' I asked Snyder.

'*I know who you are!*' he shouted, spraying spit all the way across the room. He was in a murderous rage. He looked stoned beyond comprehension.

'Who am I?' I asked him. How could he know?

'You're fucking Cross, that's who,' he said, and bared long canine teeth, the smile of a madman. His answer shook me up. 'The rest of y'all are FBI dogs! Y'all deserve to die! You will! The *Cross* don't work here, assholes.'

'Why did you kill your mother and father?' Kyle asked from his place on the stairs.

'To free'm,' Snyder sneered. 'Now, they're free as little birdies in the air.'

'I don't believe you,' I said. 'That's bullshit.'

He continued to growl like a barnyard dog. 'Smarter than you look. *Cross.*'

'Why did you use metal fangs when you bit them? What does the Tiger mean, Irwin?' I asked another couple of questions.

'You already know, or you wouldn't ask,' he said, and laughed wickedly. His real teeth were yellow and nicotine-stained. His black jeans were filthy, and looked as if they'd been dipped in ashes. The leather vest had studs missing. The cellar smelled awful, like spoiled meat. What had happened down here? I almost didn't want to know.

'Why did you kill your parents?' I asked again.

'Killed them to free myself,' he screamed. 'Killed their asses 'cause I follow the Tiger.'

'Who's the Tiger? What does the Tiger mean?'

His eyes danced with mischief. 'Oh, you'll see soon enough. You'll see. Then you'll wish you hadn't.'

He reached into his jeans and I rushed him. Irwin Snyder had a stiletto knife in his right hand. He swiped the knife at me and I pivoted away.

I wasn't fast enough, and the blade sliced my arm. It burned like hell. Snyder screeched in triumph. He lunged at me again. Fast, athletic, forward.

I managed to wrestle the knife from his hand, but he bit into my right shoulder. He went for my neck! Kyle and the others were all over him now.

'Goddamn it!' I yelled in pain. I punched his face. He bit me again. This time on the back of my hand. *Damn, it hurt!*

The FBI agents had trouble pinning him down as he

hurled a stream of curses and threats at all of us. They were afraid of being bitten.

'Now you're one of us!' he screeched at me. 'You're one of us! Now you can meet the Tiger,' he howled, and laughed, grinning like a madman.

Chapter Fifty-One

My head was aching, but I spent the next four hours questioning Irwin Snyder in a bare, white-washed claustrophobic room at a jail in Charlotte. For the first hour or so, Kyle and I interrogated him together, but it didn't work out. I asked Kyle to leave the room. Snyder was shackled, so I felt safe being alone with him. I wondered how he felt?

My arm and hand were beginning to throb, but this was more important than my flesh wounds. Irwin Snyder had known I was coming to Charlotte. How had he known? What else did he know? How was a vicious young killer in Charlotte connected to the rest of this mess?

Snyder was pale and unhealthy-looking, with a scruffy goatee and sideburns. He stared at me with eyes that were dark, very active, intelligent enough.

Then he laid his head down on the Formica table, and I

lifted him right out of his chair by his hair. He cursed at me for a full minute. Then he demanded to see his lawyer.

'Hurts, doesn't it,' I said. 'Don't make me do it again. Keep your head *off* the table. This isn't naptime. It isn't a game either.'

He gave me the finger, then put his head back down on the table. I knew he'd been getting away with this type of shit at school and in his home for years. But not here, and not with me.

I yanked him by his greasy, black hair again, even harder this time. 'You don't seem to understand the King's English. You murdered your parents in cold blood. You're a killer.'

'*Lawyer!*' he screamed. '*Lawyer! Lawyer!* I'm bein' tortured in here! I'm bein' beaten by a cop! *Lawyer! Lawyer! I want my fuckin' lawyer!*'

With my free hand I grabbed his chin. He spat on my hand. I ignored it.

'Listen to me now. *Listen!* Everybody else from the house is at the station in the city. You're the only one out here with me. No one can hear you. And you're not being beaten. But you are going to talk to me.'

I yanked his hair again – as hard as I could without actually pulling out a clump. Snyder shrieked, but I knew I hadn't hurt him much.

'You killed your mother and your father with a claw

hammer. You bit me twice. And you stink to high heaven. I don't like you, but we're going to have this talk anyway.'

'Better see somebody about those bites, pig,' he snarled. 'You been warned.'

He was still talking tough, but he cringed and pulled back when I reached out for his hair again.

'How did you know I was coming to Charlotte? How did you know my name? Talk to me.'

'Ask the Tiger, when you two meet. It'll happen sooner than you think.'

Chapter Fifty-Two

I t became clear that Irwin Snyder couldn't have committed the earlier murders. He had been out of North Carolina only once or twice in his life. Most of his contact with the outside world was over the Internet. And of course he was too young to have been involved in murder going back eleven years.

The seventeen-year-old had killed his mother and father, though. He seemed to have no remorse. *The Tiger had told him to do it.* That was all I had been able to get out of him. He refused to say how he had come into contact with the person or group who had such control over him.

While I was questioning Snyder, and then the others from the house, my shoulder and hand began to itch, and then ache. The bites were puncture wounds, but there had been little bleeding. The bite to my shoulder was the deepest, even through my jacket, and had left prominent teeth marks, which I'd had photographed at the station.

I didn't bother going to the local emergency room in Charlotte. I was too busy. But the wounds soon became extremely painful. By late morning, I had trouble making a fist. I doubted I could pull the trigger of my gun. *Now you're one of us, Cross,* Irwin Snyder had told me.

I wondered what group, or cell, or cult, Snyder was part of? Where was the Tiger? Was it only one person? I attended a meeting with the FBI and the Charlotte police that lasted until eight that evening. The net result was that we were still nowhere near a solution. The FBI was scouring the Internet, searching for messages relating to the Tiger, or any kind of tiger.

I flew back to Washington later that night, and managed to sleep a little on the plane. Not nearly enough. The phone rang minutes after I stepped inside the front door of my house. *What the hell?*

'You're back, Dr Cross. That's good. Welcome, welcome. I missed you. Did you enjoy Charlotte?'

I put down the receiver and hurried outside into the night. I didn't see anyone, no movement up or down Fifth Street, but that didn't mean he wasn't lingering near the house. How else could he have known I was here?

I ran out into the street. I stared hard into the darkness. I couldn't see anyone, but maybe he could see me. Someone had definitely been watching. Someone was out there.

'I am back,' I shouted, 'come and get me. Let's settle this right here and now. Let's settle it! Here I am, you bastard!' He didn't call back to me, didn't answer.

Then I heard a footstep behind me. I whirled around to face the Mastermind.

'Alex, *what* is going on out here? When did you get home? Who are you talking to?'

It was Nana, and she looked very small and frightened. She came up and hugged me tight.

Chapter Fifty-Three

I woke up in bad shape around six the next morning. There was blotchy redness and blistering heat around the bites. The wounds throbbed. I noticed a nasty pus-like drainage from the bite on my hand. It was swollen to nearly twice its normal size. This was not good. I was sick as a dog, and it was the last thing I needed right now.

I drove myself to the St Anthony's Hospital ER, where I found out that I was spiking a fever. My temperature was a hundred and three.

The emergency-room doctor who examined me was a tall, dark-haired Pakistani named Dr Prahbu. He could have been one of the sons in the movie *East Is East*. He said that the most likely cause of the cellulitis was staphylococcus, a common bacteria found in the mouth.

'How is it that you were bitten?' he wanted to know. I suspected that he wasn't going to like my answer, but I gave it anyway. 'I was subduing a vampire,' I said.

'No, seriously, Detective Cross. How did you come to be bitten?' he asked a second time. 'I am a serious person and this is a serious question. I need to know this.'

'I am completely serious. I'm part of the team investigating vampire killers. I was bitten by a man with fangs.'

'Okay, fine, Detective. Whatever you say.'

I was given tests in the ER: a CBC and differential count, sedimentation rate, and a culture and sensitivity test on the drainage from the wound. Blood cultures would be studied. I told Dr Prahbu that I needed copies of his findings. The hospital didn't want to give them over to me, but they finally relented and faxed the results to Quantico.

I was sent home with a prescription for a drug called Keflex. I was to keep my infected arm elevated, and administer Domeboro soaks every four hours.

I was too sick to do much of anything by the time I got home. I lay in bed and listened to 'Elliot in the Morning' on the radio. Nana and the kids hovered around me constantly. Nausea swept over me really bad; I couldn't eat. I couldn't sleep, couldn't concentrate on anything except the painful throbbing in my shoulder and hand. I became delirious for several hours.

Now you're one of us.

I finally fell asleep, but woke up around one in the morning. The witching hours. I felt even worse. I was afraid the phone would ring and it would be the Mastermind.

Someone was in the room with me.

I sighed when I saw who it was.

Jannie was sitting in the chair by my bed, keeping watch over me.

'Just like you did when I was sick,' she said. 'Now sleep, Daddy. Just sleep. Rest up. And don't you dare turn into a vampire on me.'

I didn't answer Jannie. I couldn't even manage a few words. I drifted off to sleep again.

Chapter Fifty-Four

N o one would expect this, and that was why it was so good, so excellent. The end of Alex Cross.

It was time for it to happen. Maybe it was overdue. Cross had to die.

The Mastermind was inside the Cross house, and it was as exciting and extraordinary an experience as he had imagined it would be. He'd never felt more powerful than he did standing in the dark living room at a little past three in the morning. He had won the battle. The Mastermind had triumphed. Cross was the loser. Tomorrow, all of Washington would be mourning his death.

He could do anything – so what should he do first?

He wanted to sit and think about it. No need to rush. Where would he choose to sit? Why of course, on Cross's piano bench on the sun porch. Cross's favorite spot for relaxation and escape, the place he liked to play with his children, smarmy, sentimental bastard that he was.

The Mastermind was tempted to play something, perhaps a little Gershwin, to show Cross that even his command of the piano was superior. He wanted to announce himself in a dramatic fashion. This was so good, so delicious. He never wanted tonight to end.

But was it the absolute best he could do? It had to be a night he would never forget, something to savor always. A souvenir that would have great meaning to him, only to him.

There were two triangles that explained his complex relationship with Alex Cross, and he visualized them as he sat on the porch, biding his time, enjoying himself immensely. Christ, he was smiling like a damn fool. He was in his element, and he was happy, so happy.

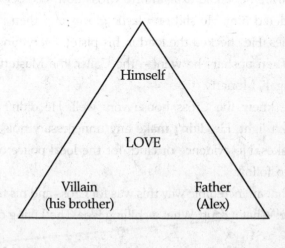

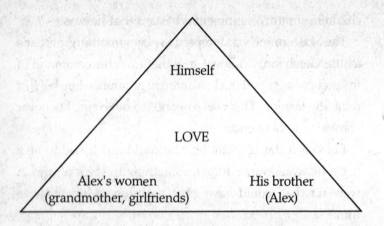

It was such a good psychological model, so concise and clear and sound. It explained everything that was going to happen tonight. Even Dr Cross would approve. It was the perfect dysfunctional family triangle.

Maybe he would explain it to Cross now. Just before he murdered him. He slid on plastic gloves and then plastic booties. He checked the load in his pistol. Everything was set. Then upstairs he went – the Caller, the Mastermind, Svengali, Moriarty.

He knew the Cross house very well. He didn't even need a light. He didn't make any unnecessary noise. No mistakes. No evidence or clues for the local police or the FBI to follow.

What an incredible way this was for Cross and his family to die. What a coup. What a chilling idea. The 'killing order' was starting to come to him as he climbed the stairs. Yes, he was sure of it.

Little Alex

Jannie

Damon

Nana

Then Cross.

He walked to the end of the upstairs hallway and stood there listening before he opened the bedroom door. Not a sound. He slowly pushed on the door.

What was this? A surprise? Christ!

He didn't like surprises. He liked precision and order. He liked to be in total control.

The young daughter, Jannie, was sitting by Cross's bed, fast asleep. Watching over her father, protecting him from harm.

He watched Cross and the girl for a long moment, maybe ninety seconds. A small nightlight had been left on in the room.

There were thick bandages on Cross's hand and shoulder. He was perspiring in his sleep. He was wounded, sick, not himself, not a worthy opponent. The killer sighed under his breath. He felt such disappointment, such sadness and despair.

No, no, no! This wouldn't do. It was all wrong, all wrong!

He closed the bedroom door, and then quickly, silently

retraced his steps out of the Cross house. No one would know he had been there. Not even the detective himself.

As usual, no one knew anything about him. No one suspected a thing.

He *was* the Mastermind, after all.

Chapter Fifty-Five

I woke several times during the night. I thought someone was in the house at one point. I felt someone there. Nothing I could do about it, though.

Then, after fourteen hours of sleep, I woke and found that I was actually feeling better. I could almost think straight again. Exhaustion still had a hold on me, though. All my joints ached. My eyesight was blurry. I could hear music playing softly in the house. Erykah Badu, one of my favorites.

There was a knock on the bedroom door and I said, 'I'm decent. Who goes there?'

Jannie pushed open the door. She was holding a red plastic tray with a breakfast of poached eggs, hot cereal, orange juice, and a mug of steaming coffee. She was smiling, obviously proud of herself. I smiled back at her. *That's my girl. What a little sweetheart she was – when she wanted to be.*

'I don't know if you can eat yet, Daddy. I brought you some breakfast. Just in case.'

'Thank you, sweetie, I'm feeling a little better,' I said. I was able to push myself up in bed, then prop a few pillows behind me with my good hand.

Jannie carried the tray over to the bed and carefully set it on my lap. She leaned in and kissed my fuzzy cheek. 'Somebody needs a shave.'

'You're being so nice,' I said to her.

'I *am* nice, Daddy,' Jannie answered back. 'You feel good enough for a little company? We'll just watch you eat – we'll be good. No trouble. Is it okay?'

'Just what I need right now,' I said.

Jannie came back with little Alex in her arms and Damon trailing behind, giving me the high sign. They climbed up on my bed and, as promised, they were very good, the best medicine around.

'You just eat your breakfast while it's hot. You're getting too skinny,' Jannie teased.

'Yeah, you are,' Damon agreed. 'You're drawn and *gaunt*.'

'Very good,' I smiled between small bites of eggs and toast, which I hoped I could keep down. I kept running my hand over little Alex's head.

'Did somebody poison you, Daddy?' Jannie wanted to know. 'What exactly happened?'

I sighed and shook my head. 'I don't know, baby. It's an

infection. You can get it from a human bite.'

Jannie and Damon grimaced. 'Nana says it's *septicemia*. They used to call it blood poisoning.' Damon contributed some scholarly research.

'Who am I to argue with Nana,' I said, and left it at that. 'I'm no match for Nana Mama right now.' *Or maybe ever.*

I looked at the puffed-up bandage and gauze covering most of my right shoulder, where I'd been bitten. The skin was a sickly yellow around the bandage. 'Something bad got into my blood. I'm okay now, though. I'm coming back.' But I remembered what Irwin Snyder had said: *You're one of us.*

Chapter Fifty-Six

I was able to make it downstairs for dinner that night. Nana rewarded my appearance at the table with chicken, gravy and biscuits and a homemade apple crisp. I made an effort to eat, and I surprised myself by doing pretty well.

After dinner, I put little Alex to bed. I went back up to my room around eight-thirty and everybody seemed to understand that I was tired, not myself yet.

I didn't sleep once I got up to my room, though. Too many bad thoughts about the murders were buzzing in my head. Right or wrong, I felt like we were getting close to something. Maybe I was just fooling myself.

I worked for a couple of hours on the computer and my concentration was fine. I was pretty certain that something had to link the cities where the murders had taken place. What was it, though? What was everybody missing? I looked at anything and everything. I studied the schedules of airplane carriers that flew into each of the cities, then bus companies, and finally railroads. It was probably just busy work, but you never know, and I had nothing better to do.

I checked out corporations that had main or branch offices in the cities and found there were a lot of matches, but it wasn't likely to get me anywhere. Federal Express, American Express, the Gap, the Limited, McDonalds, Sears, J.C. Penneys were just about everywhere, so what?

I had at least one travel book for each of the cities and I pored over them until it was almost midnight. Nothing came of it. My arm was throbbing again. I was starting to get a headache. The rest of the house was quiet.

Next, I checked on traveling sports teams, circuses and carnivals, author tours, rock-and-roll groups – and then I hit on something in the entertainment area. I had been ready to call it a night, but here was something interesting. I tried not to get excited, but my pulse quickened as I checked the West Coast information first. Then the East Coast. *Bingo. Maybe.*

I had found the kind of pattern that I was looking for – an entertainment act that worked winters and early spring on the West Coast, and then came East. Their tour cities and the murders were matching up for now. Jesus.

They had been touring for fifteen years.

I was almost certain I'd found some kind of connection to the killers.

Two magicians who called themselves Daniel and Charles.

The same ones Andrew Cotton and Dara Grey had seen on the night they were murdered in Las Vegas.

I even knew where they were scheduled to perform next. They were probably already there.

Eleven years of unsolved murders had come down to this.

New Orleans, Louisiana.

A nightclub called Howl.

A pair of magicians named Daniel and Charles.

I still couldn't travel, so I would have to remain in Washington. I hated not being able to go to New Orleans. I would miss an important time, but Kyle would be there. I knew he wanted to make this bust himself, and I couldn't blame him. This could help make his career, no doubt about it. The case was huge.

I called Kyle Craig.

Chapter Fifty-Seven

That night in New Orleans a half-dozen FBI agents circulated through the crowd that had turned out for Daniel and Charles's early performance. Howl was located in the warehouse district, off Julia Street. Usually it featured musical acts, and, even tonight, zydeco and the blues reverberated from the mortar and redbrick walls. A few tourists tried to bring 'to-geaux' cups from Bourbon Street into Howl. They were denied admission *for life*.

The used Cressidas and Colts and a few sports-utility vehicles in the parking lot were a tip-off to the presence of Tulane and Loyola college students packed inside. Smoke lay thick over the noisy and restless crowd. Several in the audience looked under-age and the club had been cited for serving minors. The owners found it easier to buy off the New Orleans police than to effectively regulate the club.

Suddenly, everything went quiet. A single voice punctuated the silence, *'Holy shit! Look at this.'*

A male tiger had walked out onto the stage, which was covered in layers of black velvet.

There was no leash on the cat. No trainer or handler was anywhere in sight. The usually raucous audience remained silent.

The big cat lazily raised his head and roared. A girl in a hot pink tank top screamed in the pit seating area. The cat roared again.

A second white tiger walked out and stood beside the first. It glared down at the crowd. The pit audience was situated directly in front of the stage. Men and women seated there scrambled away, grabbing their beer bottles.

Another unmistakable tiger roar now came from the back of the club, behind the audience. Everyone froze. How many cats were on the loose? Where were they? The crowd was silent now. What the hell was going on?

The blinding lights onstage made peripheral space a dark void. Any retreat to either side of the room was suddenly a gamble. There was a shift of the stage lights – left to right, then right to left. The lights were powerful, almost blinding. They created the visual illusion that the entire stage had moved.

The crowd's gasp was audible. Panic was in the air.

The tigers were gone!

Two magicians in shimmering black-and-gold lamé suits now stood at the center of the stage where the tigers had been just a heartbeat ago. They were both smiling; they almost seemed to be laughing at the jittery audience.

The taller of the two, Daniel, finally spoke. 'You have nothing to fear. We're Daniel and Charles, and we're the best you will ever see! That is a promise I plan to keep. Let the magic begin!'

The crowd inside Howl began to clap and cheer, and then to howl. There were two shows that night. Each was scheduled to last an hour and a half. Kyle Craig was inside the club with the FBI agents. More agents were posted outside on the street. Daniel and Charles concentrated on several trunks which they called 'Homage to Houdini'. They also performed Carl Hertz's 'Merry Widow'.

The audience response to the shows was highly favorable. Nearly everybody left the club in awe – vowing to come again, to tell friends to come. Apparently, it happened everywhere that Daniel and Charles played, coast to coast.

Now came the real work for the FBI. After the second show, Daniel and Charles were whisked away to a silver limousine idling in a sealed-off alley at the stage door. There was a lot of noise and confusion backstage. Daniel and Charles were screaming at one another.

Once the silver limousine exited the alley, a team of FBI

cars followed it through the usual crowds in downtown New Orleans, then out toward Lake Pontchartrain. Kyle Craig was in radio contact for the entire trip.

The limo pulled up in front of an antebellum mansion where a private party was in full rage. Loud rock-and-roll music, Dr John, blared across spacious lawns marked by two- and three-hundred-year-old oaks. Partygoers had spilled onto the lawns that sloped down to the dark, glimmering water of the lake.

The limo driver got out and opened one of the back doors with a theatrical flourish. As several FBI agents watched in disbelief, two white tigers jumped out.

Daniel and Charles were not in the limousine. The magicians had disappeared.

Chapter Fifty-Eight

D aniel and Charles had arrived at a small, private club inside a house in Abita Springs, Louisiana, about forty miles outside New Orleans. This particular club had never been written up in the entertainment section of the *Times-Picayune*, or in any of the glossy guide magazines available in the lobbies of just about every large and small New Orleans hotel.

A man named George Hellenga greeted his guests with great excitement and enthusiasm. Hellenga had badly pitted cheeks, the thickest black eyebrows, dark sunken eyes. He wore contacts that made his eyes appear black. Hellenga weighed more than three hundred pounds, all of it bunched tightly into black leather jacket and pants purchased at a Big & Tall shop in Houston. He bowed to the magicians as they arrived and whispered that he was honored by their visit.

'You should be,' Charles snapped. 'We're tired after a long day. You know why we're here. Let's get on with it.' Offstage, Charles often did the talking, especially when addressing someone like this pathetic underling, this cipher, George Hellenga, who immediately showed Daniel and Charles the way downstairs. They were the masters; he was the slave. There were legions of others like him, waiting in so many cities, praying for a chance to serve the Sire.

As he descended the steps, Daniel broke into a smile. He saw the captive, the slave, and he was well-pleased.

He went to the boy, who looked to be eighteen or nineteen, and spoke to him. 'I'm here now. It's so good to meet you. You're astonishing.' The boy was tall, perhaps six feet two. He had closely cropped blond hair, supple limbs, full lips that were accented with the most delicate silver rings. His lips were rosy-red, outstanding.

'He's pouting. He looks so sad. Let him loose,' Daniel commanded the slave Hellenga. 'What is the poor boy's name?'

'His name is Edward Haggerty, Sire. He's a freshman at Louisiana State. He is your servant,' said George Hellenga, who was now trembling visibly.

Edward Haggerty's slender hands were manacled to the brick wall. He wore silver thong underwear, a silver ankle bracelet. Nothing else. He was a magnificent creature, slender, toned, perfect in every way.

George Hellenga stole a nervous look at the Sire. 'He might run if we let him loose, sir.'

Daniel reached out his arms to the beautiful boy and held him tenderly, as he would a small child. He kissed his cheek, his forehead, and those astonishing red lips.

'You won't run away?' he asked in a soft, soothing voice.

'Not from you,' the boy answered, just as softly. 'You are the Sire, and I am nothing.'

Daniel smiled. It was the perfect answer.

Chapter Fifty-Nine

My phone rang early in the morning and I snatched it up. It was Kyle. In his slow and deliberate voice, he told me that Daniel and Charles had disappeared the previous night. He was furious at his agents. I'd never heard him so angry. So far, no murders had been reported in and around New Orleans. About six that morning, the magicians had showed up at their house in the Garden District. *Where had they been all night? What had happened? Something had.*

I stayed in Washington that day, still recuperating from the cellulitis. I studied Daniel and Charles and wrote a preliminary profile on them to compare with the one being done in Quantico. The first important bit of information was that the magicians had definitely performed in Savannah and Charlotte on the nights of the murders. I was working with a couple of techies in Quantico and they not only matched up the timing of the magicians' tour with about half of the murders, but verified that Daniel and Charles had definitely performed in those cities, and were there when the murders had taken place. Another useful nugget was that the tigers traveled with Daniel and Charles only for bookings that lasted at least a week. The magicians were scheduled to perform in New Orleans for the next three weeks. They also owned a house there, in the Garden District.

I shared what I had found with Quantico and they put it into the file they were amassing. I also faxed everything to Jamilla Hughes in San Francisco. She was trying her best to get down to New Orleans, but her boss hadn't made a final decision yet.

I put in another call to Kyle on the matter. He hemmed and hawed, but finally promised to see if he could get Inspector Hughes sprung for a few days. After all, it had started with her case.

I was becoming frustrated at home. I felt as if I were on a stakeout in my own bedroom – with nothing to observe firsthand. The consolation was that I was with little Alex for long patches of the day, and that I got to see more of Damon and Jannie. But I was feeling a little like the forgotten man on the murder case.

I went to see Dr Prahbu at St Anthony's that afternoon. The doctor examined me, then reluctantly gave me clearance to go back to work. He told me to take it easy for the next few days.

'How *did* you get those bites?' he asked. 'You never told me, Detective.'

'Yes, I did,' I said. 'Vampires in North Carolina.'

I thanked the doctor for his help, then went home to pack for the trip to New Orleans. I was a little unsteady, but I couldn't wait to get there. Nana didn't bother to give me the business when I left Washington this time. She was angry because I'd been so ill from the infected bites.

I flew into New Orleans International Airport that afternoon, then I took an old yellow cab to the Big Easy. A message was waiting at the front desk of my hotel, the Dauphine Orleans. I opened the small envelope hesitantly, but it was good news. Inspector Hughes was on her way to New Orleans.

The message was classic. It was pure Jamilla: *I'm coming to New Orleans, and they're going down. Don't doubt it for a second.*

Chapter Sixty

Jamilla and I met up at the Dauphine Hotel that night. She was decked out in a black leather jacket, blue jeans, a white pocket-T. She looked rested and ready for anything; I didn't feel so bad myself.

We had supper together, steak and eggs and beer, in the dining room. As always I enjoyed her company. We made each other laugh. At ten-thirty we drove over to Howl. Daniel and Charles had shows scheduled at eleven and one. And then? Maybe they had planned another clever disappearing act.

We were pumped to take them down. Unfortunately, we still needed concrete evidence that they were our killers. There were more than two hundred agents and New Orleans police involved in the case. Something had to break. Presumably, Daniel and Charles would have to feed soon.

It was a Friday night and Howl was almost full when we got there. Loud music played from speakers that seemed to be everywhere in the ceiling and walls. The crowd was mostly young and restless, drinking beer, smoking, dirty dancing. Several Goths were mixed in with the more clean-cut college kids. The two groups leered at one another and the atmosphere was charged. A photographer from *Offbeat* magazine crouched in front of the stage, waiting for the show to begin.

Jamilla and I sat down at one of the small tables and ordered Jax beers. There were at least a dozen FBI agents in the club. Kyle was outside in a surveillance car. He had been inside the night before, but it was hard for Kyle to blend in with a mostly young, hip crowd. He looked too much like a cop.

The back of my throat was already beginning to burn from the smoke and the heavy perfume in the air. A gulp of beer soothed the gullet somewhat. My arm and hand still ached some from the bites.

My head was clear, though; I definitely felt a lot better than I had. I liked having Jamilla around again. She gave good counsel.

'Kyle has a six-team surveillance on the magicians around the clock,' I told her. 'They won't lose them again. Kyle guarantees it.'

'The FBI thinks they're definitely the killers?' she asked.

'No doubt about it? Lock 'em up, throw away the key?'

'Some doubt I suppose, but not much. You never know exactly what Kyle is thinking,' I told her. 'But yes, I think he believes they are. The techies at Quantico do. So do I.'

She studied me over the lip of her bottle of Jax. 'Sounds like the two of you are pretty tight, huh?'

I nodded. 'We've worked a lot of cases together in the past few years. Our success rate is good. I can't say that I really know him.'

'I've never had much luck working with the FBI,' she said. 'That's just me though.'

'Part of my job is to make sure police relations with the Bureau run smoothly in DC. Kyle is definitely smart. He's just hard to read at times.'

She sipped her beer slowly. 'Unlike somebody else at this table.'

'Unlike two somebodies at this table,' I corrected her, and we both laughed.

Jamilla glanced toward the stage. 'What's the hold-up? Where are they? Should we start stamping our feet for them to come out and show us some magic? Show us what they've got?'

We didn't have to – a moment later one of the magicians walked out onto the stage.

It was Charles, and he *looked* like a killer.

Chapter Sixty-One

Charles was wearing a skintight black bodysuit and thigh-high patent leather boots. He had a simple diamond earring and a gold nose stud. He stared contemptuously at the audience. He did this for several uncomfortable moments, his eyes full of hatred and disdain for every case he encountered.

At least twice, I thought that he looked directly at Jamilla and me. So did she.

'Yeah, we're watching you too, asshole,' she said, raising her beer in mock salute. 'You think those two pitiful creeps know we're here?'

'Who knows? They're good at this. They haven't been caught yet.'

'I hear you. Hopefully, they both have stomach cancer and will die slowly and painfully over the next few months. Cheers,' she raised her bottle again.

Charles leaned down and spoke to a college-age couple at a table near the stage. He was miked.

'What are you two airheads staring at? Watch out, or I'll turn you into a couple of toads. Upgrade you on the food chain.' He laughed, and it was deep and throaty. To my ear, it was also unnecessarily unpleasant, way over the top. The kids in the audience laughed and cheered him on. Civility seems to be dead. Nasty is chic; nasty is so cool and *real*.

I looked over at Jamilla. 'He sees them as food. Interesting how his twisted mind works.'

The second magician sauntered onto the stage a couple of minutes later. No magic gimmicks to announce the entrance, which surprised me. I had heard this was a real light-and-sound show, but not tonight. Why the style change? Was this for us? Did they know who we were?

'For the uninitiated, I'm Daniel. Charles and I have been doing magic shows since we were twelve years old and living in San Diego, California. We're very good at magic. We can do the "Vanishing Performer" – Houdini's personal favorite; the "Sword Cabinet"; Carl Hertz's "Merry Widow"; DeHolta's "Cocoon". I can catch a bullet fired from a Colt Magnum in my teeth. So can Charles. Aren't we *special*? Don't you wish you were us?'

The crowd howled and cheered. The rock music from the speakers had been lowered some. Only the beat droned on.

'The illusion you are about to witness is the same one "Harry" Robert Houdini used to close his show in Paris and New York. We're using it to *open* our show. Need I say more?'

The lights suddenly flashed off. The stage was in total darkness. A few women in the audience screeched loudly. Mock fear. Mostly there was laughter, some of it nervous. What were these two up to?

Jamilla nudged me with an elbow. 'Don't be scared. I'm right here. I'll protect you.'

'I'll remember that.'

Tiny pinpricks of light appeared everywhere on the stage. The main spots came on again. Nothing happened for the next minute or so.

Then Daniel, riding a spirited, prancing white stallion, came out onto the stage. He was dressed in royal blue glitter from head to toe. He wore a matching top hat, and he tipped it to the cheering audience.

'I must admit this is pretty cool,' Jamilla said. 'Quite the stunt. So visual. Now what?'

Daniel was followed onstage by eight men and women in crisp, white palace uniforms. And – two white tigers. It was a pretty amazing spectacle. Two female performers in white held up a huge Oriental fan in front of Daniel and his high-stepping horse. My eyes were glued to the stage.

'Jesus,' Jamilla muttered. 'What the hell is this?'

'They're ripping off "Harry" Robert Houdini, like the man said. And they're doing it well.'

When they slowly pulled the Oriental fan away, Daniel was gone. Now Charles was seated on the white horse.

'Once again – Jesus,' said Jam. 'How do they do that?'

Somehow, Charles had changed into black trash and glitter. The smirk on his face was totally, incredibly arrogant. It showed utter disdain for the audience, but they seemed to love it, to love him. A puff of smoke, and the audience gasped as one.

Daniel was back onstage, standing alongside Charles and the spirited horse. The illusion was masterful. Everyone in the audience jumped up and clapped wildly. The screams and piercing whistles hurt my eardrums.

'And that,' Daniel announced, 'is only the beginning! You ain't seen nothing yet!'

Jamilla looked at me and her mouth sagged. 'Alex, these guys are very good, and I've *seen* Siegfried and Roy. Why are they playing at these little clubs? Why are they wasting their time here?'

'Because they want to,' I told her. '*This is where they look for prey.*'

Chapter Sixty-Two

J amilla and I watched both magic shows that night. We were amazed by the calmness and the confidence exuded by Daniel and Charles. Following the second show, the magicians went home. The agents on surveillance there said it appeared the two were settled for the night. I didn't get it, and neither did Jamilla.

Eventually, around two in the morning, she and I returned to the Dauphine. Two FBI teams would stay near Daniel and Charles's place until morning. We were becoming frustrated and confused. We had a lot of manpower working their butts off.

I wanted to ask Jamilla up for a beer, but I didn't. Too complicated for right now. Or maybe I was just getting chickenshit as I got older. Maybe I was even a little wiser. *Nah*.

I was up again at six, making notes in my hotel room. I

was learning some things I didn't want to know, and not just about magic tricks. I now knew that in the vampire underworld, the area surrounding the main home of a Regent or Elder was known as the domain. The FBI and the New Orleans police had staked out the neighborhood in the Garden District, where Daniel Erickson and Charles Defoe were staying.

Their house was located on LaSalle near Sixth. It was greystone and probably had as many as twenty rooms. The house sat on a hill, with a high, reinforced stone outer wall similar to the outer curtain of a castle. It also had a large deep cellar, which wouldn't have been possible in the swampy, sea-level terrain without the elevation of the hill. Almost no one in the task force would admit that they believed in vampires; but everyone knew that a series of brutal murders had been committed and that Daniel and Charles were the likely killers.

Jamilla and I spent the next two days surveying the house, the *domain*. We worked double shifts, and nothing could relieve the tedium. A scene that sometimes comes to mind when I'm on stakeouts is the one in *The French Connection*: Gene Hackman standing out in the cold while the French drug dealers eat an elaborate dinner in a New York restaurant. It's like that, just like that, sometimes for sixteen or eighteen hours at a stretch.

At least LaSalle Street and the Garden District were

pretty to watch. The sugar and cotton barons of the mid-nineteenth century had originally called this home. Most of the hundred- and two-hundred-year-old mansions were beautifully preserved. The majority were kept white, but a few were painted in Mediterranean pastels. Placards informing the frequent 'walking tours' about the esteemed residents were affixed to intricate wrought-iron fences.

But it was still surveillance, even sitting side-by-side with Jamilla Hughes.

Chapter Sixty-Three

D uring the stakeout on LaSalle Street, she and I found that we could talk about almost anything. That's what we did throughout the long hours. The topics ranged from funny cop stories, to investments, movies, Gothic architecture, politics, then on to more personal subjects like her father, who had run out on her when she was six. I told Jamilla that my mother and father had both died young from a lethal combination of alcoholism and lung cancer – probably depression and hopelessness, too.

'I worked for two years as a psychologist. Hung out a shingle,' I told her. 'At the time, not too many people in my neighborhood in DC could afford treatment. I couldn't afford to give it away. Most white people didn't want to see a black shrink. So I took a job as a cop. Just temporary. I didn't expect to like it, but once I started I got hooked. Bad.'

'What hooked you about being a detective?' she wanted to know. She was a good listener, interested. 'Do you remember an incident, any one thing in particular?'

'As a matter of fact, I do. Two men had been shot down in Southeast, which is where I live in Washington, where I grew up. The deaths were written off as "drug-related", which meant not much time would be spent investigating them. At the time, that was standard operating procedure in DC. Still is, actually.'

Jamilla nodded. 'I'm afraid it is in parts of San Francisco, too. We like to think of our city as enlightened, and it can be. But people out there are good at looking the other way. Makes me sick sometimes.'

'Anyway, I knew these two men, and I was almost certain they weren't involved in selling drugs. They both had jobs at a small local music store. Maybe they smoked a little weed, but nothing worse than that.'

'I know the types you're talking about.'

'So I investigated the murder case on my own. A detective friend named John Sampson helped. I learned to follow my gut. Found out that one of the men had been dating a woman who a local dealer thought he owned. I kept digging, following my instincts, digging a little deeper. Turns out, the dealer had murdered the two men. Once I solved that case, it was all over for me. I knew I was good at it, maybe because of all the psych training I'd had, and I liked making things right. Or maybe I just liked *being* right.'

'Sounds like you have some balance in your life, though. The kids, your grandmother, friends,' she said.

We let it go at that – didn't pursue the obvious – that Jamilla and I were both single and unattached. It had nothing to do with our jobs. If only it was that simple.

Chapter Sixty-Four

One comforting reality of police work is that you rarely come up against a murder situation that you've never seen or heard about before. But these killings *were* different: seemingly random, vicious, ongoing for more than eleven years, varying *modus operandi*. What made the case particularly difficult was the possibility that there were *several killers*.

I met with Kyle the following morning to talk about the case. He was in a foul mood and I couldn't wait to get out of there. We shared our pet theories and whiney complaints, then I joined Jamilla Hughes on the stakeout in the Garden District.

I brought a box of Krispy Cremes, which got major chuckles from her, and also from the FBI agents watching the house. Everybody clamored for the tasty, air-shot doughnuts, though. The entire box was gone in a matter of minutes.

'Turns out they're real homebodies,' she said as she munched on a glazed.

'It's still daylight. They're probably in their coffins,' I said.

She grinned and shook her head. Her dark eyes sparkled. 'Not exactly. The shorter one, Charles, was working in the garden out back all morning. He's certainly not afraid of the sun.'

'So maybe Daniel is the real vampire. The *Sire*. He's supposed to be the force behind the magicians' act.'

'Charles has been on the phone a lot. He's setting up some kind of party at the house. You'll love this – it's a Fetish Ball. Wear your favorite kinky things: leather, rubber, Goth, Victorian, whatever you're into. What are you into?' she asked.

I laughed, thought about it. 'Mostly denim, corduroy, jeans, a little black leather. I have a leather car coat. It's a little beat up, but it's nasty looking.'

She started to laugh. 'I think you'd look dashing as a Gothic prince.'

'How about you? Any fetishes we should know about?'

'Well . . . I'll admit to owning a couple of leather jackets, pants, one pair of long boots that I'm still paying for. I am from San Francisco, you know. A girl has to keep up with the times.'

'Same for us boys.'

It was another long day of surveillance. We continued to

watch the house until dark. Around nine o'clock, a pair of FBI agents dropped by to relieve us. 'Let's get a bite,' I said to Jamilla.

'Bad choice of words, Alex.' We both laughed a little too hard.

We didn't want to venture too far from the magicians' house, so we settled on the Camellia Grill on Carrollton Street at the River Bend. The Camellia looked like a small plantation home on the outside. Inside, it was a neat diner, with a long counter and stools screwed to the floor. A waiter in a crisp white jacket and black tie served us. We ordered coffee and omelets, which were light and fluffy and about the size of rolled-up newspapers. Jamilla had a side order of red beans and rice. When in the Big Easy.

The food was good, the coffee even better. The company was nice, too. She and I got along well, maybe even better than that. The lulls in our conversation weren't too uncomfortable, and they were infrequent. A friend of mine once defined love as finding someone you can talk to late into the night. Pretty good.

'Nothing on the beeper,' she said while we loitered over our coffee after the meal. I had heard there were lines outside the Camellia during lunch and dinner, but we had caught a slow time.

'I wonder what the two of them do inside that big, eerie

house, Alex? What do psycho murderers do in their spare time?'

I had studied enough of them. There was no set pattern. 'Some are married, even happily if you ask the spouses. Gary Soneji had a little girl. Geoffrey Shafer had three children. That's probably the scariest thing I can imagine – when a husband, or the person next door, or a dad, turns out to be a stone-cold killer. It happens. I've seen it.'

She sipped her coffee refill. 'The neighbors seem to like Daniel and Charles. They consider them eccentric but pleasant and, I love this, civic-minded. Daniel owns the house. He inherited it from his father, who was also eccentric – a portrait painter. Rumor has it that the magicians are gay, but they're often seen in the company of young attractive women.'

'Vampires aren't restricted by gender. I learned that from Peter Westin,' I said. 'These two are equal-opportunity killers, males and females. Something still isn't matching up for me, though. There's a logic hole I keep trying to fill. A few of them actually.'

'Their magical mystery tour sure matches up with a lot of the murders, Alex.'

'I know it. I can't dispute the evidence we've collected so far.'

'But you have one of your famous feelings.'

'I don't know about famous, but something feels wrong

to me. This thing isn't tracking right. The other shoe hasn't dropped. That's what worries me. Why did they get sloppy all of a sudden? They went undetected for years and now several dozen FBI agents are watching their house.'

We drank our coffee and lingered in the restaurant, which was only half full, but would be humming again when the bars closed. Nobody pressured us to leave, and we weren't in a hurry to get back to the boredom of the stakeout.

Jamilla was interesting to me for a lot of reasons, but the main one was probably that I saw so much of my own experiences in hers. We were both committed to police work. We had full lives – friends and family – and yet, in a way, we were loners. Why was that?

'You okay?' she asked. Her eyes communicated concern. I can usually intuit good people, and she was one of them. No doubt about it.

'I just went away for a minute,' I said. 'I'm back now.'

'Where do you go when you take these little mind excursions?'

'Florence,' I said. 'It's probably the most beautiful city on earth. My favorite anyway.'

'And you were just in Florence, Italy?'

'Actually, I was thinking about some of the similarities in our lives.'

She nodded. 'I've thought about it. What the heck is to

become of us, Alex? Are we both doomed to repeat the same mistakes?'

'Well, hopefully we're going to catch two real bad killers here in New Orleans. How's that?'

Jamilla reached over and patted my cheek, then she said ruefully, 'That's what I think too. We *are* doomed.'

Chapter Sixty-Five

The Mastermind watched Alex Cross get out of the car. He had him in his sights.

Cross and the lovely Inspector Jamilla Hughes had returned from a dinner break and were back on surveillance duty. Were they getting closer? Would Alex and Jamilla become lovers in New Orleans? That was an obvious flaw in Cross's character; he needed to be loved.

But now Cross was out of the car again.

Something is bothering the great Cross. Maybe he needs to walk a little after the meal. Or maybe he needs to think about the case some more, and wants to be alone. He is a loner, just like I am.

This was amazing; this was so good.

He followed Cross down a dark side street filled with modest homes in two styles – the double shotgun and the creole cottage; both were staples in this part of New Orleans.

The fragrance of honeysuckle, azaleas, jasmine and gardenias were heavy in the air. He sucked in a breath. Pleasant. A hundred years before, the scents had masked the odors of the nearby slaughterhouses. The Mastermind knew his history, knew lots about most things, and the facts flowed easily through his mind as he continued to follow Cross at a safe distance. He retained information and knew how to use it.

He could hear the rattle and hum of the St Charles Avenue streetcar as it raced along its tracks a few blocks away. It helped to cover any slight sound of his own footsteps.

He was enjoying this walk with Cross immensely. Maybe this would be *the night*. Just the thought sent adrenaline pumping through him.

He continued to move closer to Cross. Yes, this was it. Right here, right now.

He half expected Cross to spin around and look at him. That would be good, so rich, ironic, fitting. *Proof of Cross's instincts, and that he was a worthy adversary.*

The Mastermind ducked into some lurks and he circled. He was only a few yards away from Cross now. He could close the distance in an instant.

Cross came to a stop at the old Lafayette Cemetery, the

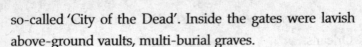

so-called 'City of the Dead'. Inside the gates were lavish above-ground vaults, multi-burial graves.

The Mastermind stopped as well. He savored this, second by second.

A New Orleans Police Department sign was posted on the gates: PATROLLED.

The Mastermind doubted that was true. And it didn't really matter, did it? He could eat the NOPD for lunch.

Cross looked around, but didn't see him in the shadows. Should he jump him now? Would they fight hand-to-hand? It didn't matter – he knew he would win. He watched Alex Cross breathe. His last breaths on this earth? What a thought.

Cross turned away from the cemetery and started down another side street. He was heading back to the surveillance car, to Inspector Hughes.

The Mastermind started forward, but then he turned away. This wasn't the night that Cross would die. He had taken mercy, spared him.

The reason – it was too dark on this street. He wouldn't be able to see Cross's eyes when he died.

Chapter Sixty-Six

Something surprising happened the next morning; an event I don't think any of us were expecting. I certainly wasn't, and it threw me for a complete loop. We had gathered at the FBI's New Orleans office for the morning briefing. There were about thirty of us in a large and sterile room that looked out on the muddy brown Mississippi River.

At nine o'clock, Kyle began to address the surveillance team that had been on the watch during the previous twenty-four hours. He finished with them and went on to the day's assignments. He handed them out and was very specific. It was a typical Craig performance: clear, to the point, efficient, never a mistake, or the hint of one.

When he was finished, or thought that he was, a hand shot into the air. 'Excuse me, Mr Craig, you didn't mention me. What am I supposed to do today?'

It was Jamilla Hughes and she didn't sound happy. Kyle was already collecting his notes, shuffling a few papers into his thick black briefcase. He barely glanced up as he said, 'That's up to Dr Cross, Inspector Hughes. Please see him.'

The remark and its delivery were unnecessarily curt, even for Kyle. I was taken aback by his rudeness, or at least the lack of any tact.

'This is complete bullshit!' She rose from her seat. 'It's unacceptable, Mr Craig. Especially that irritating, blasé tone of yours.'

The FBI agents in the room looked at her. Usually, no one dared confront Kyle on anything. After all, he was rumored to be in line for the director's job some day. Moreover, many of them felt he deserved it. He was certainly smarter than anybody else in the Bureau. He also worked harder than anyone I knew.

'Look, this is no reflection on Detective Cross,' Jamilla went on, 'but my work in California helped open this case up. I don't want anybody's pat on the back, no condescending applause, thank you, but I came all the way down here and I can contribute. So use me, and respect me. By the way, I couldn't help noticing there's only one other woman on this entire task force. Don't bother to make excuses,' she said, and waved off anything Kyle might have been ready to say in his defense.

Kyle kept his cool. 'Like the supposed vampires, Inspector Hughes, gender doesn't matter to me. I do applaud your efforts during the early stages of this case. But as I said, you can see Dr Cross about your assignment. Or you can go back home right now, if you like. Thank you, everyone,' he said as he saluted the team. 'Happy hunting. Hopefully, today will be our day.'

I was surprised, mostly by Kyle's response, but also by Jamilla's quick anger. I was uneasy when she came up to me after the meeting.

'He got me so mad. Grrrr,' she said. She shook her head and made a face. 'I have a quick temper sometimes, and he was wrong. There's something fucked-up about that man. I have a bad feeling about him. Why would he have it in for me? Because I'm working with you? So what *do* we do today, Dr Cross? I'm not leaving because he's a goddamn idiot.'

'He was wrong. I'm sorry about what happened, Jamilla. Let's talk about what we do next.'

'Don't be condescending,' she said.

'I'm not. Why don't you get off the soapbox, though.'

She still wasn't over her bad scene with Kyle. 'He doesn't like women,' she said. 'Trust me on that. He also practices the three Cs that some men are so fond of: compete, criticize, control.'

'So tell me what you *really* think about Kyle. And men in general.'

Jamilla finally managed a smile. 'I think, and I'm being pretty objective and measured about this, that your so-called friend is a total control freak and a complete asshole. As for men in general, it varies with the individual.'

Chapter Sixty-Seven

The *real* vampires had arrived and they believed they were invincible. William and Michael knew that the exotic city of New Orleans belonged to them from the instant they crossed the bridge. They were a couple of young princes with their long blond ponytails, black shirts and trousers, shining leather boots. Their mission ended here if all went well – and it would.

William drove the Red Cross van through the French Quarter – they were on the lookout for prey. The van rode slowly back and forth on Burgundy, Dauphine, Bourbon, Royal, Chartres, all of the more famous streets. The sounds of Readysexgo blared from the tape deck. 'Radio Tokyo', then 'Supernatural Blonde'.

The brothers finally got out and strolled along River-walk. They turned into the Riverwalk Marketplace, and it made William feel physically ill: Banana Republic, Eddie

Bauer, the Limited, Sharper Image, the Gap – mediocrity, tripe, utter stupidity everywhere he looked. 'What do you want to do?' William turned to Michael. 'Look at all this commercial crap in the middle of this beautiful city.'

'Let's take somebody out here in their putrid shopping mall. Maybe we should feed in a changing room at Banana Republic. I love that idea.'

'No!' William said. He grabbed hold of Michael's arm. 'We've been working too hard for this. I think we need a distraction.'

They couldn't take any more prey. Not now. Not so close to Daniel and Charles's domain. So William drove out of New Orleans on the Bonnet Carre Spillway. He continued on Interstate 10 into the real Louisiana. A distraction was definitely needed.

William found what he wanted about an hour outside New Orleans. The rock climb wasn't much, but at least the face was steep. You had to concentrate; if you didn't, you fell, and you were dead.

The brothers chose to free solo, the most extreme example of the sport. Also the most dangerous by far. In free solo, the climbers used no ropes, or any kind of backup protection.

'We are a couple of hardmen!' Michael laughed and shouted once they were halfway up the two-hundred-foot climb. Hardmen were the toughest climbers of all. They were the best, and it fit the brothers' self-image.

'Yes we are!' William shouted back to his brother. 'There are *old* climbers, and there are *bold* climbers.'

'But there are no *old, bold climbers!*' Michael roared with laughter.

The climb turned out to be more challenging than it had looked. It required lots of different kinds of skill. They had to do vertical crack climbing, then suddenly they were face climbing, pressing tight against the rock, using very small hand holds.

'We're in the climbing groove now!' Michael screamed at the top of his lungs. He had forgotten about hunting for prey, forgotten his hunger. There was nothing but the climb. Nothing but staying alive, survival of the fittest.

Suddenly, they had to commit – they were at a point in the climb where, once they made the next couple of moves, they couldn't go back the way they had come. There was nowhere to go but straight up. Or to quit right now.

'What do you think, little brother? You make a plan for us. You decide. What does your instinct tell you?'

Michael laughed so hard he had to grip the rock face with both hands. He looked down – and what he saw was certain death if he fell. 'Don't even think about quitting. We won't fall, brother. Not ever. We're never going to die!'

They climbed to the top and from there they could see New Orleans. It was their city now.

'We're immortal! We'll never die!' the brothers shouted into the wind.

Chapter Sixty-Eight

I stared out at the great, sweeping live oaks. Then I noticed the plump magnolias and sloppy, fanning banana trees of the Garden District. There was nothing else for me to do. The surveillance continued. Jamilla was starting to repeat herself. We both were, and that became a running gag between us. Sections of the day's *Times-Picayune* were all over the backseat of the car. We had read it cover to cover.

'There's no physical evidence tying Daniel or Charles to a single murder. Not in any of the cities, Alex. Everything we have on them is circumstantial, or theoretical, hypothetical bullshit. Does that make any sense to you? It doesn't to me.' She was talking, probably just to talk, but she was making sense. 'It just doesn't add up. They can't be that good. No one is.'

We were parked four blocks north of the house on

LaSalle. The *domain*. We could get there in seconds if anything developed, but so far, nothing had. That was the problem. Daniel and Charles rarely left their two-hundred-year-old mansion, and when they did, it was only to go shopping, or to a fancy restaurant downtown. Not surprisingly, they had good taste.

I tried to answer Jamilla's question. 'It makes some sense to me that we can't link them to the early murders. You know as well as I do – once a murder case gets old it's almost impossible to find witnesses, or compelling evidence. I don't understand why we haven't found anything on the recent murders, though.'

'That's what I'm thinking too. We have witnesses to the killings in Savannah and in Charleston, but no one recognizes photos of Daniel or Charles. Why not? What are we missing?'

'Maybe they don't commit the actual murders themselves,' I said. 'Maybe they used to, but not anymore.'

'Don't they want to feast on the kills? Drink the blood? What other purpose do the murders serve? Are they symbolic? Is this part of some arcane mythology? Are they creating a new mythology? Jesus, Alex, what the hell are these two monsters doing in New Orleans?'

I didn't have answers to her questions, or my own. No one did, unfortunately. So we sat in the car, tried to keep cool in the heat, and waited for Daniel and Charles to make their next move.

If they were so careful and so good then why did we know about them, why were we here?

Chapter Sixty-Nine

W illiam found this laughable. God, it was good! Priceless. He was watching the police as they in turn watched the house of horrors owned by Daniel and Charles. It was too much. The young prince walked down LaSalle, puffing on a cigarette, haughty, confident, unafraid of anyone, superior in every way he could imagine. Michael was home sleeping, so he had decided to take a stroll.

This was rich. Maybe he would see one of the local celebrities who lived in the Garden District. Like the fabulous Trent Reznor of Nine Inch Nails, or some asshole from MTV's Real World house in the Big Easy.

There were two nondescript Lincolns parked on the street. He wondered if the magicians had noticed the cars. He smiled, shook his head. He wondered what the hell Daniel and Charles were thinking. They would be careful, of course. They had been committing murders for a long time, years and years. So now what? Something had to give.

He continued to the end of the street, then walked south toward Sixth. Most of the houses there had screened-in porches crawling with vines. Along the way, he saw a fine physical specimen – a male, twenty-one or so, shirt off, pecs gleaming with sweat. That picked up his spirits. The man was hosing down a silver BMW convertible, the James Bond car.

His chiseled body, the spurting water hose and the shiny car turned William on like a light switch. But he controlled himself and walked on.

And then, just down the street, he saw a young girl. She was maybe fourteen, sitting on her front porch, gently stroking a Persian cat. She was pretty, even sultry.

The girl had long brown hair that flowed down to her small breasts. A diaphanous snakeskin-print top over a belly-length tank top. Tight, dark blue jeans, hip-hugging and flared just right. Stud and hoop earrings, both gold and silver. Toe rings. Bracelets of multiple colors on one slender arm. A typical teenager – except that she was so stunning. A complete turn-on. And arrogant, just like he was.

William stopped and called out to her. 'Your cat is beautiful.' He smiled wickedly.

She looked up, and he saw that she had the same piercing green eyes as the Persian. The girl ran her eyes all over him. He could actually feel them against his skin. He knew that she wanted him. Men and women always did.

'Why do you hold back?' he asked, and continued to smile. 'If you want something, then you should take it. Always. That's your lesson for the day, free of charge.'

'Oh, and you're a teacher?' she called from the porch. 'You don't look like any teacher I've ever had.'

'A teacher, but also a student.'

He had desire for this girl. Not only was she a physical specimen, but she had good instincts. She was sexual and knowing for her age. She used her gifts, unlike most young people, who wasted their talent and potential. She wouldn't speak again, wouldn't even smile, but she didn't look away either.

William loved her confidence, the way her bright green eyes tried to mock him, but couldn't quite do it. The way she thrust her small breasts out at him, her only weapons. He wanted to go up on the porch and take the beautiful girl right there. Bite her, drink her. Spill her blood all over the whitewashed wooden planks.

No. Not now, not yet, not here. God, he hated this, hated not being himself. He wanted to exercise his power, to use his gifts.

Finally, William began to walk away. It took all his will,

all his power, to leave this beautiful prize sitting so invit-
ingly on the porch.

It was then that the girl finally spoke again. 'Why do
you hold back?' she called, and laughed pitilessly.

William smiled and turned around.

He walked back toward the girl.

'You're very lucky,' he said. 'You've been chosen.'

Chapter Seventy

Something had to break for us. At seven in the morning, I sat alone at a table outside the Café du Monde across from Jackson Square. I ate sugar-dusted beignets and sipped chickory-laced coffee. I stared off in the direction of the spire of St Louis Cathedral and listened to the bleating horns of riverboats coming down the Mississippi.

It should have been a nice time of the morning, except that I was frustrated and angry and filled with energy that I didn't know what to do with.

I had seen a lot of bad cases, but this was possibly the most difficult to comprehend. The gruesome murders had been going on for more than eleven years, but the pattern was still unclear, and so was the motivation of the killers.

As soon as I reached the FBI offices, I got the disturbing news that a fifteen-year-old girl was missing and that she lived less than six blocks from the magicians. It was possible that she was a runaway, but it didn't seem likely to me. Still, she had been gone less than twenty-four hours.

There was a briefing scheduled and I went upstairs to find out more, and also why I hadn't been alerted earlier. When I entered the session that morning, I sensed the frustration everywhere that I looked. It was hard to imagine a worse result: we suspected that we had tracked down the murderers, but there was nothing we could do about it. And now there was a possibility they had murdered another victim right under our noses.

I sat down beside Jamilla. Both of us had containers of hot coffee plus the morning edition of the *Times-Picayune*. There was nothing about the missing girl; apparently the New Orleans police had sat on the disappearance until early that morning.

Kyle was angry. He just wasn't himself. He was storming about the front of the room, his right hand nervously combing back his dark hair. I didn't blame him – everything about the investigation depended on FBI cooperation with the local police. The NOPD had broken that trust, broken it badly.

'For once, I sympathize with Mr Craig,' Jamilla said. 'The locals were way out of line.'

'We could have been working on the girl's disappearance for hours,' I agreed. 'What a mess, and it's getting worse.'

'Maybe this is our opportunity. I wonder if we could get inside the house during the party tonight. What do you think? I'd love to give it a try,' she whispered. 'Everybody who goes to the so-called Fetish Ball will be in costume, right? Somebody needs to get inside that house. We need to do something.'

Kyle stared directly at Jamilla and me. He raised his voice. 'Can we have one meeting?'

'He means can he have *his* meeting,' she whispered. I wondered why she had taken such a dislike to Kyle. He was acting strange though; the pressure of the case was getting to him. Something had him on edge.

'Tell him what you think,' I said. 'He'll listen. Especially now that the girl is missing.'

'I doubt it. But what can he do – fire me?'

She swiveled around to face Kyle. 'I think we could probably get inside the house tonight during the party. And if we don't, what do we lose? The missing girl might be in there.'

Kyle hesitated, but then he said, 'Do it. Let's see what's in the house.'

Chapter Seventy-One

It could only happen like this in New Orleans. I spent part of the afternoon securing a couple of printed invitations and then Jamilla and I prepared our costumes for that night. The ball began at midnight, but we'd heard most of the crowd wouldn't start to arrive until closer to two.

It had already been a long night for us by the time the festivities started. We waited until just past two to approach the house. Some of the partygoers were college age, a few were even younger, but at least half of the crowd looked to be thirty or older. A few arrived in limousines and other expensive cars. The dress for the night was definitely eye-catching: antique mourning coats and top hats, velvet Victorian gowns, corsets, walking sticks, tiaras.

The Goth crowd sheathed their androgynous bodies mostly in black leather and velvet. There were body piercings everywhere; frilly white and black lace on several of the women; belly rings, dog collars, black lipstick, and gobs of mascara on both the men and women.

Blood-red eyes stared out from every direction. It was difficult to avoid them. A rock song called 'Pistol Grip Pump' played from hidden speakers outside the house. Fangs were everywhere. And stage blood. A few of the women wore black or purple velvet bands around their necks, presumably to conceal bite marks.

It got more interesting and eerie as we went inside the house. People were addressing one another with titled names, 'Sir Nicholas', 'Mistress Anne', 'The Baroness', 'Prince William', 'Master Ormson'. A statuesque woman walked by and brazenly sized-up Jamilla. She was bronzed with body paint and wore a bronze-colored thong. The iron scent of blood mingled with smoky leather and pungent oil from wall torches.

Jamilla looked ready; she was definitely tough. She had on a tight, sleek black dress with leather boots and black stockings. If she'd wanted to look sexy, she'd succeeded. She had purchased black lipstick and leather wristbands at a place called the Little Shop of Fantasy on Dumaine Street. She'd also helped me with my outfit: a mourning coat that scraped the floor, cravat, black trousers, black boots that came to my knees.

No one seemed to pay much attention to the two of us.

We checked out the main floor, then flowed with the crowd down into the basement. There were flaming torches everywhere on the stone walls. The floors were dirt and stone. It was cold and damp and musty.

'Jesus, Alex,' Jamilla whispered close to my ear. She took my arm, held it tight. 'I don't think I would have believed it if I wasn't standing right here.'

I felt exactly the same. Several of those congregating downstairs wore canine teeth that were terrifying, especially in such large numbers. Electrified candelabras and the fiery torches were the only sources of light. I saw human skulls nailed into the walls, and I was sure they were real.

I started checking to make sure we could get out of here if we had to. I wasn't sure about a quick escape. The crowd was thickening and the feeling was claustrophobic. I wondered if someone was supposed to die here tonight. If so, who would it be?

Then I heard a deep voice announce, 'The Sire is here. Bow your heads.'

Chapter Seventy-Two

The cavernous underground room was quiet and tense. I had the uncomfortable feeling that I was about to see something I wasn't supposed to. Then Daniel Erickson and Charles Defoe made their grand entrance.

The magicians epitomized outrageous bohemian royalty. The audience of faithful obediently bowed their heads. Both men were physically impressive. Charles was bare-chested and wore skintight leather pants with boots. He was an erotic-looking man with a powerful build. Daniel had on a tight black frock coat, with black trousers and a black silk cravat. He was well muscled, but slender at the waist.

Tugging against a heavy metal leash in front of them was a white Bengal tiger. Jamilla and I exchanged looks. 'This is getting interesting in a hurry,' she whispered.

Daniel stopped to talk with several of the young males. I

remembered that the earliest murder victims were all men. The tiger was less than ten feet away from me. What did it mean for the vampires? Was it just a symbol – and for what?

Charles came and stood next to Daniel against the far wall. He whispered something close to Daniel's ear. They laughed and looked around the room.

Daniel finally spoke in a loud, clear voice. I could tell he expected to be listened to. His confidence was charismatic. 'I am the Sire. What a vibrant and alive gathering this is,' he said. 'I can feel the energy coursing through this room. It excites me.

'The force harnessed here knows no limits. Believe in it. Believe in yourselves. Tonight is a special night. So come with me to the next room. The next level. Come, if you believe – or even better, if you don't.'

Chapter Seventy-Three

I had never seen anything like this. Jamilla and I were quiet and wide-eyed as we entered an even larger chamber in the basement.

The room was lit by wall sconces, most of them electric. The brutal fangs gleamed everywhere. The white tiger had begun to growl, and I recalled the bites into human flesh.

If you hunt for the vampires.

What was happening in this eerie cellar? What was the purpose of tonight's gathering? Who were these ghouls – hundreds of them?

Daniel and Charles stood beside two tall, handsome, dark-haired men in satiny black robes with capes. They looked to be in their early twenties, maybe even younger. They looked like young gods. Everyone crowded forward to see what would happen next.

'I am here to anoint two new vampire princes,' Daniel

announced with grave authority. The persona was the same one he used onstage. 'Bow before them!'

A woman at the front shrieked. 'Our princes! Dark princes! I worship you!'

'Silence!' Charles shouted. 'Take that stupid cow out of here. Banish her.'

The lights suddenly blinked once, then went out completely. The few burning torches were doused. I reached for Jamilla, and we slid back toward the nearest wall.

I couldn't see anything. I felt a cold spot at the center of my chest.

'What the hell is happening, Alex?'

'I don't know. Let's keep together.'

It got crazy very fast in the darkness. People screamed. A whip cracked nearby. It was madness. Chaos. Sheer terror.

Jamilla and I had our guns out. But there wasn't anything we could do in the dark.

A minute or so passed. Everything was inky blackness. It seemed like a very long time. Too long. I was afraid of being stabbed. Or bitten.

A generator kicked in somewhere in the house. The lights in the cellar flickered, then went on again. Then off. Then on.

I saw after-images, rings of color. And then—

The magicians had disappeared.

Someone shouted, 'Our princes are dead.'

Chapter Seventy-Four

I pushed my way through the shocked crowd and didn't meet resistance. Then I saw the bodies. The two young men in black robes lay sprawled on the cellar floor. They had been stabbed and their throats cut. Blood was pooled around the bodies. Where were Daniel and Charles?

'Police!' I called out. 'Don't touch them. Back away.'

The men and women closest to the bodies slinked away. I wondered if they had been about to drink the spilled blood. Wasn't that the ritual? The pattern for the ghoulish murders so far?

'There's only two of them! Two cops!' someone shouted.

'We *will* shoot you,' Jamilla called out in a loud, clear voice.

'Back away. Do it. Where are Daniel and Charles?' I shouted.

The crowd began to close in on us, so I fired off a

warning shot. It echoed loudly. There was chaos in the cellar. Men and women began struggling to get through the doors. No one would get away though. FBI agents were waiting outside.

Jamilla and I pushed our way into a connecting room in the basement. We started down a narrow hallway lit only by candles. Daniel and Charles could have come this way when the lights went out. It seemed likely; they knew the house.

There were small rooms crowded next to each other on either side of the dusty tunnel. The layout reminded me of ancient catacombs. Everything was closed in – musty, damp, depressing as hell, scary.

'You okay?' I glanced back at Jamilla.

'I'm fine. So far anyway. This place is starting to grow on me.' She made a wisecrack, but her eyes were darting about.

I could hear Kyle's voice calling to us. The FBI agents were inside now. 'Anything up there? Alex? You see anything?'

'Not yet. Daniel and Charles took off when the lights went off. No sign of them.'

We moved cautiously, checking each of the rooms. Most of the space seemed to be used for storage. A few were completely empty. Dank and eerie, like tombs. Atmospheric, I suppose. Spooky for sure.

I kicked open another door. Jamilla and I peered in. She gasped, her mouth open in a silent scream. 'Oh Jesus, Alex! What the hell happened?'

I reached out and held onto her arm. I couldn't believe what I was looking at. I couldn't make myself believe it. My knees went weak.

Daniel and Charles were laid out on the floor of the room. They had been murdered. I was too stunned to speak. Kyle came into the room behind us, said not a word.

We moved closer to the bodies, but I knew they were dead. The throats of both men had been cut. And there were deep bites, fang marks.

So who was the Sire?

Part Four

Hunt

Chapter Seventy-Five

L ate the following afternoon, Jamilla had to return to San Francisco. She pretty much admitted that she was burnt-out and baffled. I gave her a ride to the airport, and we continued to talk about the murder case all the way there. We realized we were both obsessing.

What had happened the night before changed everything. We had tracked down the supposed killers – and they had been killed. This was a complex and thoroughly frustrating murder mess in which anything seemed possible. The killers weren't necessarily clever, but they were full of surprises.

'Where do you go from here, Alex?' she asked as we turned into the airport.

I laughed. 'Oh, now it's where do *I* go?'

'You know what I mean. C'mon.'

'Kyle has asked me to stay down here for another day or

two to help out. Everyone who was in the house is being held by the New Orleans police. That's a lot of freaks to be interviewed. Somebody has to know something.'

'If you can get anything out of them. You think the New Orleans cops are cooperating now? They sure weren't before.'

I smiled. 'You know how stubborn local cops can be. We'll get what we need. It just might take a little longer. I'm sure that's part of the reason Kyle wants me to stay on.'

She frowned at the mention of Kyle's name. I knew she was disappointed to be leaving though. 'I have to get back home, but I'm not going to drop this one. My friend Tim at *The Examiner* is doing another big piece on the California murders. Maybe it all started out there. Think about it.'

'Eleven years ago, maybe more,' I said. 'But who were the first killers? Daniel Erickson and Charles Defoe? Someone else in the cult? *Is* there a cult?'

She threw her hands up in the air. 'I have no idea at this point. I'm practically brain dead. I'm going to get on my plane and sleep all the way home.'

She lingered for a few more minutes. We talked some more about the case. Then I asked her about Tim at *The Examiner*. 'Just a friend,' she said.

Jamilla and I shook hands at the curbside luggage drop in front of the area marked for American Airlines. Then she leaned in and kissed me on the cheek.

I slid my hand behind her neck and held her for a few seconds. It was nice. The two of us had shared a lot of pain and misery in a short time. We had also been in a life-threatening situation.

'Alex, as always, an honor,' she said as she pulled away. 'Thanks for the Krispy Cremes and everything else.'

'Keep in touch,' I said. 'Will you, Jamilla?'

'Absolutely. I plan to. You can count on it. I mean that, Alex.'

Then Inspector Jamilla Hughes turned away and walked inside the bustling terminal at New Orleans International. I was definitely going to miss her. I already thought of her as a friend.

I watched her go, then headed back to the FBI offices in New Orleans to bury my head in some work. I went over everything we had with Kyle. Then we went over everything again, just to be sure it was as fucked-up as we thought it was. The two of us agreed that there weren't even any good theories about what had happened to Daniel and Charles. We just didn't know. No one was talking so far – or maybe no one had seen anything.

'Whoever killed them wanted to show us that they were superior. To them. To us. Physically, mentally, in terms of their ruthlessness,' I said. But I wasn't really sure about that. I was just thinking out loud.

'I don't think it was an accident that the whole thing

feels a little like a magic trick,' Kyle said. 'Doesn't that strike you, Alex? Some connection to magic?'

'Yeah, but it wasn't a magic trick. Daniel and Charles are dead, and so are a lot of other people. Going back a lot of years.'

'We're nowhere. Is that what you're saying?'

'Yeah. And I don't like it here,' I said.

Chapter Seventy-Six

I worked late that night in the FBI office. So what else was new? Around nine I was feeling lonely and edgy, all messed up. I called home, but nobody was there. That worried me a little, until I remembered that it was my Aunt Tia's birthday and Nana was throwing a party at Tia's new house in Chapel Gate, north of Baltimore.

I hadn't bought Tia a present. *Damn it. Damn me.* Ever since I had come to Washington as a kid, Tia had never forgotten my birthday. Not once. This year, she had given me the watch that I was wearing now. I called her house in Maryland, and I got to talk to most of my relatives. They teased that I was missing out on some great sock-it-to-me cake. They wanted to know where I was on Tia's birthday, and when I was coming home.

I didn't have a satisfactory answer to give them. 'Soon as

I can. I miss you all. You have no idea how much I miss being there.'

I decided I needed to stop in at the magicians' house before I went back to the Dauphine. Why did I *need* to do that? I wondered. Because I was wired. Because I am obsessive. A couple of New Orleans policemen were stationed out front. They looked bored and under-utilized, and definitely not obsessive.

I showed them ID and they let me inside. No problem, Detective Cross.

I really wasn't sure why but I had a vague feeling that we had missed something in the house. Forensics had spent hours going over the place. So had I. We hadn't found anything concrete. Still, I didn't like being in the house again. The domain. Maybe I needed a gris-gris for protection.

I walked through the over-done, very ornate foyer and living room. My footsteps made the big house sound empty. I kept wondering, what were we missing? What was I missing?

The master bedroom was situated off the hall at the top of the stairs. Nothing had changed since the first time I was in there. Why in hell had I bothered to come back here? The large, open room was filled with dark, modern art, some of it hung, but several paintings were propped up against the walls. The magicians slept in a bed, not in the coffins we'd found below in the tunnels.

As I was searching through their clothes closet again, I came across something I hadn't seen before. I was sure it hadn't been there when I'd canvassed the bedroom the first time. Lying among the shoes were effigies of Daniel and Charles – miniature dolls of the magicians.

There were slash marks across the throats, chests and faces. Just like the way they were murdered.

Where the hell had the gruesome effigies come from? What did they mean? What was going on down here in New Orleans? Who had gotten into this house after we sealed it? I was tempted to call Kyle, but I held off. I wasn't sure why.

I didn't want to go back down into the tunnels alone, and at night, but I was here, and I figured I ought to take another quick look around. There were two cops posted just outside the door, right?

What were we missing? Unspeakably violent murders that went back at least eleven years.

Our two best suspects had been murdered.

Someone had put effigies in their bedroom.

I went down to the cellar, then into the tunnels that spidered out in several directions from the main area. New Orleans is about eight feet below sea level and the cellar and tunnels were probably always damp. The walls sweat.

I heard a scraping noise, and stopped. Someone or

something was walking around. I reached into my shoulder holster, took out my Glock.

I listened closely. Nothing. Then more scraping.

Mice or rats, I thought to myself. *Probably all it was. Probably. Almost definitely.*

I had to go and look further, though. That was my problem, wasn't it? I *had* to go look, had to investigate, couldn't just walk away. What was I trying to prove to myself? That I had no fears? That I wasn't like my father, who had quit on just about everything in life, including his kids and himself?

I inched forward slowly and quietly, listening to the house.

I could hear water dripping somewhere in the dank tunnels.

I used my old Zippo to light a few of the torches hung on the tunnel walls. There were really bad images in my head. The bite wounds on the bodies I'd seen. The way Daniel and Charles had been attacked. The poisonous bites I'd suffered in Charlotte. *You're one of us now.*

The anger, the rage connected to the murders was present in so many cities.

What were the killers angry about?

Where were they right now?

I never heard them coming, never saw a movement.

I was hit, twice. The attackers had come swiftly out of the darkness. One went for my head and neck. The other hit around my knees. They were a team. Efficient.

I went down hard and it took the wind right out of me. But I fell on one of the attackers, who was still wrapped around my legs. I heard a loud crack, maybe a bone breaking. Then a scream. He let me go.

I got up, but the second assailant was attached to my back. He bit me! *Oh Jesus, no!*

I cursed and slammed him into the wall. I did it again. Who the hell were these fantastic madmen? Who was the leech riding my back?

He finally let go, the sonofabitch! I spun around at him, clipping the side of his head with my gun. I hit him again with a solid left hook. He went down like a sack.

I was breathing hard, still full of fight, though. Neither of the assailants was moving much now. I kept the gun on them while I lit another candle on the wall. That was better; light always helps.

I saw a male and female, probably no more than sixteen or seventeen. Their eyes were like dark holes. The male must have been six foot six or more.

He had on a dingy white T-shirt with 'Marlboro Racing First to Finish' printed on it, and baggy, scungy black jeans.

The girl was around five two with wide hips, wide

everything. Her black hair was stringy and greasy, with reddish highlights.

I touched my neck and was surprised that the skin wasn't broken. There was no blood on my hand.

'You're under arrest,' I yelled at the two of them. 'You goddamn bloodsuckers!'

Chapter Seventy-Seven

Vampires? Is that what these twisted creeps were? Assassins? Murderers?

Their names were Anne Elo and John 'Jack' Masterson and they had attended Catholic high school in Baton Rouge until about four months ago, when they had dropped out and run away from home. Each was seventeen years old. They were just kids.

I spent three hours attempting to question the suspects that night, then another four hours the following morning. Elo and Masterson wouldn't talk to me or anyone else – not a word. They wouldn't say what they were doing inside the mansion in the Garden District. Why they had attacked me. Whether or not they had placed the sinister effigies in the closet of the dead men.

The teens simply glared across the plain wooden table in one or another of the interrogation rooms at police headquarters. The parents were notified and brought in, but Elo and Masterson wouldn't speak to them either. At one point, Anne Elo finally addressed her father with two words – 'Blow me.' I wondered how the cult of the vampire had satisfied her needs, her incredible anger.

In the meantime, there were still lots of others to talk to from the Fetish Ball. The commonality among most of them was that they held 'straight jobs' in New Orleans: they were bartenders and waitresses, hotel desk clerks, computer analysts, actors, and even teachers. Most were afraid to have their alternative lifestyles come out at work, so they eventually talked to us. Unfortunately, no one told us anything revealing about Daniel and Charles, *or their murderers*.

It was an extraordinarily busy night at the precinct house. More than two dozen homicide detectives and FBI agents conducted reinterviews. We exchanged notes and bios of the suspects with highlighted inconsistencies. We went hard at the most obvious liars in the group. We also kept a list of the witnesses who seemed the most likely to break under pressure. We switched interviewers on them, sent them to the cells, then summoned them back before they could sleep; we doubled up on them.

'All we need is a few rubber hoses,' one of the New Orleans detectives said while we were waiting for Anne Elo to be fetched from her cell for the sixth time that night.

His name was Mitchell Sams, and he was around fifty, a black man, hugely overweight, tough, effective, cynical as hell.

When Anne Elo was brought back into the interrogation room, she looked like a sleepwalker. Or a zombie. Her eye sockets were incredibly deep and dark. Her lips were chapped and caked with dried blood.

Sams went at her. 'Good morning, glory. It's nice to see your pasty-white face again. You look like total shit, babe. I'm being kind. Several of your friends, including your pathetic boyfriend, have broken down already tonight.'

The girl turned her vacant eyes toward a brick wall. 'You must be mistaking me for somebody who gives a shit,' she said.

I decided to try an idea that had been weaving through my mind for the past hour or so. I had used it on a few of the others. 'We know about the new Sire,' I told Anne Elo. 'He's gone back to California. He isn't here for you. He can't help you, or hurt you.'

Her face remained blank and unresponsive, but she folded her arms. She sagged a few inches in her chair. Her lips were bleeding again, possibly because she'd bitten into them. 'Who gives a shit. Not me.'

Just then, a bleary-eyed NOPD detective opened the door to the interrogation room where Mitchell Sams and I were working on Elo, and beckoned us out. The detective had dark sweat stains under both arms of his pale blue sports shirt. Heavy stubble covered his chin and cheeks. He looked about as exhausted as I felt.

'There's been another murder,' he told Sams. 'Another hanging murder.'

Anne Elo appeared at the open door, and slowly, rhythmically clapped her hands. 'That's great,' she said.

Chapter Seventy-Eight

I rode to the crime scene alone, feeling increasingly distant and unreal. The wheels in my head were turning slowly and methodically. Where did we go from here? I had no goddamn idea. Jesus, I was beat.

The house was an outbuilding for one of the Garden District's historic homes, a small carriage house with a second-story balcony. It looked like it could have been a cute, cozy B&B. Magnolia and banana trees surrounded it on the outside. So did an intricate wrought-iron fence, the kind I had seen everywhere in the French Quarter.

About half of the New Orleans Police Department was already at the scene. So were a couple of EMS trucks, their roof lights spinning and blazing. The press was beginning to arrive as we did – the late shift.

Detective Sams had gotten to the murder scene a couple of minutes before I did. He met me in the hallway outside the upstairs bedroom where the killing had taken place. The interior of the place had fine detailing on almost every surface – ceilings, banisters, moldings, doors. The owner had cared about the house, and also about Mardi Gras. Feathers and beads, colorful masks, costumes were tacked up on most of the walls.

'This is bad, even worse than we thought,' Sams said. 'She's a *detective* named Maureen Cooke. She's in Vice, but she was helping out on Daniel and Charles. Most of the department was pitching in.'

Sams led me into the detective's bedroom. It was small but attractive, with a sky-blue ceiling that someone had once told me was supposed to keep winged insects from nesting there.

Maureen Cooke was a redhead, tall and thin, probably in her early thirties. She had been hung by her bare feet from a chandelier. Her nails were painted red. The detective was naked except for a delicate, silver bracelet on her wrist.

Blood streaks were all over her body, but there was no sign of blood pooling on the floor or anywhere else.

I walked up close to her. 'Sad,' I whispered under my breath. A human life – gone – just like that. Another detective dead.

I looked at Mitchell Sams. He was waiting for me to speak first.

'This might not have been done by the same killers,' I said, and shook my head. 'The bite wounds look different to me. They're superficial. Something's changed.'

I stepped back from the body of Maureen Cooke and took in her bedroom. There were photographs that I recognized as part of E.J. Bellocq's study of the Storyville prostitutes. Strange, but fitting for the vice detective. A couple of Asian fans had been framed over the bed, which looked like it had been slept in. Or possibly the bed hadn't been made the previous day.

My cell phone rang. I hit a button with my thumb. I felt out of it. Numb. I needed sleep.

'Did you find her yet, Dr Cross? What do you think? Give me your best guess on how to stop these terrible murders. You must have it figured out by now.'

The Mastermind was on the line. How did he know?

Suddenly I was yelling into the phone. 'I'm going to take you down! I've figured that much out, asshole!'

I hung up on him, then I shut the phone off. I looked around the bedroom. Kyle Craig was watching me from the doorway.

'Are you all right, Alex?' he whispered.

Chapter Seventy-Nine

When I got back to the Dauphine Hotel it was almost ten-thirty in the morning. I was too tired and too worked up to sleep. My heart was still racing. There was a message for me: Inspector Hughes had called from San Francisco.

I stretched out on the bed and called Jamilla back. I shut my eyes. I wanted to hear a friendly voice, especially hers.

'I might have something good for you,' she said when I reached her at home. 'In my spare time, ha-ha, I've been taking a close look at Santa Cruz. Why Santa Cruz, you might ask? There have been several unsolved disappearances there. Too many. I plotted them out myself. Alex, something is happening up there. It fits in with the rest of this case.'

'Santa Cruz was on our original list,' I said. I was trying to focus on what she had just told me. I couldn't remember exactly where Santa Cruz was located.

'You sound tired. Are you all right?' she asked.

'I just got back to the hotel a few minutes ago. Long night.'

'Alex, *go to sleep*! This can wait. Goodnight.'

'No, I can't sleep anyway. Tell me about Santa Cruz. I want to hear it.'

'All right. I talked to a lieutenant with the Santa Cruz PD. Interesting conversation. Annoying, too. They're aware of the disappearances. They've also noted house pets and livestock disappearing in the past year. Lot of ranches in the area. Nobody believes in vampires, of course. *But* – Santa Cruz has a certain reputation. The kiddies call it the vampire capital of the US. Occasionally, the kids are right.'

'I need to see what you have so far,' I told her. 'I'm going to try and get a little sleep. But I want to read whatever Santa Cruz sends you. Can you send it to me?'

'My contact at *The Examiner* promised to send me the relevant files. Meanwhile, today's my day off. I might just take a ride.'

I opened my eyes wide. 'If you go, take somebody along. Your contact at *The Examiner*. I mean it.' I told her about the murder of the vice detective, Maureen Cooke, here in New Orleans. 'Don't go there alone. We still don't know what we're dealing with.'

'I'll take somebody along,' she promised, but I didn't know if I could believe her.

'Jamilla, be careful. I don't have a good feeling about this.'

'You're just tired. Get some sleep. I'm a big girl.'

We talked for a few more minutes, but I wasn't sure if I had gotten through to her. Like most good homicide detectives, she was stubborn.

I shut my eyes again and started to drift away, then I was gone.

Chapter Eighty

J amilla was remembering a line from a favorite Shirley Jackson novel, *The Haunting of Hill House*, which had been made into a really disappointing movie. 'Whatever walked there, walked alone,' Jackson had written. That pretty much summed up how she felt about the murder case. And maybe even about her life lately.

She drove her trusty, dusty Saab toward Santa Cruz. She gripped the steering wheel a little too firmly most of the way, and her hands felt numb. The kink in her neck was getting worse. This was a disturbing case, and she just couldn't let it go. The killers were out there somewhere. They were going to keep murdering until somebody stopped them. So maybe she should stop them.

She had tried to get Tim to go with her, but he was covering a bicyclists' protest for *The Examiner*. Besides, she wasn't sure that she wanted to spend the whole day with him. Tim was sweet, but, well, he wasn't Alex Cross. So here she was getting off Route 1, entering Santa Cruz all by her lonesome. *All by her damn lonesome again.*

At least she had alerted Tim to the fact that she was going to Santa Cruz, and of course she *was* a big girl, and armed to the teeth. *Ugh, teeth,* she thought. She cringed at the image of fangs, and the horrible deaths of all those who had been bitten.

She had always liked Santa Cruz, though. Maybe because it had been practically the epicenter of the Loma Pietra earthquake back in '89 – 6.7 on the Richter scale, fifty-seven dead – but then the area had come back. The gutsy little town and the people there had refused to fold. Lots of earthquake-proof construction, nothing higher than two stories. Santa Cruz was pure California, the best.

As she drove, she watched a big, blond surfer climb out of a VW with a surfboard strapped to the roof. He was finishing off a drippy slice of pizza, heading into the Book Shop of Santa Cruz. Pure California.

There was quite a mix of people here – post-hippies, high-tech start-up folks, transients, surfers, college kids. She liked it an awful lot. So where were the goddamn vampires hiding? Were they here? Did they know *she* was here in Santa Cruz looking for their gnarly asses? Were they among the surfers and post-hippies she was passing on the street?

Her first stop was the town's police department. The lieutenant, Harry Conover, was totally surprised to see her in the flesh. She guessed he couldn't imagine any detective going out of his or her way on the job.

'I told you I'd pass along everything I found on the Goths and wannabe vamps. Didn't you believe me?' he asked. He shook his head of longish blond curls, rolled his soft brown eyes. Conover was tall, well-built, probably in his mid-thirties. Around her age. Jamilla could tell that he was a big flirt, and that he had a high opinion of himself.

'Sure I believed you. But I had today off, and this case is burning a hole right through me. So here I am, Harry. Better than e-mail, right? What do you have for me?'

She sensed that he wanted to tell her to get a life, to enjoy her day off. She'd heard it all before, and maybe he was right. But not now, not with this case still on the boards.

'I read in a couple of the reports that some of the local ghouls might be living together commune-style. You have any idea where?' she asked.

Conover shook his head, and even pretended to be concerned. He was also checking her out, she could tell. Obviously, he was a breast man. 'We never got any confirmation of that,' he said. 'Kids crash together, of course, but I don't know about any *commune*. There are a couple of hot clubs – Catalyst, Palookaville. And lots of kids share cribs on lower Pacific Street.'

She didn't give up. Never. 'But if a lot of kids *were* living together – any ideas where that might be?'

Conover sighed, and actually looked a little annoyed with her for asking. Jamilla could tell he wasn't the kind of cop who put too much of himself into his work. She would have transferred him in a second if he worked for her, and Conover would have sworn it was a gender thing. It wasn't. He was a lazy, half-assed cop, and she hated that. Lives depended on how well he did his job. Didn't he understand that?

'Maybe out in the foothills. Or north around Boulder Creek,' Conover finally volunteered in a soft drawl. 'I really don't know what to tell you.'

Of course you don't, Harry. Duh.

'Where would *you* look first?' she persisted. *If you were worth jack shit as a cop.*

'Inspector, I just wouldn't be chasing this one too hard. Yes, there have been some curious disappearances around here. But that's true of just about every town up and down the coast of California. Kids are more restless now than they used to be when we were growing up. I don't believe anybody's getting seriously hurt in Santa Cruz, and I sure don't buy that this is the freaking *vampire* capital of the West Coast. It isn't. Believe me on that. There are no vampires in Santa Cruz.'

She nodded, pretended to agree. 'I think I'll try the foothills first,' she said.

Conover saluted her. 'If you're finished chasing ghouls before seven or so, give me a call. Maybe we could have a drink. It is your day off, right?'

Jamilla nodded. 'I'll do that. If I'm finished before seven, Harry. Thanks for all your help.' *Jackass.*

Chapter Eighty-One

S he was pissed now. Who in their right mind wouldn't be? Here she was working her butt off in somebody else's town. She parked the Saab on a funky side street, near the Metro Center, right across from the Asti bar. She had lost track of the San Lorenzo River while she was driving, but it was around here somewhere. She could *smell* it anyway.

She had just gotten out of the vehicle when two men appeared. They walked up quickly and flanked her tightly on either side.

Jamilla winced. They almost seemed to appear out of nowhere. *Blond ponytails,* she thought. *College kids? Surfers?* She sure hoped so.

They were well-built, but they didn't look like weightlifters. More like they came by it naturally. Images of Eros, Hermes, and Apollo came to mind. Muscles that were extremely well-defined. Virility. Chiseled marble.

'Can I help you fellows out?' she asked. 'Looking for the beach?'

The taller of the two spoke with tremendous confidence, or maybe it was cockiness. 'Doubt it,' he said. 'We're not surfers, actually. Besides, we're from around here. How about you?'

Both of them had the deepest blue eyes. They were incredibly intense. One looked no older than sixteen. Their movements were deliberate and controlled. She didn't like this. There was no one around to intervene on the side street.

'Maybe you could tell *me* where the beach is?' she said.

They were crowding her physically, standing too close. She wouldn't be able to get her gun out. She couldn't move without bumping into one or the other. They wore black T-shirts, jeans, rock climbers' shoes.

'You want to back off a little?' she finally said. 'Just back off, okay?'

The older one smiled. The dent between his lip and nose was a sexy round hollow. 'I'm William. This is my brother Michael. By any chance were you looking for us, Inspector Hughes?'

Oh no, oh Jesus. Jamilla tried to reach for the sidearm in the holster strapped to her back. They grabbed her. Took away her gun as easily as if she were a child. She was astonished at how fast they moved – and how strong they were. The two of them pushed her down on the sidewalk and handcuffed her. *Where did they get cuffs? In New Orleans? The murdered detective?*

The older one spoke again. 'Don't scream, or I'll snap your neck, Inspector.' He said it so matter-of-factly. *Snap your neck.*

The second one spoke then. He was right in her face. She saw the long canine fangs. 'If you hunt for the vampire, the vampire will hunt for you,' he said.

Chapter Eighty-Two

S he was gagged, then thrown roughly onto the rear
seat of a pickup truck. The truck started up and took
off with a jolt.

She was being driven somewhere. Jamilla tried to
concentrate on everything about the trip. She counted off
the seconds, kept track of the minutes. There was stop-
and-go city driving, then faster, smoother riding, possibly
on Route 1.

Then a very rough road, possibly unpaved. She figured
the trip took approximately thirty-seven minutes.

She was carried inside a building, some kind of ranch
house or roughshod farm structure. People were laughing.
At her? They wore fangs. Jesus. She was put down on a cot
in a small room and her gag removed.

'You've come looking for the Sire,' the one who called
himself William whispered, his face up close to hers.

'You've made a terrible mistake, Inspector. This one will get you killed.'

He smiled horribly, and she felt as if she were being both ridiculed, and, at the same time, seduced. William touched her cheek with his long, slender fingers. He lightly caressed her throat, stared into her eyes.

She was repulsed, wanted to run away, but couldn't do anything. There were a dozen or so vampires here – watching her like she was meat on a spit.

'I don't know anything about a Sire,' she said. 'What's a Sire? Help me out here.'

The brothers looked at each other, shared a knowing smirk. A few of the others laughed out loud.

'The Sire is the one who leads,' said William. He was so calm, so very sure of himself.

'Who does the Sire lead?' she asked.

'Why, anyone who will follow,' William answered. He laughed again, seemed to be enjoying himself immensely at her expense. 'Vampires, Inspector. Others like Michael and myself. Many others, in many, many cities. You can't imagine the extent of it. The Sire stands firm with simple directions on what to think, how to act, things like that. The Sire is not accountable to any authorities. The Sire is a superior being. Are you starting to understand? Would you like to meet the Sire?'

'Is the Sire here now?' she asked. 'Where are we?'

William continued to stare down at her. He was definitely seductive. Disgusting. Then he leaned in closer. 'You're the detective. *Is* the Sire here? Where are you? You tell me.'

Jamilla felt as if she might retch. She needed her space. 'Why are we here?' she asked. She wanted to keep them talking, keep them occupied for as long as she could.

William shrugged. 'Oh, we've always been here. This used to be a commune – California-dreaming hippies, mind-altering drugs, Joni Mitchell music. Our parents were hippies. We were isolated from other ways to live and think, so we depended on each other. My brother and I are unbelievably close. But we're nothing really. We're here to serve the Sire.'

'Was the Sire always at the commune?' she asked.

William shook his head, and gave her a serious look. 'There were always vampires here. They stayed apart, left the others alone. You had to join them, not the other way around.'

'How many are there?'

William looked at Michael, shrugged his broad shoulders, and they both laughed. 'Legions! We're everywhere.'

Suddenly William roared and went for her throat. Jamilla couldn't help it – she screamed.

He stopped inches away from her, still growling like an animal. Then he purred gently. His long tongue licked her cheek, her lips, her eyelids. She couldn't believe what was happening.

'We're going to hang you and drink every last drop. And the most amazing thing – you're going to enjoy it when you die. It's ecstasy, Jamilla.'

Chapter Eighty-Three

I had returned to Washington, and was taking a much needed day off. Why not? I hadn't seen enough of the kids lately, and it was Saturday after all.

Damon, Jannie and I went to the Corcoran Gallery of Art that afternoon. The little creeps fiercely resisted the museum at first, but once they were inside the Palace of Gold and Light they were completely entranced. Then they didn't want to leave. Typical of them.

When we eventually got home at around four, Nana told me I was to call Tim Bradley at the San Francisco *Examiner*. *Give me a break. This case wouldn't stop. Now I was supposed to call Jamilla's buddy?*

'It's important that you call. That's the message,' Nana said. She was baking two cherry pies. Reminding me how good it was to be home.

It was one o'clock in California. I called Tim Bradley at

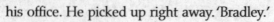

his office. He picked up right away. 'Bradley.'

'It's Detective Alex Cross.'

'Hi. I hoped you'd call. I'm a friend of Jamilla Hughes.'

I knew that much already. I interrupted. 'Is she okay?'

'Why do you ask that, Detective? She went to Santa Cruz yesterday. Did you know about that?'

'She mentioned she might go. Did somebody go with her?' I asked. 'I suggested she take company.'

His answer was curt and defensive. 'No. Like Jamilla always says, she's a big girl. And she carries a big gun.'

I frowned and shook my head. 'So what's going on? Has something happened? Is something the matter?'

'No, not necessarily. She's usually careful, precise. I just haven't heard from her, and she promised to call. *Last* night. It's been another four hours since I first called you. I'm a little concerned. It's probably nothing. But I thought you would know best . . . about this particular case.'

'Does she do things like this often?' I asked.

'Investigate a case on her day off? Yes. That's Jam. But she would definitely call me if she promised to.'

I was worried now. I thought of my last two partners. Both Patsy Hampton and Betsey Cavalierre had died, and neither of the victims had had justice. The Mastermind claimed to have killed Betsey. And also detective Maureen Cooke in New Orleans. So what about Inspector Jamilla Hughes?

'I'm going to call the local police in Santa Cruz. She gave me a name and a number. I think it was Conover. I have it written down in my notes. I'm going to call him right now.'

'All right, thank you, Detective. Will you let me know?' Tim the reporter asked. 'I'd appreciate it.'

I said that I would, then tried to reach Lieutenant Harry Conover at police headquarters in Santa Cruz. He wasn't working, but I made a fuss, and dropped Kyle Craig's name. The sergeant reluctantly gave me Conover's home number.

Someone picked up at the number, and I heard loud music that I vaguely recognized as U2. 'We're having a party at the pool. C'mon over. Or call back on Monday,' said a male voice. 'Bye, bye for now.'

The line went dead.

I redialed and said, 'Lieutenant Conover, please. It's an emergency. This is Detective Alex Cross. It's about Inspector Jamilla Hughes of the San Francisco PD.'

'Awhh shit,' I heard, then, 'this is Conover. Who is this again?'

I explained who I was and my involvement in the case in as few words as possible. I had the feeling that Harry Conover was drunk, or close to it. It *was* his day off, but Jesus – it wasn't even two in the afternoon his time.

'She went up in the hills, looking for new-wave vampires,' he said and laughed derisively. 'There are no vampires in Santa Cruz, Detective. Trust me on that. I'm sure she's just fine. She probably headed back to San Francisco.'

'There have been at least *two dozen* vampire-style murders so far.' I tried to sober Conover up, at least to get through to him. 'They hang their victims, and then drain the blood.'

'I told you what I know, Detective,' he said. 'I guess I could call out some patrol cars,' he added.

'You do that. And while you do, I'm going to call the FBI. *They* believe in vampire murders. When was the last time you saw Inspector Hughes?'

He hesitated. 'Who knows. Let me see, must be close to twenty-four hours.'

I hung up on Conover. I didn't like him at all.

I sat and thought about everything that had happened since I'd first met Jamilla Hughes. The case made my head spin. Everything about it was over the edge, completely new territory. Having the Mastermind around made it even worse.

I phoned Kyle Craig, and then American Airlines. I called Tim Bradley back and told him I was on my way to California.

Santa Cruz.

The vampire capital.

Jamilla was in trouble out there. I could feel it in my blood.

Chapter Eighty-Four

On the long flight out to California, I realized that I hadn't been tormented by the Mastermind in two days. That was unusual, and I wondered if he was traveling too. *Que pasa, Mastermind? Maybe he was on the plane to San Francisco with me?* I remembered a tired old joke about paranoia. A man tells his psychiatrist that everybody hates him. The psychiatrist says he's being ridiculous – everybody hasn't met him yet.

It got worse. At one point, I actually took a walk down the aisle and checked out the other passengers. No one looked even vaguely familiar. No Mastermind on board. No one seemed to be wearing fangs, either. I was losing it.

I arrived at San Francisco International Airport and was met by agents from the FBI. They told me that Kyle was on his way from New Orleans. Lately, Kyle had been pressuring me more than ever about making the switch to the FBI.

The change certainly made financial sense. Agents earned a lot more than detectives. The hours were usually better, too. Maybe I would talk to Nana and the kids after this was over. Hopefully soon, but why should I think that?

I left the airport with three agents in a dark blue off-road vehicle. I sat in back with the senior agent from San Francisco. His name was Robert Hatfield and he told me some of what they had so far. 'We found where some of the so-called vampires are staying. It's a ranch in the foothills south of Santa Cruz, not too far from the ocean. At this juncture, we don't know if Inspector Hughes is being held there. She hasn't been spotted.'

'What's out there in the hills?' I asked Hatfield. He could have been anywhere between thirty-five and fifty. He looked fit. His hair in a short brush cut. Appearances obviously meant a lot to him.

'Not a hell of a lot. It's rural. A couple of fairly large ranches. Rocks, desert birds of prey, a few mountain cats.'

'Not tigers?' I asked.

'Funny you should mention tigers. The ranch out there used to be a preserve for wild animals. Bears, wolves, tigers, even an elephant or two. The owners trained animals, mostly for use in feature films and commercials. They were basically hippies left over from the Sixties. The ranch was actually licensed by the Department of the Interior. It did business with Tippi Hedren, Siegfried and Roy.'

'The animals aren't still on the property?'

'Not for the past four or five years. The original owners disappeared. No one's been interested in buying the land. It's about fifty-five acres. Not good for much. You'll see.'

'What about the animals that were there? You know what happened to them?'

'Some were bought by other preserves that supply specialty animals to movies. Brigitte Bardot supposedly took some. So did the San Diego Zoo.'

I sat back in my seat and thought everything through while we drove. I didn't want to get my hopes up again. I wondered if the past owners of the ranch might have left a tiger behind. I spun a wild scenario out in my head. Actually, it was kind of interesting. Vampires in Africa and Asia supposedly changed shape into big cats rather than bats or wolves. The tiger imagery was certainly scarier than bats, and so were the ravaged bodies I had seen. Also, Santa Cruz had a reputation to uphold: the vampire capital.

We passed a farmhouse along the highway and then a small winery. Not much else to see, though. Agent Hatfield told me that in summer the hills turned brown and gold, much like the African veldt. This time of year there was lots of rain, and the terrain was a rich green, reminiscent of parts of Ireland.

I had been trying not to think about Jamilla and the

danger she might be in. *Why did she have to come up here alone? What drove her? The same things that drove me? If she was dead, I would never forgive myself.*

The car finally pulled off the main road. I didn't see a house or other building in any direction that I looked. Just barren, bright green hills. A hawk floated easily in liquid-blue skies. The scene was quiet and serene and quite beautiful.

We turned down an unpaved road and went for about a mile over bumpy, rocky terrain. We passed over the grille of a cowcatcher. A broken, split-rail fence ran alongside the road for about a hundred yards, stopped, then started again.

Suddenly, we came upon six vehicles parked on either side of the trail. All were unmarked, mostly Jeeps.

Standing right there was Kyle Craig. Kyle had his hands on his hips, and he was smiling as if he had the most amazing secret to tell me.

I suspected that he did.

Chapter Eighty-Five

'I think this is exactly what we've been working for,' Kyle said as I walked up to him. We shook hands, an old ritual that reflected on Kyle's formality. He looked calmer and more in control than he had during the past week. 'Let me show you something,' he said. 'Come.'

I followed him down along the split-rail fence until we came to a broken-down gate. He showed me a faded image. The body and head of a tiger had been branded into the gate. It was subtle, but this was it, it had to be. We had arrived at the tiger's lair.

'The group inside seems to be led by the Sire, the new and improved one, I assume. We haven't been able to establish an identity for the leader. Alex, the past Sire was the magician, Daniel Erickson. Two members of the group just returned from a trip. They were in New Orleans. Pieces are finally starting to fit.'

I looked at Kyle, shook my head. 'How did you find all of this out? When did you get here, Kyle?' *How much have you been keeping from me? And why?*

'Santa Cruz police contacted us and I came right out. We grabbed one of the "undead" when the little prick left the ranch this afternoon. He's a local high school dropout, wasn't as committed as some of the others. He told us what he knew.'

'Is the Sire in there now?'

'Supposedly. This kid has never actually seen the Sire. He's not part of the inner circle. The two males who traveled to New Orleans are in there, though. He heard they were the ones who killed Daniel and Charles. He said the two of them are total psychos.'

'Well, I believe that.' I looked down through the limbs of pine-cypress trees at the ranch. 'What about Jamilla Hughes?'

His eyes shifted. 'We found her car in town, Alex. But no sign of her. The kid we questioned didn't know about her either. He claimed there was a commotion at the ranch late last night. He was bunked in with some of the younger ghouls. They thought that someone had broken the perimeter, thought it might be the police. But then it got quiet again, according to the boy. There's no evidence that she's there.'

'Can I talk to him, Kyle?'

Kyle looked away; he didn't seem to want to answer me. 'The Santa Cruz police took him away. I guess you could go into town to see him. I talked to him, Alex. The androgynous little twerp was scared of me. Imagine that.'

Kyle was acting strange, but I reminded myself that he understood the deranged criminal mind better than any other FBI agent or police officer I had worked with. The agents who worked under him were convinced that he would run the Bureau one day. I wondered if Kyle could ever take himself out of the field, though.

'Inspector Hughes may be there. I guess we could go in right now, but I think we should wait. I want to go at them tonight, Alex. Or possibly at sun-up. I don't think she's down there.'

Kyle paused. His eyes shifted toward the distant ranch house. 'I want to find out if they hunt as a group. There are questions we need answered. What motivates these freaks? What makes them tick? I want to make sure we get the Sire this time.'

Chapter Eighty-Six

It was a long, cool, very tense night in the foothills outside Santa Cruz. I couldn't wait for it to be over, or maybe I couldn't wait for it to start. We learned something interesting right away. The woman lawyer who had been murdered in Mill Valley had been involved in a lawsuit trying to get control of this property. It was probably why she and her husband had been hung.

I watched the ranch through binoculars from the surrounding trees and rock formations. I watched until my eyes ached. No one had left as of eleven. I didn't see anyone standing lookout either. The people inside were either crazy or supremely confident. Or maybe they were innocent. Maybe this was another wrong turn.

I was trying not to worry too much about Jamilla, but it wasn't working. I couldn't bear to think that she might already be dead. Was that what Kyle thought? Was that what he was keeping from me?

At midnight, two males walked outside leading a tiger. I watched them through the night-sight glasses. I was almost certain I had seen them in New Orleans. They'd been at the Fetish Ball, hadn't they? They loped off into the flat, open fields behind the house.

One of the men got down on all fours, then rolled around in the tall grass with the cat. Jesus Christ, they were playing! How incredibly weird. I remembered that the tiger had been called off its prey in Golden Gate Park.

About twenty minutes later, the men brought the cat to a pen behind the main compound. They hugged the six-hundred-pound tiger as if it was a large dog. The lights in the main building and the bunkhouse burned brightly until past two. Loud rock-and-roll played. Then the lights were dimmed.

No one had left the house to hunt.

We still didn't know if Jamilla was inside, or even if she was alive. I stayed awake and watched. I couldn't sleep, not even for an hour or so. The FBI continued to collect information on the people inside the domain. What in God's name were they doing down there?

There was no word on the identity of the Sire. We did learn about the two blond males with the ponytails. William and Michael Alexander were the sons of a post-hippie couple who had worked at the ranch as animal handlers. The mother had been a zoologist. The boys had grown up comfortable around wild animals. They attended schools in Santa Cruz until they were ten and twelve, at which time the boys began to be home-schooled. They wore Moroccan robes and were always barefoot on their occasional trips to town. They were considered bright, but odd and extremely secretive. The boys had gotten into trouble in their early teens and been sent off to a state correctional facility for aggravated assault. They had been dealing drugs and had been caught breaking and entering.

Kyle joined me in the rocks overlooking the ranch at around three.

'You look kind of gray around the gills,' I said to him.

'Thanks. Long night. Long month. You're worried about Inspector Hughes, aren't you?' he asked me. He seemed like a detached observer now. Calm and cool. It was pure Kyle. Calculated intelligence. 'I don't know anything more, Alex. I've told you what I know.'

'I can still see the body of Betsey Cavalierre. I don't want to see something like that again. Yes, I'm worried about her. Aren't you? What are you feeling, Kyle?'

'If she's alive down there, they have no reason to murder her now. They're keeping her there for a reason.'

If she's alive.

Kyle patted my shoulder. 'Get some sleep if you can,' he

said. 'Rest up.' Then he wandered off. But when I looked his way, he was watching me.

I leaned against an oak tree and covered myself with my sports coat. I must have fallen asleep at some point between three and three-thirty. I saw Betsey Cavalierre in my dream, then my partner and friend Patsy Hampton. Finally, I saw Jamilla. *Oh Christ, not Jam. I couldn't stand that.*

I was aware of someone nearby, standing right over me. I opened my eyes.

It was Kyle. 'Time to go in,' he said. 'Time to get some answers.'

Chapter Eighty-Seven

The ranch was four to five hundred yards away. The terrain in between was too open for us to sneak up on the complex. Was this where Jamilla had been murdered?

Kyle whispered, 'She might still be alive.' It was as if he was reading my thoughts. What else did he know? What was he hiding from me?

'I've been thinking about the brothers. They never had to be careful before, so they weren't. The magicians were the careful ones. They committed murders for almost a dozen years. Never got caught. There's no record that they were even suspected of any of the murders.'

'You think the new Sire set up Daniel and Charles?'

'That's part of it, I'll bet. The brothers committed murders in towns where the magicians toured. The Sire wanted us to catch up with Daniel and Charles. It was a trap.'

'Why kill them in New Orleans?'

'Maybe because the brothers are psychopaths. Maybe they had orders to do what they did. We'll have to ask the Sire.'

'They don't think anyone can stop them. Well, they're wrong about that,' Kyle said. 'They're going to be stopped.'

Which was when we got a surprise. The front door of the ranch house opened. Several men in dark clothes hurried outside. The two brothers weren't among them. The men hurried to a grassy area where pickup trucks and vans were parked in a ragged line. They started the vehicles, then drove them toward the front of the house.

Kyle was on his Handie-Talkie. He alerted the snipers waiting in the trees and rocks behind us. 'Stand ready.'

'Kyle, don't forget Jamilla.'

He didn't answer me.

The front door opened again. Shadowy figures began to move out of the house. They were clothed in hooded black gowns and they came in pairs.

One person in each pair held a handgun to the head of the other.

'Oh shit,' I whispered. 'They know we're here.'

There was no way to tell who anybody was, or if any of the robed figures were actually hostages. I tried to pick out Jamilla's shape, her walk. Was she among them? Was she alive? My heart felt heavy in my chest. I couldn't spot her from way up here.

'Everybody move. *Now!*' Kyle spoke into his radio. 'Go. *Go!*'

The black-robed figures continued to move toward the waiting trucks and vans.

One of the hostages suddenly dropped to the ground – only one.

'That's her,' I called out.

'Take out the one over her!' Kyle ordered.

A shot rang out from one of the snipers. A hooded figure slumped over in a heap. Blood was spattered all over his hood.

We charged forward, running down the steep hill toward the ranch. Some of the hooded figures fired shots at us. No one was hit. The FBI agents didn't return fire.

Then gunfire rang out from the hills. Some of the robed figures dropped to the ground, dead or wounded. A few put their hands above their heads in surrender.

I kept my eyes fixed on one robed figure. She was up again, stumbling, almost falling. The hood was pulled back and I could clearly tell it was Jamilla. She stared up into the hills. She put her hands up high.

I started to sprint. I was looking for the brothers. And the Sire.

I moved toward Jamilla. She was massaging her wrist.

She was also shivering and I gave her my jacket. 'You okay?'

'Not sure. They hung me from a beam, Alex. What an unbelievable scene. You can't imagine. I thought I was dead.' There were tears in her eyes.

'Where's the Sire?' I asked.

'Maybe still inside. I think there's another way out of there.'

'Stay right here. I'll take a look.'

She shook her head. 'No, not on your life. This is payback. I'm coming with you.'

Chapter Eighty-Eight

Jamilla and I searched the main ranch house, then we checked a large, unattached bunkhouse. We didn't find anyone there, not a straggler, not William or Michael Alexander. And not the mysterious Sire. Jamilla was still shivering some, but she refused to turn back.

'You're sure the brothers aren't out front with the others?' she asked. 'Two blonds? Ponytails?'

'If they are, Kyle has them by now. I don't think so. Let's check the smaller shack. You know what's in there?'

She shook her head. 'I didn't get the grand tour when I arrived. Just straight to the dungeon. Then they left me hanging, so to speak.'

I threw open the door of the shack and saw heaters and a water pump. The room smelled strongly of urine. A mouse scooted into a hole in the wall. I winced and shook my head at what I saw next. Three bodies lay sprawled and spread-eagled against the far wall. They were teenagers. Two were males, both naked except for a few face and chest rings.

I bent over them and took a closer look. 'Seem like street kids to me. The blood's been drained from the bodies.' There were bite marks – not just on the necks, but on the faces and limbs. The skin of both males was as pale as alabaster.

The third body was female – a teenager of about fifteen. She matched the description of the girl who had gone missing in New Orleans. I felt deeply saddened to have found her here.

I looked away from the clouded eyes that stared up at me. There was nothing we could do for them now. I noticed a reddish-brown hatch cover among the dusty machines that provided water, heat, and probably air-conditioning to the ranch.

I moved across the room, bent down low to get a better look. The cover was loose, so I was able to pull it off.

Darkness. Silence. What else was down there? *Who else?*

I looked at Jamilla, then I shined a flashlight into the hole. It was wide enough for someone to get down inside. I saw metal stairs. A tunnel.

Then I saw footprints in the dirt below. Several pairs.

'Go, tell Kyle,' I turned to her. 'Get some help.'

Jamilla was already heading out the door. She started to run. I stared down into the abyss and wondered if anybody was looking back at me.

Chapter Eighty-Nine

I waited as long as I could, then lowered myself slowly into the black hole. I fitted easily, and started to climb down the sturdy metal ladder.

There were several steps, steep and precarious. I swept the flashlight around. I could make out a dirt floor, corrugated tin walls. The ceiling bulbs had been broken. A narrow tunnel stretched out before me.

I didn't hear any sounds up ahead, so I began to make my way down the tunnel. I moved slowly and carefully. I had the flashlight in one hand, my Glock in the other. I kept looking back for Kyle and Jamilla. Where were they?

I saw a discarded carcass a short way down the tunnel. I took a breath, shined my light on it.

A single eye stared back.

What I was looking at had been a small deer. Only the head and shoulders remained. I remembered reading that tigers eat their prey starting at the rump. They consume bone and all. There were more smudged footprints in the dirt. It looked like two pairs, but I couldn't tell for sure in the dim light. There were smaller animal tracks that might be the cat's. *Oh, Jesus*.

I kept moving, trying to adjust my eyes to the semi-darkness. There were shards of glass all over the dirt. Someone had purposely smashed the overhead light bulbs.

I heard a roar, and almost dropped the flashlight. It wasn't the smoothest move of my life, but I'd never been in a closed-off area with a tiger before. The big cat's roar echoed off the tin walls of the tunnel. It was unexpected and terrifying. I didn't know what to do next.

The cat roared a second time and I found that I couldn't move. I felt nailed to the spot. I wanted to turn around and go back, but that wasn't an option right now. I couldn't outrun a tiger in this tunnel, or anywhere else for that matter.

Somewhere in the inky blackness up ahead, the cat was watching me. I debated shutting off the flashlight, but kept it on for now. At least I would see the cat coming. I concentrated, stared out into the darkness, kept very still, as if that would help me. I had the Glock pointed straight ahead. I wondered if I could bring down a big cat with a handgun, even a powerful one. No way of knowing; no practice range for this kind of shooting. I had my doubts, though.

I couldn't see the cat, but I could almost visualize the thirty-odd teeth in its mouth. I remembered the wounds a cat had made on the two bodies in Golden Gate Park.

Someone called out. Someone was there, behind me.

'Alex, where are you? Alex?'

I heard Jamilla coming up the tunnel and I let out a breath.

'Don't move,' I whispered. 'Don't do anything. The tiger's in here.'

I didn't dare move. I wasn't even sure if I could. It was a standoff. I couldn't imagine the tiger being as frightened as I was. Was the Sire there too? The two brothers? Anybody else?

'Alex?'

It was Kyle. He was whispering. But if *I* heard him—

'Stay right there, Kyle. I mean it. Listen to me. Stay where you are unless you want me dead.'

Everything happened in a terrifying instant.

Suddenly, the cat rushed at me. Full speed? Half speed? Very goddamn fast. Shadows, a blur of fur.

It seemed to leap straight up into the cone of light shining from my flashlight. The cat was tensed muscle, raw speed, gleaming teeth, and the widest, brightest eyes – tremendous focus. It was aimed at me as surely as a deadly bullet.

Its upper body twisted athletically, showing off incredible strength. It seemed to be three to four feet off the ground, coming straight at me, unstoppable.

I had no options, and no room for error. I didn't even have to think about my next move. It just happened. I squeezed the trigger of my Glock. I fired off three quick shots. All head and upper body shots, I hoped, but I was just guessing.

The cat kept coming at me. It didn't even slow down. The gunshots couldn't stop it. I had no defense and no place to run, no place to hide.

The big cat hit me hard, brought me down like a weak prey. I waited for the powerful jaws to clamp down on me, to crush my bones. I might have screamed. I don't know what the hell I did. I'd never been more afraid. Not even close.

The cat kept going past me! It made no sense. I didn't understand. A few feet up the tunnel, I heard a loud thud. It was down. I had shot and killed a tiger.

Chapter Ninety

'**H**oly shit! Holy shit!' Jamilla said. The words exploded out of her mouth. Then she smiled. 'Jesus. I don't believe it.' She stared down at the huge, fierce animal that had tried to kill me, and was now laying at her feet.

I pushed myself up, forced my legs to move. I took tenuous steps back to where she and Kyle were standing. The cat lay twisted across the width of the tunnel. It didn't move, and it wasn't going to.

'Are they down here in the tunnel? The Lost Boys?' Kyle asked in a whisper. 'The Sire?'

'I haven't seen anybody. Just footprints, and the cat. Let's go,' I finally said.

The tunnel was much longer than I would have thought. I wasn't even sure which direction we were headed. Toward the road? The foothills? The Pacific Ocean?

'I sent men toward the perimeters of the property, about five or six hundred yards out. It spreads us thin,' Kyle said. 'I don't like it.'

I didn't answer him. I was still shaky, not quite over my moment of truth with the tiger. My heart was pumping like an engine pushed to its limit. I wondered if I might be going into shock.

'Alex?' Jamilla spoke. 'You with us? You okay?'

'Just give me a minute. I'll be fine. Let's keep going.'

Soon we could see the faintest glimmer of light up ahead. That was hopeful. But where were we coming out of the tunnel?

'Can't tell how far it is,' I said. 'Or what's between us and the light.'

My hip brushed against something. Then my shoulder. I jumped back and my whole body shuddered. But it was only a valve sticking out from the tunnel wall. Nothing. Scared the hell out of me, though.

Then I could see part of the landscape outside – a couple of cypress pines leaning away from the wind, a streak of early morning sky.

It wasn't far, maybe thirty or forty yards. Usually, the most dangerous part of a raid was breaking in; now it was getting out of this dark tunnel.

I shined the flashlight to my face, put a finger to my lips. I pointed to my chest with the same finger. *I would go first.*

I knew I was better with a gun than Kyle, and I was physically stronger than Jamilla – at least I thought so. Besides, this was the way it had been the past few years: Gary Soneji, Casanova, Geoffrey Shafer, now the Alexander brothers and their Sire. *I keep going in first. How long am I going to keep it up? Why am I doing this?*

'Don't forget, they're human,' Jamilla said. 'They bleed too.'

I wanted to believe she was right. I moved forward quietly, quickly. I hesitated at the mouth of the tunnel. Took a breath. *One, Mississippi, two . . . then out into the big, bad world.*

I don't know why, but I yelled at the top of my voice as I burst out into the pale light. No words, just a loud scream! Actually, maybe I did know why – I was afraid of these two killers, of their merciless cult, of the Sire. Maybe they bled, but they weren't human. Not like the rest of us.

I was in a pocket chasm surrounded by low-lying hills. I saw no one out there. No sign that anyone had been here recently. They had to have come this way, though. The tiger must have been in the tunnel with somebody.

Jamilla and Kyle came out of the tunnel behind me. The looks on their faces showed their disappointment, their fatigue and confusion.

I heard it before I saw anything.

A black pickup truck came roaring around the side of

one of the hills. It was headed straight for me and I had a choice: dive back into the tunnel, or hold my ground in the face of the blond killers. They were inside the truck. I could see both of them.

I held my ground.

Chapter Ninety-One

The twisted faces of the killers glared through the curved windshield of the truck. I raised my gun, held it steady as I could. Jamilla and Kyle did the same. The black Ford truck kept coming fast, almost as if they were daring us to shoot.

So we fired. The windshield splintered. Bullets pinged off the roof and hood. The roar of the guns was deafening in my ears. The acrid smell of cordite filled my nostrils.

Suddenly, the truck stopped, then shot into reverse. I kept shooting, trying to hit the driver as the target distanced itself, the vehicle backing away, veering left then right then left. I took off, running up the hill, my legs leery, as if my shoes held lead weights.

I couldn't let them get away. We'd come too far, gotten too close. These two would kill again, and again. They were madmen, monsters, and so was whoever had sent them on their mission.

Jamilla and Kyle were climbing up the steep, grassy terrain a few steps behind me. The three of us seemed to be moving in slow motion. The pickup truck was weaving wildly, its rear end fishtailing. I was hoping, praying that it would flip as it climbed in reverse up the steep side of the hill. I heard the grinding of gears and suddenly the truck flew *forward*. It was coming at us again, picking up speed.

I went down on one knee, aimed carefully, and put three shots into the windshield. The glass was blown away.

'Alex, get out of the way!' Jamilla shouted. 'Alex, move it! Now! *Alex!*'

The pickup kept coming. I didn't move away. I put a shot right where I figured the driver had to be. Then another. Then the final shot in my clip.

The big black truck was almost on top of me. I thought that I could feel heat from the engine. My face and neck were in a sweat. I had the irrational thought that a vampire can only be killed by a stake, fire, or by destroying its domain.

I didn't believe in vampires.

I believed in evil, though. I had seen it enough times to believe. The two brothers were twisted murderers. That's all they were.

I jumped sideways just before the pickup would have

run me down. I rushed down the hillside behind the truck. I was hoping it would flip – and then it did! I felt like shouting.

The truck bounced heavily on its side, then on its roof – then continued to roll over several times. Finally it stopped, resting on its passenger side, teetering slightly. Black smoke coiled up from the engine. No one got out at first.

Then the younger brother climbed out of one door. His face was streaked with blood and soot. He didn't speak, just glared at us, and then he roared like an animal. It seemed as if he had gone insane.

'Don't make us shoot you!' I shouted at him as I quickly reloaded.

He didn't seem to hear. He was in a blind rage. Michael Alexander wore long, sharp canine fangs, and they were bloody. His own blood? His eyes were red. 'You shot William! You killed my brother!' he shrieked at us. 'You murdered him. He was better than all of you!'

Then he charged – and I couldn't bring myself to shoot. Michael Alexander was insane; he wasn't responsible anymore. He kept growling, frothing at the mouth. His eyes were wild, rolling in their sockets. Every muscle on his body was tightly flexed. I couldn't kill this tortured man-child. I braced myself to tackle him. I hoped I could bring him down.

Then Kyle fired – once.

The shot struck him where his nose had been just an instant before. A dark, bloody hole appeared at the center of his face. There was no surprise or shock, just sudden obliteration. Then he crumpled to the ground. There was no doubt he was dead.

I had been wrong about Kyle – he could shoot. He was an expert, full of surprises. I needed to think about that, but not right now.

Suddenly, I heard another voice. It was coming from inside the pickup. Someone was trapped. William? Was the brother alive?

I approached the overturned vehicle slowly, gun in hand. The engine was still smoking. I was afraid the truck might blow.

I climbed onto the teetering wreck and managed to pull open a bent, badly damaged door. I saw William – shot to death, his face a sorry, bloody mask.

Then I found myself staring into the angriest, most arrogant eyes. I recognized them immediately. It was almost impossible to shock me anymore, but this was another jolt. 'So you're the one,' I said.

'You killed them, and you will be killed,' a voice threatened. 'You'll die. You *will* die, Cross!'

I was looking at Peter Westin, the vampire expert I'd met weeks before in Santa Barbara. He was cut-up, injured and bleeding. But he was in total control, even with my gun aimed at his face. He was cool and superior, so confident. I remembered sitting across from him at the Davidson Library up in Santa Barbara. He had told me he was a *real* vampire. I guess I believed him now.

I finally found the right words. 'You're the Sire.'

Chapter Ninety-Two

I tried a couple of sessions with the creepy and surreal Peter Westin that night in the jail at Santa Cruz. Kyle was attempting to get him transferred to the East Coast but I doubted he would be successful. California wanted him. Westin wore a long-sleeved black velvet shirt and black leather pants. He was as pale as paper. Thin blue veins were visible under the translucent skin of his temples. His lips were full and the pigment appeared redder than most people's. The Sire almost didn't seem human, and I was pretty sure that was the effect he wanted to convey.

It was emotionally disturbing and draining to be in the same room with him. Jamilla and I had talked about it briefly, and we both felt the same thing. Westin had none of the usual qualities that we associated with humans: conscience, sociability, deep emotion, sympathy and empathy. His entire persona was that of the Sire. He was a killer, a ghoul, a real life bloodsucker.

'I'm not going to try and scare you with interrogation room threats,' I said, low-key.

Westin appeared not to be listening. Bored? Indifferent? Smart as hell? Actually, as the Sire, he was an extraordinary person to encounter: haughty, superior, intense, physically striking. He had the most piercing eyes. He'd put on an act for me in Santa Barbara – the harmless scholar recommending books about vampires.

He cocked his head and stared intently into my eyes. He was looking for something; I couldn't tell what. I held his gaze and that seemed to irritate him. 'Fuck off,' he hissed.

'What is it?' I finally asked. 'What's on your mind, Peter? Is it that I'm not worthy to question you now?'

He smiled – and there was even a hint of warmth in it. He could be charming, I knew. I'd found that out in the library in Santa Barbara.

'*If* I talked to you, *if* I told you everything that I feel and believe, you wouldn't understand,' he said. 'You would be even more lost and confused than you are now.'

'Try me,' I said.

He smiled again, but said nothing.

'I know that you miss William and Michael. You don't show it, but you loved them,' I said. 'I know that much about you. I know you feel things deeply.'

Peter Westin nodded, almost imperceptibly. The gesture was regal. He did miss William and Michael. I was right about that. He was sad that they were dead.

Finally, he spoke again. 'Yes, Detective Cross, I *feel* more deeply than you can begin to imagine. You have no idea. You have no clue how someone like me thinks.'

Then he was quiet again. The Sire had nothing more to say. We mere mortals just wouldn't understand. I left him like that.

It was over.

Part Five

Violets Are Blue

Chapter Ninety-Three

I was feeling partially relieved, better anyway. The murder case seemed to be solved at least. Peter Westin was in jail. We'd done everything we could about his cult. The pressure had been eliminated. We'd stopped the bleeding.

Jamilla had left the previous night; we promised to keep in touch and I knew we would. I was headed out to the airport that morning to catch a flight to San Francisco, and then another to DC. I was going home and that felt good.

The details were still coming in, but I feared we would never know everything about the strange, murderous cult that had sprung up in California. It was usually that way in Homicide. You never knew as much as you wanted to. That's the basic truth about being a detective, and you never see it on TV or in the movies. I guess the endings wouldn't be as satisfying if they were closer to reality.

Peter Westin had met Daniel and Charles when they had

played in Los Angeles. Westin already had his own follow-ers in Santa Cruz and Santa Barbara, but he feigned allegiance until he felt he was strong enough to be the Sire. Then he dispatched William and Michael Alexander to do his dirty work. Supposedly there were followers in nearly a hundred cities, especially now that the Internet had brought us all so close together.

Something was still bothering me. I couldn't figure out exactly what it was, but it troubled me all the way to San Francisco. It was eating me from the inside out. Fear and dread. But about what?

There was a forty-five-minute layover, and I got off the plane. A jumble of bad thoughts played through my brain. I felt wired, itchy.

The original San Francisco vampire murders were still on my mind.

And the fucking Mastermind.

Jamilla was here in San Francisco. But that was a whole other subject.

What was bothering me?

Then I thought I knew what it was. Maybe I'd known all along. I called Jam at her office in the Hall of Justice. I was informed that she had the day off.

I called her apartment, but there was no answer. Maybe she was out on one of the five-mile runs she bragged about. Or maybe she had a date with Tim Bradley from *The*

Examiner, as if that was any of my business.

But maybe not.

Where was she?

Had something happened to her, or was I just being paranoid beyond belief? I was definitely working too hard. I didn't need this. I really didn't need this.

I couldn't take the chance. I hurried to the American Airlines counter and canceled my flight out of San Francisco. I called Nana and told her I had to stay in California for a few hours. I would be in later tonight.

'Someone out here might be in trouble,' I said.

'Yes, and that someone is you,' Nana said. 'Goodbye, Alex.' She hung up on me again. She was right to want me home; but I was right in not wanting anybody else to be hurt.

I rented a car from Budget, and I was beginning to feel that I was completely losing it. Charles Manson's words came to mind: *Total paranoia is just total awareness*. I had always thought that Manson was wrong about everything, but maybe he wasn't; maybe he was dead-on right about paranoia.

I had a powerful gut feeling that Jamilla Hughes was in danger right now. I couldn't shake it off. Couldn't ignore it, even if I wanted to. The vibrations in my head were too strong, overwhelming. It was one of my famous feelings, and I had to go with it.

I thought about my former partner, Patsy Hampton – *and her murder.*

I remembered Betsey Cavalierre – *and her murder.*

And Detective Maureen Cooke in New Orleans.

A long time ago as a homicide detective, I had just about stopped believing in coincidences. Still, I had no logical reason to believe that a psychopathic killer could be out here in California, possibly stalking Inspector Jamilla Hughes.

I just felt it.

Total awareness.

The Mastermind was out here. It was the sense I had. I waited for his call. I was ready to nail him once and for all. I was so ready.

Chapter Ninety-Four

I drove from the airport to Jamilla's apartment at several miles above the posted speed limit. On the way, I used my cell phone. There was still no answer at her place. I was already in a cold sweat. I had never followed a hunch quite like this one.

I thought about what I could do right now. One possibility was to call in help from the SFPD, but I didn't like it. Police officers are logical creatures, and coldly suspicious of gut feelings. My track record with psychopaths might buy me some credibility in Washington, but not out here in California.

I could call the FBI – but I chose not to. There were a couple of reasons why. More gut feelings that I wanted to keep to myself for a while longer.

I decided to park a block over from Texas Street, where Jamilla lived. But I took a ride up the steep Potrero Hill first. I turned onto the street about half a dozen blocks south of her place, then I toured the connecting streets. There was a mixed style of row houses: the more charming wooden ones from the early 1900s, and the boxier three- and four-story ones with lots of aluminum detail. I could see the bay, the loading docks of Pier 84, and Oakland in the distance. I passed the New Potrero Market, J.J. Mac's, the North Star restaurant – Jamilla's home turf. But where was Jamilla?

The traffic was fairly heavy. I hoped my rented sedan wouldn't be spotted easily. And that I'd see Jamilla lugging groceries, or jogging home from a nearby park where she'd worked out.

But I didn't see her. Damn it, where was she? Not that she didn't have a right to a day off.

I couldn't imagine anything happening to her, but that was the way I had felt about Patsy Hampton, and then about Betsey Cavalierre.

Two dead partners in two years.

I didn't believe in coincidences.

Patsy Hampton had been murdered by a British diplo- mat named Shafer. I was almost certain of that. Betsey's murder remained unsolved, and that was the one that worried me. I kept thinking about the Mastermind. Some- how I had become a part of his story, his fantasy world. How? Why? I had received a late phone call from him one night that summer, just after I'd learned of Betsey's murder: *'I'm the one you call Mastermind. That's a name I can live with. I am that good.'*

The killer had used a knife on her, everywhere, even between Betsey's legs. He hated women. That was clear. I had encountered only one other killer who hated women so much: Casanova in North Carolina. But I was sure Casanova was dead and couldn't have killed Betsey Cavalierre. Still . . . I felt some kind of strange link to what had happened in North Carolina. What was the connection?

I found a spot and parked about two blocks from Jamilla Hughes's apartment on the hill near 18th. Her building was older, a remodeled yellow Victorian, with the familiar three-sided bay windows you often see in San Francisco. Very nice, very homey. There were neat little signs on the trees: *'Friends of the Urban Forest.'*

I called her again on the cell. Still no answer.

My heart was pumping fast. The cold sweat continued. I had to do something. I went to the front door of the house, rang the bell, but no one answered. *Damn it. Where was she?*

Safe Neighborhood signs were stuck in bright green patches of grass up and down the street. I hoped the street was very safe. I prayed to God that it was as safe as it looked.

I went back and waited in the car. Fidgeted. Grew even more nervous and impatient. I thought about who the Mastermind might be, then about Betsey's murder. I thought about Casanova, the Gentleman Caller, about Kate McTiernan, who'd been abducted in North Carolina. Why was *that* on my mind now? What was the connection? I couldn't get the lurid and devastating murder scenes out of my head.

Not Jamilla. Don't let this happen again. Don't let her get hurt.

While I sat there worrying, my phone rang. I answered immediately.

It was him. He was playing his cruel games. He seemed so close.

'Where are you, Doctor Cross? I thought you were heading home to kith and kin. Maybe it's time that you did. Your work is done out here. There's nothing more you can do. Nothing at all. We wouldn't want anything to happen to Nana Mama and the kids, would we? That would be the worst thing, wouldn't it? *The absolute worst.*'

Chapter Ninety-Five

I immediately called Nana in Washington. Either she wasn't there, or she was still mad at me and wasn't picking up the phone. *Damn it. Answer the phone, Nana.*

I frantically called again, but there was still no answer. *Pick up, pick up! Damn it – pick up the phone!*

Sweat had begun to coat my neck and forehead. This was my darkest nightmare, my worst fear come true. What could I do from out here?

I called Sampson and told him to rush over to my house, then get back to me immediately. He didn't question me for a second.

'I'm sending a squad car now. It will be there in minutes. I'll be right behind it. I'll get back to you, Alex,' he said.

I sat in the car and anxiously waited for Sampson's call. My head was spinning with all kinds of terrible thoughts and images. There was nothing I could do – not for Jamilla, if she was in trouble; not for my own family back in Washington.

I thought about the Mastermind and the way he'd operated in the past. There were always dramatic taunts and barbs – and then, when I least expected it, he would act; he would make a strike to the heart.

When I least expected it.

Action, not words.

Horrible murders.

He knew I hadn't returned to Washington; did he know for sure that I was in San Francisco?

I couldn't focus as much as I needed to. Was it possible that he was right here on Jamilla's street? Was the killer watching me now? He had shown that he was smart enough to follow me and not be seen. Did he want a showdown?

The cell phone rang again. My heart jumped in my chest. I fumbled with the buttons.

'Cross,' I said.

'Everybody's okay, Alex. I'm at the house with Nana and the kids. They're safe and sound. They're with me now.'

I shut my eyes and sighed with relief. 'Put her on,' I told Sampson. 'Don't take no for an answer from her. I need to talk to Nana about what we're going to do next.'

Chapter Ninety-Six

S ampson promised to stay with Nana and the kids until I could get home. There was no one that I trusted more, no one in the world they would be safer with. Still, I couldn't be sure, and that was a terrible weight to carry. I didn't feel I could leave California until I had at least located Jamilla, and knew she was safe.

Finally I called Tim Bradley at *The Examiner*. He didn't know where she was, or even that she'd taken a day off work. Maybe she had needed to get away from town – to get away from being a homicide detective.

I was beginning to feel that maybe I had made a mistake by stopping in San Francisco. The longer I sat on the street, outside her house, the more convinced I was of it. Maybe the job was finally getting to me. The instincts go first.

But every time I considered leaving, I remembered the

night I arrived at Betsey Cavalierre's house, seeing her dead body.

And instincts had gotten me here in my career.

Feelings, gut reactions, experiences from the past.

Maybe just plain stubbornness.

I stayed on surveillance, stayed at my post. I got out of the car a couple of times, walked up and down the block a little. Climbed back in the car. Waited some more. I felt more than a little ridiculous, but I wouldn't give in to it. I checked in with Sampson again. Everything was okay at home. Another homicide detective I knew, Jerome Thurman, had arrived at the house, too. Double duty against the Mastermind. Was that enough protection?

Then I saw Jamilla coming up the street in her Saab. I actually clapped my hands together. I smacked the dashboard with my palm. *Yes. Thank God she was safe. There she was!*

She parked about half a block from her house on Texas Street, got out, pulling a University of San Francisco gym bag behind her. I wanted to run up and hug her, but I stayed in my car. Her hair was up in a ponytail. She was wearing a dark blue tee and loose gray workout pants. She was all right; she hadn't been hurt. *Jamilla hadn't been murdered by the Mastermind.*

I stared through the car windshield, waiting to see if anyone was watching her, stalking her. Part of me wanted to leave well enough alone now, to go home to Washington. But I kept remembering what had happened to Betsey Cavalierre after we finished our case together.

Why then? Why my partner? I almost didn't want to go there.

I gave Jamilla time to get inside – then I called her on my cell.

'This is Jamilla Hughes. Your message is important to me. Please leave it at the beep.'

Damn it! I hated those machines.

'Jamilla, this is Alex Cross. Call me. It's important. Please—'

'Hi, Alex. Where are you? *How* are you?' I could hear the smile in her voice, and it sounded inappropriate because of the emotional state I was in.

'Please be careful.' I continued with what I was going to leave her as a message. I told her why I was concerned. Finally, I had to admit the worst: that I was on the street outside her apartment.

'Well, come inside for God's sake,' she said. There were no recriminations, not even any surprise in her voice. 'I think you're over-reacting. Maybe. Let's talk about it, though. Let's talk this thing through.'

'No, let me stay out here for a while. I hope you don't think I'm being too crazy. Whoever killed Betsey has been contacting me ever since her death. The Mastermind could be here in San Francisco. He killed her right after we finished our case. Detective Cooke was murdered after the magicians were killed in New Orleans.'

That gave her pause. 'Maybe I think you're a little crazy, Alex. But I understand why you would be. I see where you're going with this. I'm also touched that you came here to watch over me. And what happened to your last partner *does* scare me.'

It helped that I knew where Jam was, and that I had actually talked to her. After we spoke, I continued watching her street. I don't know how many times I had thought about Betsey Cavalierre's murder and wondered who the killer was, but I did it again as I sat in the car.

I stayed there for several hours. Jamilla and I talked a couple of times. She urged me to come up to her apartment. I said no. 'Let me do it my way, Jam.'

It was getting late, though, and I was beginning to fade. I saw the lights in her apartment go off. Good for her. At least one of us was acting sane.

I continued to wait. Something powerful, dramatic, haunting was nagging at me. Something I almost didn't want to face. The clues had been there, but I hadn't wanted to see them for what they were. I'd wanted to follow my 'famous instincts'. Look where it had gotten me. I had blown it for so long.

Then I saw him, and everything made sense. Suddenly the puzzle was clear; all the pieces fit. Not just Betsey's murder – the Casanova murder, the stalking of Kate McTiernan, the fact that he'd been able to keep a step ahead of me.

The killer was here on Jamilla's street.

The Mastermind was here in San Francisco.

I was sure, and it made me dizzy with fear. But also with incredible disappointment, sadness, confusion. I felt like I might throw up.

It was Kyle Craig. He was watching Jamilla's place, stalking her like the madman that he was. The goddamn *Mastermind* had come here to kill her.

How could I stop him?

Chapter Ninety-Seven

'Jamilla, are you awake?' I said in a low, tense voice. I felt a shudder run through me. It couldn't get any worse than this. I still had my eye on Kyle. He was definitely watching Jamilla's building. *Goddamn him to hell.*

'I am now. No, I was awake. Where are you, Alex? Don't tell me you're still outside? Please don't tell me that. Alex, what the hell is going on?'

'Listen to me. The Mastermind is outside your place. I can see him. I think he'll try to get inside soon. I want to come up there and I don't want him to see me. Is there a back way?'

Then I told her who the killer was.

She exploded with anger, most of it directed at Kyle. 'I knew there was something seriously wrong with him – but not this wrong. We have to stop that sonofabitch. I don't care how smart he's supposed to be.'

She told me where to look for a service entrance and then a fire escape that would take me to her floor. I hurried around in the shadows. I didn't think that Kyle had seen me. I hoped not. But then – he was the Mastermind.

He was smart, as clever as anyone I'd ever worked against.

He knew about surveillance, probably a lot more than I did.

He didn't make mistakes, at least not until now.

I found the back entrance of her building easily, and I hurried up the stairs. I tried not to make a sound. I had no way of knowing where Kyle was right now.

When I got to her apartment the door was open. My stomach dropped, and I felt sick. 'Jamilla?'

She immediately peeked out through the doorway. 'Come inside. I'm fine, Alex. We've got him now, not the other way around.'

I hurried inside the apartment, and we kept all the lights off. I could still see most of the living room and kitchen, the doorway to a small terrace. A bay window with bench seating. Her home. The place where he wanted to violate her. I snuck a look outside – I didn't see Kyle on the street. He was on the move.

Jamilla didn't look frightened, just perplexed, and angry. She had her service revolver out. She was ready for whatever might happen.

I don't think that I had fully taken in what had just happened. Everything felt unreal; my vision was tunneled. My nerves were shredded and raw. Kyle Craig had been my friend. We had worked a half-dozen cases together.

'*Why* is he outside, Alex?' Jamilla finally asked. 'Why is he coming after me? I don't understand that asshole. What did I do to him?'

I stared into her eyes, hesitated a second or two, then finally spoke. 'He's not really here to get you, at least I don't think so. It's about me – it's about Kyle and me. I've become part of his fantasy, the story he tells himself every day. He's proving how much better than me he is. He has to prove that he really is the Mastermind.'

Chapter Ninety-Eight

The Mastermind had already made his next move, though he knew it was only a half-step in the greater scheme of things. He had pulled back. He was six blocks away from Jamilla Hughes's apartment, standing on a San Francisco hill past the Jackson Playground. It allowed him to watch her building, the bay windows, the small terrace on one side.

He enjoyed this – the intractable imposition of his will, his ego on the world. It had been this way for more than a dozen years. No one had come close to capturing him, or even suspecting who he really was.

Cross was inside now, and that made everything either very hard or, perhaps, easier. There was another decision to be made soon. Should he risk everything at this point? Change everything? For years, he had been living a complicated double life. He'd done whatever he wanted, wherever, whenever. He had enjoyed his freedom, and how many others had even tasted that forbidden fruit? He had been the cop and the criminal. But maybe it was time for a change? Maybe his life had become too safe, too predictable. Kyle loved the hunt – and in that way he was like Casanova and the Gentleman Caller, two very talented killers he had known well, one working in North Carolina, the other in southern California. He found that he agreed with Casanova that men needed to be hunters by nature. And so he hunted – men and women – and found he enjoyed killing both sexes; but he went an important step farther.

He hunted their killers as well. He eliminated his competition. He beat them at their own game.

He had known Casanova years before the meticulous and very nasty killer was caught by himself and Dr Cross. He had played murder games with Casanova and with the Gentleman Caller. *Kiss the girls and make them cry.* Kyle had even fallen in love with one of the victims – young Kate McTiernan. He still had a soft spot for dear, sweet Kate. He had been so many things to so many people, played so many roles, and he had only just begun.

He had been the Mastermind – but he'd also helped capture the man believed to be the Mastermind. How could you beat that for puzzle-making and puzzle-solving.

He'd been an elusive killer in Baltimore; in Cincinnati; in

Roanoke, Virginia; in Philadelphia, until he tired of those cities and the minor roles he played in them. He was husband to Louise, father to Bradley and Virginia. He was on the fast track inside the FBI, with one significant problem: he believed they were finally on to him. He was sure of it – though God, they were such obvious, plodding fools.

So many exciting roles, so many poses that sometimes Kyle Craig wondered who he actually was.

Now the game with Alex Cross had to end. He'd felt the need to taunt and torture Cross, to prove he was the homicide detective's master. And then he had gone over the edge a little himself.

It happened when he killed Betsey Cavalierre, one of his own agents. Actually, the killing couldn't be helped. Cavalierre had become suspicious of him while she was chasing the Mastermind with Cross. She had to go, had to die.

And so did Cross. Cross was loyal to his friends, trusting, and it had become his greatest flaw, his singular weakness. But Cross would have caught on to him, even if he hadn't yet. And, of course, Cross's instincts had brought him here to watch over Inspector Hughes. Cross *needed* to be a good man, an ethical cop, a protector. What a waste of intellect. What a pity that Cross couldn't have been an even better adversary.

Alex had seen him on the street – so what came next? Whatever it was, it certainly had his adrenaline flowing. This was so good. Kyle knew he had a little time to figure it out. What to do? They were inside Hughes's apartment. He had the edge on them.

He wouldn't lose his edge, his advantage.

He made his next move.

Chapter Ninety-Nine

'You know, I never liked him, Alex,' Jamilla said as we waited in the semidarkness of her apartment. 'He seemed so cold, almost mechanical to me. And I'm telling you, he doesn't like women. I felt it instantly.'

'Well, unfortunately, I did like Kyle. He's clever as hell. He even rigged calls from the Mastermind when he and I were together. Now I need to figure out who he really is. There's no psychosis involved, at least I don't think so. He's organized. He can obviously work out elaborate plans. For once, I wish he would call.'

'Be careful what you wish for,' Jamilla said.

She and I were sitting beside a shelving unit on the hardwood floor in her living room. There was also a workout bench; nothing too fancy, an older model. Five- and ten-pound free weights were scattered on the floor. So were magazines and sections of the *Chronicle*.

I hoped that Kyle couldn't see into the apartment, that he didn't have binoculars. Or possibly a nightscope attached to a rifle. I knew he could shoot from the way he'd taken down Michael Alexander. He was good at a lot of things.

Just in case, Jamilla and I tried to keep away from the windows.

'It makes me dizzy to think about what he's done so far. I wonder if we'll ever know the extent of it?' she asked.

'If we catch him, he'll want to talk. Kyle will want to show off what he's done. If he comes after us tonight, maybe we'll find everything out.'

'You think he knows you're here?'

I sighed, shrugged. 'Probably. Maybe tonight is his coming out party. I know one thing, he won't do what we expect. The Mastermind never does. That's the only real pattern he has.'

We talked about calling in reinforcements, but Jamilla thought it would probably scare Kyle off. He wanted the two of us, right? That's what he would get. *Do you want to taunt me any more, you bastard? Go for it. Bring it on, Kyle.*

So the two of us sat there in the dark, and it was almost cozy. Jamilla finally reached out and touched my hand. Then we moved together, leaned against one another. We waited.

'At least it's comfortable,' Jamilla whispered. 'As stakeouts go.'

'No place like home, right?'

It was a little before four when we heard noises above us. Jamilla turned and looked at me. We raised our guns.

For the first time, I confronted the idea of shooting Kyle, a man I had thought was my friend. I didn't like the feeling. I wasn't sure how I would react, and that scared me too.

There were soft footsteps outside on the terrace. In a way, I was relieved. This was the showdown Kyle wanted. He was coming. I figured that the story he'd been telling for so long, his fantasy life, had finally taken over. Maybe he was psychotic now. That would give us an advantage.

'Real careful,' I whispered, and touched the back of Jamilla's hand. 'Try to look at it the way he does. Kyle thinks he has us where he wants us.'

He picked the lock quickly and expertly. A minimum of effort. I realized that he had been watching her place. He knew enough to come up the back stairs, and then he'd climbed a metal ladder onto the terrace.

The lock made a soft *click*. Then nothing happened.

'We're good, everything's cool,' Jamilla whispered. 'This time, we win.'

We waited in the dark near the door. It finally opened, oh-so-slowly. Kyle came inside. He moved toward us in a low crouch. Obviously, he couldn't see where we were, but we could see him.

I hit Kyle with all my weight, full force, every ounce of strength that I had. I slammed him hard against the living-room wall. The whole apartment shook. Books and glasses fell to the floor from open shelves. I was surprised we didn't go right through the wall.

I clipped his chin with an elbow as hard as I could. Felt good. Kyle was wiry and strong, but I was pumped to take him. I hit him with a hard, short right hand. It snapped into his jaw. I hit him in the solar plexus. A real gut-wrencher.

I was going to hit him again. But then Jamilla flicked on the room lights. My brain caught fire. My body shuddered.

It wasn't Kyle Craig.

Chapter One Hundred

'**G**et down, get down! Get below the windows!' I yelled at Jamilla.

I was afraid she might be hit by rifle fire. Kyle could be out there, and I knew that he could shoot. She went down and lay facing me, and also the man I had tackled coming in the door. He looked as confused as I felt. *Who the hell was he? What had just happened? And where was Kyle?*

Jamilla had her service revolver pointed at his chest. Her hand was amazingly steady. His nose was bleeding badly from where I'd hit him. He was well-built, probably early thirties, short-haired, a light-skinned black man.

Everything was complete chaos in my brain.

'Who the hell are you? *Who are you?*' I yelled at the dazed, bleeding man on the floor.

'FBI,' he panted. 'I'm a Federal agent. Put down the gun. Put it down now.'

Jamilla was yelling too. 'I'm San Francisco PD, and I'm definitely not putting down my gun, mister. What are you doing in my apartment?' she shouted. I could almost see her mind working and she wasn't thinking nice thoughts. 'Talk to us!'

He shook his head. 'I don't have to answer your questions. Wallet's in the rear left pocket. Badge and ID. I'm FBI, goddamnit!'

'Stay down,' I yelled. 'There could be someone outside with a gun. Did Kyle Craig send you here?' I asked.

The look on the agent's face answered the question for me, but he refused to confirm or deny. 'I told you, I don't have to answer questions.'

'You sure as hell do.' Jamilla got in the last word.

I did the only thing I could under the circumstances – *I called the FBI.*

Four agents from the San Francisco office got to the apartment at a little past five in the morning. We were wary of the windows, though I doubted that Kyle was still nearby. Or even in San Francisco. The Mastermind was a step ahead. I should have known, and in a way I *had* known that he wouldn't do the expected.

During the next couple of hours, exasperated agents from the Bureau tried to reach Kyle Craig. They couldn't and it shook them up. They began to give some credence to my story that Kyle might be the man behind murders going back several years. Kyle had sent the agent to Jamilla's apartment and ordered him to break in. He'd told the agent that someone had murdered an SFPD Inspector and Alex Cross inside.

Then things started to get really hot.

I was the one who heated them up.

Chapter One Hundred and One

At seven-thirty in the morning I was on the receiving end of a phone call from FBI director Ronald Burns in Washington. Burns was cautious and wary, but I knew he wouldn't call me himself unless he had evidence that there were serious problems with Kyle. I was still confused, and hurt, but I recognized the emotions as appropriate and sane. Kyle Craig was the madman, not me.

'Tell me whatever you know, Director,' I said. 'I know a lot about Kyle, but you know things that I don't. Tell me what they are. It's important that I know everything.'

Burns didn't answer right away. There was a long pause at his end of the line. I knew him well enough to know that he was a friend of Kyle's. At least he thought he had been. We'd all been wrong for so long. We'd been fooled, and betrayed by someone we had trusted.

Finally, Burns began to speak. 'We have been getting

worried about Kyle recently. This could go back to the days of the "Kiss the Girls" case. Maybe even before it. We know his files suggest he had a troubled adolescence, but when he joined the FBI, his psychological profile showed he had got through all that. You know that Kyle was an undergrad at Duke University. It's now become apparent that he knew Will Rudolph – the Gentleman Caller – from his student days at Duke. During the case, Kyle may have been responsible for the death of a reporter named Beth Lieberman with the *LA Times*. She was closing in on Will Rudolph.'

I shut my eyes and shook my head. I had helped solve the 'Kiss' case. I knew that Kyle had attended Duke, but not about his relationship with the Gentleman Caller, a killer who had terrorized LA.

'Why didn't you talk to me?' I asked Burns. I was trying to understand the FBI's position. So far, I couldn't.

'We didn't begin to really suspect Kyle until the murder of Betsey Cavalierre. We had no proof, even then. We weren't sure if he was a possible killer or the best agent in the Bureau.'

'Jesus, Ron, we could have talked. We should have talked. He's on the run now. You should have told me. I hope you're telling me everything now.'

'Alex, you know what we know. Maybe more. I hope you're telling *us* everything.'

After I finished with Burns, I called Sampson in Washington. I told him the latest and it blew John's mind. He had moved Nana and the kids out of our house on Fifth Street. Only he and I knew where they were now.

'Everything okay there?' I asked. 'Everybody settled in all right?'

'Are you fucking kidding, Alex? Nana is pissed off like I've never seen her before. If Kyle Craig came after her, I'd put my money on Nana. The kids are cool, though. They don't know what's happening, but they've guessed it isn't good.'

I cautioned him again. 'Don't leave them for a minute, not a second, John. I'm coming back to Washington on the next flight. I don't know how Kyle could trace you there, but don't under-estimate him. He's loose. He's very dangerous. For some reason, he wants to hurt me, and maybe my family. If I can figure out why that is, maybe I can stop him.'

'And if not?' Sampson asked.

I let the question hang.

Chapter One Hundred and Two

I had to say goodbye to Jamilla Hughes again, and each time it was a little harder. We'd been through so much together in such a short time. I made her promise to be extremely careful, even paranoid, for the next few days. She promised. Finally I got on another plane out of San Francisco International.

The mysterious phone calls had stopped, but that was scary and unsettling too. I didn't know where Kyle was, or what he was doing.

Was he still watching me? Had he somehow followed me back to Washington? I shouldn't be having thoughts like that, but I was, and I couldn't stop them from coming.

Did he have binoculars focused on me as I walked up the sidewalk to my Aunt Tia's house in Chapel Gate, Maryland, about fifteen miles from Baltimore? How could he know I was here? Why, because that's what he did for a living. Could he get past Sampson and me? I didn't think so. But how could I know with complete certainty?

The kids were enjoying their short vacation with Aunt Tia. She had always spoiled them, just as she had spoiled me as a kid. 'Same old, same old,' she liked to say when she served you a piece of hot pie in the middle of the afternoon, or gave you an unexpected present. Nana was more understanding than I thought she would be. I think she liked being with her 'little sister'. Tia was younger than Nana, 'only seventy-eight', but she was spry, very contemporary in her outlook, and she was a fabulous cook. That night, she and Nana made penne with gorgonzola cheese, broccoli rabe, and sock-it-to-me cake. I ate as if it were my last meal.

Then the kids and I played and talked until the outrageous hour of eleven o'clock, way past their usual bedtime. They are by no means perfect, but the good times with them certainly outweigh the bad. I tend to talk more about the good, and why not. I'm a father and I love Damon, Jannie and little Alex more than life itself. Maybe that says something, too.

I went back to Washington the following morning. A team of FBI agents had been assigned to my family. It was the kind of attention I'd hoped we would never need. Frankly, it scared the hell out of me.

That afternoon, I attended a meeting at the FBI building

and learned that more than four hundred agents were assigned to finding and capturing Kyle Craig. So far, nothing had gotten out to the press, and Director Burns wanted to keep it that way. So did I. More than that, I wanted to catch Kyle quickly, hopefully before he killed again.

But who would he kill? Who might Kyle go after next?

Chapter One Hundred and Three

'Christine, it's Alex,' I said. I had butterflies in my stomach. 'I hate to bother you like this. It's important or I wouldn't call.' That was sure the truth. God, I hadn't wanted to make this call.

'Is little Alex okay?' she asked. 'Is it Nana?'

'No, no. Everybody's fine.' I told a half-truth.

There was a brief, uncomfortable silence. Christine and I had been engaged to be married. She was the one who had broken it off, because she couldn't handle my life as a homicide detective. Too many bad scenes just like this one.

'Alex, this isn't good news, is it? Geoffrey Shafer? Is he back in the country?' she asked. She sounded afraid and I felt for her. Geoffrey Shafer had kidnapped her.

'No, this isn't about Shafer.'

I told her about Kyle Craig. She knew him, liked Kyle, and I could tell she felt violated. She had been hurt badly by the monsters I had met in my work. She couldn't completely forgive me for that, and I didn't blame her much. I couldn't forgive myself sometimes. Talking to Christine made me remember how much I'd loved her. Probably still did.

'Is there somewhere safe you can stay for a while? It's important that you go there,' I finally said. 'I hate to do this to you. Kyle is extremely dangerous, Christine.'

'Oh, Alex. I came out here to be safe. I felt I was safe, but now you're back in my life.'

She said she would stay with somebody she trusted, a friend. I asked Christine not to say who or where it was over the phone. When she hung up, she was crying. I felt so bad for her; so terrible about what had happened. The call brought back everything that was wrong between us.

I kept calling people I cared about. I talked to everyone I could think of who had had some contact with Kyle.

I called Jamilla next. My excuse was that I wanted to remind her to be careful – even now. But I think I just wanted to talk to her. She'd been in on so much of this. Unfortunately, she was out when I called. I left a message that I was worried about her, and to please be careful.

I warned a few detective friends – Rakeem Powell and Jerome Thurman – who were still on the DC force. I doubted Kyle would go after them, but I didn't know for sure.

I phoned my chief contact at the *Washington Post*, a writer named Zachary Scott Taylor. Zach was also one of my best friends in Washington. He wanted to interview me, but I told him not to come. Kyle was jealous of the stories Zach had written about me. He had told me as much. For whatever reason, he didn't like Zach.

'This is serious,' I told Zach. 'Don't under-estimate how crazy this man is. You're on his shit list, and that's a bad place to be.'

I spoke to FBI agents Scorse and Reilly who had worked with me on the kidnapping of Maggie Rose Dunne and Michael Goldberg. They knew about the manhunt for Kyle, but hadn't been concerned for their own safety. Now they were.

I called my niece, Naomi, who'd been kidnapped by Casanova. Naomi was practicing law in Jacksonville, Florida. She was living with a good guy named Seth Samuel Taylor. They were planning to marry later this year. 'He likes to ruin other people's happiness,' I told Naomi. 'Be careful. I know you will be.'

I called Kate McTiernan in North Carolina. I remembered the meal she'd had with Kyle and me. Did it mean anything more than what it seemed on the surface? Who knew with Kyle. Kate promised to be extra careful, and reminded me she was a third-degree black belt now. Kyle had always liked Kate, and *I* reminded her of that. Actually, the more I talked to Kate, the more worried I was about her. 'Don't take any chances, Kate. Kyle is the craziest person I've ever met.'

I contacted Sandy Greenberg, a good friend at Interpol who had worked with Kyle several times. She was shocked to learn that Kyle was a murderer. She promised to be extra careful until he was caught; she also offered to help in any way that she could.

Kyle Craig was a cold, heartless murderer.

My partner at times, my friend, or so I'd thought.

I still couldn't believe it. Not completely. I tried to make up a possible hit list for Kyle.

1. Myself
2. Nana and the kids
3. Sampson
4. Jamilla

I realized I was making the list from my point of view, and although Kyle seemed focused on me, his obsessions might extend even farther. I tried another list.

1. Kyle's family – every member
2. Myself – and my family
3. Director Burns of the FBI
4. Jamilla
5. Kate McTiernan

I sat in my empty house on Fifth Street and wondered what the hell he would do next. It was driving me crazy; I felt like I was running in circles.

Kyle was capable of anything.

Chapter One Hundred and Four

He finally called again.

'I killed them, and I don't feel a thing. Nothing at all. You will, though, Alex. In a way, you're to blame. Nobody but you. I didn't even want to kill them, but I had to do it. That's the way the horror story has to go. It's out of control now. I'll admit that.'

The horrifying confession came at quarter past five in the morning. I had been asleep about three hours when the phone rang. Panic raced through my body. My heart was pounding so hard I could hear it.

'Who did you kill?' I asked Kyle. 'Who? Tell me who it was. *Tell me.*'

'What difference does it make? They're dead, slaughtered. It's someone you care about. There's nothing you can do now – except catch me. I suppose I could help you. Isn't that what you want to hear? Would that make this more interesting for you? Would it make it *fair*?' He started to laugh uncontrollably. Christ, I had never seen him lose control.

I let him go on. Inflate his ego. That's what he wanted and needed, wasn't it?

Who had Kyle killed? Oh God, who was dead? It was more than one person – slaughtered.

'We always worked as a team. In a way, it would be my crowning moment, to catch myself. I've thought about it, actually. Fantasized. What better challenge could there be? I can't think of one. Me against myself.' He started to laugh again.

I had to force myself not to ask again who he had murdered. It would just make Kyle angry. He might hang up. Still, my mind was grinding. I was incredibly afraid. Christine? Kate? Jamilla?

Someone at the FBI? Who? Oh God, who was it? Jesus, have some mercy, have pity. Show me that you're human, you bastard.

'I'm not a highly trained psychologist like yourself, but here's one amateur's theory anyway,' Kyle said. 'I think this whole rage thing might be about sibling rivalry. Could it be? You know, Alex, I have a younger brother. He came along at the height of my Oedipus complex, when I was a mere lad of two. He displaced me with my mother and father. Check into it, Alex. Consult with Quantico. Could be important.'

He was so calm, and he was ridiculing me – as a detective and as a psychologist.

My hands were starting to shake. I'd had enough. 'Who did you kill this time?' I yelled into the phone. 'Who is it?'

Kyle broke my heart. He told me in great detail about the murders he'd just committed. I was certain that he was telling the truth.

Then he hung up, even as I cursed him to hell.

Minutes later I was in my car, bleary-eyed, numb, rushing across Washington to the terrible murder scene.

Chapter One Hundred and Five

N*o, no, no!*
It was like a knife thrust into my heart, then twisted until I screamed. Kyle had hurt me badly, and he wanted me to know something: *there was worse to come. This was just the beginning.*

I stood silent and transfixed in the bedroom of Zach and Liz Taylor. My eyes were blurred by tears. Two of my dearest friends were dead. I had been to their house dozens of times before – for parties, dinner, late-night talks. Zach and Liz had visited on Fifth Street many times. Zach was Godfather to little Alex.

My only consolation was that they had died quickly. Kyle was probably nervous about getting caught. He knew he had to get in and out of their apartment in the Adams-Morgan section of Washington quickly.

Whatever his reason, he had killed the Taylors with

single gunshots to the head. He hadn't bothered to mutilate the bodies. I thought the message was clear: *This wasn't about them.*

It was about the two of us.

Zach and Liz Taylor hadn't mattered one way or the other to him. Maybe that was the worst thing of all. How easily he could kill. How much he wanted to hurt me.

This was just the start of it.

It would get worse.

There was no evidence of rage, no passion at this crime scene. I almost got the sense that once he was inside their bedroom he'd had second thoughts. *Oh Kyle, Kyle. Have mercy on us.*

I made mental notes – no need to write any of this down. I knew every horrifying detail by heart. I would never forget any of it until the day I died.

The gunshots had blown away the sides of their faces. I had to force myself to look. I remembered how in love they had always seemed to me. Zach had once told me that 'Liz is the only person I know who I enjoy being with on a long car ride.' That was the test for him. They never ran out of things to say to one another. I felt incredibly hollowed out as I stared at them. They were gone now. What a terrible waste, what a horror show.

I walked past their bodies to a large casement window that looked out on the street. I was feeling so unreal. I saw

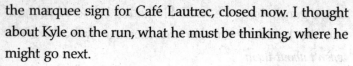

the marquee sign for Café Lautrec, closed now. I thought about Kyle on the run, what he must be thinking, where he might go next.

I wanted to catch him, to stop him. *No, I wanted to kill him. I wanted to hurt him in the worst way possible.*

Someone from the Crime Scene Unit edged up to me, a sergeant named Ed Lyle. 'Sorry about your loss. What do you want from us, Detective? We're ready to get to work here.'

'Sketch, video, photograph,' I told Lyle. But I really didn't need any of it. I didn't need any more graven images, or even any evidence.

I knew who the killer was.

Chapter One Hundred and Six

I got home around one that afternoon. I needed to sleep, but I couldn't stay down for more than a couple of hours. I got up and paced through the empty house on Fifth Street.

I kept walking from room to room. I felt the need to stop a terrible disaster from happening, but I didn't know where to start. The possible hit lists for Kyle were continually running through my head: my family, Sampson, Christine, Jamilla Hughes, Kate McTiernan, my niece Naomi, Kyle's own family.

I couldn't get the image of Zach and Liz out of my head. They had been executed in the prime of their lives – because of me. Finally, I was able to throw up, and it was the best thing that had happened to me that day. I pushed out my guts. Then I slammed the bathroom mirror with the heel of my hand and nearly broke it.

Kyle was always a fucking step ahead, right? It had been that way for so many years now. He was such an unbelievable bastard.

He had complete confidence in his abilities, including his power to elude us any time he wanted to. What would be next? Who would he kill? Who? *Who?*

How could he make himself disappear after the killings? How did he blend in and become invisible when so many people were looking for him?

He had money; he had taken care of that when he'd played the role of the Mastermind. So what was next for him?

I worked at my computer late into the night and early morning. The computer was beside my bedroom window. Was he outside watching? I didn't think even Kyle would take that kind of chance now. But hell, how could I rule anything out?

He was capable of large-scale mass murder. If that was his plan, where would he strike? *Washington? New York City? LA? Chicago? His old hometown of Charlotte, North Carolina? Maybe somewhere in Europe? London?*

Was his family safe – his wife and his two children? I had vacationed with them in Nags Head one summer. I'd stayed at their home in Virginia a few times over the years. His wife Louise was a dear friend. I had promised her I would try to bring Kyle in alive if I possibly could. But now

I wondered – did I want to keep that promise? What would I do if I ever caught up with him?

He might go after his own parents, especially since he put part of the heavy blame for his behavior on his father. William Hyland Craig had been a general in the army, then chairman of the board of two Fortune 500 companies in and around Charlotte. Nowadays, he gave lectures at ten to twenty thousand a pop; he was on half a dozen boards. He had beaten Kyle as a boy, disciplined him ruthlessly, taught him to hate.

Sibling rivalry? Kyle had brought it up himself. He had been highly competitive with his younger brother until Blake's death in a hunting accident in 1991. Had Kyle actually killed Blake? What about the older brother, who still lived in North Carolina?

Did he think of me as a younger brother? Did Kyle see Blake in me? He was competing with me, and he'd tried to control me from the start. The women in my life might have represented a threat to him, an extreme variant of sibling rivalry. Was that why he had killed Betsey Cavalierre? What about Maureen Cooke in New Orleans? And Jamilla?

I made a note to think carefully and plot out one particular angle, a dysfunctional family triangle, with both Kyle and me a part of it.

One step ahead.

So far anyway.

If he came after his family, or his parents, we would have him. They were being closely protected in Charlotte. The FBI was all over them.

Kyle knew that. He wouldn't do anything stupid – just cruel and nasty.

One step ahead.

That seemed to be the key to Kyle's fantasy life, at least as I understood it so far. He wouldn't make the obvious move. He would go at least one move, maybe two, beyond that. But how did he stay a step ahead, especially now? A very bad thought had been running through my head lately. Maybe there was someone in the FBI helping him – maybe Kyle had a partner.

I had finally drifted off to sleep when the phone in my bedroom woke me. It was three in the morning. *Goddamn him. Doesn't he ever sleep?*

I picked it up, clicked it off, then unplugged the phone from the wall.

No more phone tag, Kyle. Fuck you.

I was setting the rules now. This was my game, not his.

Chapter One Hundred and Seven

In the morning, I drank too much black coffee and thought about our last case together: the Tiger, Daniel and Charles, Peter Westin, the Alexander brothers. What did it mean in Kyle's fantasy? The macabre story he was plotting out involved both of us. He had asked me into the investigation, then used it to control me. Was that where it ended for him, and me?

I kept trying to piece together the puzzle from a psychologist's point of view. The rest might flow from that. *Might*. With Kyle, there was no knowing for sure. If he saw a clear pattern, he might reverse it; if he understood his own pathology, and maybe he did, he would use that in his favor too.

Around noon, I called Kyle's older brother, Martin, a radiologist living outside Charlotte – where we had once believed that Daniel and Charles had begun their murder spree. Did Kyle have a previous connection with them? Was that a possibility?

Martin Craig tried to help, but he finally admitted that he and his brother hadn't spoken during the past ten years. 'We saw one another at my brother Blake's funeral,' Martin said. 'That was the last time. I don't like my brother, Detective Cross. He doesn't like me. I don't know if he likes anybody.'

'Was your father especially rough on Kyle?' I asked Martin.

'Kyle always said so, but to tell the truth, I never saw much of it. Neither did my mother. Kyle liked to make up stories. He was always the big hero, or the pathetic victim. My mother used to say that Kyle had an ego second only to God's.'

'What did you think about that? Your mother's assessment of your brother?'

'Detective Cross, my brother didn't believe in God, and he wasn't second to anyone.'

The continuing theme throughout the three brothers' relationship had been competition, and Kyle had always believed that Martin and Blake won in the eyes of his parents. Kyle had been a starter on the high school basketball team, but Martin had been the clever all-county point guard, who also played bass guitar in a local band, and had an enviable social life. There had once been a feature story in the local paper about the basketball-playing brothers, but the article dealt mostly with Blake and Martin. They had all attended Duke Undergraduate, but Martin and Blake went on to medical school. Kyle became a lawyer, a career choice his father deplored. Kyle had talked to me about sibling rivalry, and maybe I was beginning to understand a little of the origins of his fantasy world.

'Martin,' I finally asked, 'is it possible that Kyle murdered your younger brother, Blake?'

'Blake died in a hunting accident – supposedly,' Martin Craig said. 'Detective Cross, my brother Blake was an incredibly responsible and careful man, *almost as careful as Kyle*. He didn't accidentally shoot himself. I've always believed with all my heart that Kyle had something to do with it. But who would believe me? That's why he and I haven't spoken in ten years. My brother is Cain. I believe he's a murderer, and I want to see him caught. I want to see my brother go to the electric chair. That's what Kyle deserves.'

Chapter One Hundred and Eight

Nothing ever starts where we think it does. I kept remembering that Kyle had done nearly all of the TV and print interviews after the capture of Peter Westin in the foothills outside Santa Cruz. He'd wanted the praise. He'd wanted to be the star, the only one. In a way, that's what he was now: the brightest star of all.

I had one decent idea about what to do next, something pro-active that might bother Kyle. I contacted the FBI and discussed it with Director Burns. He liked it too.

At four o'clock that afternoon, a press conference was called in the lobby of the FBI building. Director Burns was there to speak briefly and then to introduce me. Burns stated in no uncertain terms that I would be involved in the manhunt until Kyle Craig was brought to justice, and that Kyle would definitely be caught.

I was wearing a black leather car coat and I buttoned it

up as I stepped up to the mikes. I was playing this for all it was worth. I wanted to look self-important. I wanted to look like the star. Not Kyle. This was my manhunt. Not his. He was the prey.

There was the usual mechanical buzz and hum of cameras, the incessant flashes, and all those inquiring minds of the press, those cynical eyes staring up at me, waiting for answers that I couldn't give them. It set my nerves on edge.

My voice was as grave and important-sounding as I could make it. 'My name is Alex Cross. I'm a homicide detective in DC. I've worked closely with Special Agent In Charge Kyle Craig over the past five years. I know him extremely well.' I went into some detail on our past together. I tried to sound like a pompous know-it-all. The doctor detective.

'Kyle has been helpful in solving a few murders. He was a competent number two, excellent support for me. He was an over-achiever type, but a tireless worker.

'We will capture him soon, but Kyle, if you can hear me, wherever you are, I urge you to listen closely. Give yourself up. I can help you. I've always been able to help. Give yourself up to me. It's the only chance you have.'

I paused and stared into the TV cameras, then I stepped back slowly from the microphones. The camera flashes were everywhere. They were treating me like the star now.

Just as I had hoped they would.

Director Burns said a few more words about his concern for public safety and the extent of the FBI manhunt. He thanked me profusely for being there.

As I stood beside Director Burns, I continued to stare out into the TV cameras. I knew that Kyle would be looking right at me. I was sure that he'd see this segment, and that it would infuriate him.

I was sending Kyle a clear message, a challenge.

Come and get me, if you can. You're not the Mastermind anymore – I am.

Chapter One Hundred and Nine

N ow, I waited.

I went to visit Nana and the kids early the next morning. A team of three FBI vehicles traveled with me. We were hoping that Kyle might take the bait and follow. Not surprisingly, he didn't show. No one really expected that he would, but we were willing to try anything at this point.

Aunt Tia had a small clapboard house that was painted yellow with white aluminum shutters. It was located on a quiet street in Chapell Gate, which she called 'the country'. As I drove up to the small house, I saw no evidence of the FBI, which was a good sign, I thought. They were doing their job well.

The special agent in charge was a man named Peter Schweitzer. He had an excellent reputation. Schweitzer met me at the front door and introduced me to the six other agents inside Tia's house.

When I was fully satisfied about security, I went to see Nana and the kids. 'Hello, Daddy.' 'Hello Dad.' 'Hello, Alex.' Everybody seemed especially glad to see me, even Nana. They were having a big breakfast in the kitchen and Tia was busy making pancakes and hot sausages. She put out her arms for a hug and then everybody grabbed hold of me and wouldn't let go. I must admit, I liked the attention; I needed the hugs.

'They can't get enough of you, Alex,' Tia laughed, and clapped both hands, just the way she'd been doing for years.

'That's 'cause we don't see enough of him,' Damon taunted.

'The job's almost done,' I said, hoping that was true, not completely believing it. 'At least you're all getting three squares a day.' I laughed and gave Tia an extra hug.

I ate some breakfast and stayed at Tia's for more than an hour. We never stopped talking the whole time, but only once did anyone bring up the current difficult and scary situation. 'When can we go back home?' Damon asked.

They all stared at me, waiting for a good answer. Even little Alex held me in his gaze. 'I won't lie to you,' I said finally. 'We have to find Kyle Craig first. Then we can go home.'

'And it can be just like before?' Jannie asked.

I recognized a trick question. 'Even better than that,' I told her. 'I'm going to make some big changes soon. I promise you.'

Chapter One Hundred and Ten

I left for Charlotte, North Carolina, on a ten o'clock flight out of DC. I was heading south to visit Craig family members. Maybe Kyle was there as well. It wouldn't surprise me.

His father, William Craig, chose not to be home when I arrived at the estate where Kyle and his brothers had been raised. It was a gentleman's farm with a rambling stone and wood house set on over forty acres in horse country. Someone on the staff told me it cost over fifteen dollars a yard just to paint all the white fences running around the pastures.

I spoke with Miriam Craig on a rear porch, which overlooked wild-flower gardens and a rock-filled brook. She seemed very much in control of her emotions, which surprised me, but maybe shouldn't have. Mrs Craig told me a great deal about her family.

'Kyle's father and I had no idea, no clue about his darker side, if indeed the terrible allegations are true,' she said. 'Kyle was always distant, reserved, introspective I suppose you could say, but there was nothing to suggest that he might be this troubled. He did well in school, and in athletics. Kyle even plays the piano with a beautiful touch.'

'I never knew he played,' I said, and yet Kyle had often commented on my playing. 'Did you and his father tell him how well he was doing – in school, for example? In athletics? I suspect that boys need to hear that more than we know.'

Mrs Craig took offense. 'He didn't want to hear it. He'd say, "I know" and then walk away from us. Almost as if we had disappointed him by stating the obvious.'

'His brothers did better than Kyle in school?'

'In terms of grades, yes, but the boys were all high-honor students. Most teachers saw Kyle as being deeper. I believe that he had the highest IQ, one-forty-nine if I remember correctly. He chose not to apply himself to every subject. He had a strong will, even as a young boy.'

'But there were no obvious signs that he was severely troubled?'

'No, Detective Cross. Believe me, I've thought about it a lot.'

'Kyle's father would agree?'

'We talked about it just last night. He agrees. He's just too upset to be here. Kyle's father is a proud man, and a good one. William Craig is a very good man.'

Next, I went to see Kyle's brother in Charlotte. I talked to Dr Craig in a white-on-white conference room at the clinic where he was a partner.

'I found Kyle to be caustic and very cruel. I know that Blake did as well,' he confessed over tea.

'Cruel in what way?' I asked.

'Not to small animals or anything obvious like that – to other people. Actually, Kyle liked animals just fine. He was vicious at school, though. Both verbally and physically. A real prick. Nobody liked him much. He had no close friends that I remember. That's odd, isn't it? Kyle never had a single close friend. Let me tell you something, Detective, during Kyle's sophomore and most of his junior years, our father made him sleep in the garage because he was so unpleasant to have around.'

'That seems a little severe,' I commented. Nothing I'd heard so far was so revealing. Kyle had never mentioned the punishment, though. Neither had Mrs Craig. All she'd said was that Kyle's father was a good man, whatever that meant.

'I don't think it was severe, Detective. I think it was fair, and much less than he deserved. Kyle should have been thrown out of our house when he was around thirteen. My brother was a goddamn monster, and apparently, he still is.'

Chapter One Hundred and Eleven

Who would Kyle go after next? It was the question that obsessed me. I couldn't let it go. When I got home that night, I began to think about going out to Seattle. I had a bad feeling. Lots of them, actually. Would Kyle go after Christine Johnson next? He knew how to strike to cause the most hurt. Kyle knew me so well – but apparently, I didn't know Kyle at all.

Would he go after Christine? Or maybe Jamilla? Was I thinking the way Kyle would?

One step ahead.

God damn him to hell.

Maybe he would just come after me; maybe all I had to do was stay in the house on Fifth Street and wait for him to show up.

The question was burning inside my head. What was everybody missing? What did Kyle want – more than anything else? What motivated him? Who was on Kyle's vicious hit list – besides me?

Kyle wanted to exert his will, but he also craved the most exquisite and forbidden pleasures. What had moved him in the past was sex, rape, money – millions of dollars – revenge against those he hated.

I finally went to bed at one-thirty, but *surprise, surprise*, I couldn't sleep. I kept seeing Kyle's face every time I shut my eyes. His look was smug and confident. He was the most arrogant human being I had ever met. Possibly the most evil. I thought back about all our times together, all our long, philosophical talks, anything I could remember. I turned on the bed table light and scribbled more notes. Kyle was methodical and logical, but then he could surprise me with a tactic or strategy completely off the charts. I thought about the raid in Santa Cruz. The vampire murders seemed far away already. He had wanted me there so that I could see him be the hero. That was the whole point, wasn't it? He needed me to see how good he was. He wanted to take down Peter Westin by himself.

Suddenly, a question popped into my head. A really good one.

Where had he been unable to exert his will?

What were Kyle's darkest fantasies? What were his daydreams? His secret desires? Where had he been thwarted in the past?

The worst is yet to come. He was only starting with Zach and Liz Taylor. Was he about to go on a bloody rampage?

And then I recalled a particular fantasy that Kyle had shared with me one night after we had finished one of our worst cases. I remembered something he'd said, and couldn't get it out of my head.

I snatched up the phone and began to dial long distance. I hoped that I wasn't too late. I thought I knew who he was going to kill next.

Oh no, Kyle. Oh God, no!

Chapter One Hundred and Twelve

Maybe I was just going crazy. I drove for nearly six hours on I-95 headed to Nags Head, North Carolina. I kept changing radio stations to keep myself alert. I was thinking to myself that Kyle didn't want this to end – he was having too much fun; he was in his glory.

I had been in this part of North Carolina before, with Kate McTiernan. So had Kyle. We were trying to stop the sadistic killer named Casanova. He had kept as many as eight women captive in the woods near Chapel Hill, North Carolina. Kyle had been on our team, or so I had believed. But Kyle had also been Casanova's partner in murder.

I made it to Nags Head just before nightfall. As I drove toward the ocean, I remembered odd things: the sticky buns from the Nags Head Market; my long walks with

Kate McTiernan along Coquina Beach; the lovely, almost supernaturally picturesque beaches in Jockey's Ridge State Park. I remembered how much I admired Kate. We were still good friends, talked at least twice a month. She sent my kids imaginative presents on their birthdays and at Christmas. She was working at the Regional Medical Center in Kitty Hawk and living with a local bookseller whom she was going to marry. Their home was in Nags Head, only a couple of miles away.

Kyle had a deep, obvious crush on Kate McTiernan. He'd hinted at it: 'I could love that girl, if I didn't have Louise and the kids. Maybe I should dump them for Kate. She could make me a happy man. Kate could save me.'

He had come to visit Kate in Nags Head. I think he'd come to watch her. It bothered him that he couldn't have her, that he had been *denied* Kate McTiernan. He also knew how much Kate meant to me.

Kyle was here, wasn't he? Or he was coming.

I had warned Kate, but on the drive down I called again and explicitly told her to get the hell out of Nags Head. I didn't care how much karate she knew, or how many black belts she had accumulated. I was going to stay at her place. I thought that Kyle might be coming, too. I didn't think he wanted to *watch* anymore. If he was coming here, he wanted to kill Kate.

I took a deep breath as I finally drove into town. It all

looked so familiar, serene and beautiful, like nothing bad should ever happen here.

The worst is yet to come, I kept thinking. *That's why he killed Zach and Liz Taylor first. He set up his pattern with them. The Taylors were just the beginning. A warning of things to come.*

I drove down a narrow, paved road that weaved its way alongside wind-blown sand dunes. I was looking for any sign of Kyle. Number 1021 was a two-story clapboard beach house directly across from the ocean. Very quaint and stylish, very Kate McTiernan. If Kyle got to her, I would never forgive myself.

A Scottish flag was flying above the rooftop, and that was pure McTiernan, too. As I had asked, her six-year-old Volvo was still parked in the driveway; the houselights were on, shining like beacons to guide me – and maybe Kyle as well.

It made it look like somebody was home, and now somebody was.

Everything felt surreal to me. My nervous system was spiking. My hairs were standing on end. I had a sixth sense that Kyle was nearby. I just knew it, felt it in every inch of my body. Was he, though? Or was I just crazy? I wasn't sure which outcome would be worse.

I drove my car inside the garage and pulled down the heavy wooden door. There was a cold spot at the center of my chest. I was having difficulty catching a breath. Or thinking in a straight line.

Then I went inside Kate McTiernan's house. My sense of balance was off. I was listing to the right.

The telephone started to ring.

I pulled out my Glock and looked around the kitchen for Kyle. I didn't see anything. Not yet.

Where was he?

The worst is yet to come.

Was I ready for it this time?

Chapter One Hundred and Thirteen

I picked up the jangling phone, then hit my knee hard against the kitchen table.

'I've been looking all over for you, Alex.' Kyle was so very calm and cocksure. He had no conscience, no guilt whatsoever. His arrogance was stunning to me, even now. I wished he was here, so I could pound his face.

'Well, I guess you found me. Congratulations. I can't hide from you. You're so impressive. You *are* the Mastermind, Kyle.'

'You know, I am. You had me concerned, worried there, partner. I wanted to say goodbye in a proper and civil fashion. I'm leaving after this little adventure of ours is ended. It's almost over. *Whew.* Isn't that a relief?'

'Want to tell me where you are?' I asked him.

He paused for a half-second, and I could feel a fast river of adrenaline rushing through me. My legs were unsteady.

Suddenly I was afraid of what Kyle might have already done.

'I suppose it couldn't hurt to tell you. Let me think about it. Hmmm. There's blood everywhere, Alex. I will tell you that much. It's stunning, a masterpiece of carnage. I've outdone myself this time. Outdone Gary Soneji, Shafer, Casanova. This is my best work. I think it is, and I should know. I'm very objective about these things, but of course you know that.'

My heart was pounding and I felt dizzy. I could feel the blood rushing from my brain. I steadied myself against the kitchen counter. 'Where, Kyle? Tell me where you are. Where the hell are you?'

'Perhaps I'm at your Aunt Tia's outside Bal'more,' he said. Then he laughed like a madman. 'Chapell Gate. Such a pretty little town.'

A moan escaped from my mouth and my knees buckled. I flashed an image of my family – Nana, Jannie, Damon, Alex. I needed to be there with them. How could he have gotten past the FBI teams? And Sampson? He couldn't have. It wasn't possible.

'You're lying, Kyle.'

'Oh, am I now? Why would I lie? Think about it. What would be the point?'

The worst is yet to come. I needed to call Tia's. I should never have left them.

I heard a terrifying high-pitched scream above me in the kitchen. What in hell?

I looked up. Couldn't believe my eyes. Kyle leaped out of the trapdoor to the attic. He was still screaming. He had an ice pick clasped in his right hand, cell phone in the other.

I tried to get an arm up to shield myself. I wasn't fast enough. He'd taken me by surprise. I hadn't thought to look up there.

He plunged the blade into my chest at an odd angle. A shock of pain traveled through me. I went down hard on the kitchen floor. Had he struck my heart? Was I going to die? Was this the way it ended?

With his free hand, Kyle punched me in the face. I felt bone crunch. The left side of my face, my cheek seemed to cave in.

Kyle raised his fist to strike again. He was madman-strong, and he wanted to punish me. I was such an important character in his fantasy. He was so sick, so insane. I couldn't believe the things he'd done.

A voice inside screamed, *Take him out, find a way!*

A second punch glanced off the side of my forehead. I moved just enough to make him miss. I was in a living nightmare. This was almost surreal. The stainless steel handle of the ice pick was sticking out of my chest.

I grabbed the hood and collar of Kyle's windbreaker with one hand, his black hair with the other. I yanked him sideways, got him off me for a moment.

Somehow I managed to get up and pull Kyle with me. We were both grunting, gasping loudly for breath. I felt myself getting weaker. Blood was spreading on my shirt from the wound.

Still, I carried him forward, headfirst, right into Kate's well-organized glass kitchen cabinet. It shattered on impact. Splinters of glass and wood flew everywhere.

I pulled his head back out of the cabinet, cutting his face on nasty shards of the glass. I wanted to hurt him too. For Betsey Cavalierre, for Zachary and Liz Taylor, for all the others he had murdered along the way. So many dead at the hands of this heartless monster. The Mastermind. Kyle Craig.

He screamed, 'My eyes! My eyes!' I'd hurt him – finally.

I crunched a looping roundhouse right into his forehead. I moved in closer. I hit him again and again, then I held him up so I could hit him some more. I wouldn't let him go down. I kept body-punching Kyle Craig, body-punching him. I don't know where I got the strength. I wanted to keep hitting Kyle, for everything he'd done, the murders, the cruel betrayals, for stalking me all these months, the terrible hurt he'd inflicted on my family, on other families like mine.

He was out on his feet, so I finally let him drop to the kitchen floor. I stood over the unconscious body, exhausted, winded, afraid, and in pain. Now what? I felt as if I weren't myself anymore. Who was I? What was I becoming? What had all the brutal murders I'd seen done to me?

I stepped away from the crumpled body. The spike of the ice pick was still imbedded in my chest. It had to come out. I knew I couldn't, shouldn't, do it myself. I needed to get to a hospital. Maybe Dr Kate McTiernan would take care of me.

I made a phone call. A very important call.

This was just the *beginning*, wasn't it? Sure it was.

The Mastermind and I were alone at last. We had so much to talk about. I'd been waiting so long for this, and maybe so had he.

Chapter One Hundred and Fourteen

It was a hollow feeling to stand over Kyle and realize that I had no idea who he really was. He was an obsessively cruel psychopath; he had been stalking me for years; he had killed so many times, including friends of mine. 'You fucking bastard,' I whispered through my teeth.

The first case we had worked on together was a double kidnapping in Washington. Later, he cleared the way for me to help in the investigation of a kidnapper/killer who called himself Casanova, and who worked in the Research Triangle around the University of North Carolina and Duke. That was when we had first met Kate McTiernan. Kyle kept me close to him after that. He was the one responsible for my getting named as the VICAP liaison between the FBI and the Washington Police Department. I didn't know why at the time. Now I did.

He was conscious now. A mocking, falsely sympathetic

look crossed his face. His eyes leveled on me as he spoke. 'I know, I *know* how it hurts. You thought we were close, you thought we were friends.'

I didn't say anything, just looked into cold blue eyes edged with gray. What did I see there? Nothing except for his hatred and disdain. He was incapable of feeling guilt, or compassion.

Then Kyle smirked, and I wanted to hit him again. He began to laugh. What was the joke? What did he know? What else had he done?

He started to clap his hands together. 'Very good, Alex. You're still studying me, aren't you? You should bear in mind, I did beat you every time.'

'Except this time,' I reminded him. 'This time you lost.'

'Oh, are you so sure?' he asked. 'Are you positive that you have the upper hand, partner? How can you be certain? You can't be.'

'I'm sure. *Partner*. I do have a few questions, though. Clear some things up for me. You know what I want to hear about.'

He continued to smirk. Of course he knew. 'North Carolina. You didn't know I had attended Duke with the Gentleman Caller. I knew both killers. God, did I know them. I killed with them, hunted with them. But you let me off the hook, Detective Cross. Then there were the perfect bank robberies. The Mastermind at work. And, of course, I did kill the lovely Betsey Cavalierre. Great fun. That one's on you, Alex.'

I stared into those pitiless eyes. My voice came out in a rasp. 'Why did you have to hurt her?'

Kyle shrugged indifferently. 'That's how I win the game, by inflicting the most pain imaginable, then watching the torment and suffering. You should see the look in your eyes right now. It's priceless, a thing of beauty.

'Not that I want any pity, Doctor Cross, but did you ever see me with my shirt off? I'll answer that question. You haven't. That's because of the scars and welts there. My father, the great and respected general, the corporate chief executive officer, he beat me for years. He thought I was a very bad boy. And you know what, he was right. Father did know best. His son was a monster. Now what does that say about him?'

Kyle smiled again. Or was it a grimace? He shut his eyes.

'Getting back to Agent Cavalierre, she was investigating my whereabouts during all the robberies and kidnappings committed by the Mastermind. Smart little chippie. Pretty, too. And she really liked you, Alex. Thought you were so fine, her sweet brown sugar. I couldn't have that. She was a danger to me and a rival for your attention.

'Are you following this, Cross? Am I going too fast for you? Everything is very logical, no? I put a knife deep inside her. I was going to do the same to your friend Jamilla. Maybe I still will.'

I raised my Glock and pointed it into his face. My hand was shaking. 'No, Kyle, you won't!'

Chapter One Hundred and Fifteen

E verything had been leading up to this moment – the last few years, all of Kyle's tricks. My hand was still trembling as I moved the gun forward until it touched Kyle's forehead. To be honest, I didn't know what I would do next.

'I was hoping it might come to this. One of us in control of the situation. This is where it gets interesting to me,' he said. 'What do you do now?'

Kyle pressed his skull into the gun barrel. 'Go ahead, Alex. If you kill me like this, then I win. I like that, actually. Suddenly, *you're* the murderer.'

I let him talk – the Mastermind, the total control freak.

'Let me tell you a harsh truth,' he said. 'Can you take a little truth? How much truth can you stand?'

'Go ahead, enlighten me. I think I can take it, Kyle. I want to hear everything.'

'Oh, and you shall. What I do ... it's what all men want to do. I live out their secret fantasies, their nasty little daydreams. I completely control my environment. I don't live by rules created by my so-called peers. I live a full fantasy life. Everything I do is motivated by self-interest. It's what everybody wants, trust me on that. So stop being so self-righteous. It irritates the shit out of me.'

I shook my head. 'I have some news for you. It isn't what I want, Kyle. It's a self-centered adolescent's fantasy.'

'Oh, spare me the provincial pop psychology. And yes, it *is* what you want to do. The chase, the thrill. It's your life, too. Don't you see that? Jesus Christ, man. You love the hunt. You love it! *You love this!*'

We studied each other in the small kitchen for several minutes. The hatred between us was so obvious now. Then Kyle began to laugh again – he roared. He was laughing at my expense.

'You still don't get it, do you? You're a fool. You're so inferior. You have nothing, not a shred of solid evidence on me. I'll be out on the street in a few days. I'll be free to do whatever I like. Imagine the possibilities. Anything I can dream up. Isn't that a consoling thought, *Alex*? Old buddy, old pal.

'I *wanted* you to know who and what I am. It's no fun unless somebody knows. I wanted this to happen.

Desperately. More than anything. I set it up. And once I'm out, you'll know that I'm somewhere... waiting and watching. You see, I won this time, too. *I wanted you to catch me, you asshole.* What do you think of that?'

I stared into Kyle's eyes and it was like that game kids play – who's going to look away first? Who's going to blink?

Finally, I winked at him. 'Gotcha,' I said.

'What I think,' I continued, 'is that you just made your first big mistake. You didn't think of everything. You missed an important detail, Mastermind. Know what it is? C'mon, you're a smart guy. Figure it out.'

I stepped away from Kyle. Now I was the one who smiled, maybe even smirked. I stared into his eyes and let him think about it. I could see he had no idea. 'Watch closely.'

I took my cell phone from my pocket. I held it up for Kyle to see. I showed him that it was turned *on*.

'I called my home phone before we started to talk. The phone has been on speaker. Everything you just told me is on my voice mail. I have your confession, Kyle. Everything, every word. You lose, you sick, pitiful sonofabitch. You lose, *Mastermind.*'

Kyle suddenly sprung up from the floor at me – and then I got to knock him out again. I hit him with the best punch of my life, at least it felt that way. His body lifted up off the floor and he lost a couple of front teeth.

That was how he looked in the news photograph after his capture, the great Mastermind, missing two front teeth.

Chapter One Hundred and Sixteen

I finally got to rest up, to stop being a cop for a while. Kyle Craig was in a maximum security cell at Lorton Prison. The district attorney was confident there was more than enough evidence to convict. Kyle's expensive New York lawyer was screaming that he had committed no crimes, that he'd been framed. Isn't that amazing? The murder trial would be one of the biggest that Washington and the rest of the country had ever seen.

The thing was, I didn't want to think about Kyle, or his trial, or some other psychopathic killer anymore. I hadn't been to work in weeks, and it felt good. I felt real good. My ice pick wound was healing pretty well. The scar would be a souvenir. I was spending as much time as I could at home. I'd put on most of a new roof. I'd been to two of Damon's concerts in a row. I was on a roll.

I was working on a jump shot with Jannie; reading

Goodnight Moon and *Fox in Socks* to little Alex; taking cooking lessons from the best chef in all of Washington, or so Nana bragged. I was also making some time for myself. I'd even had a couple of nice talks with Christine Johnson. I told her I was sending the cutest pictures of Alex. Jamilla Hughes was coming East for a seminar and would visit next week. Everything was going well with her life.

It was around eleven o'clock, and I was playing the piano on the sun porch. The house on Fifth Street was quiet, everybody sleeping except for me.

The phone didn't ring, and what a sweet, simple pleasure that was.

No one came to the door with bad news that I didn't want to hear right now, or maybe ever again.

No one was watching me from outside, in the shadows, or if they were, at least they weren't being a nuisance about it.

I concentrated on getting into some songs by D'Angelo, and I was doing a pretty good job of it. 'The Line', 'Send It On', 'Devil's Pie'.

Tomorrow? Well, tomorrow was a big day, too.

I was going to resign from the DC police force in the morning.

And something else, something good for a change, I thought that maybe I was falling in love.

But that's another story, for another time.

FOUR BLIND MICE

Here's to Manhattan College on her Sesquicentennial Anniversary. Go Jaspers!

This one is also for Mary Jordan, who holds everything together, and I mean everything.

Did you ever see
such a sight in your life . . .

THE 'BLUELADY MURDERS'

Chapter One

Marc Sherman, the district attorney for Cumberland County, North Carolina, pushed the old wood captain's chair away from the prosecution table. It made a harsh scraping *eeek* in the nearly silent courtroom.

Then Sherman rose and slowly approached the jury box, where nine women and three men, six white, six African-American, waited with anticipation to hear what he had to say. They liked Sherman. He knew that, even expected it. He also knew that he had already won this dramatic murder case, even without the stirring summation he was about to give.

But he was going to give this closing anyway. He felt the need to see Sergeant Ellis Cooper held accountable for his crimes. The soldier had committed the most heinous and cowardly murders in the history of Cumberland County. The so-called 'Bluelady Murders'. The people in this county expected Sherman to punish Ellis Cooper, who happened to be a black man, and he wouldn't disappoint them.

The district attorney began, 'I have been doing this for a while, seventeen years to be exact. In all that time, I have never encountered murders such as those committed in December last by the defendant, Sergeant Ellis Cooper. What began as a jealous rage aimed at one victim, Tanya Jackson, spilled over into the shameless massacre of three women. All were wives, all were mothers. Together these women had eleven children, and of course, three grieving husbands, and countless other family members, neighbors and dear friends.

'The fateful night was a Friday, "ladies' night" for Tanya Jackson, Barbara Green and Maureen Bruno. While their husbands enjoyed their usual card night at Fort Bragg, the wives got together for personal talk, some laughter and the treasured companionship of one another. Tanya, Barbara and Maureen were great friends, you understand. This Friday night get-together took place at the home of the Jacksons, where Tanya and Abraham were raising their four children.

'Around ten o'clock, after consuming at least half a dozen shots of alcohol at the base, Sergeant Cooper went to the Jackson house. As you have heard in sworn testimony, he was seen outside the front door by two neighbors. He was yelling for Mrs Jackson to come out.

'Then Sergeant Cooper barged inside the house. Using an RTAK survival knife, a lightweight weapon favored by United States Army Special Forces, he attacked the woman who had spurned his advances. He killed Tanya Jackson instantly with a single knife thrust.

'Sergeant Ellis Cooper then turned the knife on

thirty-one-year-old Barbara Green. And finally, on Maureen Bruno, who nearly made it out of the slaughter-house, but was caught by Cooper at the front door. All three women were killed with thrusts delivered by a powerful male, who was familiar with hand-to-hand fighting techniques taught at the John F. Kennedy Special Warfare Center, headquarters for the Army's Special Forces.

'The survival knife has been identified as Sergeant Cooper's personal property, a deadly weapon he has kept since the early 1970s, when he left Vietnam. Sergeant Cooper's fingerprints were all over the knife.

'His prints were also found on the clothing of Mrs Jackson and Mrs Green. DNA from particles of skin found under the nails of Mrs Jackson were matched to Sergeant Cooper. Strands of his hair were found at the murder scene. The murder weapon itself was discovered hidden in the attic of Cooper's house. So were pathetic "love letters" he had written to Tanya Jackson – returned *unopened*.

'You have seen unspeakable photographs of what Sergeant Cooper did to the three women. Once they were dead, he "painted" their faces with ghoulish-looking blue paint. He "painted" their chests and stomachs. It is gruesome and twisted. As I said, the worst murders I have ever encountered. You know that there can only be one verdict. That verdict is guilty. Put this monster down!'

Suddenly, Sergeant Ellis Cooper rose from his seat at the defendant's table. The courtroom audience gasped. He was six feet four and powerfully built. At age fifty-five, his waist was still thirty-two inches, just as it had been when he had enlisted in the Army at eighteen. He was wearing his dress greens and the medals on his chest included a Purple Heart, a Distinguished Service Cross and a Silver Star. He looked impressive, even under the circumstances of the murder trial, and then he spoke in a clear, booming voice.

'I didn't kill Tanya Jackson, or any of those poor women. I never went inside the house that night. I didn't paint any bodies blue. I've never killed anyone, except for my country. I didn't kill those women. I'm innocent! I'm a war-hero, for God's sake!'

Without warning, Sergeant Cooper hurdled the wooden gate at the front of the courtroom. He was on Marc Sherman in seconds, knocking him to the floor, punching him in the face and chest.

'You liar, liar!' Cooper shouted. 'Why are you trying to kill me?'

When the courtroom marshals finally pulled Cooper away, the prosecutor's shirt and jacket were torn, his face bloodied.

Marc Sherman struggled to his feet and then he turned back to the jury. 'Need I say more? The verdict is guilty. Put this monster down.'

Chapter Two

T he *real* killers had taken a small risk and attended the final day of the trial in North Carolina. They wanted to see the end of this; couldn't miss it.

Thomas Starkey was the team leader, and the former Army Ranger colonel still looked the part, walked the walk and talked the talk.

Brownley Harris was his number two, and he remained deferential to Colonel Starkey, just like it had been in Vietnam, and just like it would always be until the day one or both of them died.

Warren Griffin was still 'the kid', which seemed marginally funny, since he was forty-nine years old now.

The jury had come in with a verdict of guilty less than two and a half hours after they were sent out to deliberate. Sergeant Ellis Cooper was going to be executed for murder by the state of North Carolina.

The district attorney had done a brilliant job – of convicting the wrong man.

The three killers piled into a dark blue Suburban parked

on one of the narrow side streets near the courthouse.

Thomas Starkey started up the big car. 'Anybody hungry?' he asked.

'Thirsty,' said Harris.

'Horny,' said Griffin, and snorted out one of his goofy laughs.

'Let's get something to eat and drink – then maybe we'll get into some trouble with the ladies. What do you say? To celebrate our great victory today. *To us!*' shouted Colonel Starkey as he drove down the street away from the courthouse. '*To the Three Blind Mice.*'

PART ONE

THE LAST CASE

Chapter Three

I came down to breakfast around seven that morning and joined Nana and the kids around the kitchen table. With little Alex starting to walk, things were back in 'lock-down' mode. Plastic safety locks, latches and outlet caps were everywhere. The sounds of kid chatter, spoons clattering in cereal bowls, Damon coaching his baby brother in the art of blowing raspberries, made the kitchen almost as noisy as a precinct house on a Saturday night.

The kids were eating some kind of puffed-up chocolate-flavored Oreo's cereal *and* Hershey's chocolate milk. Just the thought of all that sugar at seven in the morning made me shiver. Nana and I had eggs over-easy and twelve-grain toast.

'Now isn't this nice,' I said as I sat down to my coffee and eggs. 'I'm not even going to spoil it by commenting on the chocoholic breakfast two of my precious children are eating for their morning's nourishment.'

'You just did comment,' said Jannie, my daughter, never at a loss.

I winked at her. She couldn't spoil my mood today. The killer known as the Mastermind had been captured and was now spending his days at a maximum-security prison in Colorado. My twelve-year-old, Damon, continued to blossom – as a student, as well as a singer with the Washington Boys' Choir. Jannie had taken up oil painting, and she was keeping a journal, which contained some pretty good scribbling and cartoons for a girl her age. Little Alex's personality was emerging – he was a sweet boy, just starting to walk.

I had met a woman detective recently, Jamilla Hughes, and I wanted to spend more time with her. The problem was that she lived in California and I lived in DC. Not insurmountable, I figured.

I would have some time to find out about Jamilla and I. Today was the day I planned to meet with Chief of Detectives George Pittman and resign from the DC police. After I resigned, I planned to take a couple of months off. Then I might go into private practice as a psychologist, or possibly hook up with the FBI. The Bureau had made me an offer that was flattering as well as intriguing.

There was a loud rap at the kitchen door. Then it opened. John Sampson was standing there. He knew what I was planning to do today, and I figured he'd come by to show me some support.

Sometimes I am so gullible it makes me a little sick.

Chapter Four

'Hello, Uncle John,' Damon and Jannie chorused, and then grinned like the little fools they can be when in the presence of 'greatness', which is how they feel about John Sampson.

He went to the refrigerator and examined Jannie's latest artwork. She was trying to copy characters from a new cartoonist, Aaron McGurder, formerly from the University of Maryland and now syndicated. Huey and Riley Feeman, Caeser, Jazmine DuBois were all taped on the fridge.

'You want some eggs, John? I can make some scrambled with cheddar, way you like them,' Nana said, and she was already up out of her place. She would do anything for Sampson – it had been that way since he was ten and we first became friends. Sampson is like a son to her. His mum was in jail much of the time he was growing up, and Nana raised him as much as anybody.

'Oh no, no,' he said, and quickly motioned for her to sit back down, but when she moved to the stove, he said,

'Yeah, scrambled, Nana. Rye toast be nice. I'm starved away to nothing, and nobody does breakfast like you do.'

'You know that's the truth,' she cackled, and turned up the burners. 'You're lucky I'm an *old*-school lady. You're all lucky.'

'We know it, Nana,' Sampson smiled. He turned to the kids. 'I need to talk to your father.'

'He's retiring today,' Jannie said.

'So I've heard,' said Sampson. 'It's all over the streets, front page of the *Post*, probably on the *Today Show* this morning.'

'You heard your Uncle John,' I told the kids. 'Now scoot. I love you. Scat!'

Jannie and Damon rolled their eyes and gave us looks, but they got up from the table, gathered their books into backpacks and started out the door to the Sojourner Truth School, which is about a five-block walk from our house on Fifth Street.

'Don't even think about going out that door like that. *Kisses,*' I said.

They came over and dutifully kissed Nana and me. Then they kissed Sampson. I really don't care what goes on in this cool, unsentimental post-modern world, but that's how we do it in our house. Bin Laden probably never got kissed enough when he was a kid.

'I have a problem,' Sampson said as soon as the kids left.

'Am I supposed to hear this?' Nana asked from the stove.

'Of course you are,' John said to her. 'Nana, Alex, I've

told you both about a good friend of mine from my Army days. His name is Ellis Cooper and he's still in the Army after all these years. At least he was. He was found guilty of murdering three women off post. I had no idea about any of it until friends started to call. He'd been embarrassed to tell me himself. Didn't want me to know. He only has about three weeks to the execution, Alex.'

I stared into Sampson's eyes. I could see sadness and distress there, even more than usual. 'What do you want, John?'

'Come down to North Carolina with me. Talk to Cooper. He's not a murderer. I know this man almost as well as I know you. Ellis Cooper didn't kill anybody.'

'You know you have to go down there with John,' Nana said. 'Make this your last case. You have to promise me that.'

I promised.

Chapter Five

Sampson and I were on I-95 by eleven o'clock that morning, our car wedged between caravans of speeding, gear-grinding, smoke-spewing tractor-trailers. The ride was a good excuse for us to catch up, though. We'd both been busy for a month or so, but we always got back together for long talks. It had been that way since we were kids growing up in DC. Actually, the only time we'd been separated was when Sampson served two tours in Southeast Asia and I was at Georgetown, then Johns Hopkins.

'Tell me about this Army friend of yours,' I said. I was driving and Sampson had the passenger seat as far back as it would go. His knees were up, touching the dash. He almost looked comfortable somehow.

'Cooper was already a sergeant back when I met him, and I think he knew he always would be. He was all right with it, liked the Army. He and I were both at Bragg together. Cooper was a drill sergeant at the time. Once he kept me on post for four straight weekends.'

I snorted out a laugh. 'Is that when the two of you got close? Weekends together in the barracks?'

'I hated his guts back then. Thought he was picking on me. You know, singling me out because of my size. Then we hooked up again in 'Nam.'

'He loosened up some? Once you met him again in 'Nam?'

'No, Cooper is Cooper. He's no bullshit, a real straight arrow, but if you follow the rules, he's fair. That's what he liked about the Army. It was mostly orderly, consistent, and if you did the right thing then you usually did all right. Maybe not as well as you thought you should, but not too bad. He told me it's smart for a black man to find a meritocracy like the Army.'

'Or the police department,' I said.

'Up to a point,' Sampson nodded. 'I remember a time,' he continued, 'Vietnam. We had replaced a unit that killed maybe two hundred people in a five-month period. These weren't exactly soldiers that got killed, Alex, though they were supposed to be VC.'

I listened as I drove. Sampson's voice became far away and distant.

'This kind of military operation was called "mopping up". This one time, we came into a small village, but another unit was already there. An infantry officer was "interrogating" a prisoner in front of these women and children. He was cutting skin off the man's stomach.

'Sergeant Cooper went up to the officer and pressed his gun to the man's skull. He said if the officer didn't stop what he was doing, he was a dead man. He meant it, too. Cooper didn't care about the consequences. He *didn't* kill those women in North Carolina, Alex. Ellis Cooper is no killer.'

Chapter Six

I loved being with Sampson. Always had, always will. As we rode through Virginia and into North Carolina, the talk eventually turned to other, more hopeful and promising subjects. I had already told him everything there was to tell about Jamilla Hughes, but he wanted to hear more scoop. Sometimes he's a bigger gossip than Nana Mama.

'I don't have any more to tell you, big man. You know I met her on that big murder case in San Francisco. We were together a lot for a couple of weeks. I don't know her that well. I like her, though. She doesn't take any crap from anybody.'

'And you'd *like* to know her more. I can tell that much.' Sampson laughed and clapped his big hands together.

I started to laugh too. 'Yes, I would, matter of fact. Jamilla plays it close to her chest. I think she was knocked about somewhere along the line. Maybe the first husband. She doesn't want to talk about it yet.'

'I think she has your number, man.'

'Maybe she does. You'll like her. Everybody does.'

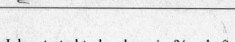

John started to laugh again. 'You do find nice ladies. I'll give you that much.' He switched subjects. 'Nana Mama is some kind of piece of work, isn't she?'

'Yeah, she is. Eighty-two. You'd never know it. I came home the other day. She was shimmying a *refrigerator* down the back stairs of the house on an oil cloth. Wouldn't wait for me to get home to help her.'

'You remember that time we got caught lifting records at Spector's Vinyl?'

'Yeah, I remember. She loves to tell that story.'

John continued to laugh. 'I can still see the two of us sitting in that store manager's crummy little office. He's threatening us with everything but the death penalty for stealing his crummy forty-five records, but we are so cool. We're almost laughing in his face.

'Nana shows up at the record store, and she starts *hitting* both of us. She hit me in the face, bloodied my lip. She was like some kind of mad woman on a rampage, a mission from God.'

'She had this warning: "*Don't cross me. Don't ever, ever cross me, ever.*" I can still hear the way she would say it,' I said.

'Then she let that police officer haul our asses down to the station. She wouldn't even bring us home. I said, "They were only records, Nana." I thought she was going to kill me. "I'm already bleeding!" I said. "You're gonna bleed more!" she yelled in my face.'

I found myself smiling at the distant memory. Interesting how some things that weren't real funny at the time suddenly get that way. 'Maybe that's why we became big, bad cops. That afternoon in the record store. Nana's vengeful wrath.'

Sampson turned serious and said, 'No, that's not what straightened me out. The Army did it. I sure didn't get what I needed in my own house. Nana helped, but it was the Army that set me straight. I owe the Army. And I owe Ellis Cooper. *Hoorah! Hoorah! Hoorah!*'

Chapter Seven

We drove onto the sobering and foreboding high-walled grounds of Central Prison in Raleigh, North Carolina.

The security housing unit there was like a prison within a prison. It was surrounded by razor-sharp wire fences and a deadly electronic barrier; armed guards were in all the watchtowers. Central Prison was the only one in North Carolina with a death row. Currently, there were over a thousand inmates, with an astounding two hundred twenty on the row.

'Scary place,' Sampson said as we got out of the car. I had never seen him look so unsettled and unhappy. I didn't much like being at Central Prison either.

Once we were inside the main building it was as quiet as a monastery, and the extremely high level of security continued. Sampson and I were asked to wait between two sets of steel-bar doors. We were subjected to a metal detector, then had to present photo IDs along with our badges. The security guard who checked us informed us that many of North Carolina's 'First In Flight' license plates were made here at the prison. Good to know, I suppose.

There were hundreds of controlled steel gates in the high-security prison. Inmates couldn't move outside their cells without handcuffs, leg irons and security guards. Finally, we were allowed to enter death row itself, and taken to Sergeant Cooper. In this section of the prison each block consisted of sixteen cells, eight on the bottom, eight on top, with a common dayroom. Everything was painted the official color, known as 'lark'.

'John Sampson, you came after all,' Ellis Cooper said as he saw us standing in a narrow corridor outside a special hearing room. The door was opened and we were let in by a pair of armed guards.

I sucked in a breath, but tried not to show it. Cooper's wrists and ankles were shackled with chains. He looked like a big, powerful slave.

Sampson went and hugged Cooper. He patted his friend's back and they looked like a couple of large, socialized bears. Cooper had on the orange-red jumpsuit that all of the death row inmates wore. He kept repeating, 'So good to see you.'

When the two men finally pulled apart, Cooper's eyes were red and his cheeks wet. Sampson remained dry-eyed. I had never, ever seen John cry.

'This is the best thing that's happened to me in a long, long while,' Cooper said. 'I didn't think anybody would come after the trial. I'm already dead to most of them.'

'I brought along somebody. This is Detective Alex

Cross,' Sampson said, and turned my way. 'He's the best I know at homicide investigations.'

'That's what I need,' said Cooper as he took my hand, 'the best.'

'So tell us about all this awful craziness. *Everything*,' Sampson said. 'Tell us from start to the finish. Your version, Coop.'

Sergeant Cooper nodded. 'I want to. It will be good to tell it to somebody who isn't already convinced that I murdered those three women.'

'That's why we're here,' Sampson said. 'Because you *didn't* murder the women.'

'That Friday was a payday,' Cooper began. 'I should have gone straight home to my girlfriend, Marcia, but I had a few drinks at the club. I called Marcia around eight, I guess. She'd apparently gone out. She was probably ticked off at me. So I had another drink. Met up with a couple of buddies. I called my place again – it was probably close to nine. Marcia was still out.

'I had another couple highballs at the club. Then I decided to walk home. Why walk? Because I knew I was three sheets to the wind. It was only a little over a mile home anyway. When I got to my house, it was past ten. Marcia still wasn't there. I turned on a North Carolina Duke basketball game. Love to root against the Dukies and Coach K. Around eleven o'clock I heard the front door open. I yelled out to Marcia, asked her where she had been.

'Only it wasn't her coming home after all. It was about a half-dozen MPs and a CID investigator named Jacobs.

Soon after that, supposedly, they found the RTAK survival knife in the attic of my house. And traces of blue paint used on those ladies. They arrested me for murder.'

Ellis Cooper looked at Sampson first, then he stared hard into my eyes. He paused before he spoke again. 'I didn't kill those women,' he said. 'And what I still can't believe, somebody obviously *framed* me for the murders. Why would somebody set me up? It doesn't make sense. I don't have an enemy in the world. Least I didn't think so.'

Chapter Eight

Thomas Starkey, Brownley Harris and Warren Griffin had been best friends for more than thirty years, ever since they served together in Vietnam. Every couple of months, under Thomas Starkey's command, they went to a simple, post-and-beam log cabin in the Kennesaw Mountains of Georgia and spent a long weekend together. It was a ritual of machismo and would continue, Starkey insisted, until the last of them was gone.

They did all the things they couldn't do at home: played music from the Sixties – the Doors, Cream, Hendrix, Blind Faith, the Airplane – *loud*. They drank way too much beer and bourbon; they grilled thick Porterhouse steaks that they ate with fresh corn, Vidalia onions, tomatoes, and baked potatoes slathered with butter and sour cream. They smoked expensive Cuban cigars. They had a hell of a lot of fun in what they did.

'What was the line in that old beer commercial? You know the one I'm talking about?' Harris asked as they sat out on the front porch after dinner.

'It doesn't get any better than this,' Starkey said as he flicked the thick ash from his cigar onto the wide-planed floor.'I think it was a shit beer, though. Can't even remember the name. 'Course, I'm a little drunk and a lot stoned.' Neither of the others believed that. Thomas Starkey was never completely out of control, and especially not when he committed murder, or ordered it done.

'We've paid our dues, gentlemen. We've earned this,' Starkey said, and extended his mug to clink with his friends.'What's happening now is well deserved.'

'Bet your ass we earned it. Couple of three foreign wars. Our other exploits over the past few years,' said Harris. 'Families. Eleven kids between us. Plus we did pretty good out in the big, bad civilian world, too. I sure never figured I'd be knocking down a hundred and a half a year.'

They clinked the heavy beer glasses again. 'We did good, boys. And believe it or not, it can only get better,' said Starkey.

As they always did, they re-told old war stories – Grenada, Mogadishu, the Gulf War, but mostly Vietnam.

Starkey recounted the time they had made a Vietnamese woman 'ride the submarine'. The woman, a VC sympathizer of course, had been stripped naked then tied to a wooden plank, face upward. Harris had tied a towel around her face. Water from a barrel was slowly sprinkled onto the towel. As the towel eventually became flooded, the woman was forced to inhale water to breathe. Her lungs and stomach soon swelled with the water. Then Harris pounded on her chest to expel the water. The woman talked, but of course she didn't tell them anything they didn't already know. So they dragged her out to a kaki tree which produced a sweet fruit and was always covered with large yellow ants. They tied the mamasan to the tree, lit up marijuana cigars and watched as her body swelled beyond recognition. When it was close to busting they 'wired' her with a field telephone and electrocuted her. Starkey always said that was about the most creative kill ever. 'And the VC terrorist bitch deserved it.'

Brownley Harris started to talk about 'mad minutes' in Vietnam. If there were answering shots from a village, even one, they would have a 'mad minute'. All hell would break loose because the answering shots *proved* the whole village was VC. After the 'mad minute', the village, or what remained of it, would be burned to the ground.

'Let's go into the den, boys,' Starkey said. 'I'm in the mood for a movie. And I know just the one.'

'Any good?' Brownley Harris asked, and grinned.

'Scary as hell, I'll tell you that. Makes *Hannibal* look like a popcorn fart. Scary as any movie you ever saw.'

Chapter Nine

The three of them headed for the den, their favorite place in the cabin. A long time ago in Vietnam, the trio had been given the code name *Three Blind Mice*. They had been élite military assassins – did what they were told, never asked embarrassing questions, executed their orders. It was still pretty much that way. And they were the best at what they did.

Starkey was the leader, just as it had been in Vietnam. He was the smartest and the toughest. He hadn't changed much physically over the years. He was six feet one, had a thirty-three-inch waist, a tan, weathered face, appropriate for his fifty-five years. His blond hair was now peppered with gray. He didn't laugh easily, but when he did, everybody usually laughed with him.

Brownley Harris was a stocky five feet eight, but with a surprisingly well-toned body at age fifty-one, considering all the beer he drank. He had hooded brown eyes with thick bushy eyebrows, almost a unibrow. His hair was still black, though flecked with gray now, and he wore it in a military-style buzz cut, though not a 'high and tight'.

Warren 'the Kid' Griffin was the youngest of the group, and still the most impulsive. He looked up to both of the other men, but especially Starkey. Griffin was six feet two, lanky, and reminded people, especially older women, of the folk-rock singer James Taylor. His strawberry blond hair was long on the sides but thinning on top.

'I kind of like old Hannibal the Cannibal,' Griffin said as they entered the den. 'Especially now that Hollywood decided he's the good guy. Only kills people who don't have nice manners, or taste in fine art. Hey, what's wrong with that?'

'Works for me,' said Harris.

Starkey locked the door into the den, then slid a plain, black-box videotape into the machine. He loved the den, with its leather seating arrangement, thirty-six-inch Philips TV, and armoire filled with tapes that were categorized chronologically. 'Showtime,' said Starkey. 'Dim the house lights.'

The first image was shaky, as someone approached a small, ordinary-looking redbrick house. Then a second man came into view. A third person, the camera operator, moved closer and closer until the shot was through a grimy, bug-specked picture window into the living room. There were three women in the room, laughing and chatting up a storm, totally unaware that they were being watched by three strangers, and also being filmed.

'Take note that the opening scene is one long camera move without a cut,' said Harris. 'Cinematographer is a genius, if I don't say so myself.'

'Yeah, you're an artist all right,' said Griffin. 'Probably some latent fagola in you.'

The women, who looked to be in their mid-thirties, were now clearly visible through the window. They were drinking white wine, laughing it up on their 'ladies' night'. They wore shorts and had good legs that deserved to be shown off. Barbara Green stretched out a leg and touched her toes, almost as if she were preening for the movie.

The shaky camera shot continued around the brick house to the back door at the kitchen. There was sound with the picture now. One of the three intruders began to bang on the aluminum screen door.

Then a voice came from inside. 'Coming! Who is it? Oohh, I hope it's Russell Crowe. I just saw *A Beautiful Mind*. Now that man is beautiful.'

'It's not Russell Crowe, lady,' said Brownley Harris, who was obviously the camera operator.

Tanya Jackson opened the kitchen door and looked terribly confused for a split second, before Thomas Starkey cut her throat with the survival knife. The woman moaned, dropped to her knees, then fell onto her face. Tanya was dead before she hit the black and olive-green checkerboard linoleum of the kitchen floor.

'Somebody's *very good* with a survival knife. You haven't lost your touch over the years,' Harris said to Starkey as he drank beer and watched the movie.

The hand-held camera shot continued, moving quickly through the kitchen. Right over the bleeding, twitching body of Tanya Jackson. Then into the living room of the

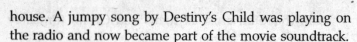

house. A jumpy song by Destiny's Child was playing on the radio and now became part of the movie soundtrack.

'What's going on?' Barbara Green screamed from the couch, and curled herself into a protective ball. 'Who are you? Where's Tanya?'

Starkey was on her in an instant with the knife. He even mugged for the camera, leered eerily. Then he chased Maureen Bruno into the kitchen, where he drove the RTAK into the center of her back. She threw both arms into the air as if she was surrendering.

The camera reversed angles to show Warren Griffin. He was bringing up the rear. It was Griffin who had brought the blue paint, and who would actually paint the faces and torsos of the three murder victims.

Sitting in the den of their cabin, the buddies watched the film twice more. When the third showing was over, Thomas Starkey removed the videocassette. 'Hear, hear!' said Starkey, and they all raised their beer mugs. 'We're not getting older, we're getting better and better.'

Chapter Ten

Hoorah!

In the morning, Sampson and I arrived at Fort Bragg, North Carolina, to begin our investigation into the Bluelady Murders. C-130s and 141s were constantly flying overhead. I drove along something called the All American Freeway, which I then took to Reilly Road. Surprisingly, there had been no security cordon around the Army base, no fence around the post, no main gate until September 11. The Army had allowed local motorists to use base roads as transit from one side of Bragg to the other.

The base itself measured twenty-five miles east–west, ten miles north–south. It was home for combat troops ready to be sent anywhere in the world within eighteen hours. And it had all the amenities: movie theaters, riding stables, a museum, two golf courses, even an ice skating rink.

There were a couple of signs as we entered at one of the new security posts. One read: *Welcome to Fort Bragg, North Carolina, Home of America's Airborne and Special Operations*

Forces. The second was common to just about every US base around the world: *You are entering a military installation and are now subject to search without a warrant.*

The grounds were dusty, and it was still hot in the early fall. Everywhere I looked I saw sweaty soldiers running PT. And humvees. Lots of humvees. Several of the units were 'singing cadence'.

'Hoorah!' I said to Sampson.

'Nothing like it,' he grinned. 'Almost makes me want to re-up.'

Sampson and I spent the rest of the day talking to men dressed in camouflage with spit-shined jump boots. My FBI connections helped open doors that might have stayed closed to us. Ellis Cooper had a lot of friends and most had originally been shocked to hear about the murders. Even now, not many of them believed that he was capable of the mayhem and cruelty involved.

The exceptions were a couple of non-coms who had gone through the Special Warfare School under his command. They told us that Cooper had physically bullied them. A PFC named Steve Hall was the most outspoken. 'The sergeant had a real mean streak. It was common knowledge. Couple of times, he got me alone. He'd elbow me, knee me. I knew he was hoping I'd fight back, but I didn't. I'm not that surprised he killed somebody.'

'Just chicken-shit stuff,' Sampson said about the training-school stories. 'Coop has a temper and he can be a prick, if provoked. That doesn't mean he killed three women and painted them blue.'

I could feel Sampson's tremendous affection and

respect for Ellis Cooper. It was a side he didn't let show often. Sampson had grown up with a mother who was an addict and a dealer, and a father who'd run out on him when he was a baby. He had never been much of a sentimentalist, except when it came to Nana and the kids, and maybe me.

'How do you feel about this mess so far?' he finally asked.

I hesitated before giving an answer. 'It's too early to tell, John. I know that's a hell of a thing to say when your friend has less than three weeks to live. I don't think we'll be welcome around Fort Bragg much longer either. The Army likes to solve its problems in its own way. It'll be hard to get the kind of information we need to really help Cooper. As for Cooper, I guess my instinct is to believe him. But who would go to all this bother to set him up? None of it makes sense.'

Chapter Eleven

I was starting to get used to the C-130s and 141s that were constantly flying overhead. Not to mention the artillery booming on the shooting range near Fort Bragg. I'd begun to think of the artillery as death knells for Ellis Cooper.

After a quick lunch out on Bragg Boulevard, Sampson and I had an appointment with a captain named Jacobs. Donald Jacobs was with CID, the Army's Criminal Investigation Division. He had been assigned to the murder case from the beginning and had been a key, damaging witness at the trial.

I kept noticing that the roads inside Fort Bragg were well trafficked by civilian vehicles. *Even now, anyone could get in here and not be noticed.* I drove to the section of the base where the main administration buildings were located. CID was in a redbrick building that was more modern and sterile-looking than the attractive structures from the Twenties and Thirties.

Captain Jacobs met us in his office. He wore a red plaid

sport shirt and khakis rather than a uniform. He seemed relaxed and cordial, a large, physically fit man in his late forties. 'How can I help?' he asked. 'I know that Ellis Cooper has people who believe in him. He helped a lot of guys when he was a DI. I also know that the two of you have good reputations as homicide detectives up in Washington. So where do we go from there?'

'Just tell us what you know about the murders,' Sampson said. We hadn't talked about it, but I sensed he needed to be the lead detective here on the base.

Captain Jacobs nodded. 'All right. I'm going to tape our talk if you don't mind. I'm afraid I think that he did it, Detectives. I believe that Sergeant Cooper murdered those three women. I don't pretend to understand why. I especially don't understand the blue paint that was used on the bodies. Maybe you can figure that one out, Dr Cross. I also know that most people at Bragg haven't gotten over the brutality and senselessness of these murders.'

'So we're causing some problems being here,' Sampson said. 'I apologize, Captain.'

'No need,' said Jacobs. 'Like I said, Sergeant Cooper has his admirers. In the beginning, even I had a tendency to believe him. The story he told about his whereabouts tracked pretty well. His service record was outstanding.'

'So what changed your mind?' Sampson asked.

'Oh hell, a lot of things, Detective. DNA testing, evidence found at the murder scene and elsewhere. The fact that he was seen at the Jackson house, although he swore he wasn't there. The survival knife found in his attic, which turned out to be the murder weapon. A few other things.'

'Could you be more specific?' Sampson asked. 'What kind of other things?'

Captain Jacobs sighed, got up, and walked over to an olive-green file cabinet. He unlocked the top drawer, took out a folder and brought it over to us.

'Take a look at these. They might change your mind, too.' He spread out half a dozen pages of copies of photographs from the murder scene. I had looked at a lot of photos like these, but it didn't make it any easier.

'That's how the three women were actually found. It was kept out of the trial so as not to hurt the families any more than we had to. The DA knew he had more than enough to convict Sergeant Cooper without using these brutal pictures.'

The photographs were right up there with the most grisly and graphic evidence I'd seen. Apparently, the women had all been found in the living room, not where each of them had been killed. The killer had carefully arranged the bodies on a large, flowered sofa. He had art-directed the corpses, and that was an element that definitely caught my attention. Tanya Jackson's face was resting in Barbara Green's crotch; Mrs Green's face was in Maureen Bruno's crotch. Not just the faces but the crotches were painted blue.

'Apparently, Cooper thought the three women were lovers. That may have even been the case. At any rate, that's why he thought Tanya rejected his advances. I guess it drove him to this.'

Finally I spoke up. 'These crime scene photos, however graphic and obscene, still don't prove that Ellis Cooper is your murderer.'

Captain Jacobs shook his head. 'You don't seem to understand. These aren't copies of the crime scene photos taken by the police. These are copies of Polaroids that Cooper took himself. We found them at his place along with the knife.'

Donald Jacobs looked at me, then at Sampson. 'Your friend murdered those women. Now you ought to go home and let the people around here begin to heal.'

Chapter Twelve

I n spite of Captain Jacob's advice, we didn't leave North Carolina. In fact, we kept talking to anybody who would talk to us. One first sergeant told me something interesting, though not about our case. He said that the recent wave of patriotism that had swept the country since September 11 was barely noticeable at Fort Bragg. 'We have always been that way!' he said. I could see that, and I must admit, I was impressed with a lot that I saw on the Army post.

I woke early the next morning, around five, with no place to go. At least I had some time to think about the fact that this could be my last case. And what kind of case was it, really? A man convicted of three gruesome murders claiming to be innocent. What murderer didn't?

And then I thought of Ellis Cooper on death row in Raleigh, and I got to work.

Once I was up, I got on-line and did as much preliminary research as I could. One of the areas I looked at was the blue paint on the victims. I checked into VICAP and got three other cases of murder victims being painted, but none of them seemed a likely connection.

I then ran down a whole lot of information on the color blue. One thing that mildly interested me was the Blue Man Group – performance artists who had started a show called *Tubes* in New York City, then branched out to Boston, Chicago and Las Vegas. The show contained elements of music, theater, performance art, even vaudeville. The performers always worked in blue, from head to toe. Maybe it was something, maybe nothing – too early to tell.

I met Sampson for breakfast at the Holiday Inn where we were staying – the Holiday Inn Bordeaux, to be more precise. We ate quickly, then drove over to the off-base military housing community where the three murders had taken place. The houses were ordinary ranches, each with a small strip of lawn out front. Quite a few of the yards had plastic wading pools. Tricycles and 'cozy coupés' were parked up and down the street.

We spent the better part of the morning and early afternoon canvassing the close-knit community where Tanya Jackson had lived. It was a working-class, military neighborhood, and at more than half the stops nobody was home.

I was on the front porch of a brick-and-clapboard house, talking to a woman in her late thirties or early forties, when I saw Sampson come jogging our way. Something was up.

'Alex, come with me!' he called out. 'C'mon. I need you right now.'

Chapter Thirteen

I caught up with Sampson. 'What's up? What did you find out?'

'Something weird. Maybe a break,' he said. I followed him to another small ranch house. He knocked on the door and a woman appeared almost immediately. She was only a little over five feet, but easily weighed two hundred pounds, maybe two-fifty.

'This is my partner, Detective Cross. I told you about him. This is Mrs Hodge,' he said.

'I'm Anita Hodge,' the woman said as she shook my hand. 'Glad to meet you.' She looked at Sampson and grinned. 'I agree. Ali when he was younger.'

Mrs Hodge walked us through a family room where two young boys were watching *Nickelodeon* and playing video games at the same time. She then led us down a narrow hallway and into a bedroom.

A boy of about ten was in the room. He was seated in a wheelchair that was pulled up to a Gateway computer. Behind him on the wall were glossy pictures of more than two dozen Major League baseball players.

He looked annoyed at the intrusion. 'What *now*?' he asked. 'That's short for *get out of here and leave me alone. I'm working.*'

'This is Ronald Hodge,' Sampson said. 'Ronald, this is Detective Cross. I told you about him when we spoke before.'

The boy nodded but didn't say anything, just stared angrily my way.

'Ronald, will you tell us your story again?' Sampson asked. 'We need to hear it.'

The boy rolled his eyes. 'I already told the other policemen. I'm sick and tired of it, y'know. Nobody cares what I think anyway.'

'Ronald,' said his mother. 'That's not true and you know it.'

'Please tell me,' I said to the boy. 'What you have to say could be important. I want to hear it in your words.'

The boy frowned and continued to shake his head, but his eyes held mine. 'The other policemen didn't think it was important. Fuckheads.'

'Ronald,' said the boy's mother. 'Don't be rude. You know I don't like that attitude. Or that kind of language.'

'Okay, okay,' he said. 'I'll tell it again.' Then he began to talk about the night Tanya Jackson was murdered, and what he'd seen.

'I was up late. Wasn't s'posed to be. I was playing on the computer.' He stopped and looked at his mother.

She nodded. 'You're forgiven. We've been over this

before. Now please tell your story. You're starting to get me a little crazy.'

The boy finally cracked a smile, then went on with his story. Maybe he had just wanted to set up his audience a little.

'I can see the Jacksons' yard from my room. It's just past the corner of the Harts' house. I saw somebody out in the yard. It was kind of dark, but I could see him moving. He had like a movie camera or something. I couldn't tell what he was taking pictures of, so it made me curious.

'I went up close to this window to watch. And then I saw there were three men out there. I saw 'em in Mrs Jackson's yard. That's what I told the police. Three men. I saw 'em just like I see two of you in my room. *And they were making a movie.'*

Chapter Fourteen

I asked young Ronald Hodge to repeat his story, and he did.

Exactly, almost word for word. He stared me right in the eye as he spoke, and he didn't hesitate or waver. It was obvious that the boy was troubled by what he had witnessed, and that he was still scared. After learning that murders had been committed in the house, he'd been living in fear of what he'd seen that night.

Afterward, Sampson and I talked to Anita Hodge in the kitchen. She gave us iced tea, which was unsweetened, with big chunks of lemon in it, and was delicious. She told us that Ronald had been born with spina bifida, an outcropping of the spinal cord that had caused paralysis from the waist down.

'Mrs Hodge,' I asked, 'what do you think about the story Ronald told us in there?'

'Oh, I believe him. At least I believe he thinks he saw what he said. Maybe it was shadows or something, but Ronald definitely believes he saw three men. And one of them with a movie camera of some kind. He's been consistent on that from the first. Spooky. Like that old Hitchcock movie.'

'*Rear Window*,' I said. 'James Stewart thinks he sees a murder outside his window. He's laid up with a broken leg at the time.' I looked over at Sampson. I wanted to make sure he was comfortable with me asking the questions this time. He nodded that it was okay.

'What happened after the Fayetteville detectives talked to Ronald? Did they come back? Did any other policemen come? Anyone from Fort Bragg? Mrs Hodge, why wasn't Ronald's testimony part of the trial?'

She shook her head. 'Same questions I had – my ex-husband and I both. A captain from CID did come a few days later. Captain Jacobs. He talked to Ronald some. That was the end of it, though. No one ever came about any trial.'

After we finished our iced teas, we decided to call it a night. It was past eight and we thought we'd made some progress. Back at the Holiday Inn Bordeaux, I called Nana and the kids. Everything was fine and dandy on the home front. They had taken up the cry that I was on 'Daddy's last case', and they liked the sound of that. Maybe I did, too. Sampson and I had dinner and a couple of beers at Bowties inside the hotel, then we turned in for the night.

I tried Jamilla in California. It was around seven her time, so I called her work number first.

'Inspector Hughes,' she answered curtly. 'Homicide.'

'I want to report a missing person,' I said.

'Hey, Alex,' she said. I could feel her smile over the

phone. 'You caught me at work again. Busted. *You're* the missing person. Where are you? You don't write, you don't call. Not even a crummy e-mail in the last few days.'

I apologized, then I told Jam about Sergeant Cooper and what had happened so far. I described what Ronald Hodge had seen from his bedroom window. Then I broached the subject that had prompted my call. 'I miss you, Jam. I'd like to see you,' I said. 'Any place, any time. Why don't you come East for a change? Or I could go out there if you'd rather. You tell me.'

Jamilla hesitated, and I found that I was holding my breath. Maybe she didn't want to see me. Then she said, 'I can get off work for a few days. I'd love to see you. Sure, I'll come to Washington. I've never been there. Always wanted to when I was a kid.'

'Not so long ago,' I said.

'That's good. Cute,' she laughed.

My heart fluttered a little as the two of us made a date. *Sure, I'll come to Washington.* I played that line of Jamilla's over and over in my head for the rest of the night. It had just rolled off her tongue, almost like she couldn't wait to say it.

Chapter Fifteen

E arly the next morning I got a call from a friend of
mine at Quantico. I had asked Abby DiGarbo to check
on rental-car companies in the area and to look for any
irregularities that took place during the week of the
murders. I'd told her it was urgent. Abby had already
found one.

It seemed that Hertz had been stiffed on the rental of a
Ford Explorer. Abby had dug deeper and discovered an
interesting paper trail. She told me that scamming a
rental-car company wasn't all that easy, which was good
news for us. The scam required a fake credit card and a
driver's license on which everything matched, including
the description of the driver renting the car.

Someone had hacked into SEC files that are main-
tained as a public record. The fake identity used on the
card was obtained and the information submitted to a
company in Brampton, Ontario, where the card was
made. A fake driver's license to match was then obtained
from a web-site, Photoidcards.com. A photograph had

been submitted, and I was staring at a copy of it right now.

White, male, nothing memorable about the face, which possibly had been changed with makeup and costume props anyway.

The FBI was still checking to see what else they could find. It was a start, though. Somebody had gone to some trouble to rent a car in Fayetteville. We had *somebody's* picture, thanks to Abby DiGarbo.

On the way over to Sergeant Cooper's house I told Sampson about the rent-a-car scam. Sampson was drinking steaming hot coffee and eating an éclair from Dunkin' Donuts, but I could tell he was appreciative in his own way. 'That's why I asked you in on this,' he said.

Cooper lived in a small, two-bedroom apartment in Spring Lake, north of Fort Bragg. He had one side of a redbrick duplex. I saw a sign: *Caution, Attack Cat!*

'He has a sense of humor,' Sampson said. 'At least he did.'

We had been given a key to open the front door. Sampson and I stepped inside. The house still smelled like cat after all this time.

'It's good not having anybody in the way for a change,' I said to John. 'No other police, no FBI.'

'Killer's been caught,' Sampson said. 'Case is closed. Nobody cares but us now. And Cooper sitting there on death row. The clock's ticking.'

Apparently, nobody had figured out what to do about the apartment yet. Ellis Cooper had felt secure enough in his posting that he'd bought the place a few years back.

When he retired, he'd planned to stay in Spring Lake.

The table in the front hallway contained photos of Cooper posing with friends in several locations: what looked like Hawaii, the south of France, maybe the Caribbean. There was also a more recent photo of Cooper hugging a woman who was probably his girl-friend, Marcia. The furniture in the apartment was comfortable-looking, not expensive, and appeared to have been bought at stores like Target and Pier One.

Sampson called me over to one of the windows. 'It's been shimmied. The place was broken into. Could be how somebody got Cooper's knife, then returned it. If that's what happened. Coop said he left it in the closet of his bedroom. The police say the knife was in the attic.'

We went into the bedroom next. The walls were covered with more photographs, mostly from places where Cooper had been posted: Vietnam, Panama, Bosnia. A Yukon Mighty Weightlifting Bench was lined up near one wall. Near the closet was an ironing board. We searched through the closet. The clothes were mostly military but there were civilian threads, too.

'What do you make of this stuff?' I asked Sampson. I pointed to a table with a grouping of odd knickknacks that looked like they came from Southeast Asia.

I picked up a straw doll that looked strangely menacing, even evil. Then a small crossbow with what looked like a claw for its trigger. A silver amulet in the shape of a watchful, lidless eye. What was this?

Sampson took a careful look at the creepy straw doll, then the eye. 'I've seen the evil eye before. Maybe in

Cambodia or Saigon. Don't remember exactly. I've seen the straw dolls, too. Think they have something to do with avenging evil spirits. I've seen the dolls at Viet funerals.'

The creepy artifacts notwithstanding, the sense I got from the apartment was that Ellis Cooper had been a lonely man without much of a life besides the Army. I didn't see a single photograph of what might be called family.

We were still in Cooper's bedroom when we heard a door open inside the apartment. Then came the sound of heavy footsteps approaching.

The bedroom door was thrown open and banged hard against the wall. Soldiers with drawn pistols stood in the doorway.

'Put your hands up! Military Police. *Hands up now!*' one of them yelled.

Sampson and I slowly raised our arms.

'We're homicide detectives. We have permission to be here,' Sampson told them. 'Check with Captain Jacobs at CID.'

'Just keep those hands up. High!' the MP in charge barked.

Sampson spoke calmly to the leader of the three MPs who now crowded into the bedroom with their guns leveled at us.

'I'm a friend of Sergeant Cooper's,' Sampson told them.

'He's a convicted murderer,' snarled one MP out of the side of his mouth. 'Lives on death row these days. But not for much longer.'

Sampson kept his hands high, but told them there was

a note from Cooper in his shirt pocket and the house key we'd been given. The head MP took the note and read:

To whom it may concern, John Sampson is a friend, and the only person I know who's working on my behalf. He and Detective Cross are welcome in my house, but the rest of you bastards aren't. Get the hell out. You're trespassing!

Sergeant Ellis Cooper.

Chapter Sixteen

I woke the next morning with the phrase 'dead man walking' repeating itself in my head. I couldn't get back to sleep. I kept seeing Ellis Cooper in the bright orange death row jumpsuit.

Early in the morning, before it got too hot, Sampson and I took a run around Bragg. We entered the base on Bragg Boulevard, then turned onto a narrower street called Honeycutt. Then came a maze of similar side streets, and finally Longstreet Road. Bragg was immaculate. Not a speck of trash anywhere. A lot of soldiers were already up running PT.

As we jogged side by side, we planned out our day. We had a lot to do in a relatively short time. Then we needed to get back to Washington.

'Tell you what's bothering me the most so far,' Sampson said as we toured the military base on foot.

'Same thing that's bothering me, probably,' I huffed. 'We found out about Ronald Hodge and the Hertz car in about a day. What's wrong with the local police and the Army investigations?'

'You starting to believe Ellis Cooper is innocent?'

I didn't answer Sampson, but our murder investigation was definitely disturbing in an unusual way: it was going too well. We were learning things that the Fayetteville police didn't seem to know. And why hadn't Army CID done a better job with the case? Cooper was one of their own, wasn't he?

When I got back to my room after the run, the phone was ringing. I wondered who'd be calling this early. Had to be Nana and the kids. It was just past seven. I answered in the slightly goofy Damon Wayans voice I sometimes use around the kids. 'Yeah-lo. *Who's* calling me so early in the morning? Who's waking me up? You have some nerve.'

Then I heard a woman's voice. Unfamiliar, with a heavy Southern accent. 'Is this Detective Cross?'

I quickly changed my tone and hoped she didn't hang up. 'Yes it is. Who's this?'

'I'd rather not say. Just listen, please. This is hard for me to tell you, or anyone else.'

'I'm listening. Go ahead.'

I heard a deep sigh before she spoke again.

'I was with Ellis Cooper on the night of the three terrible murders. We were together when the murders took place. We were intimate. That's all I can say for now.'

I could tell the caller was frightened, maybe close to panic. I had to keep her on the line if I could. 'Wait a minute. Please. You could have helped Sergeant Cooper at the trial. You can still help him. You could prevent his execution!'

'No. I can't say any more than I already have. I'm married to someone on the base. I won't destroy my family. I just can't. I'm sorry.'

'Why didn't you tell the police in town, or CID?' *Why didn't Cooper tell us?* 'Please stay on the line. Stay with me.'

The woman moaned softly. 'I called Captain Jacobs. I told him. He did nothing with the information, with the truth. I hope you do something. Ellis Cooper didn't kill those three women. I didn't believe my testimony would be enough to save him. And . . . I'm afraid of the consequences.'

'What consequences? Think about the consequences for Sergeant Cooper. He's going to be executed.'

The woman hung up. I couldn't tell much about her, but I was sure she was sobbing. I stood there staring at the phone receiver, not quite believing what I'd just heard. I had just talked to Ellis Cooper's alibi – and now she was gone.

Chapter Seventeen

Around five o'clock, Sampson and I received the terrifically good news that the commanding officer at Bragg was willing to see us at his house on the base. We were to be there at seven-thirty sharp. General Stephen Bowen would give us ten minutes, to share the information we had about the murder case. In the meantime, Sampson got through to Sergeant Cooper at Central Prison. He denied that he'd been with a woman that night. What was worse, Sampson said Cooper wasn't very convincing. But why would he hold the truth back from us? It didn't make sense.

General Bowen's quarters looked to be from the Twenties or Thirties, a stucco house with a Spanish tile roof. Up on the second floor there was a sun porch with glass on three sides, probably the master suite.

A man was watching from up there as we parked in the semicircular driveway. *General Bowen himself?*

We were met at the front door by an officer aide who identified himself as Captain Rizzo. The general's staff included an officer aide, an enlisted aide who was part of the general's security but also worked as the cook, and a driver who was also security.

We stepped into a large foyer with sitting rooms on either side. The décor was eclectic, and probably reflected the general's career around the world. I noticed a beautiful carved cabinet that looked German, a painted screen showing rolling hills and cherry trees from Japan, and an antique sideboard that suggested a possible posting in New England.

Captain Rizzo showed us into a small den where General Stephen Bowen was already waiting for us. He was in uniform. The aide leaned in to me. 'I'll return in exactly ten minutes. The general wants to talk to you alone.'

'Please sit down,' said Bowen. He was tall and solidly built, probably in his mid-fifties. He tented his fingers on top of a well-worn desk that looked like it had been with him for most of his career. 'I understand that you've come down here to try and re-open the Cooper murder case. Why do you think we should reconsider the case? And Cooper's death sentence?'

As concisely as I could I told the general what we had already found out, and also our reactions to the evidence as homicide detectives. He was a practiced listener, who punctuated what I had to say by uttering 'interesting' several times. He seemed open to other points of view and eager for new information. For the moment, I was hopeful.

When I stopped, he asked, 'Is there anything else either

of you wants to add? This is the time for it.'

Sampson seemed unusually quiet and reserved in the general's presence. 'I'm not going to get into my personal feelings for Sergeant Cooper,' he finally spoke, 'but, as a detective, I find it impossible to believe that he'd bring the murder weapon, plus several incriminating photographs, back to his house.'

Surprisingly, General Bowen nodded agreement. 'I do too,' he said. 'But that's what he did. I don't understand why either, but then again, I don't understand how a man could willfully murder three women, as he most definitely did. It was the worst act of peacetime violence I've seen in my career, and gentlemen, I've seen some bad business.'

The general leaned forward across his desk. His eyes narrowed and his jaw tensed. 'Let me tell you something about this murder case that I haven't shared with anyone else. No one. This is just for the two of you. When Sergeant Cooper is executed at Central Prison by the state of North Carolina, I will be there with the families of those murdered women. I'm looking forward to the lethal injection. What that animal did revolts and disgusts me. Your ten minutes are up. Now get the hell out of here. Get the fuck out of my sight.'

His aide, Captain Rizzo, was already back at the door.

Chapter Eighteen

The Three Blind Mice were in Fayetteville again, headed toward Fort Bragg for the first time in several months. Brownley Harris, Warren Griffin and Thomas Starkey were admitted through the security gates on All American Freeway. No problem. They had official business on post; they had an appointment.

The three men were unusually quiet as Starkey drove the dark blue Suburban across the base. They hadn't been at Bragg since the murders of the three women. Not that the place had changed one iota; change happened very slowly in the military.

'This is a trip I personally could do without,' Brownley Harris contributed from the backseat of the Suburban.

'It's not a problem,' said Starkey, taking control as he always did. 'We have a legitimate reason to be here. Be a mistake if we stopped showing our faces at Bragg. Don't disappoint me.'

'I hear you,' said Harris. 'I still don't like being back at the scene of the crime.' He decided that things needed some lightening up. 'You all hear the differential theory of the US Armed Forces – the so-called snake model?' he asked.

'Haven't heard that one, Brownie,' said Griffin, who also rolled his eyes. He knew a joke was coming, probably a bad one.

'Army Infantry comes in after the snake. Snake smells them, leaves the area unharmed. Aviation comes next, has Global Positioning Satellite coordinates to the snake. Still can't find the snake. Returns to base for re-fuel, crew rests and manicures. Field Artillery comes. Kills the snake with massive Line On Target barrage with three Formal Artillery Brigades in support. Kills several hundred civilians as unavoidable collateral damage. All participants, including cooks, mechanics, clerks, are awarded Silver Stars.'

'What about us Rangers?' asked Griffin, playing the straight man.

Harris grinned. 'Single Ranger comes in, plays with the snake, then eats it.'

Starkey snorted out a laugh, then he turned off Armistead Street into the lot for the Corps Head-quarters. 'Remember, this is just business. Conduct yourselves as such, gentlemen.'

Griffin and Harris barked, 'Yes, sir.'

The three of them gathered their briefcases, put on lightweight suit jackets, and tightened their neckties. They were the senior sales team for Hechler and Koch, and they were at Bragg to promote the sale of guns to the Army. In particular, they were trying to build common interest in the gun manufacturer's Personal Defense Weapon (PDW), which weighed just over two pounds, fully loaded, and could 'defeat all known standard issue military body armor'.

'Hell of a weapon,' Thomas Starkey liked to say during his sales pitch. 'If we'd had it in 'Nam, we would have won the war.'

Chapter Nineteen

The meeting went as well as any of them could have hoped. The three salesmen left the Army Corps offices at a little past eight that night, with assurances of support for the PDW. Thomas Starkey had also demonstrated the latest version of the MP5 submachine gun and talked knowledgeably and enthusiastically about his company's fabrications system, which made their gun parts 99.9 percent interchangeable.

'Let's get some cold beers and thick steaks,' Starkey said. 'See if we can get in a little trouble in Fayetteville, or maybe some other town down the line. That's an order, gentlemen.'

'I'm up for that,' said Harris. 'It's been a good day, hasn't it? Let's see if we can spoil it.'

By the time they left Fort Bragg darkness had fallen. 'On the road again . . .' Warren Griffin started in on his theme song, the old Willie Nelson standard that he sang just about every time they started an adventure. They knew Fayetteville, not only from business trips, but from a time when they'd been stationed at Bragg. It was only four years since the three of them had left the Army, where they'd been Rangers: Colonel Starkey, Captain Harris, Master Sergeant Griffin. Seventy-fifth Ranger Regiment, 3rd Battalion, originally out of Fort Benning, Georgia.

They were just entering town when they saw a couple of hookers loitering on a semidarkened street corner. In the bad old days Hays Street in town had block after block of rough bars and strip joints. It used to be known as *Fayettenam*. No more, though. The locals were trying to gentrify the downtown area. A billboard put up by the Chamber of Commerce read: 'Metro Living At A Southern Pace'. Made you want to throw up.

Warren Griffin leaned out the side window of the Suburban. 'I love you, and especially *you*. Stop the car this minute! Oh God, please stop the vehicle. I love you, darling. I'll be back!' he called to the two girls.

Starkey laughed, but he drove on until they reached The Pump, which had been there for at least twenty years. They strolled inside to eat and party. Why work if you couldn't get a reward? Why feel the pain unless you got some gain?

During the next few hours, they drank too many beers, ate twenty-four-ounce steaks with fried onions and mushrooms slathered on top, smoked cigars, and told the best war stories and jokes. Even the waitresses and bartenders got into the act some. Everybody liked Thomas Starkey. Unless you happened to get on his bad side.

They were leaving Fayetteville around midnight when Starkey pulled the Suburban over to the curb. 'Time for a live-fire exercise,' he said to Griffin and Harris. They knew what that meant.

Harris just smiled, but Griffin let out a whoop. 'Let the war games begin!'

Starkey leaned out his window and talked to one of the girls loitering on Hays Street. She was a tall, rail-thin blonde, wobbling slightly on silver platform heels. She had a little, pouty mouth, but it disappeared when she flashed them her best hundred-dollar smile.

'You are a very beautiful lady,' Starkey said. 'Listen, we're heading over to our suite at the Radisson. You be interested in three big tips, instead of just one? We kind of like to party together. It'll be good, clean fun.'

Starkey could be charming, and also respectful. He had an easy smile. So the blonde hooker got into the Suburban. 'You all promise to be good boys,' she said, and smiled that wonderful smile of hers again.

'Promise,' the three of them chorused. 'We'll be good boys.'

'On the road again,' Griffin sang.

'Hey, you're pretty good,' the girl said, and gave him a kiss on the cheek. She was good with men, knew how to handle them, especially soldiers from Fort Bragg, who were usually decent enough guys. Once upon a time, she'd been an Army brat herself. Not so long ago. She was nineteen.

'You hear that? This beautiful lady likes my singing. What's your name, sweetie?' asked Griffin. 'I like you already.'

'It's Vanessa,' said the girl, giving her madeup street handle. 'What's yours? Don't say Willie.'

Griffin laughed out loud. 'Why, it's Warren. Nice to make your acquaintance, Vanessa. Pretty name for a pretty lady.'

They rode out of town, in the direction of I-95. Starkey suddenly pulled the Suburban over after a mile or so and shouted, 'Pit stop!' He let the car roll until it was mostly hidden in a copse of evergreens and prickle bushes.

'The Radisson's not far. Why don't you wait?' Vanessa asked. 'You boys can hold it a little longer, can't you?'

'This *can't* wait,' said Griffin. Suddenly, he had his pistol up tight against the girl's skull.

From the front seat, Brownley Harris had his gun aimed at her chest.

'*De hai tay len dau!*' Thomas Starkey screamed, his voice deep and scary.

Hands on your head.

'*Ban gap nhieu phien phue roi do.*'

You're in serious trouble, bitch.

Vanessa didn't understand a word but she sure got the tone. Bad shit was going down. Real bad shit. Her stomach dropped. Ordinarily, she wouldn't have gotten into a car with three guys, but the driver had seemed so nice. Now why was he yelling at her? What kind of messed-up language was it? What was happening? She thought that she might throw up and she'd had a chili dog and Fritos for dinner.

'Stop, please stop!' Vanessa said, and started to cry. It

was an act, kind of, but it usually worked on the soldiers from Bragg.

Not this time, though. The insane yelling in the car got even louder. The weird language she didn't understand.

'Ra khoi xe. Ngay bay gro,' said Thomas Starkey.

Get out of the car. Do it now, bitch.

They were waving their scary guns and pointing, and she finally understood that she was supposed to get out of the car. *Oh my God, were they going to leave her out here as a sick joke? The bastards!*

Or was it worse than that? How much worse could it get?

Then the one in the front seat smacked her with the back of his hand. Why? She was already getting out of the car. Goddamn him! She almost toppled over on her silver platform shoes. Willie Nelson kicked her in the back and Vanessa gasped in pain.

'Ra khoi xe!' the man in front screamed again. Who were they? Were they terrorists or something?

Vanessa was sobbing, but she understood she was supposed to run, to hightail it into the dark woods and creepy swampland. *Jesus, God, she didn't want to go in there! There'd be snakes for sure!*

The one from the backseat punched her in the back again, and Vanessa started to run. What choice did she have?

'Lue do may se den toi!'

You're going to die.

She heard shouts behind her.

Oh God, God, God, what were they saying? What was going to happen to her? Why had she let them pick her up? Big mistake, big mistake!

Then all Vanessa could think about was running.

Chapter Twenty

'Let her go,' Thomas Starkey said. 'Let's be fair now. We told Vanessa we'd be good.'

So they leaned against the Suburban and let the frightened girl run off into the swamp, gave her a good head start.

Starkey slid on one of the Ranger's new tan berets. It had replaced the black beret of the Special Forces, once the rest of the Army had gone to black. 'Here's the first side bet of the evening. Ole Vanessa will be wearing her platform heels when we catch up with her. Or do you boys think she'll shuck the shoes?' asked Starkey. 'Bets, gentlemen?'

'Shuck 'em for sure,' said Griffin. 'She's dumb, but she's not that stupid. I'll take your bet. Fifty?'

'She'll be wearing the shoes,' pronounced Starkey. 'Girl that pretty working the street, she's dumb as a board. A hundred says so.'

Just then they saw a pair of lights veering off the highway. Someone was driving toward where they'd parked. Now who the hell was this?

'Trooper,' said Starkey. Then he raised his hand in a friendly wave at the slow-moving police car.

'Problem here?' the statie said once he'd rolled up close to the big blue Suburban. He didn't bother to get out of his car.

'Just a little pit stop, Officer. We're on our way to Fort Benning from Bragg,' Starkey said in the calmest voice. In truth, he wasn't nervous about the trooper. Just curious about how this would turn out. 'We're in the Reserves. If the three of us were on the *first* team I guess we'd all be in trouble.'

'I saw your vehicle from the road. Thought I better check to make sure everybody was all right. Nothing but swamp back there.'

'Well, we're fine, Officer. Finish our smokes and hit the road again. Thanks for the concern.'

The state trooper was just about to pull away when a woman's scream came from the woods. There was no mistaking that it was a cry for help.

'Now that's a damn shame, Officer.' Starkey swung his pistol out from behind his back. He shot the trooper point-blank in the forehead. Didn't even have to think about it. 'No good deed goes unpunished.'

He shook his head as he walked to the police car, shut off the headlights. He got into the front, pushing the dead trooper aside, and pulled the car out of sight from the main road.

'Go find the girl,' he said to Harris and Griffin. 'Pronto. She's obviously not too far. And she's still wearing her platforms, the twit. Go! Go!' he repeated. 'I'll give you chumps a couple of minutes' lead. I want to get this cruiser completely out of sight. Go. Warren is Point. Brownie is Flanker.'

When Colonel Thomas Starkey finally made his move into the woods, there wasn't a false step on his part. He went straight to where the girl had cried out for help and gotten the state trooper killed.

From that point, it was mostly instinct for him. He saw mussed leaves and grass. A broken branch of a bush where she'd passed. He noted his own internal responses – rapid breathing, surging blood flow. He'd been here before.

'*Tao se tim ra may,*' he whispered in Vietnamese. '*Lue do may se den toi.*'

I'm going to find you, honey. You're almost dead.

He was sorry that the chase after the girl had to be rushed, but the dead state trooper was an unexpected development. As always, Starkey had a calm, superaware focus. He was in the zone. Time slowed for him; every detail was precise and every movement controlled. He was moving fast, comfortable and supremely confident in the dark woods. There was just enough moonlight for him to see.

Then he heard laughter up ahead. Saw a light through the branches. He stopped moving. 'Son of a bitch!' he muttered. He moved forward cautiously, just in case.

Harris and Griffin had caught the blonde bitch. They had taken off her black hot pants, gagged her with her own scuzzy underwear, cuffed her hands behind her back.

Griffin was ripping off her silver-sequined blouse. All that was left were the sparkly silver platforms.

Vanessa didn't wear a bra and her breasts were small. Pretty face, though. Reminded Starkey of his neighbor's daughter. Starkey thought again that she was a fine little piece to be selling herself for cheap on the street. *Too bad, Vanessa*.

She struggled and Griffin let her break away, just for the fun of it. But when she tried to run, she tripped and went down hard in the dirt. She stared up at Starkey, who was now standing over her. He thought she was pathetic.

'Why are you doing this?' She was whimpering. Then she said something else through the gag as she tried to push herself up. It sounded like 'I never hurt anybody.'

'This is a game we learned a long time ago,' Starkey said in English. 'It's just a game, honey. Passes the time. Amuses us. Get the paint,' he said to Master Sergeant Griffin. 'I think red for tonight. You look good in red, Vanessa? I think red is your color.'

He looked her right in the eye and pulled the trigger.

Chapter Twenty-One

I got up at around five-thirty my first morning back in Washington. *Same old, same old,* which was fine with me.

I put on a Wizards tee-shirt and ancient Georgetown gym shorts and headed downstairs. The lights in the kitchen were still off. Nana wasn't up yet, which was a little surprising.

Well, she deserved to sleep late every once in a while.

I laced up my sneaks and headed outside for a run. Immediately I could smell the Anacostia River. Not the greatest smell, but familiar. My plan was not to think about Ellis Cooper on death row this morning. So far, I was failing.

Our neighborhood has changed a lot in the past few years. The politicians and business-people would say it's all for the good, but I'm not so sure that's right. There's construction on 395 South, and the Fourth Street on-ramp has been closed forever. I doubt it would happen for this long in Georgetown. A lot of the old brownstones

I grew up with have been torn down.

Town houses are going up which look very Capitol Hill to me. There's also a flashy new gym called Results. Some houses sport hexagonal blue ADT security signs courtesy of the huge Tyco Corporation. Certain streets are becoming gentrified. But the drug dealers are still around, especially as you travel toward the Anacostia.

If you could put on HG Wells time machine glasses, you would see that the original city planners had some good ideas. Every couple of blocks there is a park with clearly delineated paths and patches of grass. Some day the parks will be reclaimed by the people, not just the drug dealers. Or so I like to think.

A *Washington Post* article the other day proclaimed that some people in the neighborhood actually protect the dealers. Well, some people think the dealers do more good things for the community than the politicians – like throwing block parties and giving kids ice-cream money on hot summer days.

I've been here since I was ten and we'll probably stay in Southeast. I love the old neighborhood – not just the memories, but the promise of things that could still happen here.

When I got home from my run the kitchen lights still weren't on. An alarm was sounding inside my head.

Pretty loud, too.

I went down the narrow hallway from the kitchen to check on Nana.

Chapter Twenty-Two

I edged open the door and saw her lying in bed, so I quietly moved into the room. Rosie the cat was perched on the windowsill. She meowed softly. Some watch-cat.

I let my eyes roam. Saw a familiar framed poster depicting jazz musicians by Romare Bearden; it's called 'Wrapping it up at the Lafayette'.

On top of her armoire were dozens of hat boxes. Nana's collection of hats for special occasions would be the envy of any milliner.

I realized I couldn't hear Nana's breathing.

My body tensed and suddenly there was a loud roaring sound inside my head. She hadn't gotten up to make breakfast only a handful of times since I was a kid. I felt the fears of a child as I stood perfectly still in her room.

Oh God, no. Don't let this happen.

When I got close to her bed, I heard shallow breaths. Then her eyes popped open.

'Alex?' she whispered. 'What's happening? Why are you in here? What time is it?'

'Hi there, sweetheart. You okay?' I asked.

'I'm just kind of tired. Feeling a little under the weather this morning.' She squinted her eyes to look at the old Westclox on her night table. 'Seven? Oh my. Half the morning's gone.'

'You want a little breakfast? How about breakfast in bed this morning? I'm buying,' I said.

She sighed. 'I think I'll just sleep in a little longer, Alex. You mind? Can you get the kids ready for school?'

'Sure. Are you positive you're okay?'

'I'll see you later. I'm fine. Just a little tired this morning. Get the children up, Alex.' Rosie was trying to get in bed with Nana, but she wasn't having any of it. 'Scat, cat,' she whispered.

I got the three kids up, or so I thought, but then I had to rouse Jannie and Damon a second time. I put out their favorite cereals, some fruit, and then I made scrambled eggs – overdoing it a little to compensate for Nana's not being there. I warmed Alex's milk then fixed his breakfast and spoon-fed it to him.

The kids marched off to school and I cleaned up after they were gone. I changed Alex's diapers for the second time that morning, and put him in a fresh onesie covered with fire trucks. He was liking this extra attention, seemed to think it was funny.

'Don't get used to this, little buddy,' I told him.

I checked on Nana, and she was still resting. She was fast asleep, actually. I listened to her breathing for a couple of minutes. She seemed all right.

Her bedroom was so peaceful, but not old lady rosy.

There was a fuzzy, very colorful orange and purple rug at the foot of the bed. She said it gave her happy feet.

I took little Alex upstairs to my room, where I hoped to get some work done that morning. I called a friend at the Pentagon. His name's Kevin Cassidy. We had worked a murder case together a few years back.

I told him about the situation at Fort Bragg, and how little time Sergeant Cooper had on death row. Kevin listened, then cautioned me to be extremely careful. 'There are a lot of good folks in the Army, Alex. Good people, well intentioned, honorable as hell. But we like to clean up our own mess. Outsiders aren't usually welcome. You hear what I'm saying?'

'Ellis Cooper didn't commit those murders,' I told him. 'I'm almost certain of it. But I'll take your advice to heart. We're running out of time, Kevin.'

'I'll check into it for you,' he said. 'Let *me* do it, Alex.'

After I got off the phone with the Pentagon, I called Ron Burns at the FBI. I told him about the developing situation at Fort Bragg. The director and I had gotten fairly close during the troubles with Kyle Craig. Craig was a former senior agent I'd helped put away. I still didn't know exactly how many murders he had committed but it was at least eleven, probably much more than that. Burns and I had believed Kyle was our friend. It was the worst betrayal in my lifetime, but not the only one.

Burns wanted to get me over to the Bureau and I was thinking about it.

'You know how territorial local cops can be,' he said.

'The Army is even worse, especially when it comes to a homicide.'

'Even if one of their own is innocent and wrongly accused? Even if he's about to be executed? I thought they didn't leave their own out there to die.'

'If they believed that, Alex, the case would have never gone to trial. If I can help, I will. Let me know. I don't make offers that I don't keep.'

'I appreciate it,' I said.

After I got off the phone, I brought little Alex downstairs for some more milk. I was becoming faintly aware of just how much work was involved every day, every hour of every day, at the house. I hadn't even done any cleaning or straightening up yet.

I decided to check on Nana again.

Gently I opened the door. *I couldn't hear anything.*

I moved closer to the bed.

Finally, I could hear the sound of her breathing. I stood stock-still in her bedroom and, for the first time that I could remember, I worried about Nana.

She was never sick.

Chapter Twenty-Three

Nana finally got up around noon. She shuffled into the kitchen holding a thick new book, *The Bondswoman's Narrative*. I had a hot lunch ready for her and the baby.

She didn't want to talk about how she was feeling and didn't eat much, just a few spoonfuls of vegetable soup. I tried to get her over to Dr Rodman's, but she wasn't having any of it. She *did* let me cook the meals for the rest of the day, and take care of the kids, and clean the house from top to bottom per her explicit instructions.

The next morning I was up before Nana for the second day in a row. It was unheard of in all our years together.

While I waited for her to come to the kitchen, I took in the familiar sights. Paid attention, that is.

The room is dominated by her old Caloric gas stove. It has four burners and a large space she uses to hold goods cooked earlier or cooling. There are two ovens side by side. A large black skillet sits on top of the stove at all times. The refrigerator is also an older model that Nana refuses to give up for a newer one. It's always covered with notes and schedules about our life together: Damon's choir and basketball schedules; Jannie's 'whatever' schedule; emergency phone numbers for Sampson and me; an appointment card for little Alex's next pediatrician checkup; a Post-it on which she has written her latest sage advice: *You will never stumble while on your knees.*

'What are you up to, Alex?' I heard the familiar scuff of her slippers. I turned and saw her standing there, hands on hips, ready for battle, or whatever.

'I don't know. The ghost of breakfast past? How are you feeling, old woman?' I said. 'Talk to me. You okay?'

She winked and nodded her tiny head. 'I'm just fine. How 'bout yourself? You okay? You look tired. Hard work taking care of this house, isn't it?' she said, then cackled, and liked the sound of it so much that she cackled again.

I went across the kitchen and picked her up in my arms. She was so light – under a hundred pounds. 'Put me down!' she said. 'Gently, Alex. I might break.'

'So tell me about yesterday. You going to make an appointment at Dr Rodman's? Of course you are.'

'I must have needed a little extra sleep, that's all it was. It happens to the best of us. I listened to my body. Do you?'

'Yes I do,' I said. 'I'm listening to it now and it's voicing some serious concerns about you. Will you make an appointment with John Rodman, or do I have to make it for you?'

'Put me down, Alex. I'm already seeing the doctor later

this week. *Regular* visit, no big thing. Now. How do you want your eggs this morning?'

As if to show me how fine she was, Nana said that I should go back to Fort Bragg with Sampson and finish up my business there. She insisted. I did need to go to Bragg at least once more, but not before I got Aunt Tia to come and stay with Nana and the kids. Only after I was sure that everything was under control did I set out for North Carolina.

On the ride I told Sampson what had happened with Nana, and also gave a blow by blow of my day with the kids.

'She's eighty-two, Alex,' he said, but then added, 'She'll probably only be with us for another twenty years or so.' We both laughed, but I could tell John was worried about Nana, too. By his own admission, she's been like a mother to him.

Finally we arrived at Fayetteville, North Carolina, around five in the afternoon. We had to see a woman about an alibi that could maybe save Sergeant Cooper.

Chapter Twenty-Four

We drove to the Bragg Boulevard Estates, less than half a mile from Fort Bragg. The jets were still flying non-stop overhead and the artillery kept pounding away.

Just about everyone at Boulevard Estates worked on the base and lived in what is known as Basic Allowance Housing. BAH is based on rank and pay grade, the size and quality of the residence improving dramatically with rank. Most of the places we saw were small ranch houses. Several of them looked like they needed serious maintenance work. I had read somewhere that over sixty percent of the current Army was married and had children. It looked like that statistic was about right.

Sampson and I walked up to one of the brick ranch houses, and I knocked on the battered and bent aluminum front door. A woman in a black silk kimono appeared. She was heavy-set, attractive. I already knew that her name was Tori Sanders. Behind her, I could see four small children checking out who was at the door.

'Yes? What is it?' she asked. 'We're busy. It's feeding time at the zoo.'

'I'm Detective Cross and this is Detective Sampson,' I told her. 'Captain Jacobs told us you're a friend of Ellis Cooper's.'

She didn't respond. Didn't even blink.

'Mrs Sanders, you called me at my hotel about a week ago. I figured your house had to be within walking distance of the base if Sergeant Cooper stopped here on the night of the murder. I did a little checking. Found out he was here that night. Can we come in? You don't want us standing out here where all your neighbors can see.'

Tori Sanders decided to let us in. She opened the door and ushered us into a small dining area. Then she shooed her kids away.

'I don't know why you're here, or what you're talking about,' she said. Her arms were crossed tightly in front of her body. She was probably in her late thirties.

'We have other options. I'll tell you what we can do, Mrs Sanders,' Sampson spoke up. 'We can go out and ask around the neighborhood about you and Sergeant Cooper. We can also involve CID. Or you can answer our questions here in the privacy of your home. You do understand that Cooper is going to be executed in a few days?'

'God damn you. Both of you!' she suddenly raised her voice. 'You got this all wrong. As usual, the police have it wrong.'

'Why don't you straighten us out then,' Sampson said,

softening his tone some. 'We're here to listen. That's the truth, Mrs Sanders.'

'You want to be straightened out, well then here it is. You want it real? I *did* call you, Detective Cross. That was me. Now here's what I didn't say on the phone. I wasn't cheating on my husband with Sergeant Cooper. My husband asked me to make the call. He's a friend of Ellis's. He happens to believe the man is innocent. So do I. But we have no proof, no evidence that he didn't commit those murders. Ellis *was* here that night. But it was before he went drinking, and he came to see my husband, not me.'

I took in what she had said, and I believed her. It was hard not to. 'Did Sergeant Cooper know you were going to call me?' I asked.

She shrugged her shoulders. 'I have no idea. You'll have to ask Ellis about that. We were just trying to do the right thing for him. You should do the same. The man is on death row, and he's innocent as you or I. He's *innocent*. Now let me feed my babies.'

Chapter Twenty-Five

We were getting nowhere fast and it was frustrating as hell for both of us, but especially Sampson. The clock was ticking so loud for Ellis Cooper I could hear it just about every minute of the day.

Around nine that night, John and I had dinner at a popular local spot called the Misfits Pub, out in the Strickland Bridge shopping center. Supposedly, a lot of non-com personnel from Fort Bragg stopped in there. We were still nosing around for any information we could get.

'The more we know, the less we seem to know.' Sampson shook his head and sipped his drink. 'Something's definitely not right here at Bragg. And I know what you're going to say, Alex. Maybe Cooper is the heart of the problem. Especially if he put the Sanders up to calling you.'

I nursed my drink and looked around the pub. A bar dominated the room, which was crowded, loud and smoky. The music alternated between country and soul. 'Doesn't prove he's guilty. Just that he's desperate. It's hard to blame Cooper for trying anything he can,' I finally said. 'He's on death row.'

'He's not stupid, Alex. He's capable of stirring the pot to get our attention. Or somebody else's.'

'But he's not capable of murder?'

Sampson stared into my eyes. I could tell he was getting angry. 'No, he's not a murderer. I know him, Alex. Just like I know you.'

'Did Cooper kill in combat?' I asked.

Sampson shook his head. 'That was war. A lot of our people got killed too. You know what it's like. You've killed men,' he said. 'Doesn't make you a murderer, does it?'

'I don't know, does it?'

I couldn't help overhearing a man and woman who were sitting next to us at the bar. 'Police found Vanessa in the woods near I-95. Only disappeared last night. Now she's dead, she's gone. Some freaks did her with a hunting knife. Probably Army trash,' the woman was saying. She had a thick Southern accent, and sounded angry, but also frightened.

I turned and saw a florid-faced, redheaded woman in a bright blue halter top and white slacks. 'Sorry, I couldn't help over-hearing. What happened?' I asked. 'Somebody was murdered outside town?'

'Girl who comes in here sometimes. Vanessa. Somebody cut her up,' the redhead said, and shook her head back and forth. The man she was with wore a black silk shirt, cowboy hat, and looked like a failed country and western singer. He didn't like it that the woman was talking to me.

'My name is Cross. I'm a homicide detective from Washington. My partner and I are working a case down here.'

The woman's head shot back. 'I don't talk to cops,' she said, and turned away. 'Mind your own business.'

I looked at Sampson, then spoke in a lowered voice. 'If it's the same killer, he's not being too careful.'

'Or the same *three* killers,' he said.

Someone elbowed me hard in the back. I whirled around and saw a heavy-set, well-muscled blond man in a checkered sport shirt and khakis. He had a 'high and tight'. Definitely military.

'Time you two got the hell out of Dodge,' he said. Two other men stood behind him. *Three of them.* They were dressed in civilian clothes, but they sure looked like Army. 'Time you stopped causing trouble. You hear me?'

'We're talking here. Don't interrupt us again,' Sampson said. 'You hear *me*?'

'You're a big load, aren't you? Think you're a real tough guy?' the front man asked.

Sampson broke into a slow smile that I'd seen before. 'Yeah, I do. He's a tough guy, too.'

The muscular blond tried to shove Sampson off his stool. John didn't budge. One of the blond's buddies came at me. I moved quickly and he swung and missed. I hit him hard in the gut and he went down on all fours.

Suddenly, all three men were on us. 'Your asshole friend's a killer,' the blond yelled. 'He killed women!'

Sampson hit him on the chin and he sunk down on one knee. Unfortunately, these guys didn't stay down once

they were hit. Another bruiser joined in and that made four against two.

A shrill whistle sounded inside the bar. I whirled around and looked toward the door. The military police had arrived. So had a couple of eager-looking deputies from the Fayetteville police. They all had batons at the ready. I wondered how they'd gotten here so fast.

They waded in and arrested everybody involved in the bar fight, including Sampson and me. They weren't interested in who'd started it. Our heads bowed, we were escorted out in handcuffs to a black-and-white and shoved down into the squad car.

'First time for everything,' Sampson said.

Chapter Twenty-Six

We didn't need this crap – not now, especially. We were taken out to the Cumberland County Jail in a small, blue bus that sat ten. Apparently there were only a couple of cells at the jail in Fayetteville. At no time were we offered any professional courtesy because we were homicide detectives from Washington, who just happened to be working on behalf of Sergeant Ellis Cooper.

In case you're ever looking for it, the booking facility at the County Jail is located in the basement. It took about half an hour for the local police to do our paperwork, fingerprints, and take our photographs. We were given a cold shower, then 'put in the pumpkin patch'. That was the guards' clever way of describing the orange jumpsuit and slippers prisoners were made to wear.

I asked what had happened to the four soldiers who'd attacked us and was told it was none of my goddamn business, but that they'd been 'transported to the stockade at Bragg'.

Sampson and I were put in a misdemeanor block in a

dormitory cell, which was also in the basement. It was built for maybe a dozen prisoners, but there were close to twenty of us crowded in there that night. None of the prisoners were white and I wondered if the jail had other holding cells, and if they were segregated, too.

Some of the men seemed to know each other from previous nights they had spent here. It was a civil enough group. Nobody wanted to mess with Sampson, or even me. A guard walked by on checks twice an hour. I knew the basic drill. The prisoners were in charge the other fifty-eight minutes an hour.

'Cigarette?' a guy to my right asked. He was sitting on the floor with his back against a pitted concrete wall.

'Don't smoke,' I said to him.

'You're the detective, right?' he asked after a couple of minutes.

I nodded and looked at him more closely. I didn't think I'd met him, but it was a small town. We had shown our faces around. By this time a lot of people in Fayetteville knew who we were.

'Strange shit going down,' the man said. He took out a pack of Camels. Grinned. Tapped one out. 'Today's Army, man. "An army of one." What kind of bullshit is that?'

'You Army?' I asked. 'I thought they took you guys to the stockade at Fort Bragg.'

He smiled at me. 'Ain't no stockade at Bragg, man. Tell you something else. I was in here when they brought Sergeant Cooper in. He was nuts that night. They printed him down here, then took him *upstairs*. Man was a psycho killer for sure that night.'

I just listened. I was trying to figure out who the man was, and why he was talking to me about Ellis Cooper.

'I'm going to tell you something for your own good. Everybody around here knows he did those women. He was a well-known freak.'

The man blew out concentrated rings of smoke, then he pushed himself off the floor and shuffled away. I wondered what in hell was going on. Had somebody arranged the fight at the bar? The whole thing tonight? Who was the guy who had come over to talk to me? To give me advice *for my own good*?

A short while later, a guard came and took him away. He glanced my way as he was leaving. Then Sampson and I got to spend the night in the crowded, foul-smelling holding cell. We took turns sleeping.

In the morning, I heard someone call our names.

'Cross. Sampson.' One of the guards had opened the door to the holding cell. He was trying to wave away the stink. 'Cross. Sampson.'

Sampson and I pushed ourselves stiffly up off the floor. 'Right here. Where you left us last night,' I said.

We were led back upstairs and taken to the front lobby, where we got the day's very first surprise. Captain Jacobs from CID was waiting there. 'You all sleep well?' he asked.

'That was a setup,' I said to him. 'The fight, the arrest. Did you know about it beforehand?'

'You can go now,' he said. 'That's what you should do. Get your stuff and go home, Detectives. Do yourselves a big favor while you still can. You're wasting time on a dead man's errands.'

Chapter Twenty-Seven

The awful strangeness and frustration continued the day I got back to Washington. If anything, it got even worse. An e-mail was waiting for me in my office at home. The message was from someone who identified himself as 'Foot Soldier'. Everything about it was troubling and impossible for me to comprehend at this point.

It began: *For Detective Alex Cross,*

Your general interest: The Pentagon is currently taking steps to prevent some of the more than one thousand deaths each year in the 'peacetime Army'. The deaths come from car crashes, suicides and murders. In each of the past three years, at least eighty Army soldiers have been murdered.

Specifics to think about, Detective: An Army pilot named Thomas Hoff stationed at Fort Drum near Watertown, New York, was convicted of the slaying of a homosexual enlisted man on post. The convicted man claimed his innocence right up until the moment of his execution. In his defense, Hoff wasn't actually stationed at Drum until three months after the murder was committed. He had visited a friend at Hood prior to the murder, however. His prints were found at the murder scene. Hoff's service record was clean before his conviction for murder. He had been a 'model soldier' until the supposed murder.

Another case for your consideration, Detective. An Army barber, known by his friends as 'Bangs', was convicted of murdering three prostitutes outside Fort Campbell in Kentucky. Santo Marinacci had no criminal record before the killings. His pregnant wife testified that he was home with her on the night of the murders. Marinacci was convicted because of fingerprints and DNA found at the murder scene, and also because the murder weapon, a survival knife, was discovered in his garage. Marinacci swore the knife was planted there. 'For God's sake, he's a barber,' his wife called out during the eventual execution of her husband. Santo Marinacci claimed he was innocent and had been framed up to the moment that he died.

Foot Soldier

I read Foot Soldier's e-mail over again, then I called Sampson at home. I read him the message. He didn't know what to make of it either. He said he'd contact Ellis Cooper as soon as he hung up with me. We both wondered if Cooper might be behind the strange note.

For the rest of the day, I couldn't get the disturbing message out of my head. Information had been passed to me that someone thought was important. No conclusions were reached. Foot Soldier had left that up to me. What was I supposed to make of the murders at Fort Drum and Fort Campbell? The possible frame-up?

That night I took a break for a few hours. I watched

Damon's basketball team play a league game at St Anthony's. Damon scored sixteen points, and he was as smooth an outside shooter as some high school kids. I think he knew it, but he wanted to hear my opinion of his play.

'You had a real good game, Damon,' I told him. 'Scored points, but didn't forget about the rest of your team. Played tough "d" on Number Eleven.'

Damon grinned, even though he tried to hold it back. I had given the right answer. 'Yeah, he's the high scorer in the league. But not tonight.'

After we talked, Damon took off with some of his team-mates, Ramon, Ervin, Kenyon. That was a new one, but I knew I better get used to it.

When I got home, I couldn't stop thinking about Ellis Cooper and the e-mail that had come for me about other murders by Army personnel. According to Sampson, Cooper swore he didn't have anything to do with it. Who then? Someone at Fort Bragg? A friend of Cooper's?

That night in bed I couldn't stop thinking about the damn note.

Innocent men might have been executed.
Sergeant Cooper wasn't the first.
This has happened before.
Who the hell was Foot Soldier?

Chapter Twenty-Eight

I desperately needed to see someone at the Army Court of Criminal Appeals, and the FBI helped me get an appointment with the right person.

The court and its administrative offices were located in a bland-looking commercial building in Arlington. It was considerably nicer inside the building, kind of like a dignified and reserved corporate legal office. Other than the fact that most of the men and women wore uniforms, the normal touches of military culture weren't much in evidence.

Sampson and I were there to see Lt General Shelly Borislow, and we were brought to her office by an aide. It was a lengthy walk – lots of long hallways, typical of government buildings all over the Washington area.

General Borislow was waiting for us when we finally arrived. She stood ramrod straight, and was obviously physically fit. A handsome woman, probably in her late forties.

'Thanks for seeing us,' Sampson said, and shook

General Borislow's hand. I had the feeling that he wanted to handle the meeting, maybe because he had more experience with the Army than I did, but possibly because Ellis Cooper's time was running out.

'I read the transcript of the trial last night,' General Borislow said as we sat around a glass-topped coffee table. 'I also went through the CID notes from Captain Jacobs. And Sergeant Cooper's records. I'm pretty much up to speed. Now, what can I do for you, gentlemen?' I was pleased that the general was the one to bring up gender.

'I have some questions. If you don't mind, General?' Sampson said. He leaned forward so that his elbows rested on his thighs. His eyes were steady on General Borislow, who was just as focused on Sampson.

'Ask any questions you wish. I don't have another meeting until ten. That gives us about twenty minutes to talk, but you can have more time if you need it. The Army has nothing to hide in this matter, I can tell you that much.'

Sampson still held Borislow's eyes. 'Detective Cross and I have worked hundreds of homicide scenes, General. Some things about this one bother us a lot.'

'What, specifically?'

Sampson hesitated, then he went on. 'Before I get into what bothers us, I was wondering if anything about the trial or the investigation bothered you?'

General Shelly Borislow stayed in perfect control. 'A few things, actually. I suppose it could be construed as a little too pat that Sergeant Cooper held on to the murder weapon. It was a valuable souvenir, though, from his years in Vietnam. And a souvenir from the murders themselves.'

'You're aware that Sergeant Cooper's apartment was broken into a day or two before the murders? We saw signs of the break-in and Cooper confirmed it. The knife could have been taken then,' Sampson said.

Borislow nodded. 'That's certainly possible, Detective. But isn't it also possible that the sergeant created the impression that there had been a break-in at his apartment? That's what CID concluded.'

'A boy from the neighborhood saw three men in Tanya Jackson's yard around the time of the murders.'

'The boy could have seen men in the yard. That's true. He also may have seen shadows from trees. It was a dark night, and windy. The boy is ten years old. He gave conflicting accounts of the night to police officers. As I said, Detective, I studied the case thoroughly.'

'Blood that didn't match the murdered women's, or Sergeant Cooper's, was found at the homicide scene.'

General Borislow's demeanor didn't change. 'The judge in the case made the call not to allow that into evidence. If I had been the judge, I would have permitted the jury to hear about the blood. We'll never know about it now.'

'Sergeant Cooper's military record before the murders was nearly perfect,' said Sampson.

'He had an excellent record. The Army is well aware of that. It's one of the things that makes this such a tragedy.'

Sampson sighed. He sensed he wasn't getting anywhere. I did too. 'General, one more question and then we'll leave. We won't even take our allotted time.'

Borislow didn't blink. 'Go ahead with your question.'

'It puzzles me that the Army made no real effort to come to Sergeant Cooper's defense. Not before or during the trial. Obviously, the Army isn't going to try and help him now. Why is that?'

General Borislow nodded at the question, and pursed her lips before she answered it. 'Detective Sampson, we appreciate the fact that Ellis Cooper is your friend, and that you've remained loyal to him. We admire that, actually. But your question is easy to answer. The Army, from top to bottom, believes that Sergeant Cooper is guilty of three horrific, cold-blooded murders. We have no intention of helping a murderer go free. I'm afraid that I'm convinced Cooper is a murderer too. I won't be supporting an appeal. I'm sorry that I don't have better news for you.'

After our meeting, Sampson and I were escorted back through the labyrinth of hallways by General Borislow's aide. We were both silent as we walked the long walk to the main lobby.

Once we had left the building and gone outside, he turned to me. 'What do you think?'

'I think the Army is hiding something,' I said. 'And we don't have much time to find out what it is.'

Chapter Twenty-Nine

The following morning, Thomas Starkey got a clear picture of just how far things had gone for him. The clarifying incident took place less than two miles from his house in North Carolina.

He had stopped at the local strip mall for copies of *USA Today* and the *Rocky Mount Telegram*, plus some raisin cinnamon bagels from the NY Style deli. It was raining hard that morning and he stood with the newspapers and warm bagels under the overhang at the mall, waiting for the downpour to slow.

When it finally did, he started to wade through deep puddles toward his Suburban. As he did so, he spotted a couple sloshing toward him across the parking lot. They had just gotten out of an old blue pickup and they'd left the headlights on.

'Hi, excuse me. Left your lights on,' Starkey called as they came forward. The woman turned to look. The man didn't. Instead, he started to talk, and it was clear he had a speech impediment. 'Wir frum San Cros head'n La'nce.

Forgath muh wuhlet n'mah pantz . . .'

The woman cut in. 'I'm awful sorry to bother you. We're from Sandy Cross goin' to Laurence,' she said. 'So embarrassing. My brother left his wallet in his other pants. We don't even have money for gas to get back home.'

'Kin you hep's?' asked the sputtering male.

Starkey got the whole thing immediately. They'd left the goddamn truck lights on so he could be the one to make the first verbal contact, not them. The man's speech impediment was a fake and that's what really did it to him. His son Hank was autistic. Now these two shitheels were using a fake handicap as part of their cheap con to get money.

Swiftly, Starkey had his handgun out. He wasn't sure himself what was going to happen next. All he knew was that he was really pissed off. Jesus, he was steamed.

'Get on your knees, both of you,' he yelled, and thrust the gun into the male's unshaven, miserable excuse for a face. 'Now you apologize, and you better talk right or I'll shoot you dead in this fucking parking lot.'

He struck the kneeling man in the forehead with the barrel of his gun.

'Jesus, I'm sorry. We're both sorry, mister. We jus' wanted a few bucks. Don't shoot! Please don't shoot us. We're good Christians.'

'You both stay on your goddamn knees,' Starkey said. 'You stay right there, and I don't want to see you around here again. Ever, *ever*.'

He put his gun back in his jacket as he stomped off toward his car. He got to the Suburban and thanked God his teenage daughter was listening to rock music and not watching what was going on in the parking lot. Melanie was off in her own little world as usual.

'Let's skedaddle home,' Starkey said as he scrunched down into the front seat. 'And Mel, could you turn that damn music *up*?'

That was when his daughter looked up and spotted the couple kneeling in the lot. 'What's the matter with those two?' she asked her father. 'They're like, *kneeling* in the rain.'

Starkey finally managed a thin smile. 'Guess they just been saved, and now they're thanking the Lord,' he said.

Chapter Thirty

On a cold day in early October, Sampson and I made the six-hour trip by car back to Central Prison in Raleigh. We talked very little on the ride down. The clock had run out on Ellis Cooper.

Two days earlier, Cooper had been officially informed of his execution date by North Carolina's Department of Corrections. Then he had been moved to the prison's death watch area. Things were proceeding in an orderly, and deadly fashion.

Sampson and I had been authorized by the Division of Prisons to visit Sergeant Cooper. When we arrived at Central Prison, about a dozen protesters were out in the parking areas. Most were women and they sang gentle folk songs that harked back to the Sixties or even earlier. Three or four held up signs condemning capital punishment.

We hurried inside the prison and could still hear the mournful hymns beyond the heavy stone and mortar walls.

The death watch area at Central had four cells lined up side by side and opened to a day room with a TV and shower. Ellis Cooper was the only prisoner on death watch at that time. Two corrections officers were stationed outside his cell twenty-four hours a day. They were respectful and courteous when we arrived.

Ellis Cooper looked up as we entered the area and seemed glad to see us. He smiled and raised his hand in greeting.

'Hello, Ellis,' Sampson said in a quiet voice as we took chairs outside the cell. 'Well, we're back. Empty-handed, but we're back.'

Cooper sat on a small stool on the other side of the bars. The legs of the stool were screwed into the floor. The cell itself was immaculately clean, and sparsely furnished with a bed, sink, toilet and a wall-mounted writing table. The scene was depressing and desperate.

'Thank you for coming, John and Alex. Thanks for everything that you've done for me.'

'Tried to do,' said Sampson. 'Tried and failed. Fucked up is all we did.'

Cooper shook his head. 'Just wasn't in the cards this time. Deck was stacked against us. Not your fault. Not anybody's,' he muttered. 'Anyway, it's good to see the two of you. I was praying you'd come. Yeah, I'm praying now.'

Sampson and I knew that vigorous legal efforts were still proceeding to try to stop the execution, but there didn't seem much reason to talk about it. Not unless Cooper chose to bring it up, and he didn't. He seemed strangely at peace to me, the most relaxed I'd seen him.

His salt-and-pepper hair was cut short and his prison coveralls were neat and looked freshly pressed.

He smiled again. 'Like a nice hotel in here, y'know. *Luxury* hotel. Four stars, five diamonds, whatever signifies the finest. These two gentlemen take good care of me. Best I could expect under the circumstances. They think I'm guilty of the three murders, but they're pleasant all the same.'

Then Cooper leaned into the steel bars and got as close as he could to Sampson. 'This is important for me to say, John. I know you did your best, and I hope you know that too. But like I said, the deck against me was stacked so goddamn high. I don't know who wanted me to die, but somebody sure did.'

He looked directly at Sampson. 'John, I have no reason in the world to lie to you. Not now, not here on death watch. I didn't murder those women.'

Chapter Thirty-One

Twenty-four hours earlier, Sampson and I had signed an agreement to be searched before we entered the execution room. Now, at one o'clock in the morning, sixteen men and three women were led into the small viewing room inside the prison. One of the men was General Stephen Bowen from Bragg. He'd kept his promise to be there. The US Army's only representative.

At twenty minutes past one in the morning, the black drapes to the execution chamber were opened for the witnesses. I didn't want to be there; I didn't need to see another execution to know how I felt about them. On the order of the prison warden, the lethal injection executioner approached Cooper. I heard Sampson take in a breath beside me. I couldn't imagine what it would be like for him to watch his friend die like this.

The movement of the technician seemed to startle Ellis Cooper. He turned his head and looked into the viewing room for the first time. The warden asked him if he'd like to make a statement.

Cooper's eyes found us and he held contact. It was incredibly powerful, as if he were about to lose us as he fell into the deepest chasm.

Then Ellis Cooper spoke. His voice was reedy at first, but it got stronger.

'I *did not* murder Tanya Jackson, Barbara Green or Maureen Bruno. I would say so if I did, take this final injection like the man I was trained to be. I didn't kill the three women outside Fort Bragg. Someone else did. God bless you all. Thank you, John and Alex. I forgive the United States Army, which has been a good father to me.'

Ellis Cooper held his head up. Proudly. Like a soldier on parade.

The executioner stepped forward. He injected a dose of Pavulon, a total muscle relaxer which would stop Cooper's breathing.

Very soon Ellis Cooper's heart, lungs and brain stopped functioning.

Sergeant Cooper was pronounced dead by the warden of Central Prison at 1:31 A.M.

Sampson turned to me when it was over. 'We just watched a murder,' he said. 'Someone murdered Ellis Cooper, and they got away with it.'

PART TWO

JAMILLA

Chapter Thirty-Two

I was early to meet the flight coming into Gate 74 at Reagan International, and once I was at the airport I didn't know what to do with myself. I was definitely nervous, *good* nervous, with anticipation. Jamilla Hughes was coming to visit.

The airport was crowded at around four on a Friday afternoon. Lots of weary, edgy business-people sitting around ending their workweeks on the computer, or already off the clock at the bar, or reading magazines and popular novels that ranged from Jonathan Frantzen to Nora Roberts to Stephen King. I sat down, then popped up again. Finally I walked close to the large, expansive windows and watched a big American jet slowly taxi to the gate. *Well, here we go. Am I ready? Is she?*

Jamilla was in the second wave of passengers getting off the plane. She had on jeans, a mauve top, and a black leather car jacket that I remembered from our stakeouts together in New Orleans. The two of us had become fast friends on a bizarre homicide case that had started in her

hometown of San Francisco, weaved its way through the South, including the Big Easy, then ended up on the West Coast again.

We had been talking about seeing each other ever since, and now we were actually doing it. It was pretty courageous on both of our parts; I just hoped it wasn't dumb. I didn't think so, and I hoped Jam felt the same way.

Jesus, I was twitching as she came walking up to me. She looked great, though. Nice, big smile. What was I so worried about?

'Where are the thick white clouds that are supposed to be covering the city as my plane approached? God, I could see *everything* – the White House, Lincoln Memorial, the Potomac,' Jamilla grinned as she spoke.

I leaned in and gave her a kiss. 'Not every city has mountains of fog like San Francisco. You need to travel more. Your flight okay?'

'Sucked,' Jamilla grinned again. 'I don't like flying much these days, but I'm glad to be here. This is *good*, Alex. You're almost as nervous as I am. We never had trouble talking on stakeouts. We'll be fine. We'll be just fine. Now calm down, so I can calm down. Deal?' She grabbed me in both arms, hugged me, then kissed me lightly, but nicely, on the lips. 'That's much better,' she said, and smacked her lips. 'You taste good.'

'You must like spearmint.'

'No, I like you.'

We were a whole lot more comfortable during the ride into Washington in my old Porsche. We talked about everything that had been happening since we'd last seen each other. At first, it was work stuff, but then we got into the whole terrorist mess, then how my family was, and hers, and as usual neither of us shut up once we got started – which I love.

It was only as I pulled up to the house that things began to feel tense for me again. 'You ready for this?' I asked before we got out of the car.

Jamilla rolled her eyes. 'Alex, I have four sisters and three brothers back in Oakland. Are you ready for *that*?'

'Bring them on,' I said as I grabbed hold of her black leather duffel bag, which obviously held a bowling ball, and headed toward the house. I was holding my breath a little, but I was definitely glad that she was here. I hadn't been this excited in a long time.

'I missed you,' I said.

'Yeah, me too,' said Jam.

Chapter Thirty-Three

Nana had obviously been thinking about the appropriate welcoming dinner for a while. Jamilla offered to help, and of course Nana refused to let her so much as lift a little finger. So Jam trailed her into the kitchen anyway.

The rest of us followed to see what would happen next. Two immovable forces. This was high drama.

'Well all right then, all right,' Nana complained some, but I could tell she was pleased with the company. It allowed her to show off her wares, put us all to work, and test Jamilla at her leisure. She even managed to hum a little of 'Lift Every Voice and Sing' while she worked. And then, so did Jamilla.

'You okay with pork chops in apple gravy, squash casserole, over-creamed potatoes? And you're not allergic to a little cornbread, are you? Or fresh peach cobbler and ice cream?' Nana asked several loaded questions at once.

'Love the pork chops, potatoes, peach cobbler,' Jamilla said as she examined the food. 'Neutral on squash casserole. I make creamed cornbread at home. *My* grandma from Sacramento's recipe. You add creamed corn which makes it extra moist. Sometimes I throw in pork rinds, too.'

'Hmm,' Nana said. 'That sounds pretty good, girl. I'll have to try it.'

'If it ain't broke . . .' Jannie decided to contribute.

'Keep your small mind open,' said Nana, and wagged a crooked pinkie finger at Jannie. 'That's if you ever want it to grow bigger, and don't want to remain a small person all your life.'

'I was just defending your cornbread, Nana,' said Jannie.

Nana winked. 'I can take care of myself.'

Dinner was served in the dining room, with Usher, Yolanda Adams and Etta James on the CD player. So far, this was pretty good. Just what the doctor ordered.

'We eat like this every night,' Damon said. 'Sometimes, we even have breakfast out here in the formal dining room,' he told Jamilla. I could tell he already had a little crush on her. Hard not to, I suppose.

'Of course you do, like when the President stops over for tea,' Jamilla said and winked at Damon, then at Jannie.

'He comes here often,' Damon nodded. 'How did you know? My dad tell you?'

'Think I saw it on CNN. We get that on the West Coast, you know. We all have TVs out by our hot tubs.'

Dinner and the small talk were a success – at least I thought so.

The laughter was constant, and mostly relaxed. Little Alex sat in his highchair grinning the whole time. At one point Jamilla pulled Damon out of his seat and they danced a few steps to Aretha's 'Who's Zoomin' Who?'.

Nana finally rose from the table and proclaimed, 'I absolutely forbid you to help with the dishes, Jamilla. Alex can pitch in. That's his job.'

'C'mon, then,' Jamilla said to Jannie and Damon. 'Let's go out front and trade gossip about your daddy. And your Nana! You have questions, I have questions. Let's swap spit. You too, little man,' she said to Alex Jr. 'You're excused from kitchen detail.'

I followed Nana out to the kitchen with about half of the dirty dinnerware stacked in my hands and arms.

'She's pleasant,' Nana said before we got there. 'She's certainly full of life.' Then she started to cackle like one of those pesky crows in the old-time cartoons.

'What's so funny, old woman?' I asked. 'You're really getting a big kick out of yourself, aren't you?'

'I am. Why wouldn't I? You're just dying on the vine to know what I think. Well, surprise, surprise. She's a real sweetheart. I'll give you that, Alex, you pick nice girl-friends. She's a good one.'

'No pressure,' I warned her as I set dirty dishes in the sink and turned on the hot water.

'Why would I do that? I've learned my lesson with you.' Then Nana started to laugh again. She seemed more like her old self. She'd gotten a clean bill of health from her doctor, or so she said.

I went back to the dining room to clear away the rest of the dishes, but I couldn't resist taking a quick peek out the front window to check on Jamilla and the kids.

They were out in the street, tossing around Damon's football. The three of them were laughing. I also noticed that Jamilla had a real good arm, threw a tight, little spiral. She was used to playing with the boys.

Chapter Thirty-Four

Jamilla was staying in the bedroom at the top of the stairs, the room we always kept for special guests – presidents, queens, prime ministers and the like. The kids thought we were doing it for appearances, and we would have, but the unvarnished truth was that Jam and I had never been together that way, never even kissed before the airport reunion. Jamilla was here to find out if things should go any further between the two of us.

She came in through the back door of the kitchen while I was finishing up the dishes. The kids were still playing outside and Nana was straightening up God knows what upstairs. Probably the guest room, but maybe the hall bathroom. Or the linen closet?

'I can't stand it,' I finally said.

'What?' she asked. 'What's wrong?'

'You really want to know?'

'Of course I do. We're buddies, right?'

I didn't answer, but I grabbed hold of Jamilla's shoulders and kissed her on the mouth. Then I kissed her again. I was keeping an eye peeled for the kids.

And Nana, of course.

And Rosie our cat, who is a big gossip too.

Jamilla started to laugh. 'They all think we're doing a lot worse than this – the kids, your grandmother, even that nosey cat.'

'Thinking is different to knowing,' I said.

'I like your family a lot,' Jamilla said as she stared into my eyes. 'I even like the cat. Hiya there, Rosie. You gonna tell everybody about our kisses?'

'I like you,' I said as I held Jamilla in my arms.

'A lot?' she asked as she pulled away. 'You better like me a lot after I came all the way here from San Francisco. God, I hate plane rides these days!'

'Maybe I do like you a lot. I don't see you saying too much. Not a lot of reciprocation going on here.'

She grabbed me again and kissed me harder. She pressed into me and then she slid her tongue into my mouth. I liked that – a lot. I was starting to respond in kind, which probably wasn't a fantastic idea in the kitchen.

'Get a room,' we heard a voice behind us.

Nana was there, but she was laughing. 'Let me call in the kids. I want them to see this too,' she said. 'Let me get my Instamatic camera.'

'She's fooling with us,' I told Jam.

'I know,' she said.

'Heck I am,' said Nana. 'I'm rooting for Alex to get to third base.' She was cackling like a cartoon crow again.

Chapter Thirty-Five

I woke up alone in bed the next morning with the sheets thrown every which way around my body. I was kind of used to the feeling, but I didn't like it anymore than I ever had, especially with Jamilla sleeping just down the hallway in the spare bedroom. I hoped she was okay with how things were going and didn't want to go back to San Francisco already.

I lay in bed for a few minutes, thinking about other people who wake up feeling alone, even though some of them do share a bed with somebody else. Finally, I slid into some loose-fitting clothes, then tiptoed down the hall to check on Jamilla.

I tapped lightly on the door.

'I'm awake. Come in,' I heard her say.

It was a nice sound, her voice – musical, sweet. I pushed against the door and it opened with a soft whine.

'Morning, Alex. I slept great,' Jamilla said. She was sitting up in bed, wearing a white tee-shirt with SFPD printed on it in black. She started to laugh. 'Sexy, huh?'

'Actually, yeah. Detectives can be sexy. Samuel T. Jackson in *Shaft*, Pam Grier in *Foxy Brown*. Jamilla Hughes in the guest bedroom.'

She whispered, 'Come over here, you. Just for a minute. Come *here*, Alex. That's an order.'

I came forward and Jamilla reached out her arms. I slid into them like I belonged there. Kind of nice. 'Where were you when I needed you last night?' I asked her.

'I was right here in the guest room,' she smiled, and winked. 'Listen, I don't want your kids to get the wrong idea either. But.'

I cocked an eyebrow. 'But?' I asked. 'But what?'

'Just but. I'll leave the rest up to you.'

As we were finishing breakfast – in the kitchen, without the cloth napkins – I told Nana and the kids that Jamilla and I were going to tour Washington for the rest of the day. We needed a little time to ourselves. The kids just nodded over their cereal bowls; they'd been expecting as much.

'I won't expect you two home for supper then,' Nana said. 'Is that right?'

'That's right,' I said. 'We'll catch a meal in town.'

'Uh huh,' Nana said.

'Uh huh,' said the kids.

I drove about four miles from the house on Fifth. I pulled into 2020 O Street and stopped the car. Some people might have trouble finding the place, or even any information about the Mansion on O Street. There's no sign hanging outside, no indication that it isn't a private residence. Most guests come to the Mansion because of word of mouth. I happen to know the owner through friends at Kinkead's restaurant in Foggy Bottom.

Jamilla and I went inside, where I registered, and then we were brought upstairs to the Log Cabin room. Along the way, just about every surface, corner, cranny and crevice was filled with antique puppets, lithographs, jewelry in glass cases. We took it all in. Silently.

A strange thing happened to me on our way upstairs. I had the thought, *here I go again*. It almost caused me to stop walking and head back to the car. But something inside told me not to give up, not to shut feelings out, to put my trust in Jamilla.

Neither of us said a word until the bellman was gone.

Chapter Thirty-Six

'**W**ow, I could get used to this in a hurry,' Jamilla whispered when we were alone in the room. 'Let's explore this place. It's beautiful, perfect, Alex. Almost too nice.'

And so we explored.

The Log Cabin room was an amazing two stories that even included a sauna-Jacuzzi. The loft was reached by spiral stairs and had a full kitchen. The walls and floors were wood-paneled to suggest the simply hewn tongue-and-groove design of a cabin. A rough-cut, stone-framed fireplace was there to keep everything cozy. There was also an aquarium.

Jamilla did a quick, gleeful dance. She obviously approved, and so did I, mainly because she was happy. It sure was a whole lot better than the front seats of cars where we'd spent so many hours together during surveillance details in New Orleans.

As we checked out the suite, we explored each other a little, too. We stopped to kiss and I discovered once again that Jamilla had the sweetest-tasting mouth. We held each other and danced in place. We kissed some more and my head began to feel light. I was still nervous, and I couldn't quite figure out why.

Jamilla slowly unbuttoned my denim shirt and I helped her loosen and then slip out of a cream-colored silk blouse. Under her shirt, she wore a plain, thin, silver chain. Very simple and lovely.

Her hands gently unfastened my belt, then loosened my pants. I helped her out of her leather ones. 'Such a gentleman,' she said. Somewhere along the way I kicked off my shoes and she did the same with her sandals.

Which finally, somehow, brought the two of us to the centerpiece of the suite – a king-size bed.

'I like this,' she whispered against my cheek. 'Nicest bed I ever saw.'

The bed was definitely the visual focus of the room. It had four wooden columns suggesting a canopy bed, but without the frills. It was covered with a flannelly comforter and half a dozen throw pillows, which we immediately tossed onto the floor. The room looked even better a little messed-up.

'Music?' Jamilla asked.

'Be nice,' I said. 'You pick something.'

She switched on the CD player and found WPFW, 89.3. Nina Simone's 'Wild Is The Wind' was playing.

'Our song. From now on,' she said.

Jamilla and I kissed again and her mouth was soft. I was happy to see that the homicide inspector had a gentle side. Her lips continued to press into mine and I felt myself melting. Maybe that was why I was afraid. *Here I go again.*

'I'd never hurt you,' she whispered, as if she knew my thoughts. 'You don't have to be afraid. Just don't hurt me, Alex.'

'I won't.'

A few minutes later, we were dancing to 'Just The Two Of Us' and I folded Jam in real close. This was good.

She was strong, but she knew how to be tender. *Another detective. How about that?* We moved well together. My lips brushed the tops of her shoulders, then the hollow in her throat, and just lingered.

'Bite me there. Just a little,' she whispered.

I nipped her gently, slowly. I didn't want to hurry any of this. The first time with someone wasn't like any other. Not always the best, but always different, exciting, mysterious. Jamilla reminded me of my dead wife Maria, and I thought that was a good thing. She was tough on the outside, a city girl, but she could be tender and sweet. The contrast was special, and dramatic enough to give me goosebumps.

I could feel her breasts touch my chest, then her whole body was pressing into me. Our kisses became deeper and more passionate, and lasted longer.

I undid her bra and it slipped to the floor. Then I slid off her panties and she pulled down my shorts.

We stood there and looked at each other for a long time, appraising, admiring I guess, building up anticipation and passion and whatever else was going on between us. I wanted Jamilla badly now, but I waited. *We* waited.

'Disappointed?' she whispered, so low I almost couldn't hear what she said.

Her question threw me a little. 'God no. Why should I be? Who could be disappointed with you?'

She didn't say anything, but I thought I knew who she was thinking about. Her ex-husband had said things that had hurt her. I pulled Jamilla to me and her body felt hot all over. She was trembling. We slid down on the bed and she rolled on top of me. She kissed my cheeks, then my lips. 'You sure you're not disappointed?'

'Definitely not disappointed,' I said. 'You're beautiful, Jamilla.'

'In your eyes.'

'Okay. In my eyes, you're beautiful.'

I raised my head to her breasts and she lowered herself to me. I kissed one, then the other, playing no favorites. Her breasts were small, just right. In my eyes. I continued to be amazed that Jamilla didn't seem to know that she was attractive. I knew it was a terrible thing that happened to some women, and some men, too.

I lay my head down and looked at her face, studied it some. I kissed her nose, her cheeks.

She was smiling in a way I'd never seen before. Open and relaxed, beginning to trust, which I loved to see. I felt that I could stare into her deep brown eyes forever.

I eased myself inside Jamilla, and I had a thought that this was just about perfect. I had been right to trust her. Then I had another thought that I hated – *what will spoil it this time?*

Chapter Thirty-Seven

Jamilla started to laugh and then she said, 'Phew.' She ran her hand past her forehead.

'What's "phew"?' I asked her. 'Don't tell me you're tuckered out? You look in a lot better shape than that.'

'*Phew*. I was worried about the two of us being together, and now I'm not worried. *Phew*, sometimes men are really self-centered or rough in bed. Or it just feels all wrong.'

I smiled at her. 'Slept with a lot of men, huh?'

Jamilla made a little face. Cute. 'I'm thirty-six years old. I was married for four years, engaged another time. I date some. Not too much lately, but some. How about you? Was I your first?'

'Why? Did it seem like it?'

'Answer the question, smart guy.'

'I was married once, too,' I finally said.

Jamilla lightly punched my shoulder, then she rolled over on top of me. 'I'm really glad I came to Washington. Took a little nerve on my part. I was definitely scared.'

'*Oohh*, Inspector Jamilla Hughes was scared. Well, so was I,' I admitted.

'How come? What scared you about me, Alex?'

'Some women are so self-centered. Or rough in bed—'

Jamilla leaned over and kissed me – a long, lingering kiss – probably to shut me up. I was ready again, and so was she. Jamilla pulled me close and I moved inside her. This time I was on top.

'I am your love slave. Completely submissive,' she whispered against my cheek. 'I'm definitely glad I came to Washington.'

Our second time together was even better than the first, and also edged out the third time. *No, there had been nothing for either of us to be afraid of.*

Jamilla and I stayed at the hotel through the afternoon and into the early evening. It was almost impossible to leave. As it had been right from the start with the two of us, we found it easy to talk about anything on the planet.

'I'll tell you something really strange,' she said. 'And the more I'm with you, the stranger this seems to me. See, my first husband and I could never really talk. Not the way you and I do. And we still got married. I don't know what I was thinking.'

A little while later, Jamilla got up and disappeared into the bathroom. I saw the light go on the telephone on the night stand. She was making a call.

Once a detective . . . oh boy. Here we go.

When she came out, she confessed, 'I had to call work. Murder case I'm on out there is a mess. Nasty stuff. Sorry, sorry. Won't happen again. I promise. I'll be good. Or bad.

Whatever you want me to be.'

'No, no, it's fine. I understand,' I said. I did, of course. Sort of, anyway. I saw so much of myself in Jamilla. The detective! I *think* that was a good thing.

I hugged her and held her close once she got back into bed. Then the truth finally came out. It was my turn to confess. 'Long time ago,' I told her, 'I was at this hotel with my wife.'

Jamilla pulled back a little. She looked deeply into my eyes. 'That's okay,' she said. 'Doesn't mean anything. Except I really love that you were guilty about it. That's nice. I'll always remember that about my trip to Washington.'

'Your first trip,' I said.

'My first trip,' Jamilla agreed.

Chapter Thirty-Eight

O ur time together in Washington raced by like a couple of blinks of the eye, and before I knew it Jamilla had to go back to San Francisco. Sunday afternoon at a very crowded Reagan International. Fortunately, my badge got me out to the gate area. I was bummed to see her leave, and I didn't think she wanted to go, actually. The two of us hugged for a long time at the gate and we didn't much care if anyone was staring.

Then Jam had to run to her plane or miss it.

'Why don't you just stay another night?' I asked. 'Lots of planes tomorrow. And the next day. Day after that.'

'I really, *really* liked this,' she said as she pulled away from me and started to back-pedal. 'Bye, Alex. Please miss me. I liked Washington more than I thought I would.'

A flight attendant followed her in and closed the door between us. Jeez, I even liked the way Jamilla ran. She glided. And I did miss her already. I was starting to fall again and that scared me.

That night at home I was up long after midnight. At one

particularly low point I went out to the sun porch and sat at the piano playing a pretty pathetic 'Someone To Watch Over Me', thinking about Jamilla Hughes, romanticizing like hell, loving every painful second of it.

I wondered what was going to happen to the two of us. Then I remembered something Sampson had once said. *Don't ever be Alex's girlfriend. It's dangerous.* Unfortunately, he had been right so far.

A few minutes later, I became aware of banging on the screen door out front. I went around and found Sampson leaning against the doorjamb. He didn't look real good. Actually, he looked awful.

Chapter Thirty-Nine

He was unshaven, his clothes wrinkled, his eyes red and swollen. I had the feeling he'd been drinking. Then I opened the door and smelled liquor all over him, as if he'd taken a bath in the stuff.

'Figured you'd be up,' he slurred out a few words. 'Knew you would be.'

Yeah, he'd been drinking – a lot. I hadn't seen John like this in a long time, maybe ever. He didn't look real happy either.

'C'mon inside,' I said. 'C'mon John.'

'Don't need to go anywhere,' he said loudly. 'Don't need any more help from you. You helped enough, man.'

'What the hell is wrong with you?' I said, and tried to guide him inside the house again.

He shook loose, his long, powerful arms flailing. *'What did I say? I don't need your help!'* he yelled at me. 'You already fucked up enough. The great Dr Cross! Yeah, right. Not this time. Not for Ellis Cooper.'

I took a step back away from him. 'Keep your voice

down. Everybody's sleeping inside. You hear me?'

'Don't tell me what the hell to do. Don't you fucking dare,' he snarled. 'You fucked up. We fucked up, but you're supposed to be so smart.'

Finally I told Sampson, 'Go home and sleep it off.' I shut the door on him. But he pulled it open again, almost took the damn thing off its hinges.

'Don't walk away from me either!' he yelled.

Then he shoved me hard. I let it go, but Sampson pushed again. That was when I lunged at him. I'd had enough of his drunken shit. The two of us tumbled down the wood steps and onto the lawn. We wrestled on the ground and then he tried to throw a punch. I blocked it. Thank God he was too messed-up to throw a straight punch.

'You fucked up, Alex. You let Cooper die!' he yelled in my face as we both struggled to our feet.

I refused to hit him, but he struck out at me again. The punch connected with my cheek. I went down as if I didn't have any legs. I sat there, stunned, my eyes glazing over.

Sampson pulled me up, and by this time he was gasping and wheezing. He tried for a headlock. Christ, he was strong. He connected with a short, hard punch to the side of my face. I went down again but struggled back up. We were both groaning. I hurt where he'd hit me on the point of my cheekbone.

He threw a roadhouse punch that missed by an inch. Then a hard blow caught my shoulder and made it ache. I warned myself to stay away from him. He had me by four inches and forty pounds. He was drunk, angry, insane as I'd ever seen him.

But he wouldn't stop coming at me. Sampson was filled with rage. I had to take him down if I could. Somehow. But how?

Finally I hit him with an uppercut to the stomach. I jabbed his cheek. Drew blood. Then I fired a short right hand into his jaw. That one had to hurt.

'Stop it! Stop it right now! Both of you, stop!'

I heard the voice ringing in my ear. 'Alex! John! Stop this disgraceful behavior. Stop it, you two. Just *stop* it!'

Nana was pulling the two of us apart. She was wedged in between us like a small but determined referee. She'd done it before, but not since I was twelve years old.

Sampson straightened up and looked down at Nana. 'Sorry,' he mumbled. 'I'm sorry, Nana.' He looked ashamed.

Then he stumbled away without saying a word to me.

Chapter Forty

I came down to breakfast the next morning at a little before six. Sampson was sitting there eating eggs and his personal favorite, *farina*. Nana Mama was across from him at the table. Just like old times.

They were talking quietly, as if sharing a deep secret that no one else should know.

'Am I interrupting?' I asked from the doorway.

'I think we have it sorted out now,' Nana said.

She motioned for me to come sit at the breakfast table. I poured coffee first, popped in four slices of whole-wheat toast, and then finally sat across from Nana and Sampson.

He had a big glass of milk propped in front of him. I couldn't help remembering back to when we were kids. Two or three mornings a week he'd show up at around this time to break bread with Nana and me. Where else could he go? His mom was a junkie. In a way, Nana had always been like a mother or grandmother to him too. He and I had been like brothers since we were ten. That's why the fight the night before was so disturbing.

'Let me talk, Nana,' he said.

She nodded and sipped her tea. I'm pretty sure why I chose psychology for a career, and who my original role model was. Nana has always been the best shrink I've seen. She's wise, and compassionate for the most part, but tough enough to insist on the truth. She also knows how to listen.

'I'm sorry, Alex. I didn't sleep last night. I feel awful about what happened. I was way over the line,' Sampson said. He was staring into my eyes, forcing himself not to look away.

Nana watched the two of us as if we were Cain and Abel sitting at her breakfast table.

'You were over the line all right,' I said. 'That's for sure. You were also crazy last night. How much did you drink before you came over?'

'John told you he was sorry,' Nana said.

'Nana,' he turned to her, then back to me. 'Ellis Cooper was like a brother to me. I can't get over the execution, Alex. In a way, I'm sorry I went to see it. He didn't kill those women. I thought we could save him, so it's my fault. I expected too much.'

He stopped talking.

'So did I,' I said. 'I'm sorry we failed. Let me show you something. Come upstairs. This is about payback now. There's nothing left but payback.'

I brought Sampson to my office in the attic of the house. I had notes on Army murder cases pinned all over the walls. The room looked like the hideout of a madman, one of my obsessive killers. I took him to my desk.

'I've been working on these notes since I met Ellis Cooper. I found two more of these remarkable cases. One in New Jersey, the other in Arizona. The bodies were *painted*, John.'

I took Sampson through the cases, sharing everything. 'During the past year more than sixty soldiers have been murdered.' I finished up.

'Sixty?' Sampson said, and shook his head. 'Sixty murders a year?'

'Most of the violence has to do with sex and hate crimes,' I said. 'Rapes and murders. Homosexuals who've been beaten or killed. A series of vicious rapes by an Army sergeant in Kosovo. He didn't think he'd get caught because there was so much rape and killing going on there anyway.'

'Were any other bodies painted?' he wanted to know.

I shook my head. 'Just the two cases I found, New Jersey and Arizona. But that's enough. It's a pattern.'

'So what do we really have?' Sampson shook his head and looked at me.

'I don't know yet. It's hard to get information out of the Army. Something very nasty going on. It looks like soldiers may have been framed for murders. The first was in New Jersey, the latest seems to be Ellis Cooper. There are definite similarities, John. Murder weapons found a little too conveniently. Fingerprints and DNA used to convict.

'All of these men had good service records. In the Arizona murder-case transcripts, there was a mention of "two or three men" seen near the victim's house before the homicide took place. There's a possibility that innocent men have been framed and then wrongfully put to death. Framed, then wrongfully executed. And I know something else,' I said.

'What's that?'

'These killers aren't brilliant like Gary Soneji or Kyle Craig. But they're every bit as deadly. They're expert at what they do, and what they do is kill and get away with it.'

Sampson frowned and shook his head. 'Not anymore.'

Chapter Forty-One

Thomas Starkey had been born in Rocky Mount, North Carolina, and he still loved the area passionately. So did most of his neighbors. He'd been away for long stretches while he was in the Army, but now he was back to stay, and to raise his family as best he possibly could. He knew that Rocky Mount was a great place to bring up kids. Hell, he'd been brought up here, hadn't he?

Starkey was devoted to his family, and he genuinely liked the families of his two best friends. He also needed to control everything around him.

Just about every Saturday night, Starkey got the three clans together and they barbecued. The exception was the football season, when the families usually had a tailgate party on Friday night. Starkey's son Shane played tailback for the high school. North Carolina, Wisconsin and Georgia Tech were after Shane, but Starkey wanted him to put in a tour with the Army before he attended college. That's what *he* had done, and it had worked out for the best. It would work for Shane, too.

The three men usually did all the shopping and cooking for the Saturday night barbecues and the tailgate parties. They bought steaks, ribs, hot and sweet sausages at the farmers' market. They selected corn on the cob, squash, tomatoes, asparagus. They even made the salads, usually German potato, coleslaw, macaroni and, occasionally, Caesars.

That Friday was no exception, and by seven-thirty the men were in their familiar positions beside two Weber grills, staying downwind from the wafting smoke, drinking beer, cooking every meal 'to order'. Hell, they even cleaned up and did the dishes. They were proud to deliver the food just right, and to get pretty much the same kind of applause given to their sons on football nights.

Starkey's number two, Brownley Harris, tended to intellectualize. He'd attended Wake Forest and then gone to grad school at UNC. 'The irony is pretty thick here, don't you think?' he asked as he gazed at the family scene.

'Fuck all, Brownie, you'd see irony in a turkey shoot, or a clusterfuck in a rice paddy. You think too goddamn much,' Warren Griffin said, and rolled his eyes. 'That's your problem in life.'

'Maybe you just don't think enough,' Harris said, then winked at Starkey, who he considered a god. 'We're going off to kill somebody this weekend, and here we are calmly barbecuing thick sirloin steaks for our families. You don't think that's a little strange?'

'I think you're fucking strange is what I think. We've got a job to do, so we do it. No different than the way it was for a dozen years in the Big Army. We did a job in

Vietnam, in the Persian Gulf, Panama, Rwanda. It's a job. Of course – I happen to love my job. Might be some irony in that. I'm a family man and a professional killer. So what of it? Shit happens, it surely does. Blame the US Army, not me.'

Starkey nodded his head toward the house, a two-story with five bedrooms and two baths he'd built in 1999. 'Girls are coming,' he said. 'Put a lid on it.

'Hey, beautiful,' he called, then gave his wife, Judie, a big hug. Judie 'Blue Eyes' was a tall, attractive brunette who still looked almost as good as she had on the day they were married. Like most of the women in town, she spoke with a pronounced Southern accent, and she liked to smile a lot. Judie even did volunteer work three days a week at the playhouse. She was funny, appreciative, a good lover, and a good life partner. Starkey believed he was lucky to have found her, and she was lucky to have chosen him. All three of the men loved their wives, up to a point. Hell, that was another juicy irony for Brownley Harris to ponder late into the night.

'We must be doing something right,' Starkey said as he held Judie in his arms and toasted the other couples.

'You sure did,' Judie 'Blue Eyes' said. 'You boys married well. Who else would let their husbands sneak off for a weekend every month or so, and trust that they were being good boys out there in the big, bad world?'

'We're always good. Nobody does it better,' Starkey said, and smiled good-naturedly at his closest friends in the world. 'It doesn't get any better than this. It really doesn't. We're the best there is.'

Chapter Forty-Two

On Saturday night the three killers made their way north to a small town in Virginia called Harpers Ferry. During the road trip, Brownley Harris's job was to study maps of the AT, as the Appalachian Trail was called by many of the people who hiked it regularly. The spot where they were headed was a particularly popular place for hikers to stop.

Harpers Ferry was tiny, actually. You could walk from one end of town to the other in less than fifteen minutes. There was a point of tourist interest nearby called Jefferson Rock, where you could see Maryland, Virginia, and West Virginia. Kind of neat.

Starkey drove for the entire trip, no need for any relief. He liked to be at the wheel and in control anyway. He was also in charge of entertainment, which consisted of his *Best of Springsteen* tape, a Janis Joplin, a Doors, a Jimi Hendrix anthology, and a Dale Brown audiobook.

Warren Griffin spent almost the entire trip checking the team's supplies and readying the rucksacks in back. When he was finished, the packs weighed around forty pounds, a little more than half of what they used to carry on their re-con missions in Vietnam and Cambodia.

He had prepared the packs for a 'hunt and kill', the kind of ambush Colonel Starkey had planned for the Appalachian Trail. Griffin had packed standard-issue canteens; LRPs – meals which were pronounced 'lurps'; hot sauce to kill the taste of the LRPs; a tin can for coffee. Each of them would have a K-Bar, the standard military combat knife; cammo sticks, with two colors of greasepaint; boony hats; poncho liners that could do double duty as ground cover; night-vision goggles; Glocks as well as an M-16 rifle fitted with a sniper scope. When he was finished with the work, Griffin uttered one of his favorite lines, 'If you want to get a good belly laugh out of God, just tell Him about your plans.'

Starkey was the TL, or Team Leader. He was in control of every aspect of the job.

Harris was the Point Man.

Griffin was Rear Security, still the junior guy after all these years.

They didn't have to do the 'hunt and kill' exactly like this. They could have made it a whole lot easier on themselves. But this was the way Starkey liked it, the way they had always committed their murders. It was 'the Army way'.

Chapter Forty-Three

They made camp about two clicks from the AT. It was dangerous for them to be seen by anybody so Starkey established an NDP, a Night Defense Position, for the camp. Then they each kept watch in two-hour shifts. *Nostalgia rules.*

When Starkey took his shift, he passed the time thinking not so much about the job looming ahead of them, but the job in general. He, Harris and Griffin were professional killers and had been for over twenty years. They'd been assassins in Vietnam, Panama, the Gulf War, and now they were assassins for hire. They were careful, discreet and expensive. The current job was their most lucrative and involved several murders over a period of two years. The curious thing about it was they didn't know the identity of their employer. They were given new targets only after the previous job was completed.

As he stared into the dark, restless woods, Starkey wanted a cigarette, but he settled for an Altoids. Those little fuckers kept you awake. He found himself thinking about the blonde bitch they had offed near Fayetteville, pretty Vanessa. The memory got him hard and that helped the time pass. While they were still in Vietnam, Starkey had discovered that he liked to kill. The murders gave him a powerful feeling of control and elation. It was like electricity was passing through his body. He never felt guilt, not anymore. He killed for hire; but he also killed in between jobs, because he wanted to, and liked it.

'Strange, scary stuff,' Starkey muttered as he rubbed his hands together. 'Scare myself sometimes.'

The three of them were up and ready by five the next morning, which was shrouded in a thick, bluish-gray fog. The air was cool, but incredibly fresh and clean. Starkey figured the fog wouldn't burn off until at least ten.

Harris was in the best physical shape of the three, so he was designated as the scout. He wanted the job anyway. At fifty-one, he still played in a men's basketball league and did triathlons twice a year.

At 5:15 he set off from camp at a comfortable jogging pace. Christ, he loved this shit.

Nostalgia.

Harris found that he was wide awake and alert once he was on the move. He was operating beautifully after just a few minutes on the trail. The hunt and kill was a satisfying combination of business and pleasure for him, for all three of them.

Harris was the only person around this early on the AT, at least this particular stretch of it. He passed a four-person dome tent. Probably some white-bread family. Most likely 'section hikers' as opposed to 'through hikers' who would take up to six months to do the entire trail, finally ending at a place called Katahdin, Maine. Around the dome tent he noticed a camp stove and fuel bottles, ratty shorts and tee-shirts laid out to air. *Not a target*, he decided, and moved on.

Next, he came upon a couple in sleeping bags laid just off the trail. They were young, probably 'go see the world' types. They slept on inflatable air mattresses. All the comforts of home.

Harris got up close, no more than ten yards from them, before he finally decided to move on. He could tell the girl was a looker, though. Blonde, cute face, maybe twenty. Just watching her sleep with her boyfriend got his jets going pretty good. They were a definite maybe.

He saw a second couple already up and exercising near their tent about a quarter mile farther on. They had high-tech internal frame packs, $200 hiking boots, and looked like snooty city slicks. He liked them as potential targets, mainly because he *disliked* them so much immediately.

Not far past the couple's camp, he came upon a single male hiker. This guy was definitely in for the long haul. He had a high-tech pack which looked light and tight. He would probably be carrying dried food, trail mix, protein drink powder – fresh food was too heavy and difficult to haul around on your back all day. His wardrobe would be no frills too – nylon shorts, tank tops, maybe long underwear for the cold nights.

Harris stopped and watched the single hiker's camp for a couple of minutes. He let his heartbeat slow and controlled his breathing. Finally, he slipped right into the man's camp. He wasn't afraid, and he never doubted himself. He took what he needed. The hiker never stirred from his sleep.

Harris checked his sports watch and saw it was only 5:50. So far, so good. He walked back to the trail, then he began to jog again. He felt invigorated, excited about the hunt and kill out here on the nature trail. Man, he wanted to kill somebody bad. Man or woman, old or young, it didn't much matter.

The next camp he came upon was close – another couple, still asleep in a two-person dome tent. Harris couldn't help thinking how easy it would be to take them out right now. Ducks on a pond. Everybody was so vulnerable and trusting out here. What a bunch of loonies. Didn't they ever read the funny papers? There were killers on the loose in America, lots of them.

A little less than a mile beyond, he reached the camp of another family. Someone was already up.

He hid in the pine trees and watched. A fire had been started and was throwing up sparks. A woman of about forty was futzing around with a rucksack. She wore a red Speedo swimsuit and seemed in good physical shape – well-muscled arms and legs; a nice ass, too. She called out, 'Wakee, wakee!'

Moments later, two shapely teenage girls emerged from the larger tent. They had on one-piece bathing suits, and they were slapping their lithe bodies with their arms and hands, trying to get warm in a hurry, trying to 'wakee, wakee'.

'Mama bear and two baby bears,' Brownley Harris

muttered. 'Interesting concept.' Maybe too close to the murders at Bragg, though.

He watched as the three women huddled for a moment around the fire, then took off at a run. Soon he could hear a chorus of war whoops and screams, then laughter and loud splashes as they hit the small brook that ran directly behind their camp.

Brownley Harris moved quickly and silently through the trees until he reached a choice point where he could watch the mother and her pretty daughters frolic in the cold stream. They sure reminded him of the women in the massacre in Fayetteville, outside Fort Bragg. Still, they could be the secondary target.

He returned to his camp at a little past six-thirty. Griffin had prepared breakfast: eggs, bacon, plenty of coffee. Starkey was sitting in a familiar lotus position, thinking and plotting. He opened his eyes before Harris announced himself. 'How'd you do?' he asked.

Brownley Harris smiled. 'We're right on schedule, Colonel. We're good. I'll describe the targets while we eat. Coffee smells good. Hell of a lot better than napalm in the morning.'

Chapter Forty-Four

S tarkey took full command that morning. Unlike the other hikers on the AT, he kept his men deep in the woods, unseen by their fellow travelers or anyone else.

It wasn't hard to do. In their past lives they'd spent days, sometimes weeks, being invisible to enemies who were out to find and kill them, but who frequently ended up getting killed themselves. One time it had been a team of four homicide detectives in Tampa, Florida.

Starkey demanded that they treat this like a real-life combat mission, in real-life war. Total silence was imperative. They used hand signals most of the time. If someone had to cough, he did so in his neck rag, or in the crook of an arm. Their rucksacks had been packed tight by Sergeant Griffin so that nothing shook or rattled as they walked.

The three of them had slathered on bug juice, then laid on the cammo. They didn't smoke a cigarette all day.

No mistakes.

Starkey figured that the kill would take place some-where between Harpers Ferry and an area known as Lowdown Heights. Parts of the trail were densely forested there, an endless green tunnel that would be good for their purposes. The trees were mostly deciduous, leafy, no conifers. A lot of rhododendron and mountain laurel. They noticed everything.

They didn't actually make camp that night, and were careful not to leave evidence that they had been in the woods at all.

Brownley Harris was sent on another scouting mission at seven-thirty, just before it got dark. When he returned, the sun was gone and darkness had fallen like a shroud over the AT. The woods had a kind of jungle feel, but it was only an illusion. A state road ran about half a mile from where they were standing.

Harris reported in to Starkey. 'Target One is approx-imately two clicks ahead of us. Target Two is less than three. Everything's still looking good for us. I'm pumped.'

'You're always ready for a hunt and kill,' said Starkey. 'But you're right, everything's working for us. Especially this friendly, trust-your-neighbor mindset all these rec-reational hikers have.'

Starkey made the command decision. 'We'll move to a point midway between Targets One and Two. We'll wait there. And remember, let's not get sloppy. We've been too good for too long to blow it all up now.'

Chapter Forty-Five

A three-quarter moon made the going easier through the woods. Starkey had known about the moon beforehand. He wasn't just a control freak; he was obsessive about details because getting them wrong could get you killed, or caught. He *knew* they could expect mild temperatures, low wind and no rain. Rain would mean mud, and mud would mean a lot of footprints, and footprints would be unacceptable on their mission.

They didn't speak as they moved through the woods. Maybe it wasn't necessary to be so cautious out here, but it was habit, the way they had been conditioned for combat. A simple rule had always been drummed into them: *remember how you were trained, and don't ever try to be a hero.* Besides, the discipline helped them to concentrate. Their focus was on the killings that would soon take place.

The three men were in their own private worlds as they walked: Harris fantasized about the actual kills with real-life faces and bodies; Starkey and Griffin stayed very real time, and yet they hoped that Harris wasn't pulling their chain with his description of the targets. Starkey remembered one time Brownley had reported the prey was a Vietnamese schoolgirl, whom he went on to describe in elaborate detail. But when they got to the kill zone, a small village in the An Lao Valley, they found an obese woman well into her seventies, with black warts all over her body.

Their reveries were cut short by a male voice piercing the air.

Starkey's hand flew up in warning.

'Hey! Hey! What's going on? Who's out there?' the voice called. 'Who's there?'

The three of them stopped in their tracks. Harris and Griffin looked at Starkey, who kept his right arm raised. No one answered the unexpected voice.

'Cynthia? Is that you, sweetie? Not funny if it is.'

Male. Young. Obviously agitated.

Then a bright yellow light flashed in their direction, and Starkey walked forward in its path. 'Hey,' was all he said.

'What the hell? You guys Army?' the voice asked next. 'What are you doing out here? You training? On the Appalachian Trail?'

Starkey finally flicked on his Maglite flashlight. It lit up a white male in his early twenties, khaki walking shorts down around his ankles, a thick roll of toilet paper in one hand. Skinny kid. Longish black hair. A day's growth on his face. Not a threat.

'We're on maneuvers. Sorry to barge in on you like this,' Starkey said to the young man squatting before him. He chuckled lightly, then turned to Harris. 'Who the hell is he?' he whispered.

'Couple Number Three. Shit. They must have fallen behind Target Two.'

'All right then. Change of plan,' Starkey said. 'I'll take care of this.'

'Yes, sir.'

Starkey felt a coldness in his chest and knew that the others probably did too. It happened in combat, especially when things went wrong. The senses became heightened. He was acutely aware of everything going on, even at the periphery of his eyesight. His heartbeat was strong, even, steady. He loved these intense feelings, just before it happened.

'Can I get a little privacy here?' the shitter asked. 'You guys mind?'

A brighter light suddenly flashed on – Brownley Harris was shooting another video movie.

'Hey, is that a fucking camera?'

'Sure is,' Starkey said. He was on top of the crouching, shitting man before he knew what was happening. He picked the victim up by his long hair and slit his throat with the K-Bar.

'What's the woman like?' Griffin turned to Harris, who was still shooting with the hand-held camera.

'Don't know, you horny bastard. The girlfriend was sleeping this morning. Never saw her.'

'Boyfriend wasn't bad-looking,' said Griffin. 'So I'm hopeful about the chick. Guess we'll soon find out.'

Chapter Forty-Six

S ampson and I were riding on I-95 again, heading toward Harpers Ferry, Virginia. There had been a brutal double murder on the Appalachian Trail near there. So far, it didn't make sense to the FBI or the local police. But it made perfect sense to us. *The three killers had been there.*

We hadn't had this much time to talk in a long while. For the first hour we were cops discussing the murder victims, two hikers on the AT, and any possible connection to Ellis Cooper or the victims in Arizona and New Jersey. We had read the investigating detective's notes. The descriptions were bleak and horrific. A young couple in their twenties, a graphic artist and an architect, had had their throats slit. Innocents. No rhyme or reason for the murders. Both of the bodies had been marked with red paint, which was why I got the call from the FBI.

'Let's take a break from the mayhem for a while,' Sampson finally said. We had reached the halfway point of our ride south.

'Good idea. I need a break, too. We'll be knee-deep in the shit soon enough. What else is going on? You seeing anybody these days?' I asked him. 'Anybody serious? Anybody fun?'

'Tabitha,' he said. 'Cara, Natalie, LaTasha. You know Natalie. She's the lawyer with HUD. I hear your new girlfriend from San Francisco came to visit last weekend. *Inspector* Jamilla Hughes, *Homicide*.'

I laughed. 'Who told you about that?'

John furrowed his brow. 'Let's see. Nana told me. And Damon. And Jannie. Little Alex might have said something. You thinking about settling down again? I hear this Jamilla is something else. Is she too hot for you to handle?'

I continued to laugh. 'Lot of pressure, John. Everybody wants me to get hooked up again. Get over my unlucky recent past. Settle down to a nice life.'

'You're good at it. Good daddy, good husband. That's how people see you.'

'And you? What do you see?'

'I see all that good stuff. But I see the dark side, too. See, part of you wants to be old Cliff Huxtable. But another part is this big, bad, lone wolf. You talk about leaving the police department, maybe you will. But you like the hunt, Alex.'

I looked over at Sampson. 'Kyle Craig told me the same thing. Almost the same words.'

Sampson nodded. 'See? Kyle's no dummy. Sick, twisted bastard, but not dumb.'

'So, if I like the hunt so much, who's going to settle down first? You or me?'

'No contest. My role models on families are bad ones. You know that. Father left when I was three. Maybe he had his reasons. My mother was never around much. Too busy hooking, shooting up. They both knocked me around. Beat up on each other, too. My father broke my mother's nose three times.'

'Afraid you'll be a bad father?' I asked. 'Is that why you never settled down?'

He thought about it. 'Not really. I like kids fine. Especially when they're yours. I like women, too. Maybe that's the problem – I like women too much,' Sampson said, and laughed. 'And women seem to like me.'

'Sounds like you know who you are anyway.'

'Good deal. Self-knowledge is a start,' Sampson said, and grinned broadly. 'What do I owe you, Dr Cross?'

'Don't worry about it. I'll put it on your tab.'

I saw a road sign up ahead: Harpers Ferry, two miles. A man was being held there for murder.

A former Army colonel with no past record.

And currently a Baptist minister.

I wondered if anyone had seen three suspicious-looking men in the area of the murder? And if one of them had been filming what happened?

Chapter Forty-Seven

S ampson and I met with Reverend Reece Tate in a tiny room inside the modest jailhouse in Harpers Ferry. Tate was a slight, balding man with shaped sideburns down to the bottoms of his earlobes; he didn't look much like a former soldier. He had retired from the Army in 1993 and now headed a Baptist congregation in Cowpens, South Carolina.

'Reverend Tate, can you tell us what happened to you yesterday on the Appalachian Trail?' I asked him after identifying who we were. 'Tell us everything you can. We're here to listen to your story.'

Tate's suspicious eyes darted from Sampson to me. I doubt he was even aware of it, but he kept scratching his head and face as he looked around the small room. He also looked terribly confused. He was obviously nervous and scared and I couldn't blame him for that, especially if he'd been set up and framed for a double murder he didn't commit.

'Maybe you can answer a few of my questions first,' he

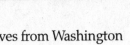

managed. 'What are homicide detectives from Washington DC doing here in Virginia? I don't understand that. Or anything else that's happened in the last two days.'

Sampson looked at me. He wanted me to explain. I began to tell Tate about our connection to Ellis Cooper and the murders that had taken place near Fort Bragg.

'You actually believe that Sergeant Cooper is innocent?' he asked when I was finished.

I nodded. 'Yes, we do. We think he was framed, set up. But we don't know the reason yet. We don't know why and we don't know who.'

Sampson had a question. 'You and Ellis Cooper ever meet while you were in the Army?'

Tate shook his head. 'I was never stationed at Bragg. I don't remember a Sergeant Cooper from 'Nam. No, I don't think so.'

I tried to remain low key. Reece Tate was an uptight, buttoned-down and formal man, so I kept our conversation as non-threatening as I possibly could.

'Reverend Tate, we've answered your questions. Why don't you answer a few of ours? If you're innocent of these murders, we're here to help you out of this mess. We'll listen, and we'll keep an open mind.'

He looked thoughtful for a moment before he spoke. 'Sergeant Cooper, he was judged guilty, I assume. Is he in prison? I'd like to talk with him.'

I looked at Sampson, then back at Reece Tate. 'Sergeant Cooper was executed in North Carolina recently. He's dead.'

Tate shook his head in a soft, low arc. 'My God, my God

in heaven. I was just taking a week off, giving myself a break. I love to camp and hike. It's a carryover from my days in the Army, but I always loved it. I was a Boy Scout, an Eagle Scout in Greensboro. Sounds kind of ridiculous, under the circumstances.'

I let him talk. The Eagle Scout in him wanted to, *needed* to get this out.

'I've been divorced for four years. Camping is my only decent escape, my release. I take off a couple of weeks a year, plus a few weekends when I can grab them.'

'Did anybody know you were planning this trip?'

'Everyone at our church knew. A couple of friends and neighbors. It wasn't any big secret. Why should it be?'

Sampson asked, 'Did your ex-wife know?'

Tate thought about it, then he shook his head. 'We don't communicate very much. I might as well tell you, I beat Helene up before we divorced. She may have driven me to it, but I hit her. It's on me, my fault. No excuse for a man to ever strike a woman.'

'Can you tell us about the day of the murders. Go through as much of what you did as you can remember,' I said.

It took Tate about ten minutes to take us through the day in detail. He said he woke up at about seven and saw that the morning was fogged in. He was in no hurry to get on the trail and so he had breakfast at camp. He started hiking by eight-thirty and covered a lot of ground that day. He passed two families and an elderly couple along the way. The day before, he'd seen a mother and her two daughters and hoped to catch up with them, but it didn't happen. Finally he made camp at around six.

'Why did you want to catch up with the three women?' Sampson asked.

Tate shrugged. 'Just crazy daydreams. The mother was attractive, early forties. Obviously, they all liked to hike. I thought maybe we could hike together for a while. That's pretty common on the AT.'

'Anybody else you saw that day?' Sampson asked.

'I don't remember anybody unusual. I'll keep thinking. I have the time in here. And the motivation.'

'All right, so there were the families, the elderly couple, the mother and her two daughters. Any other groups you saw on the trail? Males hiking together? Any single hikers?'

He shook his head. 'No, I don't remember seeing anybody suspicious. Didn't hear any unusual noises during the night. I slept well. That's one benefit of hiking. Got up the next morning, hit the road by seven-thirty. It was a beautiful day, clear as a bell and you could see for miles. The police came and arrested me around noon.'

Reverend Tate looked at me. His small eyes were pleading, searching for understanding. 'I swear, I'm innocent. I didn't hurt anybody in those woods. I don't know how I got blood on some of my clothes. I didn't even wear those clothes the day those poor people were murdered. I didn't kill anybody. Somebody has to believe me.'

His words chilled me through and through. Sergeant Ellis Cooper had said virtually the same thing.

Chapter Forty-Eight

M y *last case as a homicide detective. A real tricky one.* I'd been thinking about it pretty much non-stop for the past few days and it weighed on my mind during the numbing ride home from Harpers Ferry, Virginia.

I still hadn't given notice at work. Why not? I continued to take on homicide cases in DC, though most weren't challenging. A small-time drug dealer had been killed in the projects, but nobody cared. A twenty-year-old woman had killed her abusive husband, but it was clearly in self-defense. At least to me it was. Ellis Cooper was dead. And now a man named Reece Tate was accused of murders that he probably didn't commit.

That weekend I used air miles and took a flight out to Tempe, Arizona. I'd scheduled a meeting with Susan Etra, whose husband had been convicted of murdering two gay enlisted men. Mrs Etra was suing the Army for wrongful death. She believed her husband was innocent, and that she had enough evidence to prove it. I needed to find out if Lieutenant Colonel James Etra might have been framed for murder, too. How many victims were there?

Mrs Etra answered her front door and seemed very uptight and nervous. I was surprised to see a poker-faced man waiting in the living room. She explained that she had requested her lawyer be present. *Great*.

The lawyer was darkly tan, with slicked-back white hair, an expensive-looking charcoal-gray suit and black cowboy boots. He introduced himself as Stuart Fischer from Los Angeles. 'In the interest of possibly getting to the truth about her husband's wrongful arrest and conviction, Mrs Etra has consented to talk with you, Detective. I'm here to protect Mrs Etra.'

'I understand,' I said. 'Were you Lieutenant Colonel Etra's lawyer at his trial?' I asked.

Fischer kept his game face. 'No, I wasn't. I'm an entertainment attorney. I do have experience with homicide cases, though. I started in the DA's office in Laguna Beach. Six years down there.'

Fischer went on to explain that Mrs Etra had recently sold her husband's story to Hollywood. Now I was the one who had to be careful.

For a half-hour or so, Susan Etra told me what she knew. Her husband, Lieutenant Colonel Etra, had never been in any trouble before. As far as she knew he'd never been intolerant of gays, men or women. And yet he had supposedly gone to the home of two gay enlisted men and shot them dead in bed. At the murder trial, it was alleged that he was hopelessly in love with the younger of the two men.

'The murder weapon was an Army service revolver. It

was found in your home? It belonged to your husband?' I asked.

'Jim had noticed the revolver was missing a couple of days before the murder. He was very organized and meticulous, especially when it came to his guns. Then, suddenly, the gun was conveniently back in our house for the police to find.'

Lawyer Fischer apparently decided I was harmless enough and he left before I did. After he was gone, I asked Mrs Etra if I could take a look at her husband's belongings.

Mrs Etra said, 'You're lucky that Jim's things are even here. I can't tell you how many times I've thought about bringing his clothes to a local charity group like Goodwill. I moved them into a spare bedroom. Far as I've gotten.'

I followed her down the hall to a spare room. Then she left me alone. Everything was neat and in its place, and I had the impression that this was how Susan and James Etra had lived before murder and chaos destroyed their lives. The furniture was an odd mix of blond wood and darker antiques. A war table against one wall was covered with collectible pewter models of cannons, tanks and soldiers from various wars. Next to the models was a selection of guns in a locked display case. They were all labeled.

1860 Colt Army revolver, .44 caliber, 8-inch barrel.

Springfield Trapdoor rifle, cartridge, used in the US/Indian Wars. Has original bayonet and leather sling.

Marlin rifle, circa 1893, black powder only.

I opened the closet next. Lt Colonel Etra's clothes were

divided between his civvies and Army uniforms. I moved on, checking the various cabinets.

I was rummaging through the drawers of a highboy when I came upon the straw doll.

My stomach tightened. The creepy doll was the same kind I'd found at Ellis Cooper's place outside Fort Bragg. Exactly the same – as if they'd been bought at the same place. By the same person? *The killer?*

Then I found the watchful, lidless eye in another drawer. It seemed to be watching me. Vigilant, keeping its own nasty secrets.

I took a deep breath, then I went outside and asked Mrs Etra to come to the spare room. I showed her the straw doll and the all-seeing eye. She shook her head and swore she'd never seen either before. Her eyes revealed her confusion, and fear.

'*Who was in my house?* I'm sure that doll wasn't here when I moved Jim's things,' she insisted. 'I'm positive. How could they have gotten here? Who put those dreadful things in my house, Detective Cross?'

She let me take the doll and the eye. She didn't want them around, and I couldn't blame her.

Chapter Forty-Nine

M eanwhile, the murder investigation continued on another front. John Sampson turned his black Mercury Cougar off Route 35 in Mantoloking on the Jersey Shore and headed in the general direction of the ocean. Point Pleasant, Bay Head and Mantoloking were connecting beach communities and, since it was October, they were fairly deserted.

He parked on East Avenue and decided to stretch his legs after the drive up from Washington.

'Jesus, what a beach,' he muttered under his breath as he walked up a public access stairway and reached the crest of the dunes. The ocean was right there, less than forty yards away, if that.

The day was just about perfect. Low seventies, sunny, cloudless blue sky, the air unbelievably clear and clean. Actually, he thought, it was a better beach day than people got for most of the summer, when all these shore towns were probably jammed full of beachgoers and their transportation.

He liked the scene stretching out before him a lot. The quiet, pretty beach town made him feel relaxed. Hard to explain, but recently his days on the job in DC seemed tougher and more gruesome than usual. He was obsessing about Ellis Cooper's death, his *murder*. His head was in a real bad place lately. That wasn't true here, and it had happened instantly. He felt that he could hear and see things with unusual clarity.

He figured he better get to work, though. It was almost three-thirty, and he had promised to meet Billie Houston at her house at that time. Mrs Houston's husband had allegedly killed another soldier at nearby Fort Monmouth. The victim's face had been painted white and blue.

Let's do it, he told himself as he opened a slatted gate and walked toward a large, brown-shingled house on a path strewn with seashells. The beach house and the setting seemed too good to be true. He even liked the sign: *Paradise Found*.

Mrs Houston must have been watching for him from inside the beach house. As soon as his foot touched down on the stairs, the screen door swung open and she stepped outside to meet him.

She was a small African-American woman, and more attractive than he'd expected. Not movie-star beautiful, but there was something about her that drew his attention and held it. She was wearing baggy khaki shorts with a black tee-shirt, and was bare-footed.

'Well, you certainly picked a nice day for a visit,' she said, and smiled. Nice smile, too. She was tiny, though, probably only five feet tall, and he doubted that she weighed much more than a hundred pounds.

'Oh, it isn't like this every day?' Sampson asked, and managed a smile himself. He was still recovering from his surprise at Mrs Houston as he mounted her creaking, wooden porch steps.

'Actually,' she said, 'there are a lot of days like this one here. I'm Billie Houston. But of course you knew that.' She put out her hand. It was warm and soft in his, and so small.

He held her hand a little longer than he'd meant to. Now why had he done that? He supposed it was partly because of what she'd been through. Mrs Houston's husband had been executed nearly two years earlier, and she'd proclaimed his innocence loudly and clearly until the end, and then some. The story felt familiar. Or maybe it was because there was something about the woman's ready smile that made him feel comfortable. She impressed him about as much as the town and the fine weather had. He liked her immediately. Nothing not to like. Not so far anyway.

'Why don't we walk and talk on the beach,' she suggested. 'You might want to take off your shoes and socks first. You're a city boy, right?'

Chapter Fifty

Sampson did as he was told. No reason the murder investigation, this interview anyway, couldn't have a few nice perks. The sand felt warm and good against his bare feet as he followed her down the length of the big house, then up and over a tall, broad dune covered with white sand and waving beach grass.

'Your house is sure something else,' he said. 'Beautiful doesn't begin to do it justice.'

'I think so,' she said, and turned to look back at him with a smile. 'Of course, this isn't my house. My place is a couple of blocks inland. One of the small beach bungalows you passed driving in. I house-sit for the O'Briens while Robert and Kathy are in Fort Lauderdale for the winter.'

'That's not such bad duty,' he said. Actually, it sounded like a great deal to him.

'No, it's not bad at all.' She quickly changed the subject. 'You wanted to talk to me about my late husband, Detective. Do you want to tell me why you're here? I've been on pins and needles since you called. Why did you want to see me? What do you know about my husband's case?'

'Pins and needles?' Sampson asked. 'Who says pins and needles anymore?'

She laughed. 'I guess I do. It just came out. Dates and locates me, right? I grew up on a sharecropper's farm in Alabama, outside Montgomery. Not giving you the date. So *why* are you here, Detective?'

They had started down a sandy hill sloping toward the ocean which was all rich blues and greens and creamy foam. It was unbelievable – hardly a soul either way he looked up or down the shoreline. All of these gorgeous houses, practically mansions, and nobody around but the seagulls.

As they walked north he told Mrs Houston about his friend Ellis Cooper, and what had happened at Fort Bragg. He decided not to tell her about the other murders of military men.

'He must have been a very good friend,' she said when Sampson had finished talking. 'You're obviously not giving up easily.'

'I *can't* give up. He was one of the best friends I ever had. We spent three years in Vietnam together. He was the first older male in my life who wasn't just out for himself. You know, the father I never had.'

She nodded, but she didn't pry. Sampson liked that. He still couldn't get over how petite she was. He had the thought that he could have carried her around under his arm.

'The other thing is, Mrs Houston, I am totally convinced that Ellis Cooper was innocent of those murders. Call it sixth sense, or whatever, but I'm sure of it. He told me so just before they executed him. I can't get past that. I just can't.'

She sighed, and he could see the pain in her face. He could tell she hadn't gotten over her husband's death and how it had happened, but she still hadn't intruded on his story. That was interesting. She was obviously very considerate.

He stopped walking, and so did she.

'What's the matter?' she finally asked.

'You don't talk about yourself easily, do you?' he asked.

She laughed. 'Oh, I do. When I get going, I do. Too much sometimes, believe me. But I was interested in what you had to say, how you would say it. Do you want me to tell you about my husband now? What happened to him? Why I'm sure he was innocent, too?'

'I want to hear everything about your husband,' Sampson said. 'Please.'

'I believe Laurence was murdered,' she began. 'He was killed by the state of New Jersey. But somebody else wanted him dead. I want to know who murdered my husband, as much as you want to know who killed your friend, Ellis Cooper.'

Chapter Fifty-One

Sampson and Mrs Billie Houston stopped and sat in the sand in front of a sprawling ocean house that must have at least a dozen bedrooms. It was empty now, boarded up and shuttered, and that seemed such a monumental waste to Sampson. He knew people in DC who lived in abandoned tenements with no windows and no heat and no running water.

He couldn't peel his eyes away. The house was three stories high with wraparound decks on the upper two. A large sign posted on the dune near the house read: *These dunes are protected. Stay on walkway. $300 fine.* These people were serious about their property, or its beauty, or both, he thought to himself.

Billie Houston stared out at the ocean as she began to speak.

'Let me tell you about the night the murder happened,' she said. 'I was a nurse at the Community Medical Center in Tom's River. I got off my shift at eleven and arrived home at about half past. Laurence almost always waited

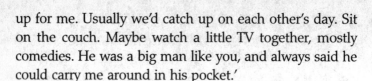

up for me. Usually we'd catch up on each other's day. Sit on the couch. Maybe watch a little TV together, mostly comedies. He was a big man like you, and always said he could carry me around in his pocket.'

Sampson didn't interrupt, just listened to her story take shape.

'What I remember the most about that night was that it was so *ordinary*, Detective. Laurence was watching *The Steve Harvey Show* and I leaned in and gave him a kiss. He sat me on his lap and we talked for a while. Then I went in to change out of my work clothes.

'When I came out from the bedroom, I poured myself a glass of Cabernet, and asked him if he wanted me to make popcorn. He didn't. He'd been watching his weight, which sometimes ballooned in the winter. He was in a playful mood, jokey, very relaxed. He wasn't tense, wasn't stressed in any way. I'll never forget that.

'The doorbell rang while I was pouring my glass of wine. I was up anyway, so I went to get it. The military police were there. They pushed past me into the house and arrested Laurence for committing a horrible murder that night, just a few hours earlier.

'I remember looking at my husband, and him looking at me. He shook his head in absolute amazement. No way he could have faked that look. Then he said to the police, "You officers are making a mistake. I'm a sergeant in the United States Army". That's when one of the cops knocked him down with his baton.'

Chapter Fifty-Two

I was trying to forget that I was on a case. Carrying around a nasty straw doll and lidless evil eye. In pursuit of killers. Relentless as I had ever been.

I walked into the lobby of the Wyndham Buttes Resort in Tempe and there was Jamilla. She had flown east from San Francisco to meet me. That had been our plan.

She was wearing an orange silk blouse with a deeper orange sweater around her shoulders, slender gold bracelets and tiny earrings. She looked just right for the 'valley of the sun', which is what I'd heard the metropolitan area of Phoenix, Scottsdale, Mesa, Chandler and Tempe was called.

'I suspect you already know this,' I said as I walked over and gave her a big hug, 'but you look absolutely beautiful. Took my breath away.'

'I did?' she asked, and seemed surprised. 'That's a nice way to start our weekend.'

'And I'm not the only one who thinks so. Everybody in the lobby is checking you out.'

She laughed. 'Now I know you're putting me on.'

Jamilla took my hand and we walked across the lobby. Suddenly, I stopped and spun her around into my arms. I looked at her face for a moment, then I gave her a kiss. It was long and sweet because I'd been saving it up on the drive over.

'You look pretty good yourself,' she said after the kiss. 'You always look good. Tell you a secret. The first time I saw you in San Francisco Airport you took *my* breath away.'

I laughed and rolled my eyes. 'Well we better take this upstairs, get a room, before we get in trouble down here.'

Jamilla leaned in and gave me another quick kiss. 'We could get in a whole lot of trouble.' And then another kiss. 'I don't do things like this, Alex. What's happening to me? *What* has come over me?'

One more hug and then we headed for the hotel elevators.

Our room was on the top floor with a view of the Phoenix skyline and a waterfall cascading into a mountainside swimming pool. In the distance, we could see jogging and hiking trails, tennis courts, and a golf course or two. I told Jamilla that a nearby football field we could see must be Sun Devil Stadium. 'I think Arizona State plays there.'

'I want to know all about Tempe and Arizona State football,' Jamilla said, 'but later on.'

'Oh, all right.'

I touched my fingers to her blouse, which was brushed silk. 'This feels nice.'

'It's supposed to.'

I slowly ran my hands over the shirt, Jamilla's shoulders, the tips of her breasts, her stomach. I massaged her shoulders and she leaned up against me and let out a long, 'Mmmm, yessssss, please and thank you.' It was like an impromptu dance, and neither of us knew exactly what was going to happen next. So nice to be back with her again.

'There's no hurry,' she whispered, 'is there?'

'No. We have all the time in the world. You know, this is called entrapment in police circles.'

'Yes, it is. I'm fully aware of that. It's also an ambush. Maybe you ought to just surrender.'

'All right, I surrender, Inspector.'

There was nothing except the two of us. I had no idea where this was going but I was learning to just go along, to enjoy each moment, not to worry too much about the destination.

'You have the softest touch of anyone,' she whispered. 'Unbelievable.'

'So do you.'

'You seem surprised.'

'A little bit,' I admitted. 'It's probably because I saw your tough-as-nails side when we were working together.'

'Is that a problem for you? My tough side?'

'No. It isn't,' I told her. 'I like your tough side. As long as you don't get too rough with me.'

Jam immediately pushed me back onto the bed, then fell on top of me. I kissed her cheeks, then her sweet lips. She smelled and tasted so good. I could feel the pulse under her skin. *There's no hurry*.

'I was a tomboy when I was a kid in Oakland. Baseball player, fast-pitch softball,' she said. 'I wanted my father and my brothers to approve of me.'

'Did they?'

'Oh yeah. Are you kidding? I was all-state in baseball and track.'

'Do they still approve?'

'I think so. Yeah, they do. My pop's a little disappointed I'm not playing for the Giants,' she said, and laughed. 'He thinks I could give Barry Bonds a run.'

Jamilla helped me with my pants while I unhooked her skirt. I shivered, couldn't control it. *All the time in the world*.

Chapter Fifty-Three

When his interview with Mrs Billie Houston was finished, it was too late for Sampson to head back to Washington, plus he liked the atmosphere at the shore, so he checked into Conover's Bay Head Inn, a bed and breakfast in town that Billie had recommended.

He had just stepped into his room on the third floor when the phone rang. He wondered who could be calling him here?

'Yeah?' he spoke into the receiver. 'John Sampson.'

There was a short silence.

'This is Billie. Mrs Houston.'

He sat down on the edge of the bed and found that he was surprised, but he was smiling. He definitely hadn't expected the call, hadn't expected to hear from her again. 'Well, hi. I haven't spoken to you . . . in minutes. Did you forget to tell me something?'

'No. Well, yes I did, actually. Here you are helping Laurence, and I do absolutely nothing to make your visit more comfortable. Would you have dinner at the house

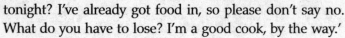

tonight? I've already got food in, so please don't say no. What do you have to lose? I'm a good cook, by the way.'

Sampson hesitated. He wasn't sure this was such a good idea. It wasn't that he thought dinner with Billie Houston would be a chore. It was just, well, a potentially uncomfortable situation, maybe a conflict of interest.

Still, the way she'd put it, what choice did he have? And what real harm could it do?

'That's a fine idea. I'd like to have dinner at the house. What time should I come by?'

'Whatever suits you is fine. It's nothing fancy, Detective. I'll start up the grill as soon as you arrive.'

'How about an hour? Is that all right? I'm John, by the way. Not Detective.'

'I think you told me that. You already know I'm Billie, and if you don't mind, I prefer that to Mrs Houston. I'll see you in about an hour.'

She hung up, and Sampson held onto the receiver for another few seconds. Now that he thought about it, dinner with Billie Houston didn't seem like a bad idea. He was looking forward to it as he stepped out of his clothes and headed for the shower.

Nothing fancy sounded pretty good.

Chapter Fifty-Four

S ampson picked up a small bouquet of flowers and a bottle of red at Central Market in Bay Head. As he got to the beach house, he wondered if he was overdoing it. *Flowers? Wine? What was going on here?*

Was he feeling guilty about the fact that this woman's husband might have been murdered? Or that she was a widow before her time? Or did it have something to do with Ellis Cooper? Or was this just about Billie Houston and himself?

He went round to the screen door that led into the kitchen of the beach house. He rapped his knuckles lightly on the wooden frame.

'Hi? Billie?' he called out.

Billie? Was that how he should be talking to her?

He had no idea why, but he was concerned for her safety. Yet no one would want to hurt Billie Houston now, would they? Still, he felt what he felt. The real killers were out there somewhere. Why not here in New Jersey?

'Door's open. C'mon in,' she called. 'I'm out on the porch.'

He came in through the kitchen and saw her setting a small dining table on the open front porch facing the ocean. Beautiful spot for dinner. Adirondack chairs, a wicker rocker painted navy blue to match the shutters.

He could see the ocean over the top of the dunes and the constantly waving sea grass.

But his eyes went back to her. She had on a crisp white shirt with faded Levi's, no shoes again. Her hair was clipped back in a ponytail. She'd put on a little lipstick, just a touch.

'Hi there. I thought that we'd eat out here. It's not too cold for you, is it?' she asked with a wink.

Sampson stepped out onto the spacious wood porch. The breeze was coming from inland, but it was comfortable outside. He could smell the ocean, but also sea lavender and asters in the air.

'It's just about perfect,' he said. That was true. The temperature was just right, as was the table she'd set, and the view of the ocean was definitely something else. There sure wasn't anything like this in Southeast DC.

'Let me do something to help,' he said.

'Good idea. You can chop vegetables and finish up the salad. Or you can cook on the grill.'

Sampson found himself smiling. 'Not much of a choice there. I'll do the salad. Nah, I'm kidding. I'd be happy to grill. Just so long as I don't have to wear a hat or apron with a snappy slogan on it.'

She laughed. 'Don't have any of those. You passed a CD player on your way from the kitchen. I left a bunch of CDs out. Pick what you like.'

'This a test?' he asked.

Billie laughed again. 'No, you already passed all your tests. That's why I asked you to supper. Stop worrying about me and you. We won't break. This is going to be fun. Better than you think.'

Chapter Fifty-Five

S he was right about the night being special. It embarrassed him, but he just about forgot Ellis Cooper for several hours. Sampson was usually quiet unless he knew somebody pretty well. Part of it was shyness, because he'd always been so tall and stood out in every social group. But he was honest enough with himself to know he didn't want to waste time on people who didn't mean anything to him, and never would.

Billie was different and he knew it, from the first time she spoke to him. The surprising thing about her was that he liked hearing her talk about anything. Her daily routine in Mantoloking; her two grown children – Andrew, a freshman at Rutgers, and Kari, a senior at Monmouth; the ocean tides and how they affected surf-casting for blues; a half dozen other things. In addition to the house-sitting, she still worked full-time as a nurse. She was in the Emergency Clinic and specialized in adult trauma. She'd flown in Med-Evac helicopters to the larger trauma units in Newark and

Philadelphia. Once upon a time, she'd even worked as a MASH unit nurse.

They didn't discuss her husband until after dinner. Sampson brought the subject up again. It had gotten cooler and they'd moved back into the living room. Billie started a fire, which was crackling and popping and warming things up inside.

'Do you mind if we talk about Laurence for a few more minutes?' he asked as they sat together on a small couch near the fire. 'We don't have to do this now if you don't want to.'

'No, it's okay. It's fine, really. That's why you came here.'

Suddenly, something caught Sampson's eye. He rose up from the couch and walked to a glass case near the fireplace. He reached inside and took out a straw doll.

Now this was definitely very strange. He examined it closely. He was sure it was a replica of the one he'd seen in Ellis Cooper's house. It scared him because it was in Billie's house. *What was the doll doing here?*

'What is it?' she asked. 'What is that creepy doll? I don't remember seeing it before. Is something wrong? You look so serious suddenly.'

'I saw this same doll at Ellis Cooper's house,' he admitted. 'It's from Vietnam. I saw lots of them in villages over there. Something about evil spirits and the dead. These dolls are bad medicine.'

She came over to the glass cabinet and stood beside him. 'May I see, please?' She examined the straw doll and shook her head. 'It looks like something Laurence might have brought home, I suppose. A souvenir.

Memento mori. I honestly don't remember ever seeing it, though. Isn't that strange. It reminds me – the other day I found a big, ugly eye in that same cabinet. It was so . . . *evil* I tossed it.'

Sampson held her gaze. 'Strange coincidence,' he said, shaking his head. He was thinking that Alex refused to believe in coincidences. 'As far as you remember, your husband never mentioned Sergeant Ellis Cooper?' he asked.

Billie shook her head. She seemed a little spooked now. 'No. He rarely talked about the war. He didn't like it when he was there. He liked it even less once he came back and had time to think about his combat experiences.'

'I can understand that. When I got back to DC I was stationed at Fort Myers in Arlington for a couple of months. I came home in my dress greens one Saturday. I got off a bus in downtown Washington. A white girl in bellbottom jeans and sandals came up and spat on my uniform. She called me a baby murderer. I'll never forget that for the rest of my life. I was so angry I turned and walked away as fast as I could. The hippie girl had no idea what happened over there, what it's like to get shot at, to lose friends, to fight for your country.'

Billie clasped her hands together and slowly rocked back and forth. 'I don't know what to tell you about Laurence. I think you probably would have liked him. Everybody did. He was very responsible, a good father to our children. He was a thoughtful, loving husband. Before he died, and I'm talking twenty minutes before he was executed, I sat with him in the prison. He stared into my eyes and said, "I did not kill that young man. Please make sure our kids know that. Make sure, Billie." '

'Yeah,' Sampson said. 'Ellis Cooper said something like that, too.'

It got quiet in the living room. A little uncomfortable for the first time.

Finally, Sampson was compelled to speak. 'I'm glad you called, Billie. Tonight was great for me. Thank you. I need to go now. It's getting late.'

She was standing beside him and she didn't move. Sampson leaned down and kissed her cheek. God, she was so tiny.

'You *do* think I'll break,' she said, but then she smiled. 'That's all right.'

She walked him out to his car. They felt compelled to talk again, mostly about the night sky over the ocean, how expansive and beautiful it was.

Sampson got into the Cougar and Billie started to walk back to the house. He watched her, and he felt sorry that the night was ending and he'd probably never see her again. He was also a little worried about her. How had the straw doll gotten into her house?

She stopped at the stairs to the house, one hand on the banister. Then, almost as if she'd forgotten something, she walked back to his car.

'I, uhm,' she said, then stopped. She seemed nervous for the first time since they'd met. Unsure of herself.

Sampson took her hands in his. 'I was wondering if I could have another cup of coffee,' he said.

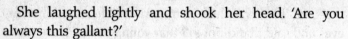
She laughed lightly and shook her head. 'Are you always this gallant?'

Sampson shrugged. 'No,' he said. 'I've never been this way in my whole life.'

'Well, c'mon back inside.'

Chapter Fifty-Six

It was almost midnight and Jamilla and I were up to our necks in the shimmering mountain pool that looked down on Phoenix in the distance and on the desert up closer. The sky over our heads seemed to go on forever. A big jet took off from Phoenix and all I could think of was the tragedy at the World Trade Center. I wondered if any of us would ever be able to look at a jet in the sky without having that thought.

'I don't want to get out of this water. Ever,' she said. 'I love it here. The desert sky goes on and on.'

I held her close to me, felt her strong heart beating against my chest. The night air was cool and it made being in the pool feel even better.

'I don't want to leave here either,' I whispered against her cheek.

'So why do we do what we do? Live in the big city? Hunt killers? Work long hours for low pay? Obsess on murders?'

I looked into her deep brown eyes. Those were good questions, ones I'd asked myself dozens of times, but especially during the past few months. 'It always seems like a good idea at the time. But not right now.'

'You think you can ever quit? Get past the adrenalin? The need to feel that what you do matters. I'm not sure that I can, Alex.'

I had told Jamilla that I was probably going to leave the police force in Washington. She nodded and said she understood, but I wondered if she really did. How many times had she faced down killers? Had any of her partners died?

'So,' she said, 'we've been beating all around it. What do you think about us, Alex? Is there hope for two cops off the beat?'

I smiled. 'I think we're doing great. Of course, that's just me.'

'I think I agree,' she smiled. 'Too early to tell for sure, right? But we're having fun, aren't we? I haven't thought about being a detective all day. That's a first.'

I kissed her lips. 'Neither have I. And don't knock fun. I could use a lot more of it in my life. This beats solving homicides.'

'Really, Alex?' She grinned and pulled me close against her. 'Is this good for you. Well, it's good for me, too. That's enough for right now. I love being here. I love tonight. And I trust you, Alex.'

I couldn't have agreed more.

At a little before midnight.

In the mountainside pool overlooking Phoenix and the sprawl of the desert.

'I trust you, too,' I said as the big American Airlines jet passed right over our heads.

PART THREE

THE FOOT SOLDIER

PART THREE

THE FOOT SOLDIER

Chapter Fifty-Seven

I got back to Washington on Sunday night at eleven. There was more of a bounce in my step and a smile plastered on my face. I'd forgotten about the rigors of the murder investigation for a couple of days and Jamilla was the reason why.

Nana was waiting up in the kitchen. What was this? She sat at the table without her usual cup of tea and with no book to read. When she saw me come in, she waved me over and gave me a hug. 'Hello, Alex. You have a good trip? You say hello to Jamilla for me? You better.'

I looked down into her brown eyes. They seemed a little sad. Couldn't hide it from me. 'Something's wrong.' Fear had grabbed at me already. Was she sick? How sick?

Nana shook her head. 'No, not really, sweetheart. I just couldn't sleep. So tell me about the trip. How was Jamilla?' she asked, and her eyes brightened. Nana definitely liked Jamilla. No hiding that either.

'Oh, she's good and she says hello too. She misses everybody. I hope I can get her to come East again, but

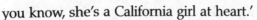

you know, she's a California girl at heart.'

Nana nodded. 'I hope she comes back,' she said. 'Jamilla is a real strong woman. You've met your match with that one. I won't hold it against her that she's from out West. Anyway, I guess Oakland is more like DC than San Francisco. Don't you think?'

'Oh, absolutely.'

I continued to look into Nana's eyes. I didn't get it. She wasn't giving me a hard time like she usually does. What was up? We were quiet for the next minute or so. Unusual for us. We usually jabber back and forth until one of us surrenders.

'You know, I'm eighty-two years old. I never felt like I was seventy, or seventy-five, or even eighty. But Alex, suddenly I feel my age. I'm *eighty-two*. Give or take.'

She took my hand in hers and squeezed it. The sadness was back in her eyes, maybe even a little fear. I felt a lump in my throat. Something was wrong with her. What was it? Why wouldn't she tell me?

'I've had a pain lately, in my chest. Shortness of breath. Angina or whatever. Not so good, not so good.'

'Have you seen Dr Rodman? Or Bill Montgomery?' I asked.

'I saw Kayla Coles. She was in the neighborhood treating a man a few houses down from us.'

I didn't understand. 'Who's Kayla Coles?'

'Dr Kayla makes house calls in Southeast. She's organized about a dozen doctors and nurses who come into the neighborhood to help people here. She's a fabulous doctor and a good person, Alex. She's doing a lot of

good in Southeast. I like her tremendously.'

I bristled a little. 'Nana, you're not some charity case. We have money for you to see a doctor of your choice.'

Nana squeezed her eyes shut. 'Please. Listen to me. And pay attention to what I'm saying. I'm eighty-two and I won't be around forever. Much as I'd like to be. But I'm taking care of myself so far, and I plan to keep doing it. I like and trust Kayla Coles. She *is* my choice.'

Nana got up slowly from the table, kissed me on the cheek and then she shuffled off to bed. At least we were fighting again.

Chapter Fifty-Eight

L ater that night, I went up to my attic office. Everyone was asleep and the house was quiet.

I liked working when it was peaceful like this. I was back on the Army case; I couldn't get it out of my mind. The bodies painted in bright colors. The eerie straw dolls. The even spookier all-seeing eyes. Innocent soldiers punished by wrongful executions.

And who knew how many more soldiers might be scheduled for execution?

There was plenty of material to go through. If even some of these executions were linked, it would be a huge bombshell for the Army. I continued my research, did some spade work on the straw doll and the evil eye. I did a search on Lexus-Nexus, which held information from most local and national newspapers and the major international ones. A lot of detectives underestimate the usefulness of press research, but I don't. I have solved crimes using information passed to the press by police officers.

I read reports about a former PFC in Hawaii. He'd been accused of murdering five men during a sex-slavery-and-torture spree that occurred from 1998 to 2000. He was currently on death row.

I moved on. I felt I had no choice but to keep going on the case.

An Army captain had killed two junior officers in San Diego less than three months ago. He'd been convicted and was awaiting sentencing. His wife was lodging an appeal. He'd been convicted on the basis of DNA evidence.

I made a note to myself: *Maybe talk to this one.*

My reading was interrupted by the sound of footsteps peppering the stairs up to the attic.

Someone was coming up.

In a hurry.

Adrenalin fired through my system. I reached into a desk drawer and put my hand on a gun.

Suddenly Damon burst into the room. He was soaked with sweat and looked like hell. Nana had told me he was asleep in his room. Obviously that hadn't been the case. He hadn't even been in the house, had he?

'Damon?' I said as I rose. 'Where have you been?'

'Come with me, Dad. Please. It's my friend. Ramon's sick! Dad, I think he's dying.'

Chapter Fifty-Nine

W e both ran down to my car and Damon told me what had happened to his friend Ramon on the way. His hands were shaking badly as he spoke.

'He took E, Dad. He's been doing E for a couple of days.'

E was one of the latest drugs of choice around DC, especially among high school and college kids at George Washington and Georgetown.

'Ramon hasn't been going to school?' I asked.

'No. He hasn't been going home either. He's been staying at a crib down by the river. It's in Capitol Heights.'

I knew the river area and I headed there with a red lamp on my car roof and a siren bleating. I had met Ramon Ramirez, and I knew about his parents: they were musicians, and addicts. Ramon played baseball with Damon. He was twelve. I wondered how deeply Damon was involved, but this wasn't the time for questions like that.

I parked, and Damon and I walked into a dilapidated

row house down near the Anacostia. The house was three stories and most of the windows were boarded.

'You been in this place before?' I asked Damon.

'Yeah, I was here. I came to help Ramon. I couldn't just leave him, could I?'

'Was Ramon conscious when you left him?' I asked.

'Yeah. But his teeth were clenched together and then he was throwing up. His nose was bleeding.'

'Okay, let's see how he is. Keep up with me.'

We hurried down a dark hallway and turned a corner. I could smell the stench of garbage and also a recent fire.

Then I got a surprise. Two EMS techs and a doctor were in a small room; they were working over a boy. I could see Ramon's black sneakers and rolled-up cargo pants. Nothing moved.

The doctor rose from her kneeling position over Ramon. She was tall and heavy-set, with a pretty face. I hadn't seen her around before. I walked up to her, showed my badge, which didn't seem to impress her much.

'I'm Detective Cross,' I said. 'How is the boy?'

The woman focused hard on me. 'I'm Kayla Coles. We're working on him. I don't know yet. Someone called nine-one-one. Did you make the call?' She looked at Damon. I realized she was the doctor Nana had talked about.

Damon answered her question. 'Yes, ma'am.'

'Did you take any drugs?' she asked.

Damon looked at me, then at Dr Coles. 'I don't do drugs. It's dumb.'

'But your friends do? Do you have dumb friends?'

'I was trying to help him. That's all.'

Dr Coles' look was severe, but then she nodded. 'You probably saved your friend's life.'

Damon and I waited in the bleak, foul-smelling room until we heard news that Ramon would make it. This time. Kayla Coles stayed there the whole time. She hovered over Ramon like a guardian angel. Damon got to say a few words to his friend before they took him to a waiting ambulance. I saw him clasp the boy's hands. It was nearly two in the morning when we finally made our way out of the row house.

'You okay?' I asked.

He nodded, but then his body started to shake, and he finally began to sob against my arm.

'It's all right. It's all right,' I consoled him. I put my arm around Damon's shoulders and we headed home.

Chapter Sixty

Thomas Starkey, Brownley Harris and Warren Griffin took separate flights to New York City, all leaving out of Raleigh-Durham Airport. It was safer and a lot smarter that way, and they always worked under the assumption that they were the best, after all. They couldn't make mistakes, especially now.

Starkey was on the five o'clock out of North Carolina. He planned to meet the others at the Palisade Motel in Highland Falls, New York, just outside the United States Military Academy at West Point. There was going to be a murder there. Two murders, actually.

Then this long mission was over.

What was it Martin Sheen's commanding officer had told him in *Apocalypse Now? 'Remember this, Captain. There is no mission. There never was a mission.'* Starkey couldn't help thinking that this job had been like that for them – a long haul, a relentless nightmare. Each of the murders had been complicated. This was Starkey's fourth trip to New York in the past two months. He still didn't even know who he was working for; he'd never met the bastard.

In spite of everything, he felt confident as the Delta flight took off that evening. He talked to the flight attendant, but avoided the kind of innocent flirting he might do under other circumstances. He didn't want to be remembered, so he stuck his face in a Tom Clancy thriller he'd picked up at the airport. Starkey identified with Clancy characters like Jack Clark and John Patrick Ryan.

Once the jet leveled off and drinks were served, Starkey went over his plan for the final murders. It was all in his head; nothing ever written down. It was in Harris's and Griffin's heads, too. He hoped they didn't get in any trouble before he got to the Point tonight. There was a raunchy strip club in nearby New Windsor called The Bed Room, but they'd promised to stay at the hotel.

Finally, Starkey sat back, closed his eyes and started doing 'the math' again. It was a comforting ritual, especially now that they were close to the end.

$100,000 apiece for the first three hits.

$150,000 for the fourth.

$200,000 for the fifth.

$250,000 for West Point.

$500,000 bonus when the entire job was done.

It was almost over.

And Starkey still didn't know who was paying for the murders, or why.

Chapter Sixty-One

Sharp, steep cliffs of granite overlooked the Hudson River at West Point. Starkey knew the area well. Later that night he drove down the main drag in Highland Falls, passing cheesy-looking motels, pizza shops, souvenir stands. He went through Thayer Gate with its turreted sentry tower and stone-faced MP on guard. *Murder at West Point*, he thought. *Man oh man*.

Starkey put the job out of his mind for another few moments. He let impressions of West Point wash over him. Impressions and memories. Starkey had been a cadet here, been a first-year plebe like the two youngsters he saw jogging back to barracks now. In his day he'd shouted the cadet motto 'Always the hard way, sir!' over a thousand times if he'd shouted it once.

God, he loved it here: the attitude, the discipline, the whole physical plant.

The Cadet Chapel stood high on a hillside overlooking the Plains. A cross between a medieval cathedral and a fortress, it still dominated the entire landscape. The campus was filled with mammoth gray-stone buildings and emphasized the fortress effect. An overwhelming sense of solidarity and permanence. *Soon to be shaken badly.*

Harris and Griffin were waiting for him on the grounds. For the next hour, they took turns watching the Bennett house on Bartlett Loop, an area of West Point reserved for officers and their families. The house was redbrick with white trim and plenty of ivy creeping the walls. Smoke curled lazily from the stone chimney. It was a four-bedroom, two-bath unit. On the housing map it was designated as Quarters 130.

Around nine-thirty the three killers reconnoitered on the seventeenth fairway of the West Point golf course. They didn't see anyone on the hilly course that formed one of the boundaries of the military academy. Route 9-W was just to the west.

'This might be easier than we thought,' Warren Griffin said. 'They're both home. Relaxing. Guard down.'

Starkey looked at Griffin disapprovingly. 'I don't think so. There's a saying here, "Always the hard way, sir". Don't forget it. And don't forget that Robert Bennett was Special Forces. This isn't some big city architect having a sleep-over on the Appalachian Trail.'

Griffin snapped to attention. 'Sorry, sir. Won't happen again.'

Just before ten o'clock, the three of them made their way through the bramble and woods that bordered the backyard of Quarters 130. Starkey pushed back a stubborn branch of a pine tree and saw the house.

Then he spotted Colonel Robert Bennett in the kitchen. War-hero, father of five, husband for twenty-six years, former Special Forces in Vietnam.

Bennett was holding a goblet of red wine and seemed to be supervising the preparation of a meal. Barbara Bennett stepped into view. She was doing the real work. Now she too took a sip of his wine. Robert Bennett kissed the back of her neck. They seemed loving for a couple married well over twenty years. *That's too bad*, Starkey thought, but kept it to himself.

'Let's do it,' he said. 'The last piece in the puzzle.'

And it truly was a puzzle – even to the killers.

Chapter Sixty-Two

Robert and Barbara Bennett were just sitting down to dinner when the three heavily armed men burst through the back door into the kitchen. Colonel Bennett saw their guns, camouflage dress, and also noted that none of the men wore masks. He saw *all of the faces* and knew this couldn't be worse.

'Who are you? Robert, who are they?' Barbara stuttered out a few words. 'What's the meaning of this?'

Unfortunately, Colonel Bennett was afraid that he knew exactly who they were, and maybe even who had sent them. He wasn't sure, but he thought he recognized one of them from a long time ago. He even remembered a name – *Starkey. Yes, Thomas Starkey. Good God, why now? After all these years?*

One of the intruders pulled shut the colorful curtains on the two kitchen windows. He used a free arm to sweep the dinner plates, chicken, salad and wine glasses onto the kitchen floor. Bennett understood this was for dramatic effect.

Another man held an automatic weapon pressed to Barbara Bennett's forehead.

The kitchen was totally silent.

Colonel Bennett looked at his wife and his heart nearly broke. Her blue eyes were stretched wide and she was trembling. 'It's going to be all right,' Bennett said in the calmest voice he could manage.

'Oh, is it, Colonel?' Starkey spoke for the first time. He signaled the third intruder, and the man grabbed the front of Barbara's white peasant blouse and tore it off. Barbara gasped and tried to cover herself. The bastard then yanked off her bra. It was for effect, again, but then the man stared at Barbara's breasts.

'Leave her alone! Don't hurt her!' Bennett yelled, and it sounded like a command, as if he were in a position to give them.

The one he knew to be Starkey hit him with the butt of his handgun. Bennett went down and thought that his jaw was broken. He almost blacked out, but managed to stay conscious. His cheek was pressed into the cold tile of the kitchen floor. He needed a plan – even a desperate one would do.

Starkey stood directly over him. And now it got insane. He spoke in Vietnamese.

Colonel Bennett understood some of the words. He'd done enough interrogations during the war, when he'd run several Kit Carson scouts in Vietnam and Laos.

Then Starkey spoke in English. 'Be afraid, Colonel. You'll suffer tonight. So will your wife. You have sins to pay for. You know what they are. Tonight your wife will know about your past, too.'

Colonel Bennett pretended to pass out. When one of the gunmen leaned over him, he pushed off the floor and grabbed at his handgun. Getting the gun was the only thought in Bennett's brain. *He had it!*

But then he was struck viciously on the head. Then on the shoulders and back. He was being screamed at in Vietnamese as the severe beating continued. He saw one of the bastards punch his wife right in the face. For no reason at all.

'Stop it. Don't hurt her for Christ sakes.'

'May se nkin co ay chet,' Starkey yelled in Vietnamese.

Now you get to watch her die.

'Trong luc tao hoi may.'

While I interrogate you, pig.

'May thay cank nay co quen khong, Robert?'

Does that sound familiar, Robert?

Starkey then forced his pistol inside Colonel Bennett's mouth. 'Remember this, Colonel? Remember what happens next?'

Chapter Sixty-Three

S ampson and I got to West Point at a little past five o'clock on Friday evening. All hell had broken loose there.

I'd received an urgent heads-up from Ron Burns at the FBI. There'd been a murder-suicide at the Point that had immediately aroused suspicions when the news got to Quantico. A highly decorated colonel had supposedly killed his wife, then himself.

Sampson and I flew into Stewart Field in Newburgh, then I drove eighteen miles by car to West Point. We had to park our rented car and walk the last several blocks to the officers' housing.

The streets were roped off and closed to through traffic. The press was on hand, but they were being kept away by military police. Even the cadets couldn't help looking curious and concerned.

'You're getting chummy with Burns and the FBI,' Sampson said as we walked to the murder scene on Bartlett Loop. 'He's giving a lot of help.'

'He has it in his head that I might want to work with them,' I told Sampson.

'And? Might you?'

I smiled at Sampson, didn't confirm or deny.

'I thought you were getting out of police work, sugar. Wasn't that the big master plan?'

'I don't know anything for sure right now. Here I am though, headed to another completely fucked-up murder scene with you. Same shit, different day.'

'So you're still hooked, Alex. Bad as ever, right?'

I shook my head. 'No, I'm not *hooked* on the case, John. I'm helping you out. Remember how this started? Payback for Ellis Cooper?'

'Yeah, and you're also hooked. You can't figure out this puzzle. That makes you angry. And curious as hell. That's who you are, Alex. You're a hunter.'

'I yam what I yam,' I shook my head and finally smiled, 'said Popeye the sailor man. The killers were here, John. The three of them were here.'

Chapter Sixty-Four

The Bennett house was roped off and secured. Sampson and I identified ourselves to a nervous-looking MP at the perimeter of the crime scene. I could tell that he'd never seen anything like this before. Unfortunately, I had.

After we put on disposable paper boots, we were permitted to climb three stone steps that led into the house. Then we went looking for a CID officer named Pat Conte. The Army was 'cooperating' because of the other cases. They'd also let in a couple of FBI techs to show their good faith.

I found Captain Conte in the narrow hallway leading from the living room. The murders had apparently taken place in the kitchen. Techies were dusting for fingerprints and photographing the scene from every angle.

Conte shook hands and then he told us what he knew, or thought that he knew at this point.

'All I can give you so far is the obvious. From the looks of things, Colonel Bennett and his wife were engaged in an argument that seems to have turned violent. For a while, she must have given as good as she got. Then Bennett retrieved his service revolver. He shot her in the temple, then shot himself. Friends say that he and his wife were close, but that they fought a lot, sometimes violently. As you can see, the shooting took place in the kitchen. Some time last night.'

'That's what you think happened?' I asked Conte.

'At this point, that's my statement.'

I shook my head and felt my anger rising. 'I was told that because of the possible connection between these deaths and the others that we could expect cooperation here.'

Captain Conte nodded. 'That's what you just got, my full cooperation. Excuse me, I have work here.' He walked away.

Sampson shrugged as we watched the CID officer shuffle off. 'Can't say that I blame him too much. I wouldn't want you and me messing around at my crime scene either.'

'So, let's go mess around.'

I went over to see if I could get anything from the FBI people, the *Evidence Response Team*, also known as ERTs. They were being their usual thorough selves in the kitchen, where the murders had taken place. Given the normal level of dislike for the FBI, it's remarkable how much respect is given to ERTs. The reason is, they're very, very good.

Two members of the ERTs were taking Polaroid shots in the kitchen. Another, wearing a white coverall called a 'bunny suit', was looking for fibers and hairs using an alternative light source. Everybody had on rubber gloves and paper booties over their shoes. The head man was named Michael Fescoe, and I had already met him down on the Appalachian Trail, where he had supervised the crime scene investigation in the woods.

'CID giving you their full cooperation too?' I asked.

He scratched his light brown crew cut. 'I can tell you my version, and it's a little different from Captain Conte's.'

'Please,' I said.

Fescoe began, 'The killers, whoever they were, did a thorough job with both the setup and the cleanup. They've done this before. They're professionals through and through. Just like the killers in Virginia.'

'How many of them?' I asked.

Fescoe held up three fingers. 'Three men. They surprised the Bennetts at dinner. And then they murdered them. These men, they bring force to bear without conscience. You can quote me on that.'

Chapter Sixty-Five

It was time to celebrate! The war was over. Starkey, Harris and Griffin ordered obscenely large, very rare Porterhouse steaks topped with jumbo shrimp at Spark's restaurant on West Forty-sixth Street in Manhattan. For anyone with wads of the green stuff, there was no better place to get happy in a hurry than in New York City.

'Three years, but it's finally over,' said Harris, and raised a glass of cognac, his fourth after-dinner drink of the evening.

'Unless our mysterious benefactor changes his mind,' cautioned Starkey. 'It could happen. One more hit. Or maybe a complication that we didn't plan on. Which doesn't mean we shouldn't party tonight.'

Brownley Harris finished his cheesecake and dabbed his mouth with a cloth napkin. 'Tomorrow we go home to Rocky Mount. The good life. That's not so terrible bad. We're finally out of the game, undefeated and unscored on. Nobody can touch us now.'

Warren Griffin just grinned. He was pretty well plowed.

They all were, except Starkey, who said, 'But tonight, we party. We damn well deserve it. Just like the old days, Saigon and Bangkok, Hong Kong. The night is young, and we're full of mischief, piss and vinegar.' He leaned in close to his friends. 'I want to rape and pillage tonight. It's our right.'

After they left the restaurant, the three friends strolled to East Fifty-second, between First and York. The brownstone they stopped at was a walk-up that had seen better days. Four stories. No doorman. Starkey knew it as 'Asia House'.

He rang the front buzzer and waited for the intercom. He had been here before.

A woman answered in a sultry voice. 'Hi. May I have your code please, gentlemen.'

Starkey gave it in Vietnamese. *Silver. Mercedes Eleven.*

They were buzzed inside. '*Xin moi len lau. Cac em dang cho,*' the voice said in Vietnamese. The ladies are waiting, and they are stunning.

'So are we,' Thomas Starkey said, and laughed.

Starkey, Harris and Griffin climbed the flight of red-carpeted stairs. As they reached the first landing, a plain gray door opened.

An Asian girl, slender and young, no more than eighteen, and gorgeous, stood legs akimbo in the doorway. She had on a black bra and matching panties, thigh-high stockings, sling backs with high-heels.

'Hi there,' she said in English. 'I'm Kym. Welcome. You're very good-looking men. This will be fun for us, too.'

'You're very beautiful, Kym,' Starkey said in Vietnamese.

'And your English is flawless.' He then pulled out a revolver and pointed it between the girl's eyes. 'Don't say another word or you die. Right here, right now, Kym. Your blood all over the carpet and those walls.'

He shoved the girl into a living room, where three other girls were seated on two small couches. They were also young, Asian, very pretty. They wore silk negligees, lavender, red and pink, with color-coordinated high-heels and stockings. Victoria's Secret.

'Don't speak, ladies. Not a word,' Starkey said, and pointed his gun at one then the other.

'Shhh,' Brownley Harris held a finger to his lips. 'Nobody gets hurt. We don't want that either. Trust me, my little Asian dolls.'

Starkey threw open the door at the rear of the living room. He surprised an older woman, probably the voice over the intercom, as well as a husky bouncer in gym shorts and black tee-shirt with CRUNCH stenciled on it. They were greedily eating Chinese food out of cardboard containers.

'Nobody gets hurt,' Starkey said in Vietnamese as he shut the door behind him. 'Hands up high.'

The man and woman slowly raised their hands, and Starkey shot them dead with the silenced revolver. He wandered over to some high-tech equipment and calmly removed a tape. The surveillance camera at the front entrance had recorded their arrival, of course.

Starkey left the slumped, bloody bodies and returned to the living room. The party had begun without him. Brownley Harris was kissing and fondling the pretty young girl who had answered the door. He had lifted Kym up and held her tiny mouth pressed against his. She was too frightened to resist.

'*May cai nay moi dem lai nhieu ky niem,*' Starkey said, and smiled at his friends, but also at the women.

Memories are made of this.

Chapter Sixty-Six

They had done this many times before, and not just in New York. They'd 'celebrated' victories in Hong Kong, Saigon, Frankfurt, Los Angeles, even in London. It had all started in South Vietnam when they were just boys in their teens and early twenties, when the war was on and the madness was everywhere around them. Starkey called it 'blood lust'.

The four Asian girls were terrified, and that was the thrill for Starkey. He totally got off on the look of fear in their eyes. He believed that all men did, though few would admit it.

'*Bon tao muon lien hoan!*' he shouted.

We want to party now!

'*Chi lien hoan, the thoi.*'

It's a celebration.

Starkey found out the girls' names: Kym, Lan, Susie and Hoa. They were pretty, but Kym was truly beautiful. A slender body with small breasts; delicate features – the best of a complicated heritage that could be

Chinese, French and Indian.

Harris found bottles of Scotch and champagne in a small kitchen. He passed the hootch around and made the girls drink, too.

The alcohol calmed them, but Kym kept asking about the owner. Occasionally, the bell rang downstairs. Kym's English was the best and she was told to say that the girls were busy for the night – a private party. 'Come back another time, please. Thank you.'

Griffin took two of the girls upstairs to another floor. Starkey and Harris looked at each other and rolled their eyes. At least he'd left two pretty ones for Brownley and himself. Kym and Lan.

Starkey asked Kym to dance. Her eyes were gleaming slants of dark purple. Except for her three-inch heels, she was naked now. An old song by the Yardbirds played on the radio. As he danced, Starkey remembered that Vietnamese women had a thing about their height, at least when they were around American men. Or maybe it was American men who had a thing about height? Or length?

Harris was speaking in English to Lan. He handed her a bottle of champagne. 'Drink,' he said. 'No, drink it down there, babe.'

The girl understood, either the words or lewd gestures. She shrugged, then dropped onto the couch and inserted the champagne bottle in herself. She poured the champagne, then comically wiped her lips. 'I was thirsty!' she said in English.

The joke got a good laugh. Broke the tension.

'Ban cung phai wong nua,' the girl said.

You drink, too.

Harris laughed and passed the bottle to Kym. She lifted one leg and put it inside without sitting down. She kept it there while she danced with Starkey, spilling champagne all over the carpet and her shoes. Everybody was laughing now.

'The bubbles tickle,' Kym said. 'I have an itch inside me now. You want to scratch it?' she asked Starkey.

The switchblade seemed to come from nowhere. Kym jabbed it at Starkey without actually stabbing him. She screamed, 'You go! Leave right now. Or I cut you bad!'

Then Starkey had his gun out again. He was so cool and calm. He reached and shut off the loud music. Silence. And dread. Incredible tension in the room. Everywhere except on Thomas Starkey's face.

'Dung, dung!' cried Kym. *'Hay dep sung ong sang mot ben di bo.'*

No, no! Put the gun away.

Starkey moved toward little Kym. He wasn't afraid of the switchblade, almost as if he knew he wasn't going to die like this. He twisted the knife out of her hand, then he held the revolver against the side of her skull.

Tears ran down the girl's smooth cheeks. Starkey brushed them away. She smiled up at him. *'Hay yew toi di, ank ban,'* she whispered.

Make love to me, soldier man.

Starkey was there in the apartment, but his head was in Vietnam. Kym was shaking and he loved that, the total control he felt, the evil he was capable of, the electricity it could bring into his system.

He looked at Harris and his friend knew. He just *knew*.

They fired the guns simultaneously.

The girls flew back against the wall and then slid down onto the floor. Kym was shaking all over, very close to death. 'Why?' she whispered.

Starkey just shrugged at her.

Upstairs there were two more *pffthts*. The sound of falling bodies, Susie and Hoa. Warren Griffin had been waiting for them. He knew, too.

It was just like in the An Lao Valley, Vietnam.

Where the madness had started.

Chapter Sixty-Seven

When we finished up at Colonel Bennett's house, Sampson and I checked into the Hotel Thayer, right on the grounds of West Point. I continued to think about the three killers and how they kept getting away. *Force without any conscience.* That was what Agent Fescoe had called it.

In the morning I met Sampson for breakfast in the hotel dining room overlooking the majestic Hudson, which appeared almost steely gray in the distance and was topped by whitecaps. We talked about the grisly Bennett murders and wondered if they were connected to the others, and if the killers had changed their pattern.

'Or maybe there are more murders that we just don't know about,' Sampson said. 'Who knows how many have been killed at this point, or how far back the murders go?' He poured himself another steaming cup of coffee. 'It has to come down to the three killers. They were here, Alex. It has to be the same three men.'

I couldn't disagree with him. 'I have to make a few calls,

then we're out of here. I want to make sure the local police are checking into whether anybody actually saw three men who don't belong on the grounds or in Highland Falls.'

I went upstairs to my room and called Director Burns. He wasn't in, so I left a message. I wanted to call Jamilla, but it was too early in California so I logged onto my computer and sent her a long e-mail.

Then I found that I had a new message. *Now what?*

It turned out to be from Jannie and Damon. They were breaking my chops about being away from home again, even for a night. When was I coming back? Would they get a neat souvenir from West Point? How about a shiny new sword for each of them? And one for little Alex, too.

There was a second message for me.

It wasn't from the kids.

Or Jamilla.

Detective Cross. While you are at West Point, you ought to see Colonel Owen Handler. He teaches political science. He might have some answers for you. He's a friend of the Bennetts. He might even know who killed them.

I'm just trying to be helpful. You need all the help you can get.

Foot Soldier.

Chapter Sixty-Eight

The three killers had been right here. I couldn't get the thought out of my head, but the feeling was in my bones, my blood.

Sampson and I walked along the main drag toward Thayer Hall. Several cadets were out practicing for parade on the Plains. As we got closer, I saw that wooden pegs were driven into the ground to show the cadets exactly where to turn their faultlessly sharp corners. I had to smile. It reminded me that so many things in life were an illusion. Maybe even the 'facts' I was collecting on this case.

'So what do you think about this help we're getting? The mad e-mailer? The Foot Soldier?' Sampson asked. 'I don't like it, Alex. It's too convenient, too pat. This whole case is about being set up.'

'You're right, we don't have any reason to trust the information we're getting. So I don't. On the other hand, we're here. Why not talk to Colonel Handler? It can't hurt.'

Sampson shook his head. 'I wish that was so, Alex.'

I had called the History Department immediately after I received the 'helpful' e-mail from Foot Soldier. I was told that Colonel Handler had a class that met from eleven until noon. We had twenty minutes to kill, so we took in a few sights: Washington Hall, a cavernous three-story building where the entire Corps of Cadets could sit simultaneously for meals; the Eisenhower and MacArthur Barracks; the Cadet Chapel; plus several incomparable river vistas.

Cadets flowed past us lickity-split on the sidewalk. They wore long-sleeved gray shirts with black ties, gray trousers with a black stripe, brass belt buckles shined to perfection.

Everybody was moving in double time! It was contagious.

Thayer Hall was a huge gray building that was virtually windowless. Inside, the classrooms all looked identical, each with desks arranged in a horseshoe so that everyone was in the front row.

Sampson and I waited in a deserted hallway until Handler's class was finished and the cadets filed out.

They were incredibly orderly for college students, which didn't surprise me, but it was still impressive to watch. Why aren't students in all universities orderly? Because no one demands it? Well hell, who cares? But it was a striking scene. All these young kids with so much purpose and resolve. On the surface anyway.

Colonel Handler trailed his students out of the class-room. He was a burly man, around six feet one with short-cropped, salt-and-pepper hair and a full beard. I already knew he'd served two tours of duty in Vietnam, had an MA from the University of Virginia and a doctorate from Penn State. That much was on the West Point web-site.

'We're Detectives Cross and Sampson,' I said as I walked up to him. 'Could we talk to you for a moment?'

Handler grimaced. 'What's this about, Detectives? One of our cadets in trouble?'

'No, no,' I shook my head. 'The cadets seem beyond reproach.'

A smile broke across Handler's face. 'Oh, you'd be surprised. They only look blameless, Detective. So if it isn't one of our charges, what is it you'd like to talk to me about? Robert and Barbara Bennett? I've already spoken to Captain Conte. I thought CID was handling that.'

'They are,' I told him. 'But the murders might be a little more complicated than they appear. Just like the cadets here at West Point.'

As concisely as I could, I told Handler about the other murder cases that Sampson and I had been investigating. I didn't tell him about the e-mail from the Foot Soldier that had led us to him. As I spoke, I noticed a professor in the classroom next to Handler's. He had a bucket with water and a sponge, and he was actually washing the blackboard before the next class. All the classrooms had identical buckets and sponges. Hell of a system.

'We think there's a connection to something pretty bad that took place in Vietnam,' I said to Colonel Handler. 'Maybe the murders actually started there.'

'I served in Southeast Asia. Two tours,' Handler volunteered. 'Vietnam and Cambodia.'

'So did I,' said Sampson. 'Two tours.'

Suddenly, and for no apparent reason, Colonel Handler seemed nervous. His eyes narrowed and darted around the hallway. The cadets were gone now, no doubt rushing off to Washington Hall for lunch.

'I'll talk to you,' he finally said, 'but not on the grounds. Pick me up at my place tonight. It's Quarters ninety-eight. We'll go somewhere else. Come by at eight sharp.'

He looked at Sampson and me, and then Colonel Handler turned and walked away.

In double time.

Chapter Sixty-Nine

I had the feeling that we were close to something important, at West Point, and maybe with Colonel Handler. It was something ineffable that I'd seen in his eyes when the subject had turned to Vietnam. *Maybe the murders started there.*

The colonel had made reservations at what he called an 'extraordinarily misplaced' northern Italian restaurant in Newburgh, Il Cenacolo. We were on our way there, riding the Storm King Highway, a winding rollercoaster with incredible views of the Hudson, which stretched out hundreds of feet below.

'Why didn't you want to talk to us closer to home?' I finally asked the colonel.

'Two of my best friends were just murdered there,' Handler said. He lit up a cigarette, blew out a stream of smoke. It was pitch black outside and the mountainous road had no lights to guide our way.

'You believe the Bennetts were murdered?' I asked.

'I *know* they were.'

'Do you know why?'

'I might. You've heard of the blue wall of silence with the police? In the Army, it's the same, only the wall is gray. It's higher, thicker, and has been here for a hell of a long time.'

I had to ask another question. I couldn't hold back. 'Are you Foot Soldier, Colonel? If you are, we need your help.'

Handler didn't seem to understand. 'What the hell is Foot Soldier? What are you talking about?'

I told him that a mysterious someone had been periodically slipping me information, including Handler's own name. 'Maybe you thought it was time we met face to face,' I said.

'No. I *may* be a source for you now. But it's only because of Bob and Barbara Bennett. I'm not Foot Soldier. I never contacted you. You came to see me. Remember?'

As convincing as he sounded, I didn't know whether to believe him, but I had to pursue the identity of Foot Soldier. I asked Handler for names, others who might be helpful in the investigation. He gave me a few, some Americans, even a couple of South Vietnamese who might be willing to help.

Handler spoke from the darkened backseat of the sedan. 'I don't know who's been contacting you, but I'm not so sure that I'd trust whoever it is. Right about now, I'm not sure that I'd trust anyone.'

'Not even you, Colonel?'

'*Especially* not me,' he said, and laughed. 'Hell, I'm a college professor.'

I glanced up into the rearview mirror and saw a single

pair of headlights approaching. I hadn't noticed much traffic so far and most of it had been speeding in the opposite direction, heading south.

Suddenly Sampson raised his voice and turned to Handler. 'Why don't you tell us what's really going on, Colonel? How many more have to die? What do you know about these murders?'

That's when I heard a gunshot, then the sound of glass breaking. The car behind was already on us, and passing on the right shoulder.

My eyes darted and I saw a driver, then a gunman leaning out the window of the backseat.

'Get down!' I yelled at Handler and Sampson. 'Cover up!'

More shots came from the pursuing car. I swerved the wheel violently to the left. We skidded hard across double-yellow lines, heading for the cliffs, and the Hudson River far below. Handler yelled, *'Watch it, Jesus! Watch it!'*

We hit a straight part of the highway, thank God. I stomped on the accelerator, picked up some speed. But I couldn't lose the other car.

He was in the right-hand lane now.

I was in the *wrong* lane, the one meant for oncoming traffic.

Sampson had gotten to his gun and returned fire. More shots struck our car.

The other sedan stayed right with us. I couldn't shake loose. I was doing over ninety on a twisty road built for fifty or sixty. On my right side was a shoulder and then the mountain wall; on my left, a sheer drop down toward the Hudson River and certain death.

I was going too fast to see faces in the other car. Who the hell was it?

Suddenly I stomped on the brakes and our car skidded badly. Then it fishtailed! We wound up facing in the opposite direction, south.

I took off that way. Back toward West Point.

I floored it again, got back up to ninety in an awful hurry.

I passed two cars heading north, both blaring their horns at me. I couldn't blame them. I was over the double line and racing at about forty miles an hour over the speed limit. They must have thought I was drunk, or mad, or both.

When I was sure no one was following, I slowed down.

'Handler? Colonel?' I called out.

He didn't answer. Sampson hung over the backseat to check on him. 'He's been hit, Alex.'

I pulled to the side of the road and turned on the interior lights. 'How bad? Is he alive?'

I saw that Handler had been shot twice. Once in the shoulder. And once in the side of the head.

'He's dead,' Sampson said. 'He's gone.'

'You all right?' I asked.

'Yeah,' he said. 'I wasn't the target, and that boy in the car could shoot. He was after Handler. We just lost our first real lead.'

I wondered if we had lost Foot Soldier as well.

Chapter Seventy

There's nothing like an attempt on your life to get you properly focused – and to get the blood boiling.

It was an exercise in futility, but Sampson and I rushed Owen Handler to the ER at West Point Hospital. He was pronounced dead at around nine. I'm certain he was dead when we brought him in. The shooter in the other car was a chillingly good marksman, a professional killer. *Had three men actually been in the pursuing car? I didn't think so.*

We were questioned by the local police and also CID officers from West Point. Captain Conte even came to see us, spouting off his concern for our safety, but also playing twenty questions with us, almost as if we were suspects. Conte informed me that the commanding officer at West Point, General Mark Hutchinson, was personally supervising the investigation now. Whatever that was supposed to mean.

Then General Hutchinson actually showed up at the hospital. I saw him speaking to Captain Conte, then a few other grim-faced officers gathered in the hallway. But

Hutchinson never came over to see Sampson and I. Not a word of condolence or concern.

How goddamn strange, and inconsiderate. It was maddening. *The gray wall of silence*, I thought, remembering Owen Handler's words. General Mark Hutchinson left the hospital without making contact with us. I wasn't going to forget that.

All the while I was at West Point Hospital, I couldn't get one thought out of my head: *There is nothing like an attempt on your life . . . to get your blood boiling.* I was shaken by the attack on Colonel Handler, but I was also angry as hell.

Wasn't that part of the motive behind the massacres at My Lai and others like it? Anger? Fear? The need for retribution? Unthinkable things happened during combat. Tragedies were inevitable. They always had been. What was the Army trying to cover up now? Who had sent the killers after us tonight? Who had murdered Colonel Handler, and why?

Sampson and I spent the night at the Hotel Thayer again. General Hutchinson decided to put MPs on the second floor to protect us. I didn't think it was necessary. If the gunmen had been after us, they wouldn't have driven off and left us alive.

I kept thinking: *two* men had been in the car that attacked us.

There had been *three* men involved in the earlier killings.

I couldn't get that fact out of my head either.

Three, not two.

Eventually, I called Jamilla and shared everything that had happened with her. Detective to detective, friend to friend. She didn't like the actions of General Hutchinson and the Army either. Just talking it through with her helped tremendously.

I was thinking about doing it more often, like maybe every night.

Finally, I fell asleep on that thought.

Chapter Seventy-One

The following morning the New York papers were filled with a story about the murder of four call girls, a madam and a bouncer on the East Side of Manhattan. The women were Vietnamese and Thai, and because of that I talked to the detective in charge of the investigation in Manhattan. So far, the NYPD was nowhere on the grisly case. I thought about going to New York, but there were other pressing things on my mind.

There was an important lead I hadn't even begun to satisfactorily check out. The Foot Soldier. Who the hell was he? Or she? And why had Foot Soldier contacted me by e-mail? What was the mystery person trying to tell me?

Owen Handler had given me a few names, and once I returned to Washington, I dug around until I tracked a few of them down. The most interesting to me was Tran Van Luu, a former Kit Carson scout who was now living in the United States.

There was a catch, a big one. Tran Van Luu was on death

row in Florence, Colorado. He'd been found guilty of murdering nine people in Newark and New York City. I knew a little about the federal prison at Florence and had even been there once. *That was the second catch*. Kyle Craig was imprisoned there, my old nemesis. Kyle was also on death row.

The Florence ADX was one of the so-called 'supermax' prison facilities. Thirty-six states now had them. Death row was located in the Security Housing Unit, a kind of prison within a prison. It turned out to be a bland, sand-colored building with extraordinarily heavy security inside and out. That was comforting, since Kyle Craig was being held inside, and Kyle had nothing but disdain for prison security.

Two heavily armed guards accompanied me to death row. As we walked down the otherwise empty, fluorescent-lit hallways, I heard none of the usual chaotic noise of a prison. My mind was somewhere else anyway.

I had arrived in Colorado around noon. Everything was running smoothly on the home front, and hopefully I'd be back in DC that night. Nana wasn't missing any opportunities, though. Before I left the house she sat me down and told me one of her story-parables. She called it *The story of the thousand marbles*. 'I heard this on NPR, Alex. It's a true story, and I'm passing it along to you for what it's worth. Seems there was this man who lived in Southern California, around San Diego I believe it was. He had a family, nice family, and he worked very hard, long hours, lots of weekends. Sound familiar?'

'Probably familiar to a lot of people,' I said. 'Men and women. Go ahead, though, Nana. This hardworking man with the extraordinarily nice family living outside San Diego. What happened to him?'

'Well anyway, this man had a kindly grandfather who adored both him and his family. He'd noticed that his grandson was working too hard, and he was the one who told him about the marbles. He told it this way. He said that the average life span for men was around seventy-five years. That meant thirty-nine hundred Saturdays – to play when you were a kid, and to be with your family when you got older and wiser.'

'I see,' I said. 'Or to play once you got older. Or even to give lectures to anyone who'll listen.'

'Shush, Alex. Now, listen. So the grandfather figured out that his grandson, who was forty-three, had about sixteen hundred and sixty Saturdays left in his life. Statistically speaking. So what he did was he bought two large jars and filled them with beautiful cat's-eye marbles. He gave them to his grandson. And he told him that every Saturday, he should take one marble out of the jar. Just one, and just as a reminder that he only had so many Saturdays left, and that they were precious beyond belief. Think about that, Alex. If you have the time,' said Nana.

So here I was at a supermax prison – on a Saturday. I didn't think I was wasting the day, not at all. But Nana's message had sunk in anyway.

This was my last murder case. It had to be. This was the end of the road for Detective Alex Cross.

I focused my mind on the baffling case as I walked toward the cell of Tran Van Luu. He would make my trip worth at least one marble.

Or so I had to hope.

Chapter Seventy-Two

Tran Van Luu was fifty-four years old and he informed me that he spoke Vietnamese, French and English fluently. His English was excellent and I couldn't help thinking that he looked more like a college professor than a prison inmate convicted of several murders. Luu wore gold wire-rim glasses and had a long, gray goatee. He was philosophical – about everything apparently. But was he the Foot Soldier?

'Nominally, I am a Buddhist,' he said as he sat in a cell that was only seven by twelve feet. A bed, a stool and a fixed writing shelf filled more than half of the space. The fixtures were all made of poured concrete so they couldn't be moved or disassembled by the inmates.

'I will give you some history,' he said. 'The back story.'

I nodded. 'That would be a good place to start.'

'My birthplace is Gon Track Village in the Quang Bihn Province, just north of what was the DMZ. This is one of the country's poorest provinces, but they are all relatively poor. I started work in my family's rice fields at five.

Everyone was always hungry, even though we grew food. We had one real meal a day, usually yams or cassava. Ironically, our rice was handed over to the landlord. All loyalty was to family, including ancestors, a plot of land and the village. Nationalism was non-existent, a Western notion imported by Ho Chi Minh.

'My family moved south in nineteen sixty-three and I enlisted in the Army. The alternative was starvation, and besides, I had been brought up to hate the Communists. I proved to be an excellent scout and was recommended to MAC-V/Recondo school run by US Army Special Forces. This was my initial encounter with Americans. I liked them at first.'

'What happened to change that?' I asked Luu.

'Many things. Mostly I came to understand that many of the Americans looked down on me and my country-men. Despite repeated promises, I was left behind in Saigon. I became a boat person.

'I finally got to America in seventy-nine. Orange County in California, which has a very large Vietnamese population. The only way we could survive was to recreate the family/village structure from our own country. I did so with a gang – the Ghost Shadows. We became successful, at first in California, then in the New York area, including Newark. They say I murdered members of rival gangs in New York and Jersey.'

'Did you?' I asked Luu.

'Oh, of course. It was justifiable, though. We were in a war.' He stopped talking. Stared at me.

'So now you're here in a supermax prison. Have you

received a date for the execution?'

'No. Which is very humorous to me. Your country is afraid to execute convicted murderers.'

'It's comical? Because of things you saw in Vietnam?'

'Of course. That is my frame of reference.'

'Atrocities committed in the name of military activity.'

'It was war, Detective.'

'Did you know any of these men in Vietnam: Ellis Cooper, Reece Tate, James Etra, Robert Bennett, Laurence Houston?'

Luu shrugged. 'It was a long time ago. Over thirty years. And there are so many American surnames to remember.'

'Colonel Owen Handler?'

'I don't know him.'

I shook my head. 'I think you do. Actually, Colonel Handler was in charge of the MAC-V/Recondo school when you were there being trained as a Kit Carson scout.'

Luu smiled for the first time. 'Believe it or not, Detective Cross, the scouts didn't usually get to meet the man-in-charge.'

'But you met Colonel Handler. He remembered you to the day he was killed. Can you help me stop the murders?' I asked Luu. 'You know what happened over there, don't you? Why did you agree to see me?'

He gave another indifferent shrug. 'I agreed to see you . . . because my good friend asked me to. My friend is Kyle Craig.'

Chapter Seventy-Three

I could feel a cold spot where my heart was supposed to be. This couldn't all be leading to Kyle Craig. I had put him here in Florence for all the murders he had committed – and now, somehow, he'd gotten me to come and visit.

'Hello, Alex. I thought you'd forgotten all about me,' Kyle said when he saw me. We met in a small interviewing room near his cellblock. My head was full of paranoid thoughts about the 'coincidence' of seeing him again. He couldn't have set this up. Not even *he* could do that.

Kyle had changed physically, so much so that he resembled one of his older brothers, or maybe his father, more than himself. When I had been pursuing him, I'd met everyone in Kyle's family. He'd always been gaunt, but in prison he had lost at least twenty pounds. His head was shaven and he had a tattoo on one side of his skull: it was part dragon, part snake. He actually looked like a killer now.

'Sit down, Alex. I missed you even more than I thought

I would. Sit, please. Let's talk the talk. Catch up with the catch up.'

'I'll stand, thanks. I'm not here to make small talk, Kyle. What do you know about these murders?'

'They've all been solved by the police or the Army, Alex. The guilty have been charged, and in some cases executed. Just as I will be eventually. Why waste your time on them? I'm a hundred times more interesting. You should be studying me.'

His words were delivered in a low-key manner, but they went through me like a powerful electric current. Was Kyle the missing goddamn connection? He couldn't be behind the murders? They had started long before he'd been arrested. *But did that really matter?*

'So, you don't know anything that can help me? Then I'm leaving. Have a nice life.'

Kyle raised a hand. 'I'd like to help, Alex. I mean that sincerely. Just like the old days. I miss it. The chase. What if I *could* help?' he asked.

'If you can, then do it, Kyle. Do it right now. We'll see where it goes from there.'

Kyle leaned back in his chair. Finally, he smiled, or maybe he was laughing at me? 'Well, since you didn't ask, it's better here in prison than I could have hoped. Believe it or not, I'm a minor celebrity. And not just among my peers. Even the kick-ass guards cater to my wishes. I have lots of visitors. I'm writing a book, Alex. And, of course, I'm figuring out some way to get out of here. Trust me, I will some day. It's just a matter of time. It almost happened a month ago. *This* close. I would have come to visit, of course. You and Nana and those sweet children.'

'Does Luu know *anything*?' I asked.

'Oh, absolutely. He's very well read. Speaks three languages fluently. I like Luu very much. We're dear friends. I also like Ted Kaczynski; Yu Kikimura, the Japanese terrorist; and Ramon Matta, formerly with the Medellin cartel. Interesting inmates, fascinating lives, though more conservative than I would have expected. Not Ted, but the others.'

I'd had enough. Of Kyle Craig. Luu. Florence.

'I'm going,' I said. I started to walk away.

'You'll be back,' Kyle whispered. 'Or maybe I'll come and visit you next time. At any rate, best of luck with your fascinating murder case.'

I turned back. 'You'll be in here for the rest of your life. Not too long, I hope.'

Kyle Craig laughed heartily. More than ever, he gave me the creeps.

Chapter Seventy-Four

A s John Sampson drove into Bay Head, New Jersey, he felt his spirits rise dramatically, and the very pleasant sensation inside made him smile to himself. He was doing a lot of that lately. Hell, he was going to ruin his tough guy image if he kept this shit up much longer.

He drove along Route 35, past sprawling beach houses, Central Market, and a couple of picturesque, whitewashed churches. This part of the Jersey shore was quiet and undeniably pretty. He couldn't help but appreciate the serenity and the well-preserved beauty. A slight breeze from the ocean blew through the open windows of his Cougar. Geraniums and rose hips bloomed along the side of the road, obviously planted by the village itself.

What was not to like? He was glad to be here again.

Long ways from DC, he found himself thinking. *And it's not all bad. For a change of pace anyway. For a break from all the murders.*

During the drive up from DC, Sampson had tried to convince himself that this excursion to the Jersey shore was all about Ellis Cooper and the other murders, but that wasn't the whole truth. Coop was definitely a big part of it, but this was also about Billie Houston.

He thought about her all the time. What was it about that wisp of a woman?

Actually, he knew at least part of the answer. From the moment he'd met her, he was completely comfortable. She was the female friend he'd been hoping to meet for a long time. It was hard to describe the feeling, but he knew he'd never had it before. He felt that he could tell Billie things about himself that he'd held inside for a long time. He trusted her already. When he was with her he could come outside of himself, leave the castle he had constructed to guard the person he really was from being hurt.

On the other hand, John Sampson had never had a successful long-range relationship with any woman. Never been married, not even seriously tempted. So he wasn't going to delude himself, or get too soppy and sentimental about Billie. He had good reasons to be here in Jersey. A few more questions had to be asked about her husband's time in Vietnam. He and Alex had learned things from Owen Handler that needed filling in. He *was* going to solve these murder cases. Somehow, some way.

Well, hell, that cynical little introspection had sure dampened his spirits, and any burgeoning romance in his soul.

Then he happened to see her up ahead on East Avenue. *Yep, it was her!*

Billie was climbing out of her light green convertible

with an armful of groceries. He'd called ahead and said he might be coming.

Now who had she been shopping for? Did she expect him to stay for dinner? Oh brother, he needed to calm himself down. *Slow down. You're on the job, that's all. This is just police business.*

Then Billie saw his car and waved her free arm, and he found himself leaning out of the window of the Cougar, calling up the street, 'Hey there, little one.' *Hey there, little one?*

What the hell had happened to smooth and cool and detached John Sampson? What was happening to him?

And why did he feel so good about it?

Chapter Seventy-Five

$\mathbf{B}$illie understood that she and John Sampson needed to talk about her husband and his murder. That was why he'd come back, probably the only reason. She made a pitcher of sweetened iced tea, and they went out to the oceanside porch. Might as well be comfortable. *Try not to make an ass out of herself.*

'Another perfect day in paradise,' he said, and smiled brilliantly. Billie couldn't keep herself from staring a little at the policeman. He was strong and good-looking and his smile was dazzling whenever it came. She had the sense that he didn't smile enough, and wondered why that was. What had happened to him growing up in Washington? And then living and working there? She wanted to know everything about him, and that natural curiosity was something that had been missing since Laurence had died.

Don't make this into something it isn't, she reminded herself. *He's a policeman on a murder case. That's all this is. You just have a silly crush on him.*

'Average day in paradise,' she laughed. Then she got a little more serious. 'You wanted to talk some more about Laurence. Something else happened, didn't it? That's why you're back here.'

'No, I came to see you.' *There was that amazing smile of his again.*

Billie took a little swing at the air with her hand. 'Sure you did. Anyway – your murder case?'

He told her about the recent deaths of Robert and Barbara Bennett in West Point, and then the shooting of Colonel Owen Handler. He shared his and Alex's theory that three men might be responsible for at least some of the murders. 'Everything seems to point back to Vietnam. Something incredible happened, something so bad that it's probably the root cause of all these murders in the present. Your husband may have been involved in some way. Maybe he didn't even know it, Billie.'

'He didn't like to talk about his experiences over there.' She repeated what she'd told him during his first visit. 'I always respected that. But then something strange happened. Several years ago, he brought home books about the war. *Rumors Of War* was one that I remember. He rented the movie *Platoon*, which he'd always insisted he wouldn't watch. He still didn't want to talk about the war, though. Not to me anyway.'

Billie sat back in the navy blue wicker rocker she'd chosen. She stared out at the ocean. Several gulls floated over the tall dunes. Picture pretty. Miles away, she could see the blurred outline of an ocean liner on the horizon.

'He always drank, but during those last years, he drank

much more. Hard liquor, wine. He wasn't ever abusive, but I felt he was drifting farther and farther away.

'One night around dusk he took off down the beach with his fishing pole and a pail for anything he might catch. It was early September, and the bluefish were running. He could have caught them with his pail.

'I waited for him to come back, but he didn't. Finally, I went out looking for him. Most of these houses on the beach empty out after Labor Day. That's the way it is here. I walked south a mile or so. I was getting a little scared.

'I had brought a flashlight, and as I headed back, I turned it on and worked my way up closer to the dunes and the deserted beach houses. That was where I found him.

'Laurence was laying in the sand beside his fishing pole and the bait bucket. He'd finished off a pint of whiskey. Looked like a street bum who'd lost his way and wound up sleeping it off on the beach.

'I lay down beside him and held him in my arms. I asked him to please tell me why he was so sad. He *couldn't*. It broke my heart that he couldn't tell me. All he said was that "you can't outrun your past". It looks like he was right.'

Chapter Seventy-Six

They talked about Vietnam, and her husband's Army experiences after the war, until Sampson was starting to get a headache. Billie never complained. Around four in the afternoon they took a break and watched the high tide coming in. It amazed Sampson that the long stretch of beach could be so empty on such a sunny and blue-skied day.

'Did you bring a suit?' she asked, and smiled.

'Actually, I did throw a suit in the car,' Sampson said, and returned her smile.

'Want to take a swim?'

'Yeah. Be nice.'

They slipped into their suits and met back on the front porch. She had on a black one-piece. He figured she must do a lot of swimming, or maybe worked out. She was little, but she didn't look like a young girl. She was probably in her early forties.

'I know I look okay,' Billie said, and twirled around. 'So do you. Now let's hit the water before you chicken out on me.'

'Chicken out? You know I'm a homicide detective?'

'Uh-huh. Water's sixty-seven today, tough guy.'

'What? Is that cold?'

'You'll soon find out.'

They walked to the top of the dune in front of the house. Then they broke into a full-out run. Sampson was laughing, mostly at himself, because he didn't *do* this kind of thing.

They high-stepped their way through the low surf like kids on vacation, ignoring that the water was in the sixties, cold as hell, absolutely freezing.

'You *can* swim?' Billie asked as a huge swell moved toward them. She thought she saw him nod.

'John?' she asked again.

'I can swim. Can *you*?'

Then they both dove under the wave as it crested high above their heads. A short way out past the first wave, they re-surfaced. Billie started to stroke her way out to a point past the breakers. Sampson followed, and he was a good, strong swimmer. That delighted her for some reason.

'Sometimes, kids from the cities,' she said as they bobbed heads together, 'they don't learn to swim.'

'That's true. I have this good friend. When we were growing up in DC, his grandmother made sure we knew how. She used to take us to the city pool. She said, "You swim, or you drown".'

Then Sampson found himself taking Billie in his arms. She used a forefinger to wipe beads of water off his face. Her touch was gentle. So were her eyes. Something was going on here and whatever it was, he didn't know if he was ready for it.

'What?' Billie asked.

'I was just going to say,' he said, 'that you're surprising in a lot of ways.'

She closed her eyes for a second, nodded. Then she opened her eyes again. 'You're still here. Good. I'm glad you came back. Even if you came to interrogate me.'

'The reason I came was to see you. I told you.'

'Whatever you say, John.'

Nobody but Alex and Nana called him John.

They swam back toward shore and played in the creamy surf for a while. Even though it was late afternoon they took a walk to the south, passing more large houses that were shut up tight for the coming winter. They fell into a nice rhythm along the way. They had to stop and kiss at each house.

'You're getting kind of corny,' Billie finally said. 'It becomes you. You have a tender side, John Sampson.'

'Yeah. Maybe I do.'

They ate dinner on the front porch again. Sampson put on the radio. Afterward, they snuggled in the loveseat, and again he was struck by how tiny she was. She fit against him, though.

'One Night With You' came on the radio. Luther Vandross. Sampson asked her to dance. He couldn't believe it – *I just asked Billie to dance on the porch.*

He tucked her in close. She fit nicely standing up, too. They moved well together, totally in synch. He listened to her breathing and could feel her heartbeat as well.

An old Marvin Gaye tune came on the radio and they danced to that, too. It all seemed dreamlike to him. Completely unexpected.

Especially when they went upstairs together at around ten-thirty. Neither of them said a word, but Billie took his hand and led him into the bedroom. A three-quarter moon was lighting the whitecaps. A sailboat lazily drifted by out beyond the line of surf.

'You okay?' she whispered.

'I am much more than okay. Are you, Billie?'

'I *am* Billie. I think I wanted this to happen from the first time I saw you. You ever done this before?' she asked. There was that sly grin of hers again. She was playing with him, but he liked it.

'First time. I've been saving myself for the right woman.'

'Well, let's see if I'm worth the wait.'

Sometimes, he could be in a hurry, and that would be okay, the way of the world in Washington, but not tonight. He wanted to explore Billie's body, to get to know what pleased her. He touched her everywhere; kissed her everywhere. Everything about her seemed right to him. *What's happening here? I came to ask this woman about some murders. Murders! Not love-making in shimmering moonlight.*

He could feel her small breasts rising and falling, rising and falling. He was on top of her, supporting his weight on his hands.

'You won't hurt me,' she whispered.

'No, I won't.'

I won't. I couldn't hurt you. And I won't let anybody hurt you.

She smiled, rolled over, and then slid up on top of him. 'How's that? Is that better for you?'

He ran his strong hands up and down her back and over her buttocks. She hummed 'One Night With You'. They began to move together, really slowly at first. Then faster. And faster still. Billie rose and fell hard on him. She liked it that way.

When they finally collapsed with the pleasure of it all, she looked into his eyes. 'Not bad for your first time. You'll get better.'

Later, Sampson lay in the bed with Billie snuggled up against his side. It still made him smile to see how small she was. Small face, small hands, feet, breasts. And then the thought hit him – stunned him: he was at peace for the first time in years. Maybe ever.

Chapter Seventy-Seven

I was pumped up to see Nana and the kids when I got home from my trip to Florence prison that night. It was only seven and I'd been thinking we might go to the IMAX theater, or maybe the ESPN Zone – some nice treat for the kids.

As I climbed the front steps of the house, I spotted a note stuck onto the screen door, flapping in the breeze.

Uh-oh.

Messages left at the house always make me a little queasy. There'd been too many bad ones during the past few years.

I recognized Nana's handwriting: *Alex, we've gone to your Aunt Tia's. Be back by nine or so. Everybody misses you. Do you miss us? Of course you do – in your own way. Nana and the kids.*

I'd noticed that Nana Mama had been unusually sentimental lately. She said she was feeling better, back to her old self again, but I wondered if that was true. Maybe I should talk to her doctor, but I didn't like interfering in her business. She'd been doing an excellent job of taking care of herself for a long time.

I shuffled on into the kitchen and grabbed a cold beer from the fridge.

I saw a funny drawing of a pregnant stork that Jannie had stuck up on the door. Suddenly, I felt lonely for everybody. The thing about kids for some people – for me anyway – is that they complete your life, make some kind of sense out of it, even if they do drive you crazy sometimes. The gain is worth the pain. At least in our house it is.

The telephone rang and I figured it was Nana.

'Hooray, you're home!' came a welcome voice. *Well, surprise, surprise*. It was Jamilla, and that cheered me right up. I could picture her face, her smile, the bright shine in her eyes.

'Hooray, it's *you*. I just got home to an empty house,' I said. 'Nana and the kids deserted me.'

'Could be worse, Alex. I'm at work. Caught a bad one on Friday. Irish tourist got killed in the Tenderloin district. So tell me, what was a fifty-one-year-old *priest* from Dublin doing in one of the seediest parts of San Francisco at two in the morning? How did he get strangled with a pair of extra-large pantyhose? My job to find out.'

'Sounds like you're enjoying yourself anyway.' I found myself smiling. Not at the murder, but at Jamilla's enthusiasm for the Job.

Jamilla was still laughing. 'Well, I do enjoy a good mystery. How's your case going? Now that sucker is nasty. I've been thinking about it in my free moments.

Somebody "murdering" Army officers by framing them for crimes they didn't commit.'

I brought her up to speed, detective to detective, then we talked about more pleasant subjects, like our time together in Arizona. Finally, she said she had to run, to get back to her case. I thought about Jam after I hung up the phone. She loved police work, and she said so. I did too, but the demons were getting to me.

I grabbed another beer out of the fridge, then I headed upstairs. I was still ruminating about Jamilla. Nice thoughts. Nothing but blue skies . . .

I opened the bedroom door, then I just stood there, shaking my head back and forth.

Sitting on my bed were two large glass jars. Pretty ones. Maybe antiques. They were filled with what looked to be hundreds of cat's-eye marbles.

I went over to the bed. Took one out.

I rolled the marble between my thumb and forefinger. I had to admit that it felt precious.

The Saturdays I still had left.

How did I plan to use them?

Maybe that was the biggest mystery of all.

Chapter Seventy-Eight

I had the feeling that I was being followed around in Washington during the next few days. *Watched*. But I couldn't seem to catch them at it. They were either very good, or I was completely losing it.

On Monday I was back at work. All that week I put in my time at the precinct, on the Job. I made sure I spent extra hours at home with the kids before I did overtime in my office in the attic. A colonel named Daniel Boudreau at the Pentagon was cooperating somewhat. He'd sent me Army records from the Vietnam War. Lots of paperwork that appeared not to have been looked at in years. He also suggested I contact the Vietnamese Embassy. They had records, too.

I read through the old files until I couldn't stay awake any longer and my head was throbbing severely. I was searching for anything that might link Ellis Cooper, Reece Tate, Laurence Houston, James Etra, Robert Bennett, or even Tran Van Luu to the string of murders.

I found no connection, nothing remotely promising. Was that possible?

None of the men had ever served together in Asia.

Late that night I got another e-mail from the Foot Soldier. Jesus Christ. Obviously, he wasn't Owen Handler. So who was sending the messages? Kyle Craig? Was he still trying to play with my head? How could he get the messages out of a supermax prison?

Somebody was sending them and I didn't like it. I also didn't trust the information I was getting. Was I being set up, too?

Detective Cross,

I am a little disappointed in your progress. You get on a good track, then you get off it. Look back at where you've been already. The answers are all in the past. Isn't that always the way it works out?

The note was signed *Foot Soldier*.

But there was something else at the bottom of the page. A very disturbing icon – *a straw doll*. Just like the ones we'd found.

After work on Wednesday of that week I visited the Vietnamese Embassy on Twentieth Street in Northeast. The FBI had made a call for me. I arrived at a little before six and went up to the fourth floor. I was met there by a translator named Thi Nguyen. At her desk were four large boxes of old records kept by the government of her country.

I sat in her small office and Thi Nguyen read passages to me. She didn't want to be doing this, I could tell. I supposed she'd been ordered to work late. On a wall behind her was a sign: *Embassy Of The Socialist Republic of Vietnam.* Also a portrait of Ho Chi Minh.

'There's nothing here, Detective. Nothing new,' she complained as she went through dusty files that were over thirty years old. I told her to please stay with it. She would sigh loudly, adjust her odd, black-rimmed glasses, and sullenly dig into another file. This pouty ritual went on for hours. I found her incredibly unpleasant.

At around nine o'clock, she looked up in surprise. 'There's something here,' she said. 'Maybe this is what you're looking for.'

'Tell me. Don't edit, please. Tell me exactly what you're reading.'

'That's what I've been doing, Detective. According to these records, there were unauthorized attacks on small villages in the An Lao Valley. Civilians seem to have been killed. This happened half a dozen times. Somebody must have known about it. Maybe even your Military Advisory Council.'

'Tell me everything that's in there,' I repeated. 'Please don't leave anything out. Read from the texts.'

The boredom and exasperation she had shown before were gone. Suddenly the translator was attentive, and also seemed a little frightened. What she was reading now was disturbing her.

'There are always unfortunate incidents during a war,' she lectured me. 'But this is a new pattern in the An Lao Valley. The killings seem to have been organized and methodical. Almost like your serial killers here in America.'

'There are serial killers in Asia, too,' I said.

Ms Nguyen bristled at my comment. 'Let me see. There were formal complaints made to your government and the US Army by officers in the ARVN. Did you know that? There are also repeated complaints from what was then called Saigon. This was a murder case, according to the ARVN. Murder, not war. The murder of innocent civilians, including children.' She frowned and shook her head. 'There's more about the precise pattern of the murders. Men, women and children, innocent villagers were killed. Often the bodies were painted.'

'Red, white, blue,' I said. 'The painting was a calling card left by the killers.'

Ms Nguyen looked up in alarm. 'How did you know? Did you already know about these horrible murders? What is your role in all this?'

'I'll tell you when we're finished. Don't stop now. Please. This could be what I've been looking for.'

About twenty minutes later, Ms Nguyen came upon something that I asked her to read a second time. 'A team of Army Rangers was sent into the An Lao Valley. It's unclear, but it seems they were dispatched to the area to investigate the murders. I'm sorry, Detective. It's also unclear here whether they succeeded or not.'

'Do you have any names?' I asked. 'Who was on this team?' I could feel the adrenalin ripping through my body now.

Ms Nguyen sighed and shook her head. Finally, she rose from her desk. 'There are more boxes on the fifth floor. Come with me, Detective. You say that people are still being killed?'

I nodded, then I followed Thi Nguyen upstairs. There was an entire wall of boxes and I helped her carry several of them down to her office.

The two of us worked late on Wednesday, then again on Thursday night, and we even got together during her lunch hour on Friday. She was hooked now, too. We learned that the Rangers sent to the An Lao Valley were military assassins. Unfortunately, none of the paperwork had been organized according to dates. It had just been thrown into boxes and left to collect dust, never to be read by anyone again.

Around two-fifteen on Friday we opened another few boxes crammed with papers pertaining to the investigation in the An Lao Valley.

Thi Nguyen looked up at me. 'I have names for the assassins,' she said. 'And I think I have a code name for the operation. I believe it was called *Three Blind Mice*.'

PART FOUR

EXIT WOUNDS

Chapter Seventy-Nine

I had three names now – three men who had been dispatched to the An Lao Valley to stop the murder of civilians there. I needed to be extremely careful with the information, and it took Sampson and I another week to track the men down and find out as much as we could about them.

The final confirmation that I needed came from Ron Burns at the FBI. He told me that the Bureau had suspected these men of doing two other professional hits: one a politician in Cincinnati, the second a union leader's wife in Santa Barbara, California.

The names were:

Thomas Starkey.

Brownley Harris.

Warren Griffin.

The Three Blind Mice.

The following weekend, Sampson and I went to Rocky Mount, North Carolina. We were chasing men who had played a part in mysterious violence in the An Lao Valley thirty years before. What in hell had really happened there? Why were people still dying now?

Less than five miles outside the city limits of Rocky Mount, tracts of farmland and crossroad county grocers still dominated the landscape. Sampson and I drove out into the country, then back to town again, passing the Rocky Mount-Wilson Airport and Nash General Hospital, as well as Heckler and Koch where Starkey, Harris and Griffin worked as the sales team for several military bases, including Fort Bragg.

Sampson and I entered Heels, a local sports bar, at around six o'clock. Race-car drivers as well as a few basketball players from the Charlotte Hornets frequented the place, so it was racially mixed. We were able to fit into the crowd, which was noisy and active. At least a dozen TVs blared from raised platforms.

The sports bar was less than a mile from Heckler and Koch US, where some of these men and women worked. Other than the thriving high-tech business community, Heckler and Koch (pronounced 'Coke') was one of the largest places of employment in town, just behind Abbott Laboratories and Consolidated Diesel. I wondered if the gun company might have some connection to the murders. Probably not, but maybe.

I struck up a conversation with a plant supervisor from H and K at the bar. We talked about the plight of the Carolina Panthers, and then I worked in the subject of the gun manufacturer. He was positive about his company, which he referred to as 'like a family' and 'definitely one of the best places to work in North Carolina, which is a good state to work in'. Then we talked about guns, the MP5 submachine gun in particular. He told me the MP5 was used by the Navy SEALS and elite SWAT teams, but it had also found its way into inner-city gangs. I already knew that about the MP5.

I mentioned Starkey, Harris and Griffin, casually.

'I'm surprised Tom and Brownie aren't here already. They usually stop in on a Friday. How do you know those boys?' he asked, but didn't seem surprised that I did.

'We served together a long time ago,' said Sampson. 'Back in sixty-nine and seventy.'

The supervisor nodded. 'You Rangers too?' he asked.

'No, just regular Army,' said Sampson. 'Just foot soldiers.'

We talked to some other H and K employees, and they spoke positively about the company. The guys we talked to knew Starkey, Harris and Griffin, and everybody knew they'd been Rangers. I got the impression that the three men were popular and might even be local heroes.

Around quarter past seven, Sampson leaned in close and whispered into my ear. 'Front door. Look who just blew in,' he said. 'Three business suits. Don't much look like killers.'

I turned slowly and looked. *No, they didn't look like killers.*

'But that's what they are,' I said to Sampson. 'Army assassins who look like the nicest guys in the bar, maybe in all of North Carolina.'

We watched the three of them for the rest of the night – just watched the trio of hit men.

Chapter Eighty

S ampson and I were staying out at a Holiday Inn near
the Interstate. We were up the next morning by six.

We had a potentially heart-stopping, but rather tasty
breakfast at a nearby Denny's (omelets and 'home fries
covered and smothered'). Then we planned out our big
day. We'd learned the night before that Heckler and Koch
had a big family-style picnic going that afternoon. We were
planning to crash it. Cause a little trouble if we could.

After breakfast we took a spin past the houses of the
three murder suspects. A slick DC group we liked called
Maze was playing from the CD. Nice contrast to the
folksiness of Rocky Mount. City meets country.

The killers' houses were in upscale developments called
Knob Hill, Falling River Walk, and Greystone. It looked as
if a lot of young professionals with families lived there.
The new South. Quiet, tasteful, civilized as hell.

'They know how to blend in,' Sampson said as we drove
by Warren Griffin's two-and-a-half story Colonial. 'Our
three killer boys.'

'Good at what they do,' I said. 'Never been caught. I really want to have a chat with them.'

Around eight, we went back to the Holiday Inn to get ready for the picnic and whatever else might happen today. It was hard to believe that the three killers fit so well into Rocky Mount. It made me wonder about pretty, innocent-looking small towns and what might be lurking behind their façades. Maybe nothing, maybe a whole lot of everything.

Sampson and I were originally from North Carolina, but we hadn't spent that much time here as adults, and unfortunately, most of it had been working on a couple of celebrated murder cases. The gun-company picnic was scheduled to start at eleven, and we figured we would show up at around one when the crowds were large. We knew from the night before that just about everybody from H and K, from the mailroom to stockroom to the corporate suite, would be on hand for the big day.

That included Starkey, Harris, Griffin – and their families.

And of course, Sampson and I.

It was time for a little payback.

Chapter Eighty-One

I t was a hot, humid day and even the cooks at the company picnic were checking the grill infrequently. They much preferred to stay in the shade and sip cold Dr Pepper soft drinks in their *'BBQ from Heaven'* aprons. Everybody seemed to be taking it easy, having a good time on a pretty Saturday. *Another cat's-eye marble bites the dust.*

Sampson and I sat under an ancient, leafy oak tree and listened to the symphony of local birds. We drank iced tea from Lucite cups that looked like real glass. We wore *H and K Rules* tee-shirts and looked as if we belonged, and always had.

The smell of ribs was strong in the air. Actually, the smoke from the grills was probably keeping the bugs from becoming an immediate problem.

'They sure know how to cook those ribs,' Sampson said.

They did, and so did I. Ribs, to cook properly, need indirect heat, and the fires had been built with two piles of charcoal – one in front, one in the back, but none in the middle where the racks with the ribs had been placed. I had learned about ribs, and all kinds of cooking, from Nana. She'd wanted me to be as good in the kitchen as she was. That wasn't going to happen real soon, but I was decent, at least. I could fill in when needed.

I even knew that there was a standing argument in the grilling world about the relative merits of the 'dry rub' versus the 'wet mop'. The dry rub was a mixture of salt, pepper, paprika and brown sugar, which was said to have both the heat and the sweetness to bring out the true flavor of the meat. The wet-mop mix had a base of apple cider, with added shallots, jalapeno peppers, ketchup, brown sugar and tomato paste. I liked the mop *and* the rub just fine – so long as the meat was cooked until it just about fell off the bone.

'Everybody is having such a good, all-American time,' Sampson said as we sat and watched the world go by. 'Remind me to tell you about Billie in Jersey.'

'Billie?' I asked. 'Who's Billie?'

'Tell you later, partner. We're working now. On the trail of three stone-cold killers.'

That we were. We were busy watching the families of Starkey, Harris and Griffin from a safe distance. I noticed that Thomas Starkey looked our way once or twice. Had he spotted us? If he had, he didn't seem overly concerned.

'You think they're the ones who killed Colonel Handler? Think they know who we are, sugar?' Sampson asked.

'If they don't, they probably will soon.'

Sampson didn't seem to mind. 'That's your big plan? Get us killed down here in Rocky Mount?'

'They won't do anything with their families around,' I said.

'You sure?'

'No,' I said. 'I'm not sure. But that's what my gut tells me.'

'They're killers, Alex.'

'Professional killers. Don't worry, they'll pick their spot.'

'Oh, I'm not worried,' Sampson said. 'I'm just anxious to get it on with these boys.'

As the afternoon progressed, we talked casually to some more H and K employees and their families. The people were easy to talk to and we were real friendly. Most of them said they liked where they worked a lot. Sampson and I passed ourselves off as new to the company and nobody questioned it. In fact, most everyone was cordial and welcoming, almost to a fault. Hard not to like the folks in Rocky Mount, most of them anyway.

Lunch was followed by team sports and other competitive games: swim races, volleyball, soccer, softball, and organized contests for the kids.

Starkey, Harris and Griffin eventually headed off toward one of the adjoining softball fields.

Sampson and I followed at a distance.

Let the games begin.

Chapter Eighty-Two

'Need a couple more to fill out this team. You big fellows play any ball?' asked an old man wearing a dusty Atlanta Braves shirt and ball cap. 'You're welcome to join in. It's a friendly little game.'

I glanced over at Sampson. He smiled and said, 'Sure, we'll play some ball.'

The two of us were put on the same team, which seemed the more ragtag and needier of the two. Starkey, Harris and Griffin were on the other team. Our worthy opponents for the friendly game.

'Looks like we're the underdogs,' Sampson said.

'We're not down here to win a softball game,' I said.

He grinned. 'Yeah, and we're not here to lose one either.'

The game was good-natured on the surface, but everything was heavily stacked against our team. Starkey and Harris were good athletes, and everybody on their team seemed decent and knew how to play. Our group was uneven, and they exploited our weaknesses. We were behind by two runs after the first inning, and four runs after the third.

As we jogged off the field to take our turn at bat, Sampson patted my butt. 'Definitely not down here to lose,' he said.

Sampson was scheduled to bat third that inning. I would be up fourth if somebody got on base. A skinny, older Mexican man led off with a bunt single and got razzed by our macho opponents for not having any *cojones*. The next batter, a big-bellied accountant, blooped a single just over the second baseman's head. More semi-good-natured razzing came from our opponents.

'Rather be lucky than good,' our guy yelled back from first base as he slapped his big beer belly.

Now Sampson stepped to the plate. He never took a practice swing, just touched the rubber base with the tip of the longest and heaviest bat he could find on the rack.

'Big power hitter. Better move back those fences!' Starkey called from shortstop. He looked like a ball-player, moved easily and fluidly at bat and in the field, bent the peak of his cap just so.

Sampson just stood there with the bat on his shoulder. Nobody except me knew what to expect from the big man, and even I couldn't always tell with him. The two of us had played a lot of ball together when we were kids. Sampson had been an all-city receiver as a junior in high school, but he didn't go out for the football team in his senior year. He was an even better baseball player, but he never played organized ball after Little League.

I stood on deck, trying to figure how he would play it.

Actually, there weren't any fences at the field, so he couldn't hit one out of the park if he wanted to. So what would he do?

The first pitch floated up to the plate, fat and juicy, but Sampson never took his bat off his shoulder. It was hard to imagine a more tempting pitch would come his way.

Warren Griffin was doing the pitching for their team. He was a decent-enough athlete, fielded his position well.

'Didn't like that one?' he called to Sampson. 'What's the matter with it?'

'No challenge.'

Griffin smiled. He signaled for Harris to come out to the mound. Brownley Harris was doing the catching, and he looked like a slightly shorter version of the old Red Sox great, Carlton Fisk. *Pudge.*

On the next pitch, Griffin wound up and delivered a windmill-style fastball toward home plate. He was real quick, what they call sneaky fast.

But so was Sampson.

He dropped his bat and sent a near-perfect drag bunt down the third-base line. They were so surprised, he could have walked to first base and made it easily. He was on, the bases full.

'Up to you, sugar,' Sampson called from first base. He was grinning at me, winking, pointing an imaginary six-gun my way.

I started to smile as I strolled to the plate. He'd put me on the spot, just like he'd planned it.

'You like a challenge, too?' Warren Griffin called from the pitcher's mound.

'You a bunter or a hitter?' Starkey taunted from his spot at shortstop.

The catcher, Brownley Harris, settled in behind me. 'What's it going to be, hot-shot? How you want it?'

I looked back at him. 'Surprise me,' I said.

Griffin set up for a windmill-style pitch so I figured he was coming with heat. *What the hell?* I thought. *Just a friendly little game.*

The fast pitch came in a little high, but it was close enough to my power wheel that I couldn't resist taking a whack. The bat cracked and the ball shot straight over the pitcher's head, still picking up speed and altitude. It flew over the center fielder's head, too. Our team of misfits was going crazy, screaming and cheering from the bench. Suddenly, there was some joy in Mudville.

I was on my horse, rounding the bases. Starkey gave me a look as I touched second and raced past him. It was as if he knew something. *Did he?*

I made it to third and saw Sampson ahead of me; he was waving me home. I didn't even look toward the outfield – I was coming no matter what happened out there.

I curled around third base, and then I accelerated. I probably hadn't moved this fast in years.

I was really motoring.

Brownley Harris was waiting for me at home plate – but where was the ball? I was moving like a runaway train when I saw the throw from the outfield skipping through the infield on two hops. Hell, it was going to beat me home. Goddamn it.

Harris held his ground as he took the perfect throw from the center fielder. He had me dead to rights.

I kept barreling toward him. Harris was blocking home plate with his beefy body. If I hit him hard it might shake the ball loose. His dark, hooded eyes held mine. He was ready for impact, whatever I could give him. He looked like he'd played some football; still looked tough and in shape. Army Ranger. Killer. His eyes bordered on mean.

I was bearing down on Harris and, as I got close, I lowered my shoulder. Let him see what was coming his way.

Then, at the last possible instant, I went wide and low. I did a pretty hook-slide around the catcher. With my left hand I touched home plate between his thick legs and muddy cleats.

'Safe!' the umpire yelled and spread his arms wide.

As I was getting up, I caught sight of Harris out of the corner of my eye. He was moving toward me fast. This could be trouble. No more friendly little game.

His right arm suddenly shot forward and he slapped me 'five'.

'Nice play,' he said. 'You got us that time, partner. Be ready for you next time. Hell, we're all on the same team anyway, right? H and K all the way.'

Jesus, he actually seemed like a nice guy.

For a killer.

Chapter Eighty-Three

'**Y**ou run pretty good for a washed-up cop in his early forties,' Sampson said as we walked through a dusty lot filled mostly with minivans and trucks. We'd seen enough at the company picnic. After our show of respectability we'd lost the softball game by seven runs, and it could have been even worse.

'At least I don't have to bunt to get on base,' I said.

'Last thing they expected, sugar. Worked, didn't it? Pissed'm off, too.'

'We lost the game.'

'But not the war,' said Sampson.

'This is true. Not the war. Not yet anyway.'

I drove from the picnic site out to the Falling River Walk development. I parked right around the corner from Thomas Starkey's house. It was redbrick with white trim on the windows, black shutters. The lot looked to be about an acre and was landscaped with rhododendron, hemlock and mountain laurel. It was well kept. We walked past a mass of yellow chrysanthemums to the side door.

'This how it's going to be from here on?' Sampson asked. 'Breaking and entering in broad daylight?'

'They probably know who we are,' I said. 'Know we're here for them.'

'Probably. Rangers are the premier light-infantry unit in the Army. Most are good guys, too. "Rangers lead the way." That's been their motto since Omaha Beach, D Day. Tip of the spear.'

'How about in Vietnam?' I asked.

'Lots of Rangers over there. They performed the heavy re-con missions. Seventy-fifth Ranger Regiment, three battalions. Exemplary soldiers, the best. Most of them. Probably had the best military assassins, too.'

It took me less than a minute to get inside the side door of the Starkey house, which led into a small laundry room that reeked of bleach and detergent. We didn't hear any alarm going off, but that didn't mean we hadn't tripped one coming inside.

'Could the three of them still be in the Army? Special assignment?' I asked.

'The thought had crossed my mind. I hope this isn't about something the Army is trying to hide.'

'But you think it might be?'

'Like I said – I hope it's not. I *do* like the Army, sugar. Hoo-hah!'

The house was only a few years old, and it was immaculate and strikingly ordered inside. Two fieldstone fireplaces on the first floor, vaulted ceilings, a game room with a wet bar and a pool table. I figured the house was probably around five thousand square feet and cost maybe four hundred thousand. Thomas Starkey lived pretty well for a salesman. So did Griffin and Harris from the look of their new houses.

Everything was neat and clean; even the kids' toys were stacked and arranged on shelves. Starkey and his wife sure ran a tight ship.

The kitchen was high tech, with a big Below Zero refrigerator. Shiny, stainless-steel All-clad pots and pans hung above the work station. A giant cast-iron skillet had a place of pride on the right back burner of the stove.

Off the master bedroom was a small room that turned out to be Starkey's den. Lots of Army souvenirs and pictures. I looked at the photographs on the walls, saw Harris and Griffin in several. *But none of the men whom they had set up*. I didn't really expect to see Ellis Cooper in a picture on Thomas Starkey's wall, but that didn't stop me from hoping.

Sampson was opening desk drawers and examining the contents of several cabinets built into the wall. He came to a closet with a padlock on it. He looked over at me.

I shrugged. 'Go for it. That's what we're here for.'

'No turning back now.'

He took out his Glock and smashed down with the butt. The padlock held, but he had snapped the hinge off the wall. Obviously, the lock was just to keep out Starkey's kids, and maybe his wife.

'Dirty pictures,' Sampson said as he rummaged around inside. 'Skin magazines, some nasty bondage. One with really young girls. Here the women are shaved. Lots of Asian girls. Fancy that. Maybe they did those girls in New York.'

He checked the closet for false sides. 'Nothing. Just the sleazy porn collection. He's not the husband and daddy of the year, but I guess we knew that already.'

I kept looking, but I didn't think I'd find anything incriminating. 'He must keep the good stuff somewhere else. I guess we should go. Leave everything the way it is. I want Starkey to know we were here.'

'Might get Tom in some trouble with the missus,' Sampson said, and winked.

'Good deal. He should be in trouble with somebody.'

Sampson and I walked back through the house and out the side door again. Birds were chirping in the trees. How sweet. The sun was a brilliant white-gold orb in blue skies. Nice town, Rocky Mount.

A blue GMC Suburban was parked out front. Starkey, Harris and Griffin were waiting for us.

Three Blind Mice.

Also, three against two.

Chapter Eighty-Four

No point in being subtle. Sampson and I took our guns out. We held them with the barrels down, not pointed at anyone. The three of them didn't appear to be armed. *Just a friendly little game, right.*

'Nothing's going to happen here,' Starkey called to us. 'This is where my wife and children live. It's a good neighborhood. Decent people in all these houses up and down the street.'

'And it's also where you keep your porn collection,' I said. 'S&M, bondage. Memories of your sweethearts from the war.'

He smiled thinly, nodded. 'That too. You're detectives, right? DC? Friends of Sergeant Ellis Cooper. Seems to me that you're a long ways from home. Why don't you go back to Washington? It's safer there than here in Rocky Mount. Believe it or not.'

'We know what you've done,' I told him. 'Most of it anyway. We don't know why yet. That'll come. We're getting close. The An Lao Valley in Vietnam? What happened there, Colonel Starkey? It was real bad, right? Things got out of control. Why is Three Blind Mice still working?'

Starkey didn't deny the murders or anything else I said. 'There's nothing you can do to us. Like I said, I think you should go home now. Consider this a friendly warning. We're not bad guys. We're just doing our job.'

'What if we don't go?' Sampson asked. 'What if we continue the investigation here in Rocky Mount? You killed a friend of mine.'

Starkey clasped his hands together, then he looked at Harris and Griffin. I could tell they weren't into friendly warnings.

'Don't come near any of our houses again,' Starkey said. His eyes were cold and hard. The assassin. *We're not bad guys. We're a whole lot worse than that.*

Brownley Harris pushed himself away from the hood of the Suburban. 'You hear what the man said? You two niggers listening? You *oughtta* be. Now clear the fuck out of here and don't ever come back. You don't come to a man's house with this shit. Not the way it's done, you hear? You fucking hear me?'

I smiled. 'You're the hothead. That's good to know. Starkey is the leader. So what does that make you, Griffin? You just muscle?'

Warren Griffin laughed out loud. 'That's right. I'm just muscle. And artillery. I'm the one who eats guys like you for breakfast.'

I didn't move a muscle. Neither did Sampson. We continued to stare at the three of them. 'I am curious

about one thing, Starkey. How do you know about us?
Who told you?'

His answer shook me to the core.

'Foot Soldier,' he said. Then Colonel Thomas Starkey
smiled and tipped his ball cap.

Chapter Eighty-Five

Sampson and I rode the Interstate back to Washington late that afternoon. I was really starting to dislike, or at least tire of I-95 and its thundering herd of slip-sliding, exhaust-spewing tractor-trailers.

'The circumstances could be better, but it's good spending all this time with you,' I said as we tooled along in the passing lane. 'You're too quiet, though. What's up? Something's bothering you.'

He looked my way. 'You remember a time – you were about eleven – I came over? Spent a couple of weeks with you and Nana?'

'I remember a lot of times like that,' I told him. 'Nana used to say we were brothers, just not flesh and blood ones. You were always at the house.'

'This time was different, sugar. I even know why you don't remember. Let me tell it.'

'All right.'

'See, I never used to go home after school. Reason being, nobody was there most of the time. That night I got home around nine, nine-thirty. Made myself corned beef hash for dinner. Sat down to watch some tube. I used to like *Mission Impossible* back then, wait for it all week. There was a knock at the door.

'I went to see who was there, and it was Nana. She gave me a big hug, just like she still does when she sees me. Asked me if I had some corned beef hash for her, too. Said she liked hers with eggs on top. Then she cackled her cackle, you know.'

'I don't remember any of this. Why was she at your house so late at night?'

Sampson continued with his story. 'That afternoon my mother was convicted for possession of heroin to sell. She'd been sentenced. Social Services came by, but I was out. Somebody called Nana Mama.

'So Nana came over, and she actually ate a little of the hash I'd cooked. Told me it was pretty good. Maybe I would be a famous chef one day. Then she said I was coming over to your house for a while. She told me why. She had done some of her magic with Child Welfare. That was the first time that Nana saved me. The first of many times.'

I nodded. Listened. Sampson wasn't finished with his story.

'She was the one who helped get me into the Army after high school. Then into the police academy when I got out of the service. She's your grandmother, but she's more a mother to me than my own flesh. And I never had a father, not really. Neither of us did. I always thought that held us together in the beginning.'

It wasn't like Sampson to go on and open up like this. I still didn't speak. I had no idea where he was headed, but I let him go as much as he wanted to.

'I always knew I didn't have it in me to be a father or a good husband. It was just something I felt inside. You?'

'I had some fears before I met Maria,' I said. 'Then they just went away. Most of them anyway. I knew Maria and I would be good together. First time I held Damon the rest of the fears pretty much disappeared for good.'

Sampson began to smile, then he was laughing. 'I met somebody, Alex. It's strange, but she makes me happy and I trust her with my secrets. Look at me, I'm grinnin' like a goddamn Halloween pumpkin.'

Both of us were laughing now. Why not? It was the first time I'd seen Sampson in love, and we'd been friends for a long time.

'I'll mess it up somehow,' he said. But he was still laughing. We joked and laughed most of the rest of the way home. Jesus, John Sampson had a girlfriend.

Billie.

Chapter Eighty-Six

Nana Mama always used to say, '*Laugh before breakfast, cry before dinner.*' If you raise a family, you know there's some truth to that, crazy as it sounds.

When I got back to Fifth Street that night there was a red-and-white EMS truck sitting in front of our house.

I shut down the Porsche and bounded out of it.

It was raining, and the bracing wind and water whipped at my face. Partially blinded by the rain, I hurtled up the front steps and entered the house. My heart was hammering and a voice inside whispered *no, no, no*.

I heard voices coming from the living room and rushed in there expecting the worst.

Nana Mama and the kids were sitting on the old sofa. They were all holding hands.

Across from them sat a woman in a white lab coat. I recognized Dr Kayla Coles from the night with Damon's sick friend, Ramon.

'You missed all the excitement,' Nana said as she saw me enter the room.

'Imagine that, Daddy,' said Jannie. '*You* missed the excitement.'

I looked toward the doctor sitting in the easy chair. 'Hello, Doctor.'

She had a good smile. 'Nice to see you again.'

I turned to Nana. 'Exactly what excitement did I miss? For starters, what's the EMS truck doing outside?'

She shrugged. 'I thought I had a heart attack, Alex. Turns out, it was just a fainting spell.'

Dr Coles spoke. 'Nana doesn't remember passing out. I was down the street at the time. I work with a group that brings health care into the neighborhoods of Southeast. Makes it easier for some people to get good care. More personal, and definitely more affordable.'

I interrupted. 'Nana passed out. What happened to her?'

'Damon saw the EMS truck and he came and got me. Nana was already up on her feet. She had an irregular heartbeat. Rapid, threading. The pulse in her wrist wasn't as fast as the actual heart rate, so there could be some diminished circulation. We took her over to St Anthony's for a few tests.'

Nana shrugged the whole thing off. 'I fell down, went boom, in the kitchen. Always hoped it would be there. Damon and Jannie were just great, Alex. About time they started taking care of me for a change.'

She laughed, and so did Dr Coles. I was glad they both saw the humor in the situation.

'You're still here. It's past nine,' I said to the doctor.

She smiled. Good bedside manner, or whatever this

was. 'We were having so much fun I decided to stay for a while. I still have one more stop, but Mr Bryant doesn't get off work until ten.'

'And,' I said, 'you were waiting for me to get home.'

'Yes, I thought that would be the best idea. Nana says you work late a lot of nights. Could we talk for a minute?'

Chapter Eighty-Seven

The two of us stepped out onto the front porch. Heavy rain was pelting down on the overhang and the air was damp and cool. The good doctor pulled a gray car sweater around herself.

'I've already had this chat with your grandmother,' she said. 'Nana asked that I talk to you, answer all your questions. I would never go behind her back, or condescend to her in any way.'

'That's a good idea,' I said. 'I think you'd find that she's awfully hard to condescend to.'

Kayla suddenly laughed. 'Oh, *I know*. I had your nana – sorry, Mrs Regina Hope Cross in eighth grade. She's still probably the most inspirational teacher I've had. That includes undergraduate at Brandeis and medical school at Tufts. Thought I would flash my resume by you.'

'Okay, I'm impressed. So what's the matter with Nana?'

Kayla sighed. 'She's getting *old*, Alex. She admits to eighty-two. The tests we took at St Anthony's won't come back until some time tomorrow or the next day. The lab boys will call me, then I'll call Nana myself. My concern? She's been having palpitations for several weeks. Dizziness, lightheadedness, shortness of breath. She tell you?'

I shook my head. Suddenly I felt more than a little embarrassed. 'I had no idea. She told me she was feeling fine. There was a rough morning a couple of weeks back, but no complaints from her since.'

'She doesn't want you to worry about her. When she was at St Anthony's we did an EKG, an echocardiogram, routine lab work. As I mentioned, her heartbeat is irregular.

'On the positive side of things, there's no sign of edema. Her lungs are clear. No evidence that she's suffered a stroke, even a slight one. Nana has very good general muscle strength for somebody her age, or even younger.'

'So what happened to her? You have any idea?'

'We'll have the test results in a day. Dr Redd in the lab was in Nana's class, too. If I was to hazard a guess, I would say atrial fibrillation. This involves the two small upper chambers of the heart, the atria. They seem to be quivering, rather than beating effectively. There's some risk of clotting.'

'I take it she's okay to be here tonight,' I said. 'I don't want her stubbornness to keep her out of the hospital if she needs to be there. Money isn't a consideration.'

Kayla Coles nodded. 'Alex, my opinion is that it's safe for her to be home right now. She said her sister will be coming from Maryland tomorrow. I think that's a wise precaution. Someone to help with the kids and the house.'

'I'll help with the kids,' I said. 'And the house.'

She raised an eyebrow. 'I believe we've already established that you work too hard.'

I sighed and shut my eyes for a couple of seconds. The news was finally hitting me, sinking in. Now I had to force myself to deal with it. Nana was in her early eighties, and she was sick.

Kayla reached out and lightly patted my arm. 'She's getting up there, but she's strong, and she wants to be around for a long time. That's important. Alex, Nana believes that you and the children need her.'

I finally managed a thin smile. 'Well, she's right about that.'

'Don't let her do too much right now.'

'Hard to keep her down.'

'Well, *tie* her if you have to,' Kayla Coles said, and then she laughed.

I didn't, couldn't right then. I knew a fair amount about heart disease from my days at Johns Hopkins. I would definitely keep a closer watch on Nana. 'What about you, Dr Coles? What about your work schedule? Nearly ten o'clock and you still have more house calls.'

She shrugged, and seemed a little embarrassed by the question. 'I'm young, I'm strong, and I believe the people in these neighborhoods need decent, affordable health care. So that's what I'm providing – trying to. Goodnight, Alex. Take good care of your grandmother.'

'Oh, I will. I promise.'

'The road to hell,' she said.

'Paved with good intentions.'

She nodded and walked off the porch. 'Say goodnight to everybody for me.' Dr Coles headed down Fifth Street to her final appointment of the day.

Chapter Eighty-Eight

I did some more background work on the Three Blind Mice the next day, taped notes to my wall in the attic, but I couldn't get into it, couldn't concentrate worth a damn. Nana's lab tests came back in the afternoon, and as Kayla Coles had promised, she did call the house. The two of us had a talk on the phone after she spoke to Nana.

'I just wanted to thank you for your help,' I said as I got on the line. 'I'm sorry if I was rude the other night.'

'What makes you think you were rude? You were a little frightened is all. I don't think "rude" is part of your makeup. Anyway, let me tell you about your grandmother. She *is* suffering from atrial fibrillation, but given the options, that's not such bad news.'

'Tell me why I should be happy about it,' I said.

'Not happy. But the treatment is non-invasive and has a good success rate. I think we can treat her with a catheter ablation. We'll start there. She'll be able to go home the next day, and hopefully be her old self in a week.'

'When should she go in for the procedure?' I asked.

'That's up to her. I wouldn't wait more than a couple of weeks. She sounded a little stubborn when I brought up a hospital stay. Says she's too busy.'

'I'll talk to her. See if it helps. What do we do until then?'

'Just baby aspirin, believe it or not. One eighty-one milligram tablet a day. She also has to limit her caffeine – coffee and tea. And she should avoid stress-related situations. Good luck on that one.'

'That's it?' I asked.

'For now, yes. Please watch the stress on her. I'll stay involved if she wants me to.'

'I know she does.'

Kayla Coles laughed. 'Good. She's a smart woman, isn't she? We're going to make sure she sees a hundred.'

I laughed. 'I hope *I* get to see her reach a hundred. So, no special precautions until we go in for the procedure?'

'No, not really. Just try not to bring too much excitement into her life.'

'I'll do my best,' I said.

'You do your best and try not to get *shot*,' said Kayla Coles before she hung up.

Chapter Eighty-Nine

No way I was going to get shot staying at home – or so I believed. A couple of mornings after my conversation with Dr Kayla Coles, I came downstairs to make breakfast for the kids. Nana was sitting at her spot at the kitchen table, a large brown mug steaming in front of her.

'Unh, uh.' I wagged a finger at her.

'Decaffeinated,' she said. 'Don't start in on me, Alex.'

'Nope. I won't even say that you're a little touchy this morning. Sleep okay?'

'Nobody my age sleeps okay. I did set up an appointment for the catheter ablation. I go in a week from today. Happy?' she asked.

'Very happy,' I said, then I went and gave her a hug, which Nana returned in kind. Dr Kayla was right – she was strong for her age.

Later that morning I had a pretty good talk with FBI Director Burns. He told me he had someone trying to track the e-mail from the Foot Soldier, but so far no luck on it. He asked if I'd given serious consideration to his offer to work at Quantico. I'd been expecting the question.

'I've thought about it some. My life is suddenly a little complicated. For one thing, I need to get some kind of closure on this case with the Army.'

'They helping or getting in the way? The Army?' Burns asked.

'A little of both. I've met some good people. Army's like everybody else, though. They want to solve their own problems. There's something incredibly nasty going on with this murder case. They know it, and so do I. I feel it in my bones. There will be more murders. That's my fear.'

'If I can help,' Burns said. 'No strings attached, Alex. This is a big case. I think it's important, too.'

'I appreciate that.'

After I got off the phone, I went in search of Nana. She was futzing around in the kitchen as usual. *Her* kitchen. *Her* house.

'I need a rest. So do you,' I said to her. 'Where do you want to go after your procedure?'

'Paris,' Nana said without blinking an eye. 'Then maybe Rome. Venice, of course. Florence would be real nice. Then come home through London. Stop in and see the Queen. What do you think? Sound too rich for your blood? Maybe you were thinking of a train ride to Baltimore?' she asked, and laughed at her own joke. She was a funny lady, always had been.

'I have some money put away,' I told her.

'Me too,' she said. 'Mad money. What about Jamilla? What about your job?'

'If Jamilla could take some time off, that would be great. She likes her job, though.'

'That sounds familiar, doesn't it? How's *your* marble collection? Maybe you should buy a couple of jars for her.'

I laughed. Then I went over and put my arms around Nana. Couldn't help myself lately. 'I love you, old woman,' I said. 'I don't tell you that enough, and when I do, it isn't with the passion I feel.'

'That's nice to hear,' she said. 'You can be so sweet sometimes. I love you too, and I always say it with the passion that I feel.'

'You feeling all right?' I asked.

'Today's good. Tomorrow, who knows?' She shrugged. 'I'm making some lunch. Don't ask if you can help. I'm fine. Still on the right side of the grass.'

After lunch, I went upstairs to my office in the attic to think about what my next steps should be. There was a fax waiting. I wagged my finger at it. '*Unh, uh.*'

It was a copy of a news story in the *Miami Herald*. I read about the execution last night of a man named Tichter at the Florida State Prison in Starke. Abraham Tichter had been in Vietnam. Special Forces.

Scrawled at the bottom of the fax was the following:

Innocent of these murders in Florida. Wrongfully accused, convicted and executed. Abraham Tichter makes six. In case you aren't keeping count.

Foot Soldier

I was keeping count.

Chapter Ninety

E ver since Nana had been under the weather I'd been doing the grocery shopping and most of the household chores. Usually I took little Alex with me to the small Safeway on Fourth Street. That's what I did early in the afternoon.

I carried him high on my shoulders, out the kitchen door and down the driveway to my car.

Alex was giggling and yapping as he always does. The boy never shuts up or sits still. He's a bouncing ball of pure energy and I can't get enough of him.

I was absently thinking about the last message from Foot Soldier, so I don't even know why I happened to notice the black Jeep traveling down Fifth.

It was moving at around thirty, right about the speed limit.

I don't know why I paid it much attention, but I did. My eyes never left it as it came toward little Alex and me.

Suddenly, the barrel of a black Tec protruded through the side window of the Jeep. I pulled down the baby, then

dropped to the ground, whipping my body sideways to avoid landing on Alex.

The shooting started.

Pop-pop-pop-pop-pop.

I bellied across the lawn, shielding my baby under my left arm, and then dragging him behind a shade tree. I needed cover between us and the gunman.

I didn't get a good look inside the Jeep, but I did see that the driver and the shooter were white. Two of them – not three.

I couldn't tell if they were the men from Rocky Mount. Who else could it be, though? The shooters from West Point? Were they the same? What was happening now on Fifth Street? Who had ordered it?

Pop-pop-pop-pop-pop.

Pop-pop-pop-pop-pop.

Bullets cracked into the walls of the house and a front window shattered. I had to stop the attack somehow. *But how?* I crawled to the porch, and made it just before another round of fire.

Pop-pop-pop-pop-pop.

Unbelievable, even for Southeast.

I pushed Alex down behind the porch. He was screaming bloody murder now. Poor frightened little boy. I kept him down on the ground. Then lifted my head and got a quick peek at the Jeep stopped in front of my house.

Pop-pop-pop-pop-pop-pop-pop.

I returned fire. Three carefully aimed shots, so as not to hit someone in the neighborhood. Then two more shots. *Yes!* I knew that I got the shooter. Possibly in the chest, but maybe the throat. I saw him jerk back hard and then slump over the seat. No more shots came.

Suddenly the Jeep took off, tires screeching, backside shimmy-shaking as it skidded around the nearest corner.

I carried Alex inside and herded Nana and the baby into her room. I made them stay down on the floor. Then I called Sampson and he was at the house in minutes. I was just about past being shocked and afraid for my family, when I became as angry as I'd ever been. My body shook with rage and the need for retaliation.

'Lot of broken windows, some bullet holes in the walls. Nobody hurt,' Sampson said after a quick walk around the house.

'It was a warning. Otherwise I think they would have killed me. They came to the house to deliver a message. Just like when we went to Starkey's house in Rocky Mount.'

Chapter Ninety-One

It was just past four in the morning when Thomas Starkey waltzed out the kitchen door of his home. He walked across a dewy patch of lawn, then climbed into his blue Suburban. It started right up. Starkey always kept it in perfect condition, even serviced it himself.

'I'd like to take a few potshots at the fucker right now,' Sampson said at my side. We were parked in deep shadows at the end of the street. 'Blow out a few windows in his house. Spread a little terror his way.'

'Hold that thought,' I said.

A few minutes later, the Suburban stopped and picked up Warren Griffin, who lived nearby in Greystone. It drove on to Knob Hill and picked up Brownley Harris. Then the Suburban sped out of Rocky Mount on US-64, heading in the direction of Raleigh.

'None of them look shot up,' Sampson said. 'That's too bad. So who'd you shoot on Fifth Street?'

'I have no idea. Complicates things though, doesn't it? These three know something. They're in this conspiracy we've been hearing about.'

'The silent gray wall?'

'That's the one. Seems to work pretty well, too.'

I didn't have to follow too closely, didn't even have to keep the Suburban in sight. Earlier that morning, around three o'clock, I'd slapped a radio-direction-finding device under the vehicle. Ron Burns was helping me in any way he could. I'd told him about the shooting at my house.

I kept a good distance behind the killers. The Suburban stayed on US-64 past Zebulon, then I-440 to 85th South. We went by Burlington, Greensboro, Charlotte, Gastonia and then entered South Carolina.

Sampson sat beside me on the front seat, but he fell asleep before we got to South Carolina. He had worked a shift the day before and he was exhausted. He finally woke up in Georgia, yawned, and stretched his big body as best he could in the cramped space.

'Where are we?'

'Lavonia.'

'Oh, that's good news. Where's Lavonia?'

'Near Sandy Cross. We're in Georgia. Still hot on their trail.'

'You think this is another hit coming up?'

'We'll see.'

At Doraville we stopped at a diner and had breakfast. The state-of-the-art device attached to the Suburban was still tracking. It seemed unlikely that they'd check and find it at this point.

The breakfast – cheese omelets, country ham and grits – was a little disappointing. The diner looked just about

perfect, and it sure smelled good when we walked inside, but the generous portions were bland, except for the country ham, which was too salty for me.

'You going to follow up with Burns? Maybe become an FBI man?' Sampson asked after he'd downed his second coffee. I could tell he was finally waking up.

'I don't know for sure. Check with me in a week or so. I'm a little burnt out right now. Like this food.'

Sampson nodded. 'It'll do. I'm sorry I got you involved in all this, Alex. I don't even know if we can bring them down. They're cocky, but they're careful when they need to be.'

I agreed. 'I think they did the hits solely for money. But that doesn't explain enough. What happened to start the killing? Who's behind it? Who's paying the bills?'

Sampson's eyes narrowed. 'The three of them got a taste for killing in the war. Happens sometimes. I've seen it.'

I put down my knife and fork and pushed the plate away. No way could I finish off the omelet and ham. I'd barely touched the grits, which needed something. Maybe cheddar cheese? Onions, sautéed mushrooms?

'I owe you. This is big debt, Alex,' Sampson said.

I shook my head. 'You don't owe me a thing. But I'll probably collect on it anyway.'

We went back out to the car and followed the signal for another two hours. The trip had taken from morning into the early afternoon.

We were on I-75 which we took to US-41, and then *old* 41. Then we were on some narrow, meandering country road in Kennesaw Mountain Park. We were following three killers in northern Georgia, about eight hours from Rocky Mount, close to five hundred miles.

I passed the turn-off the first time and had to go back. A turkey vulture was sitting there watching us. The hills around here were heavily forested and the foliage was thick and ornery-looking.

'We ought to park somewhere along the main road. Hide the car as best we can. Then walk on in through the woods,' I said.

'Sounds like a plan. I hate the fucking woods, though.'

I found a little turn-in that would keep the car hidden. We opened the trunk and took out guns, ammo and night-vision goggles for each of us. Then we walked about half a mile through the thick woods before we could see a small cabin. Smoke was curling out of a fieldstone chimney.

A very cozy spot. For what, though? A meeting of some kind? Who was here?

The cabin was near a small lake that was fed by the headwaters of the Jacks River, at least that was how it was marked. A stand of hemlocks, maples and beech trees enveloped the clearing in deep green. Some of the trees were easily six feet wide.

The blue Suburban was parked in front of the cabin – but so was a silver Mercedes station wagon. It had North Carolina plates.

'They've got company. Who the hell is this?' Sampson asked. 'Maybe we caught a break.'

We saw the front door open and Colonel Thomas

Starkey stepped outside. He had on a green tee-shirt and baggy fatigue pants.

Right behind him was Marc Sherman, Cumberland County's district attorney. *Christ.*

It was the lawyer who had prosecuted and convicted Ellis Cooper for the murders of three women that he didn't commit.

Chapter Ninety-Two

'**W**hat the hell is this? You *know* who he is?' Sampson asked. His temperature was rising fast.

'I remember him. Like you said, maybe we caught a little break. But why would Marc Sherman be here?'

Sampson and I were crouched behind a couple of ancient beech trees about a hundred yards from the cabin. The forest was eerily dark and almost seemed primitive. The roots of the huge trees all around us were carpeted by small ferns. On the walk there our legs got a good lashing from the catbrier and blackberry stickers.

'We're in deep shit somewhere around Kennesaw, Georgia. We traveled a lot of hours to get here. Now what?' John asked.

'Now we wait. We *listen*,' I said.

I reached into a cloth duffel bag and pulled out a black box attached to what looked like a silver wand. The apparatus was a long-distance microphone, compliments of my new good buddies at the Bureau in Quantico.

Sampson nodded when he saw what it was. 'FBI wants you *real* bad.'

I nodded back. 'That they do. This is a state-of-the-art unit. But we should get a little closer.'

We made our way up toward the cabin, crawling on our hands and knees between the towering trees. Besides the long-distance mike, Sampson and I had rifles, and 9-millimeter Glocks.

'Take one of these,' I said. 'In case you don't like the NVGs.' I handed him a pocket scope that worked in day or night. Fully extended, it was less than six inches long. Another valuable loan from the FBI.

'Only fair, I guess,' Sampson said. 'The boys probably have a couple of war toys of their own inside that log cabin.'

'That's what I was thinking. It's the argument I used with Burns. That and the fact that they came after me at my house. Burns has three kids of his own. He was sympathetic.'

Sampson glanced over at me. 'I thought you didn't know it was them in Washington?' he whispered.

'I don't. I'm not so sure it was. I had to tell Burns something. I don't know that it *wasn't* them.'

Sampson grinned and shook his head. 'You're gonna get fired before you get hired.'

I stayed close to the ground and trained one end of the mike at the cabin. We were only fifty yards away now. I worked the microphone around until the voices were as clear as if they were just a few feet away from us.

I recognized Starkey's voice. 'Thought we'd party a little

tonight, Counselor. Tomorrow we're going to hunt deer up on the mountain. You in?'

'I have to go back tonight,' said Marc Sherman. 'No hunting for me, I'm afraid.'

There was a brief silence, then a burst of laughter. Three or four men joined in.

Brownley Harris spoke up. 'That's just fine, Sherman. Take your blood money and run, why don't you? You hear this one? The Devil takes a meeting with this lawyer.'

'I heard it,' said Sherman.

'Funny, Marc. Now listen. Devil is slick as shit, you know. I mean, *you know*, right, Counselor? Devil says, "I'll make you a senior partner right now. Today." Young turk lawyer asks, "What do I have to do?" Devil says, "I want your immortal soul. Beat. And also the immortal souls of everyone in your family." The young lawyer stops and thinks, and he eyes the Devil something fierce. Then the lawyer says, "What's the catch?" '

There was raucous laughter from inside the cabin. Even Sherman joined in.

'That's even funny the fourth time. You *do* have the rest of my money?' he asked once the laughter had stopped.

'Of course we do. We've been paid, and you're going to be paid in full. We keep our deals, Mr Sherman. You can trust us. We're men of honor.'

Suddenly, I heard a loud noise off to the left of where we were crouched. Sampson and I swiveled around in a hurry. What the hell was this? A red sports car was coming fast up the dirt road. Too fast.

'Now who the hell is this?' Sampson asked in a whisper.

'More killers? Maybe the shooters from Washington?'

'Whoever it is, they're moving.'

We watched as the red car bounced up the badly rutted dirt road. It pulled in behind the Suburban, screeched to a stop.

The front door of the cabin opened. Starkey, then Harris stepped outside onto the porch.

The doors of the sports car were flung open simultaneously, almost as if the action was choreographed.

Two dark-haired women stepped out. Asian and very pretty. They were wearing skimpy tops and short skirts. Both had on outrageous shoes with high-heels. The driver held up a bottle in silver wrapping paper, smiled, and waved it at Starkey.

'*Chao mung da den voi to am cua chung toi*,' Starkey called from the front porch.

'Vietnamese,' Sampson said. 'Starkey said something like, "Welcome to our hootch." '

Chapter Ninety-Three

We had been observing the rustic cabin for more than two hours, and now we watched the sun dip behind the mountains. It had gotten much colder and my body was feeling stiff and I was tired from the drive. The wind whistled through the forest, whistled and sometimes roared. It felt like it was blowing right through me.

'We're going to get them,' Sampson whispered hoarsely. I think he was trying to cheer me up. 'Maybe tonight, maybe not. They're making mistakes, Alex.'

I agreed with that. 'Yes, they are. They're not invincible. I'm not even sure if they have the whole story themselves. They're just a piece of this.'

We could hear them inside the cabin – every word. Marc Sherman had apparently decided to stay for the party. Rock music echoed from the cabin. Janis Joplin was wailing, and one of the Asian women sang along. It sounded like bad karaoke, but nobody complained. Then the Doors came on. Memories of Vietnam, I suppose. 'This is the end . . .'

Occasionally, someone would pass by a window. The Asian women had both taken off their tops. The taller of the two stepped outside for a few minutes. She smoked a joint, taking greedy puffs.

Harris came out and joined her. They spoke English on the porch.

'I used to know your mama-san,' he said, and giggled.

'You're kidding?' the girl laughed and blew out jets of smoke. 'Of course you're joking. I get it. Sort of.' She looked to be in her late teens, maybe early twenties. Her breasts were large and too round, augmented. She wobbled slightly on the high-heels.

'No, I knew her. She was my hootch mama. I made it with her, and now I'm going to make it with you. See the irony?'

The girl laughed again. 'I see that you're stoned.'

'Well, there's that too, my smart little dink. The thing is, maybe you're my daughter.'

I tuned out on the conversation and stared at the outline of the A-frame cabin. It looked like some family's vacation house. We'd heard that the three of them had been using the place since the mid-eighties. They'd already talked about murders committed in these woods, but it wasn't clear who had been killed, or why. Or where the bodies were buried.

Jim Morrison was still singing 'The End'. The TV was on too, a University of Georgia football game. Georgia versus Auburn. Warren Griffin was rooting loudly and obnoxiously for Auburn. Marc Sherman had apparently gone to Georgia and Griffin was breaking his chops.

Sampson and I stayed in a culvert, a safe distance away. It was getting even colder, the wind screaming through the large hemlocks and beech trees.

'Starkey doesn't seem to be partying,' Sampson finally said. 'You notice that? What's he doing?'

'Starkey likes to watch. He's the cautious one, the leader. I'm going to move a little closer. We haven't seen or heard from the other girl in a while. Makes me nervous.'

Just then, we heard Marc Sherman raise his voice. 'Jesus, don't cut her. Be careful! C'mon, man. Put away the K-Bar!'

'Why the hell not cut her?' Harris yelled at the top of his voice. 'What the hell is she to you? You cut her, then. Try it, you'll like it. You cut her, Counselor. Get your hands dirty for a change!'

'I'm warning you, Harris. Put the goddamn knife down.'

'You're warning *me*? That's pretty rich. Here – take the knife. *Take it!* Here you go!'

The lawyer groaned loudly. I was pretty sure he'd been stabbed.

The girls began to scream. Sherman was moaning in excruciating pain. Chaos had taken over inside the cabin.

'*Cockadau!*' Harris suddenly yelled in Vietnamese. He sounded a little nuts.

'*Cockadau* means kill,' Sampson told me.

Chapter Ninety-Four

Sampson and I were up in a flash and sprinting full-out toward the cabin. We reached the front door together. He went in first with his gun drawn.

'Police!' he yelled over the blaring rock music and TV. 'Police! Hands in the air. Now!'

I was right behind Sampson when Starkey opened up with an MP5. At the same time, Griffin fired a handgun from across the room. The two Asian women were screaming as they scampered out the cabin's rear door. They had enough street smarts to get out of there fast. I saw that the smaller woman had a deep gash across her cheek. Her face was dripping blood.

Marc Sherman lay on the floor, motionless. There were dark splatters of blood on the wall behind the lawyer's body. He was dead.

The big gun erupted again, noise and smoke filling the room. My ears were ringing. I wasn't even sure if I'd been hit or not.

'Move out!' Sharkey yelled to the others.

'*Di di mau!*' Brownley Harris shouted, and actually seemed to be laughing. Was he completely mad? Were they all insane?

The three killers bolted out the back door. Warren Griffin covered the retreat with heavy fire. They didn't want a final shootout inside the cabin. Starkey had other plans for his team.

Sampson and I fired at the retreating men, but they made it out. We approached the back door slowly. Nobody was waiting there, and no more shots were fired at us for the moment.

Suddenly there was the sound of shooting away from the cabin. Half a dozen hollow *pops*. I heard the shrill screams of the two women cut through the trees.

I peeked my head around the corner of the cabin. I didn't like what I saw. The two women hadn't made it to their car. Both lay on the dirt road. They'd been shot in the back. Neither of them moved.

I turned to Sampson. 'They'll come back for us. They're going to take us out here in the woods.'

He shook his head. 'No they're not. We're going to take *them* out. When we see them, we open up. No warnings, Alex. No prisoners. Do you understand what I'm saying?'

I did. This was an all-or-nothing fight. It was war, not police work, and we were playing by the same rules as them.

Chapter Ninety-Five

It was awfully quiet all of a sudden. Almost as if nothing had happened, as if we were alone in the woods. I could hear the distant roar of the Jacks River, and birds twittering in the trees. A squirrel scampered up the trunk of a hemlock.

Otherwise, nothing moved. Nothing that I could see, anyway.

Eerie as hell.

I was getting a really bad feeling – we were in a trap. They knew we would come here after them, didn't they? This was their turf, not ours. And Sampson was right, this was war. We were in a combat zone, behind enemy lines. A fire fight was coming our way. Thomas Starkey was in charge of the opposition and he was good at this. All three of them were pros.

'I think one woman is moving a little,' he said. 'I'm going to check on her, Alex.'

'We both go,' I said, but Sampson was already slipping away from the cover of the trees.

'John?' I called, but he didn't look back.

I watched him run forward in a low crouch. He was down close to the ground, moving fast. He was good at this – combat. He'd been there, too.

He was about halfway to where the women lay when gunfire erupted from the woods to his right.

I still couldn't see anybody, just whispers of gun smoke wafting up into tree branches.

Sampson was hit and he went down hard. I could see his legs and lower torso just over a bramble. One leg twitched. Then nothing.

Sampson didn't move anymore.

I had to get to him somehow. But how? I crawled on my stomach to another tree. I felt weightless and unreal. *Completely* unreal. There was more gunsmoke. Pinging off rocks, thudding into nearby trees. I didn't think I was hit, but they'd come damn close. The fire was heavy.

I could see sheets of smoke from the rifles rising to my right. I could also smell the gunsmoke in the air.

It struck me that we weren't getting out of this one. I could see Sampson where he lay. He wasn't moving. Not even a twitch. I couldn't get to him. They had me pinned down. *My last case.* I had said that right from the start.

'John,' I called. 'John! Can you hear me?'

I waited a few seconds, then I called out again. 'John! Move something. John?'

Please say something. Please move.

Nothing came back to me.

Except another round of heavy fire from the woods.

Chapter Ninety-Six

I hadn't experienced anything like the explosive rage, but also the fear, that I felt. This happened in combat, I realized, and considered the irony. Soldiers lost buddies in the war and went a little mad, or maybe a great deal mad.

Is that what had happened in the An Lao Valley? There was a noisy buzzing inside my head, bright flashes of color in front of my eyes. Everything around me felt completely surreal.

'John,' I called again. 'If you can hear me, move something. Move a leg. John!'

Don't die on me. Not like this. Not now.

He didn't move, didn't respond. There was no sign that he was alive. He didn't shiver or twitch.

Nothing at all.

More rifle fire suddenly erupted from the woods, and I hugged the ground, digging my face into leaves and dirt.

I tried to put Sampson out of my mind. If I didn't, I would wind up dead. I had a terrible thought about John and Billie. Then I let it go. I had to. Otherwise, I'd die out here for sure.

Trouble was, I didn't see how I was going to out-maneuver three Army Rangers in the woods, especially on terrain they were familiar with. These were experienced combat veterans. So they wouldn't risk closing in on me right away. They'd wait until dark.

Not too long from now. Maybe a half-hour. Then I was going to die, wasn't I?

I lay behind a big hemlock, and a lot of disconnected thoughts shunted through my head. I thought about my kids, how unprepared I was to die, and how I would never see them again. I'd had so many warnings, so many close calls, but here I was.

I checked on Sampson again – he still hadn't moved.

I raised my head a couple of times. Just for a second. I turkey-necked a look across the horizon.

There were no moving shadows in the woods. I knew they were there though, waiting me out. Three Army assassins. Led by Colonel Thomas Starkey.

They'd been here before; they were patient as death itself.

They had killed a lot of people. In the Army. And out of it.

I thought of something Sampson had said before he went to help the two women. *When we see them, we open up. No warnings, Alex. No prisoners. Do you understand what I'm saying?*

I understood perfectly.

Chapter Ninety-Seven

*P*atience.

This was a waiting game, right? I understood that much about tonight. I even knew the military jargon for what I had to do next.

EE. Evade and escape.

I studied the rough terrain behind me and saw that I could slide down into a hollow that would give me some cover but would also allow me to move laterally, east or west. I could change my position without their knowing it.

That would give me a small advantage.

But I'd take anything I could get right now. I felt that I was a dead man. I didn't see any way out of this. So the hollow or gully looked awfully good to me.

I thought about Starkey, Griffin and Harris. How good they were; how badly I wanted to bring them down, Starkey in particular. He was the smart one, the leader, the cruelest of the three. Then I thought of what Sampson had said: *No prisoners.* Only they had to be thinking the same thing.

I started to slide backward. I call it a slide, but I was almost burrowing into the wet leaves and soft ground.

At least I made it down into the hollow without being shot. Catbrier was stuck all over my legs and chest. I wasn't sure, but I didn't think I could be seen from the woods. No one shot me in the head anyway. *That was a good sign, right? A victory in itself.*

I crawled sideways in the hollow – slowly – with my face pressed deep into the cold dirt and leaves. I couldn't breathe very well. I kept moving until I was a good fifteen or twenty yards from my original position. I didn't risk looking up, but I knew my angle to the woods and the house had changed significantly.

Could they be watching me from somewhere close by? I didn't think so. But was I right?

I listened.

I didn't hear a twig break or brush being pushed aside. Just the steady whistle of the wind.

I pressed my ear to the ground, willing to try anything for an advantage. It didn't help.

Then I waited some more.

Patience.

Things Sampson had told me about the Army Rangers surfaced in my head. Odd facts. They had supposedly killed fifty-five VC for every Ranger in the war. That was the story anyway. And they took care of their own. In the Vietnam War only one Ranger was listed MIA. All the others were accounted for, every single one.

Maybe they had gone, fled from the woods, but I doubted it. Why would they leave me here alive? *They wouldn't . . . Starkey wouldn't allow it.*

I felt guilty that I'd left Sampson, but I wouldn't let myself dwell on it. I couldn't think about him. Not now. Later. If there was a later.

When we see them, we open up.

No warnings, Alex.

Do you understand what I'm saying?

I moved again, circling to the northeast, I figured. Were they moving on me, too?

I stopped.

New position.

I waited there some more. Every minute seemed like ten. Then I saw something move. *Jesus! What the hell?* It was a bobcat, eating its own droppings. Maybe twenty, twenty-five yards away. Unconcerned with me. In its own world.

I heard someone coming, and he was very fucking close.

How had he gotten so close without my hearing him before?

Shit, he was right on top of me!

Chapter Ninety-Eight

H ad he heard me, too?

Did he know I was right there, a few feet away?

I didn't dare breathe. Or even blink my eyes.

He moved again.

Very slow, very careful, a professional soldier. No, a professional killer. There was a big difference. Or was there?

I didn't move an inch.

Patience.

No prisoners.

He was so close – almost to the hollow I was lying in. He was coming for me. He had to know my position.

Which one of them was it? Starkey? Griffin? Harris – who I had avoided crashing into during a softball game? Was he going to kill me now? Or would I kill him?

Somebody was going to die in a minute or less.

Who could it be?

Who was up there over my head?

I shifted my body so I'd see him the instant he came

over the edge. Was that what he would do? What were his instincts? He'd done this kind of tracking before. I hadn't. Not in the woods. And not in a war zone.

He moved again. Inches at a time.

Where the hell was he going? He was just about on top of me.

I watched the uneven ridge of the hollow and I held my breath. Tried not to blink. I felt the sweat streaming through my hair and down the back of my neck, down my back. An incredible cold sweat. The buzzing in my ears returned.

Someone rolled over the edge!

Brownley Harris. His eyes widened when he saw me waiting there for him, my gun aimed at his face.

I fired just one shot. *Boom.* Then there was a dark hole where his nose had been an instant before. Blood spurted from the center of his face. His M-16 dropped from his hands.

'No warnings,' I whispered as I took the rifle. Were the others close behind him? I waited for them. Ready as I'd ever be for a shootout.

Sergeant Warren Griffin.

Colonel Thomas Starkey.

The woods were so eerie. Silent again. I scuttled away under the cover of darkness.

Chapter Ninety-Nine

A three-quarter moon was out and that was both good and bad news. I was sure they would come for me now. It seemed logical, but was my logic the same as theirs?

I was back close to my original position in the woods. I thought so anyway.

Then I was certain.

My eyes teared involuntarily. I saw Sampson, lying still, right where he'd been shot. I could see the body so clearly in the moonlight. And I started to shake. What had happened was finally hitting me with its full force. I swiped at my eyes. A fist seemed to clench my heart and hold it tight, wouldn't let go.

I could see the dead women lying in the dirt road. Flies were buzzing around the bodies. An owl hooted from a nearby tree. I shuddered. In the morning perhaps a hawk or turkey vultures would come to feed on the bodies.

I slipped on the night goggles I'd brought with me. I hoped they would give me an advantage. Maybe not, probably not. Starkey and Griffin would have the best, too. They worked for a company that manufactured high-tech equipment, didn't they?

I kept reminding myself that I'd taken out Brownley Harris. It gave me some confidence. He'd looked so utterly surprised to see me. Now he was dead, his arrogance gone, exploded in an instant by a bullet.

But how could I surprise Starkey and Griffin? They must have heard the shot. Maybe they thought it came from Harris. No, they had to know he was dead.

For a couple of minutes I considered a flat-out run. Maybe I could get to the road. I doubted it, though. More likely I'd be shot down trying.

They were good at this, but Harris had been good, too. He was experienced, and now he was lying dead in a ditch. I had his rifle in my hands.

Patience. Wait on them. They have questions and doubts, too.

I watched Sampson's body for another few seconds, then I had to turn away. I couldn't think about him now. I mustn't, or I would die as well.

I never heard it coming – a sudden blast of deafening gunfire. One or both of them had gotten between me and the cabin. I spun in the direction of the shots. Then a voice pierced the darkness.

Close behind me.

'Put down the gun, Cross. I don't want to kill you. Not just yet.'

Warren Griffin was down in the hollow with me. I saw him now. He had a rifle aimed at my chest. He wore night goggles and looked like an alien.

Then Thomas Starkey appeared, also wearing goggles. He was above the gully, staring down. He had an M-16 aimed right at my face and he was smiling horribly. His victory grin.

'You couldn't leave it alone, asshole. So now Brownley's dead. So's your partner,' said Starkey. 'You satisfied yet?'

'You forgot the two women. And the lawyer,' I said.

It was strange to be looking at Griffin and Starkey through the night vision glasses, knowing that they were seeing me the same way. I wanted to take them down so much it hurt. Unfortunately that wasn't going to happen.

'What the hell happened in Vietnam?' I asked Starkey. 'What started all of this? What the hell was it?'

'Everybody who was over there knows what happened. Nobody wants to talk about it. Things got out of hand.'

'Like what, Starkey? How did it get this bad?'

'At first, there was a rogue platoon on the loose. That's what we were *told* anyway. We were sent to the An Lao Valley to stop them. To clean it up.'

'You mean murder our own soldiers? Those were your orders, Starkey? Who the hell is behind this? Why the murders now?'

I was going to die, but I still wanted answers. I needed to know the truth. Hell of an epitaph. *Alex Cross. Died seeking the truth.*

'I don't even fucking know,' Starkey hissed. 'Not all of it. I'm not going to talk about it anymore either. Maybe what I'm going to do . . . is cut you into little pieces. That happened over there. I'll *show* you what was done in the

An Lao Valley. See this knife. It's called a K-Bar. I'm really good with it. I've had some practice recently.'

'I know you have. I've seen some of your butchery.'

Then the strangest thing I could ever imagine happened. It blew my wheels off, completely blew my mind into a thousand pieces.

I was staring past Starkey. But something was different in the background. At first I didn't know what, then I did and my knees became weak.

Sampson was gone!

I didn't see his body anyway. At first I figured I was just disoriented. But then I was sure I wasn't. His body had been over there – near a tall beech tree. Now it wasn't there.

No warnings, Alex.

No prisoners.

Do you understand what I'm saying?

I heard his words echo inside my head. I could hear the exact *sound* of it.

'Put down your guns,' I said to Starkey and Griffin. 'Drop them right now. Now!'

They looked puzzled, but kept their guns aimed at me.

'I'm going to cut you everywhere,' Starkey said. 'This is gonna take hours. We'll be here 'til morning. I promise.'

'*Put down the guns!*' I heard Sampson's voice before I saw him walk out from behind a tree. 'And the knife, Starkey! You're not cutting anybody.'

Warren Griffin spun around. Two shots instantly caught him in the throat and upper chest. His gun went off as he fell over backwards to the ground. Arterial blood pumped from his wounds as he died.

'Starkey, no!' I yelled. 'No!'

Thomas Starkey had raised his gun at me. Then he took one high in the chest. It didn't stop him. A second shot stung him in the side and spun him full around. A third blasted through his forehead and he went down for good in a bloody heap. His gun and K-Bar fell into the gully near my feet. His blank eyes stared into the night sky.

No prisoners.

Sampson was weaving toward me. As he came forward he rasped, 'I'm okay, I'm okay.'

Just before he collapsed into my arms.

PART FIVE

FOUR BLIND MICE

Chapter One Hundred

A s it turned out, Jamilla was a life-send after the shootings in Georgia.

She called every day, often two or three times, and we talked until she could tell I was healing some. Sampson was the one who'd been physically wounded, and he was healing now too, but I was the one who seemed hurt the most. There had been too much killing, for too long, in my life.

Early one morning Dr Kayla Coles arrived at the house on Fifth Street. She marched right into the kitchen where Nana and I were eating breakfast.

'What's that?' she pointed an accusatory finger and asked with an arched eyebrow.

'It's decaf. Just terrible. A memory of real coffee, and a bad one at that,' Nana told her with a straight face.

'No, I'm talking about *Alex's* plate. What are you eating?'

I pointed out the ingredients for her. 'These are two eggs, over-easy. What's left of two hot sausage patties.

Home fries, slightly burned. The remains of a homemade sticky bun. Mmm mmm good.'

'You made this for him?' She looked at Nana in horror.

'No, Alex made it for himself. He's been cooking most of the breakfasts since my fainting spell. He's treating himself this morning because his big murder case is finally over. And he's feeling better.'

'Then I take it you don't always eat like this?'

I smiled at her. 'No, Doctor. I don't usually eat eggs, sausage, sticky buns and greasy potatoes. I was almost killed down in Georgia, and I'm celebrating that I wasn't. I guess that I prefer death by breakfast. Care to join us?'

She laughed out loud. 'I thought you'd never ask. I smelled something heavenly when I opened the car door. I followed it all the way to the kitchen.'

Kayla Coles asked a few questions about the case while she ate – a single egg, orange juice, just a bite of a sticky bun. I glossed over most of the details of the case, but I gave her a feel for the three killers and what they had done, and what I knew about *why*, which wasn't enough, but that's the way it goes sometimes.

'Where's John Sampson now?' she wanted to know.

'Mantoloking, New Jersey,' I said. 'He's recovering from his wounds, among other things. He has a nurse. A live-in, I hear.'

'She's his girlfriend,' said Nana. 'That's what he really needed anyway.'

After breakfast Dr Coles gave Nana a physical right there in the house. She took her temperature, pulse, blood pressure, listened to her chest with a stethoscope, then did a P and A. She checked for fluid buildup in Nana's ankles, the tops of her feet and hands, under her eyes. She looked into Nana's eyes and ears, tested her reflexes, looked at the color of her lips and nail beds. I knew all the elements of the test and possibly could have done the exam myself, but Nana liked getting visits from Kayla Coles.

I couldn't take my eyes off Nana during the checkup. She just sat there, and she seemed like a little girl to me. She never said a word, never complained.

When Kayla was finished, Nana finally spoke up. 'Am I still alive? I haven't passed, have I? Like that scary movie with what'shisname Willis.'

'Bruce Willis . . . Yes, you're still with us, Nana. You're doing beautifully.'

Nana took a deep breath and sighed out loud. 'Then I guess tomorrow's the big day. Go in for my catheter ablation, my radio-frequency ablation, whatever it is.'

Dr Coles nodded. 'You'll be in and out of the hospital in a snap. I promise you that.'

Nana narrowed her eyes. 'You keep your promises?'

'Always,' said Kayla Coles.

Chapter One Hundred and One

In the early evening, Nana and I took a ride out to Virginia in the old Porsche. She'd asked if we could take the drive, just the two of us. Aunt Tia was home with the kids.

'Remember when you first got this car? We used to take a ride just about every Sunday. I looked forward to it all week,' she said once we were out of Washington and on the highway.

'Car's almost fifteen years old now,' I said.

'Still runs pretty good, though,' Nana said. She patted the dash. 'I like old things that work. Long, long time ago, I used to go for a car ride every Sunday with Charles. This was before you came to live with me, Alex. You remember your grandfather?'

I shook my head. 'Not as much as I'd like to. Just from the photographs around the house. I know the two of you came to visit in North Carolina when I was little. He was bald and used to wear red suspenders.'

'Oh, those awful, awful suspenders of his. He had a couple dozen pairs. All red.'

She nodded, then Nana seemed to go inside herself for a moment or two. She didn't talk about my grandfather very often. He had died when he was just forty-four. He'd been a teacher, just like Nana, though he taught Math, and she was English. They had met while working at the same school in Southeast.

'Your grandfather was an excellent man, Alex. Loved to dress up and wear a nice hat. I still have most of his hats. You go through the Depression, things we saw, you like to dress up sometimes. Gives you a nice feeling about yourself.'

She looked over at me. 'I made a mistake, though, Alex.'

I glanced over at her. '*You* made a mistake? This is a great shock. I'd better pull over to the side of the road.'

She cackled. 'Just one that I can recall. See, I knew how good it could be to fall in love. I really loved Charles. After he died, though, I never tried to find love again. I think I was afraid of failing. Isn't that pathetic, Alex? I was too afraid to go after the best thing I ever found in this life.'

I reached over and patted her shoulder. 'Don't talk like you're leaving us.'

'Oh, I'm not. I have a lot of confidence in Doc Kayla. She would tell me if it was time for me to start collecting on all my old debts. Which I plan to do, by the way.'

'So, this is a parable, a lesson?'

Nana shook her head. 'Not really. Just an anecdote while we're taking this nice ride in your car. Drive on, young man. Drive on. I'm enjoying this immensely. We should do it more often. How about every Sunday?'

The whole ride out to Virginia and back, we never once

talked about Nana's procedure in the hospital the next morning. She obviously didn't want to, and I respected that. But the operation, at her age, scared me as much as any murder case could. No, actually it scared me more.

When we got back to the house I went upstairs and called Jamilla. She was at work but we talked for nearly an hour anyway.

Then I sat down at my computer. For the first time in over a week I pulled up my notes on the Three Blind Mice. There was still one big question I needed to answer if I could. Big *if*.

Who was behind the three of them?

Who was the real killer?

Chapter One Hundred and Two

I fell asleep at my work desk, woke up around three in the morning. I went down to my bedroom for a couple of hours. The alarm sounded at five.

Nana was scheduled to be at St Anthony's Hospital at six-thirty. Dr Coles wanted her to be one of the first operations of the day, while everybody on the staff was fresh and alert. Aunt Tia stayed at the house with little Alex, but I brought Damon and Jannie with me to the hospital.

We sat in the typically antiseptic-looking waiting room, which really started to fill up with people around seven-thirty. Everybody in there looked nervous and concerned and fidgety, but I think we were probably right up there with the worst of the lot.

'How long does the operation take?' Damon wanted to know.

'Not long. Nana might not have gone in first, though. It all depends. It's a simple procedure, Damon. Electrical energy is delivered to the AV node. The electricity is a little like the heat in a microwave. It disconnects the pathway between the atria and the ventricles and will stop the extra impulses causing Nana's irregular heartbeat. Got all that? Don't hold me to it, but that's fairly close to what's happening.'

'Is Nana wide awake while it's happening?' Jannie wanted to know.

'Probably. You know your Nana. They gave her a mild sedative and then local anesthesia.'

'Won't touch her,' Jannie said.

So we talked and waited, and fretted and worried, and it took longer than I thought it should take. I tried not to let my mind wander to bad places. I wanted to stay in touch with the moment.

I conjured up good memories of Nana, and they were a little like prayers. I thought about how much she meant to me, and also to the kids. None of us would be where we were without Nana's unconditional love, her confidence in us, and even her needling – irritating as it could be sometimes.

'When is she coming out?' Jannie looked at me. Her beautiful brown eyes were full of uncertainty and fear. It struck me that Nana had really been a mother to all of us. Nana Mama was more mama than nana.

'Is she all right?' Damon asked. 'Something's wrong, isn't it? Don't you think this is taking too long?'

Unfortunately, I did. 'She's just fine,' I said to the children.

More time passed. Slowly. Finally, I looked up and saw Dr Coles coming into the waiting room. I took a quick breath and tried not to let the kids see how anxious and nervous I really was.

Then Kayla Coles smiled. What a beautiful, glorious smile that was, the very best I've seen in a long while.

'She's all right?' I asked.

'Aces,' she said. 'Your nana is a tough lady. She's asking for you already.'

Chapter One Hundred and Three

We visited with Nana in the recovery room for an hour, then we were asked to leave. She needed to rest up.

I dropped the kids off at school around eleven that morning. Then I went home to do a little more scud work in my office.

I was looking into something for Ron Burns, a strange but intriguing case involving convicted sex-offenders. In return he'd gotten me some US Army records that I wanted to check out. Some of it had come off ACIRS and RISS, but most had come straight from the Pentagon. One of the subjects was the Three Blind Mice.

Who was the real killer? Who gave orders to Thomas Starkey? Who sanctioned the murders?

I kept thinking about Nana, and how tough she was, and how much I would have missed her if something had gone wrong that morning. The terrible, guilt-ridden fantasy kept running through my head that I was going to get a call from Kayla Coles and she would say, *I'm sorry, Nana passed away. We don't know what went wrong. I'm so sorry.*

The call didn't come, and I threw myself into the work. Nana would be home tomorrow. I needed to stop worrying about her and put my mind to better use.

The Army records were interesting, but also about as depressing as an IRS audit. Obviously there had been rogue activity in Vietnam, Laos and Cambodia. The Army, at least officially, seemed to turn away and not look too closely at what had happened. There weren't civilian review boards, of course, like the police departments had to investigate misconduct. The press had no way to judge what was going on either. They rarely interviewed victims' families in the small villages. Plus, few of the American reporters spoke much Vietnamese. The good and the bad of it was that the Army had sometimes fought fire with fire. Maybe it was the only way to effectively fight a guerrilla war. But I still didn't know what had happened over there to inspire the murders stateside during the past few years.

I spent several grueling hours looking through more records of Colonel Thomas Starkey, Captain Brownley Harris and Sergeant Warren Griffin. I saw that their Army careers were exemplary, at least in written form. I went back as far as Vietnam and the pattern continued. Starkey was a highly decorated officer; Harris and Griffin were good soldiers. There was nothing in the records about assassinations in Vietnam committed by the trio. Not a single word.

I wanted to know when they had met and where they had served together. I kept leafing through records, hoping, but not finding the connect point. I knew they'd fought together in Vietnam and Cambodia. I went through every page a second time.

But there was nothing in any of the records to indicate they'd worked together in Southeast Asia. Not a goddamn word.

I sat back and stared out onto Fifth Street, letting my eyes glaze over. There was only one conclusion I could come up with, and I didn't like it.

The Army records had been doctored.

But why? And by whom?

Chapter One Hundred and Four

I t wasn't over yet.

I could feel it in the pit of my stomach, and I hated the queasy feeling, the uncertainty, the lack of closure. Or maybe I just couldn't let go. All those unsolved murders. *Who was the real killer? Who was behind the strange murders?*

A week after the shootings in Georgia, I sat in Ronald Burns's office on the fifth floor of FBI headquarters in Washington. Burns's assistant, a crew-cut male in his mid-twenties, had just brought us coffee in beautiful china cups. There were also fresh mini-pastries on a silver tray.

'Pulling out all the stops?' I asked the director. 'Hot coffee and Danish.'

'You got it,' he said, 'shameless manipulation. Go with it.'

I'd known him for years, but it was only during the past few months that I'd worked closely with Burns. What I'd seen so far, I liked, but I'd been fooled before.

'How's Kyle Craig doing?' I asked him.

'We're trying to make it as uncomfortable as possible for him out in Colorado,' Burns said. He allowed himself a smile. 'We have to keep him in solitary most of the day. For his own protection, of course. He hates being by himself. Drives him crazier. No one to show off to.'

'No psychiatrists in there trying to figure him out?'

Burns shook his head. 'No, no. Not a good idea. That would be too dangerous for them.'

'Besides, Kyle would like the attention. He craves it. He's a junkie for it.'

'Exactly.'

We smiled at the image of Kyle locked away in seclusion, hopefully for the rest of his life. Unfortunately, I knew he had made contact with others in the max security unit – particularly Tran Van Luu.

'You don't think Kyle had anything to do with these killings?' Burns finally asked.

'I checked that out as much as I could. There's no evidence he knew Luu before he was assigned to Florence.'

'I know he visited out there, Alex, when he was still with the Bureau. He was definitely on the max security unit as well as death row. He could have met Luu. It's possible. I'm afraid you never know with Kyle.'

I almost didn't want to think about the possibility that Kyle might be behind the diabolical murder scheme somehow. But it *was* possible. Still, it seemed so unlikely that I didn't give it much credence.

'You had any time to think about my offer?' Burns asked.

'I still don't have an answer for you. I'm sorry. This is a big decision for me and my family. If it's any consolation, once I land I don't jump around.'

'Okay, that's fine with me. You understand I can't leave the offer on the table indefinitely?'

I nodded. 'I appreciate the way you're handling this. You always this patient?'

'Whenever I can be,' Burns said, and left it at that. He picked up a couple of manila folders from the coffee table between our chairs and slid them my way.

'I have something for you, Alex. Take a look.'

Chapter One Hundred and Five

'More of the Bureau's resources that you want me to see?' I said, and smiled at Burns.

'You'll like this. It's real good stuff. I hope it's helpful. I want to see you get some closure on this Army case. We're interested in this one, too.'

I reached into one of the folders and pulled out what looked like a faded patch off of a jacket. I held it up to examine the cloth more closely. The patch was green khaki with what looked like a crossbow sewn into the fabric. *There was also a straw doll on the patch. An eerie, awful straw doll. The same kind I'd first seen in Ellis Cooper's house.*

'The patch came from the jacket of a sixteen-year-old gang member in New York City. The gang he belonged to is named Ghost Shadows. They use different coffee shops on Canal Street in New York as headquarters. It's called roving turf,' Burns said.

'A task force we ran with the NYPD brought the gangbanger in. He decided to trade some information he thought might be valuable to them. It wasn't. But it could be valuable to you.'

'How so?' I asked.

'He says he's sent you several e-mails during the past month, Alex. He used computers at a technical high school in NewYork.'

'He's Foot Soldier?' I asked, and shook my head in amazement.

'No. But he may be a messenger for Foot Soldier. He's Vietnamese. The symbol of the crossbow is from a popular folktale. In the story, the crossbow could kill ten thousand men every time it was fired. The Ghost Shadows think of themselves as very powerful. They're big into symbols, myth, magic.

'As I said, this kid and his fellow gangbangers spend most of their time in the coffee shops. Playing ding lung, drinking Café Su Da. The gang moved to New York from Orange County in California. Over one hundred fifty thousand Viet refugees have settled in Orange County since the seventies. The gang in New York favored Vietnamese-style criminal activities. Smuggling illegal aliens – called snakeheads – credit card fraud, software and computer parts heists. That help you?'

I nodded.'Of course it does.'

Burns handed me another folder.'This might help too. It's information about the former leader of the Viet gang.'

'Tran Van Luu.'

Burns nodded.'I did a tour in sixty-nine and seventy. I was in the Marines. We had our own re-con people. They'd get dropped into hostile territory, just like Starkey and company. Vietnam was a guerrilla war, Alex. Some of our people acted like guerrillas. Their job was to wreak havoc behind enemy lines. They were tough, brave, but more than a few of them got incredibly desensitized. Sometimes they practiced situational ethics.'

'Wreak havoc?' I said. 'You're talking about terrorism, aren't you?'

'Yeah,' Burns nodded. 'That's what I just said.'

Chapter One Hundred and Six

The FBI flew me out to Colorado this time. Ron Burns had made this his case now. He wanted the person or persons behind the long string of murders.

The isolation unit at Florence seemed as oppressive as it had been on my first visit there. As I entered the Security Housing Unit, guards in khaki uniforms watched me through bulletproof-glass observation posts. The doors were either bright orange or mint green – odd. There were cameras every ten feet along the bland, sand-colored walls.

The cell where Tran Van Luu and I met had a table and two chairs, which were dead-bolted to the floor. Three guards in body armor and thick gloves brought him to me this time around. I wondered if there had been trouble recently. Violence?

Luu's hands and ankles were cuffed for our meeting. The gray hairs hanging from his chin seemed even longer than at our last visit.

I took the jacket patch Burns had given me out of the

pocket of my coat. 'What does this mean? No more bullshit.'

'Ghost Shadows. You know that already. The crossbow is just folklore. Just a design.'

'And the straw doll?'

He was silent for a moment. I noticed that his hands were curled into fists. 'I believe I told you that I was a scout for the American Army. Sometimes, we left calling cards in villages. One, I remember, was a skull and crossbones with the words *"When you care enough to send the very best"*. The Americans thought that was very funny.'

'What does the straw doll mean? Is it your calling card? Was it left at all the murder scenes? Or afterwards at the soldiers' homes?'

He shrugged. 'Perhaps. You tell me, Detective. I wasn't at the murder scenes.'

'What would this particular calling card mean? The straw doll?'

'Many things, Detective. Life is not so simple. Life is not merely sound bites and easy solutions. In my country, popular religion is flexible. Buddhism from both China and India. Taoism. Confucianism. Ancestor worship is the oldest and most indigenous belief throughout Vietnam.'

I tapped my finger on the jacket patch.

'Straw dolls are sometimes burnt or floated away on a river as part of rituals honoring the dead. Evil spirits are the ghosts of those who were murdered or who died without proper burial. The straw doll is a threatening message reminding the offending person it is *they* who should rightfully be in the doll's place.'

I nodded. 'Tell me what I need to know. I don't want to have to come back here.'

'Nor should you. I don't have any need for confession. That's more of a Western concept.'

'You don't feel any guilt about what's happened? Innocent people have died.'

'And will continue to. What is it that you really want to know? Do you believe I owe you something because of your crackerjack detective work?'

'You admit that you used me?'

Luu shrugged. 'I don't admit anything. Why should I? I was a guerrilla fighter. I survived in the jungles of An Lao for nearly six years. Then I survived in the jungles of California and New York. I use whatever is provided to me. I try to make the most of the situation. You do the same, I'm sure.'

'Like at this prison?'

'Oh, especially in prison. Otherwise, even a reasonably bright man could go mad. You've heard the phrase "cruel and unusual". A cell that is seven by twelve feet. Twenty-three hours a day in it. Communication only through a cell slot in the door.'

I leaned across the table, my face close to Luu's. Blood was pounding inside my head. Tran Van Luu was the Foot Soldier. He had to be. And he had the answers that I wanted. Was he also responsible for all these murders?

'So why did you kill Sergeant Ellis Cooper? The others? Why did they have to die? Is it all just revenge? Tell me what the hell happened in the An Lao Valley. Tell me and I'll go away.'

He shook his head. 'I've told you enough. Go home, Detective. You don't need to hear anymore. Yes, I am Foot Soldier. The other answers you seek are too much for the people in your country to hear. Let these murder cases go. Just this once, Detective, *let them go.*'

Chapter One Hundred and Seven

I made no move to get up and leave.

Tran Van Luu stared at me impassively, then he smiled. Had he expected this? Stubbornness? Obtuseness? Was that why he'd involved me in the first place? Had he talked to Kyle Craig about me? How much did he know? Everything, or just more pieces of the puzzle?

'Your continuing journey is interesting to me. I don't understand men like you. You want to know why terrible things happen. You want to make things right, if only occasionally.

'You've dealt with vicious killers before. Gary Soneji, Geoffrey Shafer, Kyle Craig, of course. Your country has produced so many killers, Bundy, Dahmer, all the others. I don't know why this happens in such a civilized country. A place with so many blessings.'

I shook my head. I really didn't know either. But Luu wanted to hear what I had to say on the subject. Had he asked Kyle the same questions?

'I've always felt it has something to do with high

expectations. Many Americans expect to be happy, expect to be loved. When we aren't, some of us go into a rage. Especially if it happens to us as children. If instead of love, we experience hatred and abuse. What I don't understand is why so many Americans abuse their children.'

Luu stared at me, and I could sense his eyes probing into mine. Was he a strange new kind of killer – a lord executioner? He seemed to have a conscience. He was philosophical. A philosopher-warrior? *How much did he know? Did the case end here?*

'Why did someone orchestrate the murder of Ellis Cooper?' I finally asked. 'Simple question. Will you answer it for me?'

He frowned. 'All right. I will do that much. Cooper lied to you and your friend Sampson. He had no choice but to lie. Sergeant Cooper was in the An Lao Valley, although his records don't say so. I saw him execute a girl of twelve. Slender, beautiful, innocent. He killed the girl after he had raped her. I have no reason to lie about that. Sergeant Cooper was a murderer and rapist.

'They all committed atrocities; they were all murderers. Cooper, Tate, Houston, Etra, Bennett and Tichter. Harris, Griffin and Starkey, too. The Blind Mice. They were among the worst, the most bloodthirsty. That's why I chose them to hunt down the others. Yes, *I was the one*, Detective. But I'm already condemned to death here. There's nothing more you can do to me.

'Colonel Starkey was never told why the murders were taking place in the US. He didn't know my identity. He was an assassin; he never asked. He just wanted his money.

'I believe in rituals and symbolism, and I believe in revenge. The guilty have been punished and their punishments fit the crimes. Our unburied dead have been revenged and their souls can finally rest. Your soldiers left their calling cards, and so did I. I had plenty of time to think about it in here, plenty of time to make my plans. I hungered for revenge, and I didn't want it to be simple or easy. As you Americans say, I wanted payback. I got it, Detective. Now I am at peace.'

Nothing was as it seemed. Ellis Cooper hadn't been entirely straight with us from the start. He'd proclaimed his innocence to Sampson and me. But I believed Tran Van Luu. The way he told the story was entirely convincing. He had witnessed atrocities in his country, and maybe even committed them himself. What was the phrase Burns had used – wreak havoc?

'There was a saying the Army had in the An Lao Valley. Do you want to hear it?' he asked.

'Yes. I need to understand as much as I can. It's what drives me.'

'The phrase was, *If it moves, it's VC.*'

'Not all our soldiers did that.'

'Not many actually, but some. They came into villages in the out country. They would kill everyone they found. *If it moves* . . . They wanted to frighten the Viet Cong, and they did. They left calling cards – like the straw dolls, Detective. In village after village. They destroyed an entire country, a culture.'

Luu paused for a moment, possibly to let me think about what I had heard so far. 'They liked to paint the faces and bodies of the dead. The favorite colors were red, white and blue. They thought this was so humorous. They never buried the bodies, just left them for their loved ones to find.

'I found my family with their faces painted blue. Their *ghost shadows* have been haunting me since that day.'

I had to stop him for a moment. 'Why didn't you tell anyone? Why didn't you go to the Army when this was happening?'

He looked straight into my eyes. 'I did, Detective. I went to Owen Handler, my first CO. I told him what was happening in An Lao. He already knew. His CO knew. They all knew. Several teams had gotten out of control. So had the assassins sent in to clear up the mess.'

'One more question,' I said to Luu while everything he'd told me was boiling inside my head.

'Ask. Then I want you to leave me alone. I don't want you to come back.'

'You didn't kill Colonel Handler, did you?'

'No. Why should I put him out of his misery? I wanted Colonel Handler to live with his cowardice and shame. Now go. We are finished.'

'Who killed Handler?'

'Who knows? Perhaps there is a fourth blind mouse.'

I got up to leave and the guards came into the cell. I could see they were afraid of Luu, and I wondered what he had done in his time here. He was a scary and complicated man, a Ghost Shadow. He had plotted several murders of revenge.

'There's something else,' he finally said. Then he smiled. The smile was horrible – a grimace – no joy or mirth in it. 'Kyle Craig says hello. The two of us talk. We even talk about you sometimes. Kyle says that you should stop us while you can. He says that you should put us both down.' Luu laughed as he was led from the cell. 'You *should* stop us, Detective.'

'Be careful of Kyle,' I offered some advice. 'He isn't anybody's friend.'

'Nor am I,' said Tran Van Luu.

Chapter One Hundred and Eight

As soon as Luu was taken away, Kyle Craig was brought into the interview room in the isolation unit on death row. I was waiting for him. *With bells on.*

'I expected you'd stop by and visit, Alex,' he said as he was escorted inside by three armed guards. 'You don't disappoint. Never, ever.'

'Always one step ahead, isn't that right, Kyle?' I asked.

He laughed, but without a trace of mirth as he looked around at the cell, the guards. 'Apparently not. Not anymore.'

Kyle sat across from me. He was so incredibly gaunt and seemed to have lost even more weight since I'd seen him last. I sensed that his mind was going a mile a minute inside that bony skull.

'You were caught because you wanted to be caught,' I said. 'That's obvious.'

'Oh Christ, spare me the psycho-babble. If you've come as Dr Cross, the psychologist, you can turn around and leave right now. You'll bore me to tears.'

'I was talking as a homicide detective,' I said.

'That's a little better, I suppose. I can stomach you as a sanctimonious cop. You're not much of a shrink, but then again it's not much of a profession. Never did anything for me. I have my own philosophy: *Kill them all, let God sort'm out*. Analyze that.'

I didn't say anything. Kyle had always liked to hear himself talk. If he asked questions, he often wanted to ridicule whatever you said in response. He lived to bait and taunt. I doubted that anything had changed with him.

Finally, he smiled. 'Oh, Alex, you are the clever one, aren't you? Sometimes I have the terrifying thought that you're the one who's always a step ahead.'

I didn't take my eyes away from his.

'I don't think so, Kyle.'

'But you're persistent as an attack dog from hell. Relentless. Isn't that right?'

'I don't think about it much. If you say so, I probably am.'

His eyes narrowed. 'Now you're being condescending. I don't like that.'

'Who cares what you like anymore?'

'Hmmm. Point taken. I must remember that.'

'I asked before if you could help me with Tran Van Luu, the murders he's involved in. Have you changed your mind? I suspect there's still one murderer out there.'

Kyle shook his head. His eyes narrowed. 'I'm not the Foot Soldier. I'm not the one trying to help you. Some mysteries just never get solved. Don't you know that yet?'

I shook my head. 'You're right,' I said. 'I am relentless. I'm going to try to solve this one, too.'

Then Kyle slowly clapped his hands, making a hollow popping sound. 'That's our boy. You're just perfect, Alex. What a fool you are. Go find your murderer.'

Chapter One Hundred and Nine

Sampson was recuperating on the Jersey shore with Billie Houston, his own private nurse. I called him just about every day, but I didn't tell John what I'd heard about Sergeant Ellis Cooper and the others.

I also called Jamilla every day, sometimes a couple of times a day, or she'd call or e-mail me. The distance separating us was becoming more and more of an issue. Neither of us had a good solution for now. Could I ever move the family to California? Could Jamilla move to Washington? We needed to talk about it face to face, and pretty soon.

After I returned from Colorado I spent a couple of days working in Washington. I knew that I had one more important trip to make, but I needed some more preparation first. *Measure twice, cut once.* Nana had always preached that to me.

I spent countless hours on Lexis, but also the military databases, ACIRS and RISS. I made a visit to the Pentagon and talked to a Colonel Peyser about violence against civilians committed by American soldiers in Southeast Asia. When I brought up the An Lao Valley, Peyser abruptly cut off the interview, and then he refused to see me again.

In a strange way, that was a very good sign. *I was close to something, wasn't I?*

I talked to a few friends who had served in Vietnam. The phrase, *'If it moves, it's VC'* was familiar to most of them. Those who knew about it justified it, since violent outrages were constantly being committed by the North Vietnamese. One Army vet told this story: He'd overheard other soldiers talk about a Vietnamese man, in his mid-eighties, who'd been shot down. 'Got to hand it to him,' a gunnery sergeant had joked, 'man his age and he volunteers for the Viet Cong.'

And one name kept coming up whenever I talked about the An Lao Valley.

In the records.

Everywhere I looked.

One name that was a link to so much that had happened – there, and here.

The fourth of the blind mice?

I had to find that out now.

Early on Thursday morning I left for West Point. It would be about a five-hour drive. I was in no particular hurry. The person I wanted to see there wasn't going anywhere. He didn't think he had any reason to run and hide.

I loaded up the CD player with the blues mostly, but also the new Bob Dylan which I wanted to hear at least once. I brought along a thermos of coffee as well as sandwiches for the road. I told Nana that I would try to be home tonight, to which she curtly replied, 'Try harder. Try more often.'

The drive gave me time to think. I needed to be sure that I was doing the right thing by going to West Point again. I asked myself a lot of tough but necessary questions. When I was satisfied with the answers, I gave some more thought to taking a job with the FBI. Director Ron Burns had done a good job showing me the kind of resources I'd have at Quantico. The message was clear, and it was also clever: *I would be better at what I did working with the FBI.*

Hell, I didn't know what I wanted to do, though.

I knew that I could make it in private practice as a psychologist, if that was what I really wanted. Maybe I could do a better job with the kids if I had a regular job instead of *the Job*. Use those marbles wisely, savor those precious Saturdays. Make a go of it with Jamilla, who was constantly in my thoughts, and should be.

Eventually, I found myself on Route 9W, following road signs for Highland Falls and West Point.

As I got close to the Point, I checked my Glock and put a clip in. I wasn't sure if I'd need a gun. Then again, I hadn't thought I'd need one the night Owen Handler was murdered near here.

I entered West Point through the Thayer gates at the north end of Highland Falls.

Cadets were all over the Plains, practicing for parade, still looking beyond reproach. Smoke curled lazily from a couple of chimneys on top of Washington Hall. I liked West Point a lot. I also admired most of the men and women I'd met in the Army. But not all of them, and everybody knows what a few bad apples can do.

I pulled up in front of a redbrick building. I had come here for answers.

One name was left on my shopping list. A big name. A man beyond reproach.

General Mark Hutchinson.

The commandant of West Point.

He had avoided me the night Owen Handler had been murdered, but that wasn't going to happen again.

Chapter One Hundred and Ten

I climbed steep stone steps and let myself into the well-kept, redbrick building that housed the offices of the commandant of West Point. A soldier with a 'high and tight' haircut was sitting behind a dark wood desk that held a highly polished brass lamp and orderly stacks of papers and portfolios.

He looked up, cocking his head like a curious and alert grade-school student. 'Yes, sir. Can I help you, sir?'

'My name is Detective Alex Cross. I believe General Hutchinson will see me. Please tell him that I'm here.'

The soldier's head remained tilted at the curious angle. 'Yes, sir, Detective. Could you tell me something about your business with the general, sir?'

'I'm afraid that I can't. I believe the general *will* see me, though. He already knows who I am.' I went and sat on a stuffed chair across the room. 'I'll be right here waiting for him.'

The soldier at the desk was clearly frustrated; he wasn't used to civil disobedience, especially not in General

Hutchinson's office. He thought about it, then he finally picked up the plain black phone on his desk and called someone farther up the chain of command. I figured that was a good thing, a necessary next step.

A few minutes passed before a heavy wood door behind his heavy wood desk opened. An officer in uniform appeared and walked straight over to me.

'I'm Colonel Walker, the general's adjudicator. You can leave now, Detective Cross,' he said. 'General Hutchinson won't be seeing you today. You have no jurisdiction here.'

I nodded. 'But I do have some important information General Hutchinson should listen to. It's about events that took place during his command in the An Lao Valley. This was in sixty-seven through seventy-one, but in particular sixty-nine.'

'I assure you, the general has no interest in meeting with you or hearing any old war stories you have to tell.'

'I have a meeting set up with the *Washington Post* about this particular information,' I said. 'I thought the general should hear the allegations first.'

Colonel Walker nodded his head once, but he didn't seem impressed or worried. 'If you have someone in Washington who wants to listen to your story, you should go there with it. Now please leave the building or I'll have you escorted out.'

'No need to waste the manpower,' I said, and got up from the cushy armchair. 'I'm good at escorting myself.'

I went outside on my own steam and walked to my car. I got in and slowly drove up the pretty main drag that cuts through West Point. I was thinking hard about

what to do next. Eventually I parked on a side street
lined with tall maples and oaks that had a majestic view
of the Hudson.

I waited there.

The general will see me.

Chapter One Hundred and Eleven

It was past dark when a black Ford Bronco turned into the driveway of a large Colonial-style house that was flanked by elm trees and ringed by fort-style fencing.

General Mark Hutchinson stepped out of his vehicle. The interior lights illuminated his face for a few seconds. He didn't look one bit worried. Why should he? He had been to war several times, and he'd always survived.

I waited about ten minutes for him to put the house-lights on, then get settled in. I knew that Hutchinson was divorced and lived alone. Actually, I knew a lot about the general by now.

I walked up the front steps, much as I'd gone up the steps to the general's office earlier that afternoon. The same deliberate pace. Relentless, unstoppable, stubborn as hell. I was going to talk to Hutchinson today, one way or the other. I had business to finish. This was my 'last case', after all.

I banged the front door's iron knocker a couple of

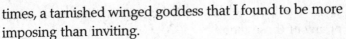

times, a tarnished winged goddess that I found to be more imposing than inviting.

Hutchinson finally came to the door in a blue-checked sport shirt and pressed khaki slacks. He looked like a corporate executive caught at home by a pesky door-to-door salesman, and none too happy about the interruption at this time of night.

'I'm going to have you arrested for trespassing,' he said when he saw me. As I'd told the soldier in his reception area, the general knew who I was.

'That being the case—' I pushed my way in the front door. Hutchinson was a broad-shouldered man, but in his sixties. He didn't try to stop me, didn't touch me at all.

'Haven't you caused enough trouble?' he asked. 'I believe you have.'

'Not really. I'm just getting started.'

I walked into a spacious living room and sat down. The room had deep couches, brass floor lamps, curtains in warm blues and reds. His ex-wife's taste, I assumed.

'This won't take too long, General. Let me tell you what I know about An Lao.'

Hutchinson tried to cut me off. 'I'll tell you what you *don't* know, mister. You don't know how the Army works, and you don't seem to know much about life in power circles either. You're out of your depth here. Leave. Now. Take your goddamn stories to the *Washington Post*.'

'Starkey, Griffin and Brownley Harris were military assassins assigned to you in Vietnam,' I began.

The general frowned and shook his head, but finally seemed resigned to hearing me out. He sat down. 'I don't know what the hell you're talking about. I've never heard of any of those men.'

'You sent ten-person teams into the An Lao Valley specifically to intimidate the Vietnamese. It was a guerrilla war, and your teams were instructed to act like guerrillas. They committed murders, mutilations. They slaughtered non-combatants. They had a calling card – they painted their victims red, white or blue. It got out of control, didn't it, General?'

Hutchinson actually smiled. 'Where did you dig up this ridiculous shit? You have some fucking imagination. Now get the hell out of here.'

I continued. 'You destroyed the records showing that these men were even in the An Lao Valley. The same was true of the three assassins, Starkey, Griffin and Harris, the ones you sent to clean up the mess. That's how I first found out about the deception. They *told* me they were there. But their Army records said otherwise.'

The general looked disinterested in what I had to say. It was all an act, of course. I wanted to get up and punch him until he told me the truth.

'The records *weren't* destroyed, General,' I went on.

Finally, I had his attention. 'What the hell are you talking about?'

'Just what I said. The records weren't destroyed. A Kit Carson scout named Tran Van Luu brought the atrocities to the attention of his CO. None other than Colonel Owen Handler. No one would listen, of course, so Luu stole copies of the records – and took them to the North Vietnamese.

'Those records were held in Hanoi until nineteen ninety-seven. Then the CIA happened to obtain copies. I got my copies from the FBI, as well as the Vietnamese Embassy. So maybe I do know a little about life in Washington's power circles. I even know that you're being considered for the Joint Chiefs. But not if any of this started to come out.'

'You're crazy,' Hutchinson huffed. 'You're out of your mind.'

'Am I? Two teams of ten men each committed a hundred or more civilian murders in villages during nineteen sixty-eight and sixty-nine. You were the commanding officer. You gave the orders. When the teams got out of control, you sent in Starkey and his men to tidy up. Unfortunately, they killed a few civilians themselves. More recently, you gave the order to have Colonel Handler killed. Handler knew about your role in the An Lao Valley. Your career would have been ruined and you might have even gone to jail.

'You went up country with Starkey, Harris and Warren Griffin yourself. You were there, Hutchinson, in the An Lao Valley. You're responsible for everything that went wrong. You were there – the *fourth* Blind Mouse.'

Hutchinson suddenly turned around in his chair. 'Walker, Taravela,' he said, 'you can come in now. We've heard more than enough from this bastard.'

Two men entered through a side door. They both had guns drawn, pointed at me.

'Now you don't get to leave, Dr Cross,' said Colonel Walker. 'You don't get to go home.'

Chapter One Hundred and Twelve

My hands were cuffed tightly behind my back. Then I was pushed outside and shoved down into the trunk of a dark sedan by the two armed men.

I lay curled up like a blanket in there. For a man my size, it was a tight squeeze.

I could feel the car back out of Hutchinson's driveway, bump over the gutter, then turn onto the street.

The sedan rode inside West Point at a reasonable speed. No more than twenty. I was sure we were leaving the grounds as the car finally sped up.

I didn't know who was up front. Whether General Hutchinson had come along with his men. It seemed likely that I was going to be killed soon. I couldn't imagine how I could get out of this one. I thought about the kids and Nana, and Jamilla, and I wondered why I'd risked my life again. Was it a sign of good character, or a serious character flaw? And did it really matter anymore?

Eventually, the car turned off the smooth highway surface onto a seriously bumpy road that was probably unpaved. I estimated we were about forty minutes from West Point. So how much longer did I have to live?

The car rolled to a stop and I heard the doors open and slam shut. Then the trunk was sprung.

The first face I saw was Hutchinson's. There was no emotion in his eyes. Nothing human looked back at me.

The two others were behind him. They had handguns pointed my way. Their stares were blank as well.

'What are you going to do?' I asked a question that I already knew the answer to.

'What we should have done the night you were with Owen Handler. Kill you,' said Colonel Walker.

'With extreme prejudice,' added the general.

Chapter One Hundred and Thirteen

I was lifted out of the car trunk and unceremoniously dropped on the ground. I landed hard on my hip. Pain lanced my body. Just the beginning, I knew. These bastards were out to hurt me before they killed me. I was handcuffed and there was nothing I could do to stop them.

Colonel Walker reached toward me and ripped my shirt open. The other man was pulling off my shoes, then my pants.

Suddenly, I was naked and shivering in the woods somewhere in upstate New York. The air was cold, probably in the low forties.

'Do you know what my real crime is? Do you know what I did that was so wrong in Vietnam?' Hutchinson asked. 'I gave the fucking order to fight back. They killed and maimed our men. They practiced terrorism and sadism. They tried to intimidate us in every way they could. I wouldn't be intimidated. I fought back, Cross. Just like I'm fighting back now.'

'You also murdered non-combatants, disgraced your command,' I spat the words at him.

The general leaned in close. 'You weren't there, so don't tell me what I did or didn't do. We *won* in the An Lao Valley. Back then, we used to say there were only two kinds in the world, the motherfuckers and the mother-fucked. I'm a motherfucker, Cross. Guess what that makes you?'

Colonel Walker and the other man had paint and brushes. They began to swab cold paint onto my body. 'Thought you would appreciate this touch,' Walker said. 'I was in the An Lao Valley, too. You going to tell the *Washington Post* on me?'

There was nothing I could do to stop this. No one could help me either. I was naked in the world, and all alone, and now I was being painted. Their calling card before they killed me.

I shivered in the cold. I could see in their eyes that killing me meant nothing to them. They'd murdered before. Owen Handler for one.

So how much longer did I have? A few minutes? Maybe a couple of hours of torture? No more than that.

A gunshot rang out in the blackness. It seemed to come from beyond the headlights of the sedan we'd driven there in. *What the hell?*

A dark hole opened in Colonel Walker's face, just below his left eye. Blood spurted. He flopped over backwards, landing with a heavy thud on the forest floor. The back of his head was gone, just blown away.

The second soldier tried to duck, and a bullet drilled his

lower spine. He screamed, then fell and rolled right over me.

I saw men come swarming out of the woods – at least half a dozen. I counted nine, ten of them. I couldn't see who they were in the darkness. Who in hell was rescuing me?

Then, as they came closer, moonlight illuminated some of the features. My God! I didn't know them, but I knew where they had come from and who had sent them – either to follow me, or to kill Hutchinson.

The Ghost Shadows were here.

Tran Van Luu's people had been tracking me. Or Hutchinson.

They were speaking in Vietnamese. I didn't understand a word they were saying. Two of them grabbed the general and threw him to the ground. They began to kick him in the head, the chest, stomach, and the genitals. He cried out in pain, but the beating continued, almost as if they couldn't hear him.

They left me alone. But I had no illusions – I was a witness to this. I lay with my face pressed against the ground. I watched the attack from the lowest vantage point. The beating of General Hutchinson seemed unreal and almost inhuman. They were kicking Colonel Walker and the other soldier now as well. *Beating the dead!*

One of them took out a serrated knife and cut Hutchinson. His scream pierced the night. It was obvious they wanted to hurt the general, but not kill him. They meant to torture and terrorize, to wreak havoc.

One of Luu's men pulled out a straw doll. He threw the

doll at Hutchinson. He then stabbed the general in the lower stomach. Hutchinson screamed again. The stomach wound wouldn't be fatal. The torture was going to continue. And sooner or later they would paint all of our bodies.

I believe in rituals and symbolism, and I believe in revenge. Tran Van Luu had told me that in prison.

One of his men finally came for me. I curled into a protective ball. No one could save me now. I knew the Ghost Shadows' plan – wreak havoc, get revenge for ancestors who had been murdered but never buried.

'You want watch? Or go?' the man asked. His voice was surprisingly calm. 'You free to go, Detective.'

I looked into his eyes. 'Go,' I said.

The Ghost Shadow helped me to my feet, took off my cuffs, then he led me away. He threw me rags to clean up with. A second man brought my clothes and shoes. They were both respectful.

Then I was brought to the gates of West Point, near 9W, where I was released unharmed. I had no doubt that those were Tran Van Luu's explicit orders.

I ran to get help for General Hutchinson and his men, but I knew I was already too late.

The Foot Soldier had killed them.

Chapter One Hundred and Fourteen

R on Burns finally reached me at home the following afternoon. I was up in my office, standing at the bay window looking down on Fifth Street and the rest of the neighborhood.

Jannie was on the front lawn teaching little Alex how to play tag. She was even letting her brother win, but that wouldn't last long.

Burns was saying, 'Alex, I just got off the phone with a special agent named Mel Goodes. He called me from a small town in upstate New York called Ellenville. You ever hear of Ellenville?'

'Actually, no. But I think I've been there recently,' I said. 'Have I?'

'Yeah, you have,' Burns said. 'That's where they took you from West Point.'

'What was Agent Goodes doing in Ellenville?' I asked.

'We were called in by the local police from up that way. They were puzzled and, frankly, shocked, by a mess some local deer hunters found in the mountains this morning.'

'I'll bet they were. Three murder victims. A grotesque death scene. Ritualistic.'

'Three unidentified males. It really shook up the locals. They blocked off half the mountain. The victims had severe cuts and electrical burns all over their bodies. The initial police report said they'd been "sodomized slash cauterized." The faces had been painted.'

'Red, white and blue.'

I was only half listening now. Jannie was teaching little Alex how to *lose* at tag. He started to cry, and she picked him up and hugged him. She looked up at my window and waved. She had it all under control. That was Jannie. Meanwhile, I was thinking about torture, terrorism, things that happen in the name of war. Jihad. Whatever. When would it stop? Probably never, or not until somebody blew up our beloved planet. How totally insane of us.

'I was wondering if you could shed any more light on the three murders?' Burns asked. 'Can you, Alex?'

I waved back to the kids, then I walked over to my desk and sat down. There was a picture of Maria with Jannie and Damon when they were little. I wondered what she would have thought of all this. The kids? Me? Jamilla? Murder victims painted the colors of the American flag?

'Two of the victims are probably General Mark Hutchinson and a Colonel named Walker. The third man is a PFC at West Point. I didn't catch his name. Hutchinson was responsible for some atrocities over thirty years ago in Vietnam. It finally caught up with him.'

I told Burns almost everything I knew about the night

before. As always, he was a good listener. I appreciated that more and more. And I was beginning to think that I trusted him.

'You know who killed the three West Pointers?' he finally asked.

I thought about that for a moment, then I said that I didn't. Technically, that was true. Burns asked a few more questions, but he accepted what I'd told him. I liked that. It meant that he accepted my judgment. I made another judgment then and there about the FBI director.

'I'll come and work for you,' I told him. 'I'll join the FBI. Like you said, it'll be fun.'

'Who says the offer is still open?' Burns said, and laughed. I liked that, too.

EPILOGUE

THE GARTER

Chapter One Hundred and Fifteen

The last thing I expected this year was a big, joyful wedding. I stood holding Jamilla's hand and looking out over the beautiful grounds in Church Falls, Virginia.

The setting was a sprawling meadow behind a small restaurant-inn. Yellow and white lights had been strung in the elm trees and along the patio rails. Everywhere I looked there were roses, and marigolds, and simple but quite beautiful English daisies.

The bride was absolutely gorgeous in a simple white satin gown, with no fussy train or veils. The dress was in the Empire style and draped elegantly on Billie's small frame. She wore a necklace and earrings made from brightly colored courie shells to celebrate her African-American heritage. Her hair was swept back in a chignon with sprigs of baby breath tucked in just so. Billie couldn't have looked happier. Her smile was radiant all through the day.

Sampson never stopped smiling either. He was dressed in a dove gray suit, and I swear he looked like a prince. A friend of ours, Reverend Jeffrey Campbell, had agreed to perform the ceremony in front of nearly a hundred of us who loved John and Billie with all our hearts.

Reverend Campbell asked if we would do everything in our power to support this new family in the community? *'We will!'* everyone answered with great enthusiasm and warmth.

The reception followed and I got to say a few words in a champagne toast.

'I have known this large man since we were both small boys. At least *I* was a boy. He has always been a part of our family, and always will be. John is loyal to his friends, his word is the truth, he's honorable, kind, generous, sweet – believe it or not – which is why he is my best friend in all the world. I have not known Billie quite as long. But I already like her a lot better than John.

'To a long, happy life together. I love you, John and Billie. Now let's hear some music. Let's dance until tomorrow.'

John and his wife danced to 'Let's Stay Together'. Then Jamilla and I joined in with several other couples. 'Nice wedding,' she said. 'I like John and Billie as a couple. They're great.' Folks started to stack their plates with food – coconut chicken, and cornbread stuffing, dumplings, dirty rice, greens. Everybody was snapping pictures with the single-use cameras left on each table. Billie's best friend from nursing school sang 'Our Love Is Here to Stay' and it was good. John and I got together on 'Sexual Healing' and it was pretty bad, which was why it was so good. The children were underfoot at all times. And

Sampson still hadn't stopped smiling.

Late in the afternoon, Damon and Jannie each grabbed one of my arms and escorted me out into the yard. 'I'll be right back,' I said to Jamilla. 'I hope.'

Billie was seated on a wooden chair with her back to half a dozen woeful-looking, even terrorized single males.

'You don't have to actually catch the garter,' she said turning and winking. 'The first one who *touches* it is the lucky winner.'

I stood on one side of the rag-tag boys club, winking and making ridiculous faces at Damon and Jannie, and, of course, Jamilla. Suddenly, they all pointed toward the sky.

I looked up – and the purple garter was spinning and spiraling down toward me. I couldn't get out of the way if I wanted to.

So I caught it and I twirled it around my outstretched finger. 'Doesn't scare me,' I said.

I looked to my left – and there was Jamilla with Nana. Jam was laughing and clapping her hands, and her smile said, doesn't scare me either.

I looked away – and by God, there was Dr Kayla Coles. And she wasn't clapping, just smiling coyly. Then she winked at me. Now what did that mean?

I shook my head, still laughing, but then I saw one more face. Director Ron Burns of the FBI.

My new boss was motioning for me to come over and see him. He had some kind of thick folder under his arm, which I had absolutely no plans of reading that Saturday.

But I did.